THE
TREASURE
SEEKERS

LAND OF THE FAR HORIZON

Voyage of the Exiles
Angel of the Outback
The Emerald Flame
Beyond the Wild Shores
The Treasure Seekers

THE TREASURE SEEKERS

PATRICIA HICKMAN

BETHANY HOUSE PUBLISHERS
MINNEAPOLIS, MINNESOTA 55438

The Treasure Seekers
Copyright © 1998
Patricia Hickman

Cover illustration by William Graf
Cover design by the Lookout Design Group

All rights reserved. No part of this publication may be reproduced, stored in a retrieval system, or transmitted in any form or by any means—electronic, mechanical, photocopying, recording, or otherwise—without the prior written permission of the publisher and copyright owners.

Published by Bethany House Publishers
A Ministry of Bethany Fellowship International
11300 Hampshire Avenue South
Minneapolis, Minnesota 55438
www.bethanyhouse.com

Printed in the United States of America by
Bethany Press International, Minneapolis, Minnesota 55438

Library of Congress Cataloging-in-Publication Data

CIP data applied for

ISBN 1-55661-545-0   CIP

To Jared.

At a time when life threw me a lot of curves,
God sent you to me as a reminder
of His grace and undeserving love.
Always be His faithful servant,
little man.

PATRICIA HICKMAN is an award-winning novelist and the wife of a pastor. She is the author of numerous fiction novels for both adults and children. Her works have been translated in foreign editions and have been featured selections for The Christian Herald Family Bookshelf. She and her husband, Randy, have three children, Joshua, Jessica, and Jared.

CONTENTS

PART ONE

1. April Blue 13
2. Annie's Powder Keg 30
3. Empty-Handed Orphans 44
4. The Suspect 56
5. Mistaken Love 70
6. The Dowry 84
7. Rogan's Reprieve 93
8. Courting a Rogue 104
9. Gold in California 116

PART TWO

10. A Prayer for Rogan 127
11. Abbot's Convict 137
12. Annie's Fitting 144
13. From This Time Forth 153
14. The Engagement 165
15. No Secret Wedding 176

16. Melancholy and Lace 182
17. Candle Carolers 193
18. A Sad Silence 204
19. The Invitation 215
20. Dog and Peacock 229
21. Thy Will Be Done 241

PART THREE

22. Moonlight Nuptials 253
23. A Place to Pray 264
24. The Rescue 275
25. The Mountain's Shadow 288
26. A Reasonable End 296
27. A Wilderness Gentleman 306
28. The Best-Dressed Laundress 315
29. Night of a Thousand Stars 324
30. Saint Rogan 335
31. Wanted Dead 345
32. Lewis Pond's Creek 354
33. A Season for Love 361

But lay up for yourselves treasures in heaven,
where neither moth nor rust doth corrupt,
and where thieves do not break through nor steal:
For where your treasure is,
there will your heart be also.

MATTHEW 6:20–21

PART ONE

So is he that layeth up treasure for himself,
and is not rich toward God.
Luke 12:21

1
APRIL BLUE

England 1844

"Isabelle says a man's coming by tomorrow, Mother. Who is he?" Annie Carraway peered from the loft where she and her younger sisters slept, her flaxen curls a cushion for her tawny cheeks. A thin shaft of April sunlight had insinuated itself through the hole in the roof. She lay still for a moment, allowing Wednesday's morning light to heat her right cheek until it burned as hot as the anger pent up inside of her.

"Just a farmer paying his respects."

"But he's coming to see you?"

"Annie, have you gathered the eggs this morning?"

"I have, Mother. See, in the kitchen." She sat up, acknowledging her mother, Constance, who spoke from the parlor below.

"I wish I'd stop feeling so tired all the time." Her mother sighed.

"Is the farmer a married man?"

"What is it you're trying to say, Annie?"

"I just thought I should know why a complete stranger would be coming to our home." Annie, London-born, never minced words, and her clipped British accent made her sound older than her age of twelve. She didn't offer her mother so much as a glance, but lay on her back again, a wave of caution braiding itself about her anger.

"Stop fiddling with that shoe, Annie. You'll only make the hole worse."

She had removed her right shoe to examine it, rubbing her finger around the hole worn through the sole. "I hate being poor." Throwing the shoe aside, she picked up some string and twined it around her fingers until she had a tangled snarl. She could never make a proper cat's cradle, and now the task seemed a childish waste of time. With one impatient flick of her wrist, the heavy string hurtled to the floor below. She sat up and dangled her legs over the edge of the loft's rectangular opening.

"What have you done to yourself?" her mother demanded. "Your legs are black and blue."

"I never remember." Annie drew up her legs and lifted them into the air.

"Well, keep your skirts down. The ladies from church will think that I beat you."

"Why do they have to come?"

"I'm a widow. They believe it's their duty, I suppose."

"They never have anything good to say."

"Hush, you! I won't have you speaking ill of them."

Annie dropped her bare feet back through the opening. She had spent the last five years of her young life in Devonshire, and not once could she remember the women visiting when her father was still alive. But Ralph Carraway had never darkened the door of a church. After years of taking the children to church by herself, Annie's mother had given in to his ways and stayed home with him on Sundays. After his death, the Carraway family hadn't missed a single Sunday.

"I wonder how your cousin Doris is faring in Paris by now. Lucky girl."

"I'm sure she hates it. Doris hates everything."

Annie didn't know why it made her so miserable that her wealthy cousin Doris Dearborn had been sent away to Paris to study. Since her father was a well-to-do magistrate, Doris and her siblings had never known hard times. In spite of her inbred civility, Doris had her own irritating way of letting her poorer cousins know that she only offered them her attention out of obligation.

Annie, however, judged Doris to be plain, a slow wit, and not worthy of the well-educated suitors who would surely come her way. Not that Annie desired suitors. She was too obsessed with caring for her widowed mother, an obligation she had taken upon herself the week her father had passed on.

Annie noticed her mother had grown quiet, so she sat up and found her staring out the window. Anxiety, the choking kind, seized her every time she caught her staring so sadly out the window.

"I hope those women don't stay long," said Constance.

"Let's go see your sister today, Mother, after the church ladies leave. Aunt Sybil loves it when you come. The sun is shining and—"

"I don't feel like seeing anyone today."

Annie pulled herself to the edge of the loft's opening, dropped her head down, and stared at her mother, the disapproval evident in her scowl. She hung from the hole for a moment until she felt her cheeks flush.

"If you're gaping at me behind my back, I'd ask you to please stop." Constance sat in the tattered chair she kept by the window, an observation point for the grave of her husband. When Annie had tried to move the chair once, Constance had made her put it back.

"I hate it here," Annie muttered under her breath.

"Move, please." Her youngest sister, Clarisse, scrambled up the ladder, tripping as she came. A long, exaggerated sigh deflated Annie's whole being. She longed for a few more uninterrupted moments of solace in her loft. She closed her eyes and dragged herself over as Clarisse bounded up beside her. Clarisse, always breathless, habitually raced about the cottage, a constant ball of emotion and movement.

"Oh me, I daren't be late or Mrs. Gunneysax will fuss at me!" Clarisse exclaimed.

"Who said you could don my best church dress?" Annie cocked her head and peered up at her.

"I'm having tea with Mrs. Gunneysax." Clarisse held up her doll with the broken face, then fidgeted in the oversized lace frock, causing her blond curls to coil like nervous springs about her cherubic face.

"Clarisse—"

"We're giving our mother a grand birthday and—"

"Please take it off. I don't want to have to launder it again before Sunday."

"What are you doing, Annie?"

"Dying."

"You say such dreadful things."

"But I *am* dying here, Clarisse." She spread her arms onto the blankets, tilted her head back, and rolled her eyes to feign a corpse.

"Mother, make her stop!" Clarisse shouted.

"Annie, don't torment your sister."

"Why must you be such a snitch, Clarisse?"

"I want you to come and play with me."

"I can't. I've got to clean the house. You should help me. Some ladies from the church are dropping by today."

"Why doesn't our mother do the chores anymore?"

"Because she's already dead. She just hasn't made it to heaven yet, like Papa."

"I'm leaving. I don't like you today, Annie, and neither does Mrs. Gunneysax. Mother! Annie called you 'dead' . . ."

"Take off my dress!" Annie watched her sister stumble down the ladder, glad to see her go. She looked over the edge of the loft floor again at her fragile-looking mother. Her hair had taken on more gray than in the past. The sight of her sitting with her knees up in the chair made Annie want to cry. The tension between them had worsened in the last few weeks. With the anniversary of her father's death only eight weeks away, guilt pricked at her emotions. She wanted to make every effort to quell the war between herself and her mother. In a recurring form of self-punishment, she once again reminded herself of her mother's plight.

Nearing her fortieth birthday, Constance Carraway had not counted on being left to find her own way in the world. Annie reminded herself of that fact often enough. Constance had died on the inside the same day, the very hour, that her beloved Ralph had given up the ghost. Determined to unearth a dead tree from their land, Ralph had miscalculated the slant of the tree and the swing of the ax, and he was buried two days later. He had not planned on his death. Nor had Annie's mother.

All of these things caused Annie to feel guilty, although reason told her they were not her fault.

Isabelle, Annie's younger sister and the one closest to her age, entered the parlor bearing a bowl of gruel with bacon on the side.

"Eat something, Mother. You're looking wan."

"I'm not hungry," Constance said wearily.

"I insist, Mother. And while you eat, I'll read to you from the Scriptures."

Annie pressed her chin against her folded fingers until they hurt. She pondered Isabelle's perfect auburn hair, forever pulled up in a large flowered ribbon. Isabelle had won the heart of Aunt Sybil, Doris's mother, and therefore had garnered many gifts from her, including a full basket of hair ornaments.

"You're so good to me, Isabelle. If all the world had your goodness, then we would have heaven on earth," Constance said.

" 'As for God, his way is perfect; the word of the Lord is flawless. . . .' "

"You're flawless, Isabelle," Annie murmured. She knew it was true. For every instance that arose, for every trauma she faced, Isabelle knew a Scripture. Annie sighed, rolled onto her back once more, and held the worn-out shoe to her chest while she listened to Isabelle's distant reading. She batted away an angry tear. *Father God, I am not good. Make me good for Mother's sake.*

Before the sun had fully lightened the English hills beyond her father's grave, Annie arose early on Friday to gather eggs and make hot biscuits before poring over her borrowed schoolbooks. The sun never invaded the downstairs room as it did Annie's loft. The once sunny parlor, now a prison of heavy drapes and locked doors, had taken on an odd shade of blue. "April Blue," Clarisse had called it.

"I'm off to the well!" Annie paused at the door, a bucket in her hand. She noticed her papa's gloves were still lying on the windowsill, where her mother had left them earlier that morning. Her brother Thomas had worn them the day before. And until she herself removed the gloves from the parlor, Annie knew they would sit there like a ghost, yet another haunting reminder of her private torment.

As much as Annie fought it, resentment roiled within her mind and her emotions. Papa had left them all, suddenly and without a farewell. He had been the skillful navigator for the Carraways. He had barked out the orders and they had followed in obedience, but with a surety. In spite of his hard directives, Annie had adored him. But she had not been allowed to grieve his death. Whenever she cried, Mother would burst into tears and take to her bed for days. Therefore, Annie could only cry on the inside of her soul, where her mother could not see nor hear. Memories of sunlit days spent collecting blue four o'clocks down by the garden gate fell into the dust of her twelve-year-old mind. No matter how hard Annie willed it, her mother would not enter the land of the living— not even when the banker came bearing the news of the foreclosure on their farm.

Ralph Carraway, dead ten months now, wouldn't have wanted their home to fall into disarray, or their lives into such a pitiful state. Annie knew it was true but couldn't awaken her mother to the fact. She had resumed her studies at home in order to help with the farm while her four siblings attended the one-room school in the borough. But she could not create money from the dust she swept from the floor. Mother yet struggled to sleep at night and often remained abed until well past dawn.

Annie, however, had noticed a few encouraging signs over the past few weeks. Constance had taken to working in the garden, even though she had yet to offer a glimmer of the once jovial smile Annie longed to see. Annie tossed her worn woolen coat about her shoulders—a winter habit—and made fast to draw water before bringing in the eggs and cooking breakfast. Hurrying back from the well, she felt a tickle of warmth on her neck that alerted her to the change in seasons. The time had arrived to put away her coat, she decided. The thought also came to her that perhaps she had other matters she should lay to rest as well.

Her eyes, a wilderness of blue longing, searched the silent land for solutions. The farmer, Jock Carver, had visited Mother yesterday as planned. He had taken a keen interest in Constance—an unsettling interest, in Annie's estimation. She veered off the path that led straight to the cottage and took the longer route instead. Her father had often taken walks along the dirt paths and returned with answers. But the hills, thrusting their early green shoots of life from the thawing earth, laughed down at her now. The fresh colors and scents of a lively spring only shouted their condescension that life goes on even when you will it to stop.

"Annie?"

She whirled around and found her eight-year-old brother, Thomas, peering up at her.

"You haven't left for school yet?"

"We'll be leaving shortly, but I wanted to ask you something."

"Go on."

"Is Mother going to marry Mr. Carver?"

"No!"

"Don't have to be so testy. How do you know?"

"He's just a farmer who paid her a visit. That's all—and nothing more."

"Good. I don't like him."

"I don't either."

"Will we lose our farm?"

"No." She silently prayed for God to forgive her lie.

"I'm glad of it. I never want to leave Papa here alone."

"He's not alone. He's in heaven. Now, off with you, before you're late for school." She noticed his hesitation.

"I love you, Annie."

"I love you too, Thomas." Annie hugged her younger brother, hating the anxiety she saw in his haunted face.

"Bye, see you this afternoon."

"Good-bye. Before you go, please take Papa's gloves and put them back in the barn. I don't want them lost."

"When I'm finished with school today, I will."

She bit her lip and watched him head for the group of farm children, all of them collected on the hillside like new spring crocuses. She hoped her siblings would keep their worries private. If the neighbors found out about the Carraways' plight, the gossip would begin. Or worse yet, the simpering charity. Certain that they already suspected their difficulties, Annie felt it all the more reason to move away and start again somewhere else.

The problem was, Mother refused to move. The thought distressed Annie. Papa had never accepted charity. Carraways, the decent and proper ones, made their own way, the same as their ancient Celtic forefathers whose blood had bought and paid for the farmland the Carraways owned. Annie would protect Mother from herself, even if it meant rationing out their meals in order to stretch what remained of their farm income.

Thomas's worries shadowed her mind and caused anxiety to flutter around her insides. If an eight-year-old had noticed Jock Carver's interest in their mother, she had reason to believe her own fears were well founded. The man had stayed into the candlelight hours on Thursday evening. Observing him from her loft, she concluded that although he spoke often of his good intentions, something made her mistrust him. He had a smiling face, but it was not one that gladdened her. He had glanced up at her more than once, but she had ignored him. Annie had sized him up as a commoner dressed in a gentleman's cloak.

Jock Carver did not have a clever mien or intelligent eyes like Papa. Carver's eyes, close set, had a color indefinable. His unkempt hair hung straight and long over his ears and fell unevenly around the top of his collar. His hands and fingernails were never clean, a fact that bothered Annie. To her, he looked more like an outlaw, but she had only said such things to Isabelle. He had talked at length about how he hated to see Mother lose the farm. Annie didn't like the familiar way he spoke to Mother or how he moved from the chair near the window to the settee next to her. It didn't seem proper at all. Nor did she feel he should be calling her mother Constance so early on. Annie noticed, too, that, although he wore a costly coat, his old leather shoes had lived past their years. Whenever she didn't know a person, she would always study their shoes and then draw her conclusions about them. She concluded right away that she didn't care for Carver.

The days were passing too quickly. Annie knew that time would soon pounce upon them with cruel ferocity if Mother wouldn't shake off her grief. Her mother would be left with only one choice—to marry a man whom Annie loathed. She determined at once that Mother had to listen to reason. Annie returned to the cottage and prepared breakfast. After pouring them each a bowl of gruel, she popped a napkin into the air and whisked it onto her mother's lap.

"Thank you, Annie. You're awfully quiet this morning."

"I've been thinking. Have you spoken to your sister this week?"

"My sister? You mean your aunt Sybil? Whatever for?" Constance sighed and rested her forehead against her clasped hands. The shadows under her eyes revealed the weight of her situation.

"Aunt Sybil has ideas about what we should do."

Isabelle rushed past, bearing her homemade satchel. "Did you say Sybil?"

"Her ideas are foolish rubbish!" Constance said. "She has the money to gamble. We don't."

"We can't leave our farm—Papa's farm," Isabelle said.

"Isabelle, you'll be late." Annie pointed at the door with her gaze.

"Mother, I want you to know that I understand why you want to remain here," Isabelle said.

"Good day, Isabelle!" Annie stood and walked her to the door.

"I'm going—don't rush me!" Isabelle shut the door fast.

"We have such a small farm anyway, Mother. Why not let your sister's family help us? They possess the means and since we don't—"

"I'm not leaving, Annie." Constance's tone and faraway look revealed she had already resolved the matter, independent of her daughter's wishes.

"The land is your brother-in-law's for the asking. You know that's true. Women cannot own property."

"Abbot Dearborn respected your father too much. My brother-in-law would never take it without paying me."

"Then let Uncle Abbot pay you! We could settle elsewhere. I hate it here!"

"You don't understand. Your father and I wanted you to have a section of the farm one day. It was our dowry for you, Annie. We wanted it for all of our children."

"I don't need a dowry because I don't need a husband. I'm going to live with you and take care of you. That's what Papa would have wished. I knew him better than anyone."

"You didn't know him better than I. He would want you to marry—and marry well."

"And would he want the likes of that Carver fellow lurking about like a pirate?" She hung the kettle upon the hook.

"You'll not show me disrespect, young lady! You'd best stick to your own affairs and leave the more important matters to your elders."

"*You* are all that matters to me, Mother! Please ask Mr. Carver to stop calling on you. He makes me nervous." Annie stood behind her mother, feeling suddenly awash with emotion. She wrapped her arms around her neck and pressed her head against her mother's.

"He's a good man, Annie. He's spoken well of you." Constance gripped Annie's hands in a loving way but spoke with unwavering composure.

"And well he should. It would do Mr. Carver good to add the Carraway land to his own. If indeed he has any. We don't know anything about him, you know."

"I've had little time, Annie. I've only just met the man!"

"But you know what he wants!"

"You're judging him too harshly. He only wants to help us, help with the farm."

"I'd rather see Aunt Sybil set fire to it than see the likes of him snatch it up."

"Hester Parker says her brother has had some dealings with him. He pays his bill on time at the mercantile."

"But he looks like a criminal."

"We've few choices, Annie. What am I to do?"

"Aunt Sybil's told you of free land being given to settlers in New South Wales."

"It's for convicts. Not the likes of good people."

"It's for everyone, Mother. Aunt Sybil says—"

"Bah! Aunt Sybil!"

"England will give settlers a loan until the first harvest. We could hire men to do the work in New South Wales, Sybil says. We could have a farm three times the size of this one. Uncle Abbot says he'll sign for us. We'll be rich."

"We'd be fools in a land of strangers and criminals. It's not Christian, I say."

"And is it Christian to stay and live out the dreams of a dead man?" Annie paused, observing the distress in her mother's face. Realizing she had spoken out of turn, she raised her hand to her mouth and looked away.

"Annie Carraway, you ought to be ashamed! And you're only repeating what your aunt has said."

"But she's right! Papa can't manage our lives from heaven, Mother. We've got to do for ourselves. Please say you'll at least ask more questions about New South Wales."

"I won't." Constance pushed aside her breakfast and went to stand at the window.

Annie hated to see the pain in her mother's face. She longed to wipe it from their lives and begin anew. If she would be honest with herself, she would admit that the promise of free land held no meaning for her. She only wanted to pull her mother away from a man she would soon agree to marry for reasons other than love. But instead of confessing her fears, she had hurt her mother with stinging words. She hated herself almost as much as she loathed Jock Carver. He was such a far cry from the only man they had grown up idolizing.

Her papa's memory only offered another reason to pack up and leave for the new land: Too many reminders here of Papa forbade them any joy or any hope. The house, the farm, the tools in the barn, his gloves—they all whispered his name. It was the land that had killed Papa. She hated it and wanted to wake up in a more forgiving place. She imagined New South Wales as a beautiful wilderness that beckoned the world's wanderers to come and taste of its unsullied treasures.

Silent and apologetic, she stole up behind her mother and wrapped her arms around her waist. Burying her face in the soft folds of her bodice, she felt a sob rise in her throat. The two of them cried without words while the morning went about its own business.

Jock Carver came to visit again on Saturday.

"Good mornin', Constance, Annie," he said. Annie noticed that he had doffed his hat and tossed it onto her father's favorite chair. She couldn't bring herself to reply.

"Good day, Jock," Constance said, closing the door behind him, her eyes chastening her oldest daughter without words. Mother still wore the black mourning frock, but her widow's attire deterred him no more than Annie's impudence.

The more Annie saw of him, the more she felt him too homely for Mother. He was not cut from the same cloth as Papa. A far cry from the well-bred Carraways, his ill-use of the language and common mannerisms sent her running more than once for her tidy loft sanctuary. She wanted him to go away and never return. Nonetheless, he always returned. He stayed for an hour on Saturday morning, joined them in their noon meal, and departed with few words to Annie or any of her siblings. By the following Friday, Annie had wearied of his unexpected visits. He appeared without warning, with little understanding of decorum.

"Time to wake up, Mother." Annie had arisen early, having started a secret project she wanted to finish. She would never complete it with her mother always home.

"Is it morning already?" Constance said sleepily.

Annie handed her mother a paisley frock, just pressed, along with her bonnet.

"What are you up to, Annie Carraway?"

"Aunt Sybil says I should make you pay her a visit. Besides, it isn't proper the way we keep accepting gifts from Aunt Sybil and offering nothing in return. Let's bake some of our bread dough. You and Isabelle can return her generosity."

"But Mr. Carver might drop by."

" 'Might?' You'd do well to teach the man some lessons in etiquette. If he comes by, I'll tell him you had errands to run. He should understand that you're not here at his beck and call."

"By the saints, you're right, Annie . . . I suppose."

Annie had already stoked the fire. While Constance shaped the bread loaf, Annie awakened her sister and told her that she would have to miss school for the day. Isabelle, although groggy, hurried about seeing that the other siblings dressed themselves for the school day. At times, she would toss Annie a suspicious glance.

"Thank you for going with Mother today, Mussy." Annie used Isabelle's affectionate name, a name they had called her most of her life.

"You're not wanting Mother to visit Aunt Sybil at all, are you?"

"Of course I am."

"Then join us."

"I can't." Annie took her by the elbow and led her onto the porch.

"Why not?"

"I have to finish her birthday gift. It's only a few weeks away."

"You're afraid Jock Carver will show up again, aren't you?"

"If he does, I'll set the dogs on him."

Isabelle laughed.

"Now, don't give away our surprise, Mussy. It's hard enough hiding surprises from Mother. She always manages to find out."

"I won't. I swear it."

While Constance dressed herself, Annie brought out the hot bread, wrapped it for the short jaunt by wagon, and placed it in a basket with a sampling of jams.

She kissed her siblings and bid them a good day. It seemed to her that her mother took longer than usual to dress herself. She kept looking through the window, hoping that Jock Carver would not appear again unannounced. Soon Constance appeared, looking more lovely than she had in almost a year.

"Finally! Here's the basket for Aunt Sybil. Please give the twins my best," Annie said.

"You're certain you don't want to go with us?" Constance asked.

"No. I've too much to do here."

"You work too hard," Constance said.

" 'And whatsoever ye do, do it heartily, as to the Lord, and not unto men—' "

"Thank you, Isabelle. I'll remember that verse," Annie interrupted her.

Annie watched them leave, then breathed a relief-filled sigh. She ran to her loft bed and pulled out a small box. She had started a needlework design that she hoped to finish before her mother's birthday in May. Her secret handicraft had been contrived to the delight of her younger sisters, who wanted to surprise their mother with a gift. She hastened to thread her needles. The day passed without incident, and Annie's eyes burned from staring at the needlework. She set it down and began to watch for the return of her siblings. The sound of the hens clucking out in the yard caused her to stand to her feet. She readied herself for the squealing entourage of laughter from her sisters and the mischief of her unruly younger brothers. Instead, she heard a rap at the door. She tucked the needlework under a book and opened the door.

"Afternoon."

"Mr. Carver." A feeling of disappointment darkened her gaze. She mustered as much sincerity as her spirit would allow.

"Is the missus about?"

"We—Mother wasn't expecting you today."

"You'll tell 'er I'm 'ere, then?"

Annie began to answer but hesitated. As often as she had met the man, something in his exaggerated mannerisms caused her to exercise caution. She wouldn't tell him that she was alone.

"She's gone, then?"

"She's about somewhere. Didn't you see her out in the yard?" She prayed her voice did not betray her lie.

"No. But I'll wait for 'er. You'll excuse me, girl, while I 'elp meself to some o' your mother's fine vittles."

Annie didn't widen the door to allow him inside, but he walked past anyway and strode toward the aroma of beans simmering. With a deliberate sigh, she waited at the open doorway, tapping her fingers. A distinct odor caught her senses. *Rum?* Annoyance clouded her young eyes.

"Have ye a bit o' grog, girl? Fetch some for me, will you, and a bowl o' them beans I can smell."

"Mr. Carver, you know Mother doesn't partake of strong spirits. Nor is she expecting you today. She looks a fright, and I am certain she would be displeased with me if I didn't ask you to return at another hour."

"Aye. I know your mum well. Constance is always pleased to see me and knows ol' Carver don't take no stock in matronly frills."

Seeing that she could not persuade the man to leave, Annie shut the door fast and walked past him without a word. Pulling her skirts aside, she stopped. Seeing the whites of his eyes tinged with a scarlet cloud, she felt certain that he had been drinking.

"I sees the way you look at me, girl," Carver muttered.

Annie kept walking straight toward the kitchen. Fearing the man sought an encounter with her, she needed to dismiss herself at once.

"Answer your elder, girl!"

"I am neither looking your way nor giving thought to you, sir." She lifted the needlework from her chair, rolled it up, and slid it into a cloth bag for safekeeping.

"You don't want Mr. Carver callin' on your mum, do you, now?"

"It is no secret. I want no gentleman to call on my mother. Who is worthy to replace our father? Neither you, nor any caller, in my eyes."

Carver considered her response. He twisted his mouth to one side, nodded, and glanced down at his feet as though he were weighing her words.

"If you'll excuse me, sir."

"Your mum's felt the weight o' lookin' after all you waifs since your papa died. It kills 'er soul to see you all doin' without. But if she up and marries me, she could buy you lots o' pretties. Carver's got some money. You be thinkin' otherwise, but your thinkin' be muddled. That's wot."

Sighing once more, Annie walked away. When Papa was alive, a man like Carver would have been handed a penny at the door and sent on his way. To find herself conversing with him about personal matters offended her strong sense of propriety. She walked into the kitchen and busied herself with washing and chopping a large bowl of vegetables. Little time had passed before the kitchen door swung open. She whirled around. "Mr. Carver, I must ask that you confine yourself to our parlor. We have rules about gentleman callers—"

"Quiet, little wench!"

"My mother will arrive at any moment. To find you—in such a way will upset her. Leave now! Do you hear me, Mr. Carver?"

"Pretty little wench."

"I said leave *now*!" Annie heard her voice rise. Her heart fluttered and she felt a twinge of nausea rise in her stomach.

"Your mum's gone, eh? You been foolin' ol' Mr. Carver, ain'tcha?"

Annie backed away, attempting to keep her footing, but she stumbled on the floor's cracks. She glanced around, deciding quickly that she could run through the kitchen doorway to escape out the back. But then she remembered with regret how her mother had asked a carpenter to board up the back door after Papa had died, for fear of robbers.

"You be needin' some new dresses, eh, my sweet? You want Mr. Carver to take care o' you? Don't be frightened. I'll teach you some new ways—"

"No! Go away! Mother will have you hanged if you touch me!"

"It's lies you been tellin' about me. Everyone knows Mr. Carver's a good man. All children tell lies. You shouldn't be runnin' from the one who could 'ave you dressed more stylish than your auntie Sybil's girl."

"Don't speak of my family! You don't know us well enough!"

"I know everythin'. You want to move your mum away from 'ere. Want to run your poor mother's life. Wot you need, girl, is to be broken."

Annie shrieked. Bolting for the door, she tried pushing her way past him. She felt him grip her arm and pull her powerfully toward him. Her emotions roiled and the bile rose in her throat. "Mother! Papa!"

The Carraway children raced to the top of the hill that overlooked their farmhouse. They had found a wounded bird. The boys chased it along the ground, having sport with the poor creature.

"Let's tie a string to its leg," Linus yelled.

"Stop it, I say! You're mean! Both of you!" Clarisse exclaimed.

"He's wounded, Clarisse. We should put him out of his misery," Thomas said.

"You're horrid, you are! Let it go or I shall tell Mother that the teacher kept you both after today for scuffling."

"You'll not or I'll smack your hands, Clarisse!" Linus retorted.

"Set the bird free, Linus! It isn't worth a scolding. Let us hurry.

I see our mother standing yonder. See?" Thomas stood, arms crossed. He pointed in the opposite direction. While the others looked away, he scooped up the bird and ran down the hill laughing. His siblings called after him, having realized he'd played them all for fools. But none were as swift as he. He ran into the farmyard. He would have raced for the barn with his prize, but he heard a peculiar sound.

"No, let me go! Stop!"

He stopped and gazed toward the house. Usually Annie or his mother stood out on the porch waiting for them all to bound into the Carraway house. But seeing the empty porch and hearing the cry sent his heart racing. He laid the bird upon a stump and bolted for the house.

"Thomas, where are you going?" Clarisse shouted.

"Annie!" Thomas shrieked.

As Thomas ran toward the house, Constance appeared upon the hill's crest in the wagon with Isabelle. She called after Thomas, but he didn't hear her.

"Annie! Annie!" Thomas shouted, then tore into the house with terror in his throat.

"Thomas . . ." Annie could say no more. She staggered away from Carver just as Thomas kicked open the door and bounded inside. He rushed to her side as Annie stumbled against the wash table. Her clothes torn, she cried and struggled to speak. A moan from the floor behind the large oak table sent Thomas running to the other side. He shouted and pulled a butcher knife from the table.

"He meant to do me harm! I had to stop him!" Annie pointed at the man on the floor, who was groaning and pulling broken pottery from his bruised head.

The kitchen filled with squealing, hysterical children, followed by their worried mother. "What is it, Thomas?" Constance cried.

"Get the pistol, Linus! We've a robber. Annie's whipped herself a robber!"

"I'll go fetch Uncle Abbot!" Isabelle said.

Constance, horrified, snatched the pistol from Linus.

"Whoever you are, we are the Carraways and we will shoot you if we must!" Constance held the weapon in her trembling grasp.

Annie stumbled to her mother's side and helped her steady the pistol.

"He's moving!" Clarisse said.

"He's a horrible man! I told you, Mother! Didn't I say it first?" Annie's tears saturated her cheeks.

"Who, Annie? Who is the brute?" Cautiously, Annie guided her around the table, all the while keeping the pistol leveled at the perpetrator.

A moan escaped his lips. Constance lifted her petticoats and glanced warily around the table while Thomas stood aiming the knife at the man. Recognizing Carver, she shrieked and dropped the pistol. Annie retrieved the fumbled weapon and held Carver at bay.

They maintained this uncomfortable position until Uncle Abbot arrived with two other men. They bound Carver and led him away while their wives tended to the hysterical Carraway children.

Constance nursed her terrified daughter with tea and honey as she wiped her face with a damp cloth. Between her sobs, she uttered prayers and chastened herself.

"He was going to, to . . ." Annie couldn't stop sobbing. The memory of him touching her, tearing at her clothes, brought the horror rushing back at her.

"There, there. But he didn't, Annie. God kept his hand on you."

"And helped her clout the bloke!" Thomas said.

"We should have left long ago." Constance wiped her eyes.

"What did you say?" Annie asked.

"Your fine uncle has offered us good money for our land. It's about time we Carraways took our leave."

Annie pushed aside her tea and held her mother's fingers to her lips. With gentle regard she kissed them and closed her eyes as another soft blanket of guilt settled around her shoulders.

2
ANNIE'S POWDER KEG

"Here, Isabelle. Help me with this one, will you?" Annie tied some rope around a small box.

"I remember that hatbox," Isabelle said.

"Mother's Easter bonnet from a few years ago."

"Yes, you're right. The feathers are all in tatters now."

"As are all of our belongings. No matter, though." Annie tied the knot while Isabelle held it taut.

"Will we be rich in New South Wales?"

"Richer than Uncle Abbot himself!" Annie said.

"Good. We shall both marry well, then."

"Why marry at all?" Annie looked up from her packing. Isabelle's distant stare caused her to sigh.

"I want to be loved. Don't you?"

Annie shrugged, watching Isabelle hug herself. Isabelle was such a needy person. The young men had not even begun to notice her, Isabelle being only eleven years of age. But she had already started noticing them.

"On what Scripture do you base that wish?" Annie asked.

"Song of Solomon."

"Hush, both of you, talking like tawdry old maids!"

"Hello, Mother." Annie steadied the stack of boxes so they wouldn't topple.

Constance pressed her toe against a large crate and shoved it against the wall. Instead of packing another empty crate, she turned and walked out onto the porch, her silence drawing the girls' attention.

"Mother's scarcely spoken all morning," Isabelle said in a hushed voice.

"Let's keep working." Annie dug out the next crate.

While Annie and her siblings had busied themselves all week with crating up a fifteen-year collection of worn-out belongings, she noticed her mother would take moments to stroll to the front porch, her eyes caressing the land in an apologetic farewell. After paying off the banker, she had set aside a minuscule portion of the money that her brother-in-law had paid her for the farm and bought herself a traveling dress. It was a fine-looking frock, tailored at the shoulders and hips, a blue suit actually. It had hung on her door all week while all the family admired it. But even the new dress had not cheered her days.

By Wednesday morning, in the predawn shadows of the first day of June, Constance had lit the candles to illuminate the parlor and said her morning prayers. But as the Carraway children had clambered around the breakfast table, she said little to any of them. Annie noticed that she had frayed the ends of her apron ties, having wound them many times around her fingers. Reality had finally struck. Mother would leave behind the hundred-year-old farm by week's end. It all brought a disillusioning close to a legacy that had never reached its potential. Papa's farm was gone.

"Isabelle, I feel guilty," Annie confessed. She prayed that her mother would find peace in the new land and made it her personal obligation to see that Mother would never feel alone. But she might never shake the nagging fear that she had caused it all. She tied up another small crate with rope and asked Isabelle to hold it fast while she knotted it.

" 'There is therefore now no condemnation to them which are in Christ Jesus, who walk not after the flesh, but after the Spirit.' "

"Ouch!" Annie wagged her finger. A splinter stuck fast. She ran to find her sewing kit.

"Let me do it." Isabelle rifled through the threads until she found a needle.

"Will we ever finish?" Annie glanced toward the entry, saw Mother's shadow against the windowpane.

"Hold still."

"You're hurting me worse!"

"Stop wiggling. There. It's out."

"Mother hates me, doesn't she?"

"No. She's glad for you. It's because of you that she found out the truth about Jock Carver."

"Jock Carver's in jail!" Linus skittered past, dragging a rope behind him with a noose about a doll's head.

"Linus!" Annie rankled.

"They going to hang him 'til he's dead!" Linus dangled the doll at the end of the rope.

"Stop! You're killing Mrs. Gunneysax!" Clarisse shrieked.

"Linus, give Clarisse back her doll at once!" Annie shouted.

"He's in jail with the rats!" Linus began a singsong.

"*Now*, Linus!" Annie persisted until the doll had been returned to Clarisse.

After Linus and Clarisse had paraded from sight, Isabelle put away the needle and positioned another crate in front of herself.

"Let's fill this crate with Mother's things," Annie said.

"Annie, did you hear that Jock Carver had escaped from jail to come here? You were right about him. He really was an outlaw."

"Really? I knew it all along. Why was he in jail?"

"Train robbery. Almost got away with it. That's why he was flashing around his money. He had hidden it—buried it, they say. When he escaped jail he dug it up, bought a horse and a piece of land here, thinking he'd never be found out."

"Mother was duped by an outlaw."

"Feel better now?" Isabelle nodded.

"How do you know all this?"

"Doris told me."

"Doris? But she's in Paris."

"Paris? You mean you didn't know—"

"Annie, I see your aunt and uncle approaching." Constance stood at the door waving her shawl. "Quick-like! Put on the kettle!"

"We're packing, Mother. They'll not be expecting tea—"

"Don't argue with me! We should be civil to them for all they've done."

Annie heaved a sigh, but she felt relieved too. Jock Carver had been thrown in jail. He wouldn't be hanged, in spite of Linus's assumptions. He'd be free someday, but by that time, the Carraways would be raising grandchildren in another land. However, watching her mother agonize about being uprooted from her homeland sent waves of anxiety through her. She felt responsible for the entire move now. She even felt responsible somehow for the incident with Carver.

"What on earth are you thinking about?" Isabelle asked.

"Isabelle, do you think that I've caused all of this? Our moving away, I mean."

"No, and please stop asking me that, will you?"

"I want to know what you think."

"I think that Mother is better off without the likes of that Jock Carver. I think you're much smarter than all of us, that's what I think."

"I didn't make Jock Carver attack me, Mussy. If you think that's true, then I want to die. Take a knife and kill me now before I breathe another wicked breath!"

"You're insane, aren't you? Like that woman who lives next to Aunt Sybil."

Annie assured herself many times that she couldn't have caused Jock Carver to appear out of nowhere, to make his ill-fated move. She worried that the same thought had crossed Mother's mind. Aunt Sybil had scolded Annie for allowing such thoughts to consume her, said she did Mother a favor in the long run. Hoping Sybil's words would take root, she mulled them over daily. But it was futile. Guilt now consumed her.

"Give me that, Thomas!" Isabelle shouted.

"It isn't your book! It was Father's," Thomas answered.

"Thomas, you know Papa read that one to me. He would want me to have it," Isabelle insisted.

"He read it to all of us, Isabelle. I'll keep it for all of us. You'd be selfish with it."

"Isabelle! Allow Thomas to pack the book. He'll forget about it later. He always does." Annie blew out a hard, ponderous sigh.

"No, I won't!" Thomas took swift defense on his own behalf.

Annie had noticed the tension rising among her siblings for the last several weeks. Trying to keep the peace, she handed Isabelle Ralph Carraway's worn Bible, one his father had left to him. One seldom read unless Mother picked it up.

"Look, Annie. Look what he wrote." Isabelle showed her the handwriting inside the front cover.

" 'To be given to my daughter Isabelle, upon my death. Ralph Carraway.' "

"I never noticed," Annie said. "Strange that he would think of such a thing."

"I'll take care of it." Isabelle found a cloth to wrap it in.

The front door opened. The early light of dawn beckoned the fresh, cool scent of the summer morning into the parlor and drew all of their attention to the entry. Mother stood with a lightweight fichu wrapped about herself. She had a curious smile. The gold of sunrise glinted off her face, her hair. She looked somehow young again, Annie decided.

"What is it, Mother?" Isabelle asked.

"Your uncle and aunt are here. They've something to tell all of you."

Sybil and Abbot Dearborn strolled into the room. Sybil untied her bonnet and assisted her husband with his hat while the children clustered about them. Their twin daughters, Amy and Rosalyn, hair piled with ribbons and waists cinched with lace, sauntered in behind their parents. Seeing them matched from top to bottom, Annie had always felt that two identical smug faces was almost more than a person should be asked to bear.

Annie smiled at her aunt. She loved Aunt Sybil in spite of her interfering ways. But in this instance, her interference had brought about good. Abbot Dearborn had not been so easy to know. Recognizing his reputation as a stern man, she surmised that his being a magistrate gave reason for his solemnity.

"Hello." Sybil greeted each of them.

Amy and Rosalyn, both seven years of age, allowed their aunt Constance to kiss them, then glanced up, expectant of their father's words.

"I've an opportunity I want to tell all of you about. Constance, join us, will you?" Abbot allowed Sybil to take his gloves.

Seeing the sudden light in her mother's face encouraged Annie. Nonetheless, she guarded her feelings.

"As you know, your aunt Sybil and I have, for your sakes, investigated the colonization of New South Wales. We've made arrangements for your mother to occupy a twenty-acre tract of land. It will be difficult in the beginning but, we feel, an enormous opportunity."

Steadying her eyes first on her uncle and then back to her mother, Annie allowed a faint smile to play around the corners of her mouth. She enjoyed the manner in which Uncle Abbot spoke to all of them, as though he delivered a message from young Queen Victoria herself. Annie needed to feel important again.

"Opportunity presents itself in many forms. I, too, have been offered land in New South Wales and a new position as magistrate in Sydney. I turned it down at first."

Annie noted the hint of gratification that wrapped itself around Aunt Sybil's face. If Uncle had power, then Sybil was surely omnipotent.

"It isn't far from the land you will be settling, and if it gives your aunt comfort for us to follow, then . . ."

"You're going with us?" Elation swept through Annie, and her excitement proved contagious for her siblings. As her brothers and sisters squealed with excitement, she dabbed at a tear. Embracing Mother, she then turned and hugged her aunt.

"What's all this?" Sybil asked as tears ran unchecked down Annie's cheeks.

"Thank you, Aunt Sybil." Sobs rose in her throat. She couldn't admit to anyone until now how frightened she was of settling so far from Devonshire.

"Does Doris know yet?" Constance wiped her own eyes.

"Yes. As a matter of fact, she'll be joining us. She's found no suitors that interest her, and so she decided . . ."

While Sybil babbled on, Annie sighed. Why should anyone be surprised to know that Doris had no suitors? The girl was a veritable bonanza of whining, complaining dread.

"Doris wasn't happy in Paris," Isabelle said.

"You knew?" Annie whispered.

Isabelle nodded but kept her eyes on her aunt as they whispered to each other.

"Why didn't you tell me?" Annie, almost demanding, felt angered that Isabelle knew something but kept it from her.

"I thought you knew."

"How could I know if you didn't tell me?"

"I knew. I thought that you knew."

"I feel ill."

"Hush!"

Realization sank in. Annie's little piece of Eden had been tainted.

"Aren't you girls excited?" Constance asked.

Annie and Isabelle both nodded, Isabelle smiling with more sincerity than Annie.

"But what of her studies in France?" Annie asked, showing no trace of emotion.

"She's—"

"No longer interested in art?" Annie could read through her aunt's protective screen.

Sybil's brows lifted and she pursed her mouth. "Not anymore."

"Oh."

"Bah, the girl's homesick!" Abbot interjected.

"What of our farm, Uncle Abbot?" Annie asked.

"Annie, it is no longer our farm," Constance interjected.

"Not to worry," Uncle Abbot said. "The girl has a right to know. You all do. Ernest and Victor are going to manage the land here." He referred to his two oldest sons. Both now married, they had absorbed their father's strong material ambitions.

"They've plans to bring in a new breed of cattle," Sybil added.

Annie battled the jealousy that rose inside of her. The thought of a Dearborn making their struggling farm succeed left her feeling sour, but she couldn't raise a note of protest now.

"They're jolly satisfied and so am I." Abbot's gaze indicated he had lost interest in conversing with the women.

"So there we have it." Constance lifted her brows and gave a dismissive nod to Annie.

"Back to work, Isabelle. Let's finish up in the loft." Annie took Isabelle's arm and led her up the ladder before an impertinent comment escaped the younger girl's lips.

"What's wrong with you? I thought you wanted Uncle Abbot to buy our land."

"I do."

"You're acting peculiar about it."

"I just thought they would keep the land for our brothers' sakes."

"After paying us for it?"

"All right, I didn't know what to think. I'm just surprised is all."

"His sons will make it a fine farm."

"Doesn't it strike you as odd that Uncle Abbot would follow us to Sydney?"

"I don't understand your suspicions, Annie. Why can't you just accept his deed as kindness?"

"It's just odd. That's all that I'm saying."

"Why else would he go?"

"I don't know."

"Don't you like Abbot?"

"I'm just a little angry. You should have warned me about Doris—about all of this!"

"You're too testy with Doris. She likes you."

"She doesn't like anyone."

"Doris likes *you*."

"She only likes to have me around to show off her new dresses."

"I like her new dresses."

"They're frivolous."

"You *are* jealous, aren't you?"

"Of Doris?"

"Of Doris, of the Dearborns. You should—"

"If you quote another Scripture—"

"Who said I was going to quote Scripture?"

"You always do!"

"I'm going back downstairs. With the adults!"

Annie whirled around, turning her back to her sister as Isabelle made her way down the ladder.

The sound of laughter below annoyed Annie even more. Slowly, it occurred to her that Aunt Sybil's constant prodding must have been full of selfish purpose. Annie felt duped. Surely Mother realized that her brother-in-law had seized another opportunity. Annie gazed down at her mother and tried to read her face. Always perfect in manner to the outside world, Mother's actions showed nothing but indebtedness toward Abbot. Yet in the midst of their dilemma, he stood to make a fortune. If she knew him as well as she thought, he would not only make money off the Carraway farm that he had purchased for a pittance, but would also collect another bundle in New South Wales. While the Carraways hacked away to stave off poverty's ravenous appetite, Abbot would rise above all the others and add more wealth to his already burgeoning coffers.

Annie could say nothing, however, for it was at her own prodding that her mother had given in. Annie had gotten her wish. It sickened her to realize that Mother had been right all along about Uncle Abbot's opportunistic ways. A tiny seed of resentment embedded itself in the temperamental folds of her emotions. She gazed down at Abbot again. *Why are you really going to Sydney, Abbot? You aren't saying, are you?*

The sun was hot, hotter than most autumn days on the southern coast of England. The citizens milled about the docks of Southampton, greeting the new passengers who had arrived and waving farewells to the ones who were parting. Cloistered about a wagon, several people bartered and haggled over the price of a fresh fish.

"Don't dawdle, girls," Sybil's voice rose above the clamor.

"Coming!" Rosalyn grabbed her sister's wrist and dragged her along.

Sybil herded the twins through the crowd, picking at them and fiddling with their hair ribbons. Uncle Abbot hurried to keep up with his wife, and their eldest daughter, Doris, followed behind.

"Why must we leave so early?" Doris shaded her eyes with her hand.

"Have you shown your cousins your new wardrobe from Paris?" Sybil glanced back and, ignoring Doris's complaints, chose instead to admire her fashionable seaside frock.

"They don't care about my Paris fashions. What would they know of fashion?"

"I suppose you're right, Doris dear."

"You should have eaten your breakfast, Doris," Abbot muttered. "You know how ill you become aboard ship."

"Everything makes me ill, so what does it matter?" Doris whined.

Sybil had gotten them all up earlier than the Carraways. She wanted a hotel-cooked breakfast before leaving England. Having heard of the primitive accommodations in New South Wales, she craved a taste of culture before departing. Knowing the tight purse strings of her husband, she had predicted that if her sister and children met them in town, Abbot would not agree to the hotel breakfast. It would be improper to dine in their presence without offering an invitation, but to pay the bill for all of them would not sit well with him either. She had found the perfect inn and dragged Abbot inside. She fed her impatient brood and justified her cause. *Constance probably cares little for hotel fare.*

"Where's Aunt Constance?" asked Amy, "and all our cousins?"

Rosalyn ran behind her, her red ringlets bouncing in a comical fashion as she hurried to keep up with her twin.

"They'll be along shortly. Your father's sent a man out to the farm to bring them into town." She glanced up at the *Lady Franklin*. Colored flags flying from the topsails popped in the wind, a seeming welcome to come aboard.

"Let's board, shall we?" Glancing right and left, Abbot took his wife's arm.

"But what of Constance? We should wait for them, shouldn't we?"

"Constance will find her way, Sybil. Besides, you wanted to view the harbor from the ship. Here's your chance!"

"Oh, bother, you're right! Let's do board, Abbot. Your coachman will see they arrive safe and sound. I can't wait to set sail."

Abbot placed his hands behind the twins' heads to propel them forward.

"Buy me a doll first, Father!" Rosalyn saw a window full of toys.

"Me too!" Amy parroted.

"You have new dolls, both of you," Sybil said.

"On we go, then. I'll stand at the bow and watch for the Carraways, Sybil. You ladies go and explore the ship."

"Thank you, dearest." Sybil popped open her parasol and tugged at her short, stylish blue jacket.

"I think I feel ill," Doris moaned as she followed her mother up the boarding plank.

Annie alighted from the carriage, allowing the coachman to assist her. She rather enjoyed the fact that Uncle Abbot had sent a coachman. In secret, she hoped that some of the ladies from church would arrive to see them off, but not for her own sake. Mother looked so fashionable in her tailored frock. All of her brothers and sisters had donned their Sunday best, much to the boys' dissatisfaction. To see them all dressed in tasteful finery, any casual observer would not hesitate to believe them to be anything less than comfortably settled in society. Annie made great show of smoothing her skirt and snugging her white gloves against her fingers. She watched the coachman turn aside to tend to one of his horses before her sisters alighted.

"Look at the ship!" Thomas bellowed.

"Thomas, do aid your sisters. They can't muss themselves, now, can they?"

"Let them jump down. Like this!" He leaped from the carriage.

"You're horrid, Thomas!"

"Do as Annie asks, Thomas," Constance affirmed.

"But she's taking on airs—"

"Thomas!" Grasping the side of the carriage, Constance grew impatient with her oldest boy.

"Yes, Mother!" The lad dragged his heels but waited at the carriage door.

"I'll assist the young ladies, madam. Beggin' your pardon." The driver dropped the horse's hoof he had been examining.

Annie waltzed past Thomas, ignoring his red-hot glare.

"Think you're so lofty. You'll fall from your perch soon enough," the boy muttered.

"You've said enough!" Constance rankled.

The stroll through the harbor invigorated Annie. She wanted to run but restrained her impulses, reminding herself that she wasn't a child. The coachman assisted them in finding the *Lady Franklin*. Abbot and Sybil being nowhere in sight, Constance instructed Annie to wait on the dock for them while she settled the children aboard. Annie adjusted her hat of sienna red straw, thrusting the pin into her coif. Mother had fussed, but only a little, when she had coifed her hair. She had tired of her girlish ringlets. She was as much a lady as Doris, who was only two years her senior. Doris had worn a stylish coiffure for several years, although the style had scarcely done justice for the girl, in Annie's cultivated estimation.

Gazing over the heads of the harbor frequenters, she strained to find the faces of her aunt and uncle. Although Sybil made it her custom to arrive late, Annie still hoped they fared well and had not met with misfortune. The lull of boredom soon engaged her senses. The harbor winds had gained strength, forcing her to keep her hand atop the straw hat. She glanced up at the ship and then out once more over the harbor. She heard a voice lifting above the others, and it caused her to turn and look.

"But I need to speak with a passenger aboard, sir!"

"The *Lady Franklin*'s about to leave port. I can't allow ye aboard without a ship's passage, miss. Now, along wif ye, afore I summon the law!" The mariner stood holding a passenger list. It was his duty to see that no one stepped upon the boarding plank without proper proof of passage.

Annie observed the woman engaged in argument. She was a young woman, quite attractive. Attired in a French walking dress of brown suede and velvet, the woman was fast losing her genteel composure.

"But I must see this passenger!" she persisted.

"Not without proper passage, lady. Now I'm askin' ye once again to leave."

"Excuse me." Pity swept over Annie.

The stylish woman and the mariner turned to look at her.

"I'm about to board the *Lady Franklin*. If I can deliver your message to the captain, perhaps we could at least send word to your friend aboard ship." Annie awkwardly adjusted her hat once more.

"No, thank you, young lady." The woman shook her head, her face flushed with an unspoken sorrow.

"If you'd leastwise give me the passenger's name, miss . . ." the mariner persisted.

Turning to make her way up the plank, Annie grasped the taut rope to guide her way. She had taken only one step when she heard the woman answer. "Mr. Abbot Eugene Dearborn."

Annie whipped around. Her brows knit and her eyes widened. She continued moving toward the woman, listening as the lady poured out her complaint.

"I must find Eugene!"

"Miss? Did you say Abbot Dearborn?" Annie tried to conceal her surprise. She had never heard Uncle Abbot called by his middle name.

The woman nodded.

"Now, there we 'ave it! The man's already boarded along wif 'is good wife and 'is youngsters." The mariner slapped the list with the backs of his fingertips.

"I know Mr. Dearborn. What is wrong, miss?" Annie asked.

"It's that—well, I heard only this morning that Eugene had come to the harbor. I assumed he'd be visiting someone or tending to his affairs. But never this!"

"Please tell me what troubles you, miss. I'll try to help." Seeing the woman overcome with grief, Annie glanced around, feeling helpless. Hoping to see a familiar face, her eye fell on her mother, who beckoned her to come aboard. Instead, she gestured with her gloved hand and admonished her to join her at the foot of the plank.

"I never thought he'd leave like this. Eugene knows that I'm carrying his child."

"What did you say?" Annie asked.

"Perhaps I've chased him away. I shouldn't have told him so soon. But I never intended for this to happen. Abbot's abandoned me now." Her emotions bursting, the woman began to sob without inhibition.

"Annie?"

Hearing her mother's voice, Annie turned her head, but her eyes stayed fastened on the distraught lady. Stunned by the woman's charges against her uncle, she pursed her lips, not knowing what to say.

"Uncle Abbot and Aunt Sybil have already boarded," Constance told her. "We must go now." She placed her arm around Annie.

"But—"

"Uncle? *You're* his *niece*?" The woman's voice quivered.

Offering a silent nod, Annie opened her mouth to reply. But the stranger gathered her skirts and disappeared into the milling throng.

"Whatever is wrong?" Constance demanded.

"It's . . . Uncle Abbot. That woman . . ."

Constance's face filled with an unreadable emotion. She turned to head up the gangplank.

"Mother, wait!"

"Come along, Annie."

"That woman says she's with child. She—"

"Annie! I want you to forget everything that woman's said to you. Never utter a word! Understand?"

"But, Mother, Uncle Abbot is a—" Holding her skirts as she marched up the plank, she swished them back and forth, her anger conspicuous.

"Not a word!"

"You're asking me to hide all this from Aunt Sybil?" She stopped at the edge of the ramp, shocked by her mother's reaction. Constance walked straight ahead and never answered her.

Annie finally joined Sybil and her mother at the top of the ramp. Sybil had gathered together the Carraway children along with her own twins. Doris stood behind them, mopping her brow with a lace handkerchief.

"Annie! There you are, dear child," Sybil exclaimed. "I was beginning to worry!"

Annie gazed into her aunt's eyes. *Trusting eyes*. She saw her uncle standing in the midst of a group of men, blowing cigar smoke, collecting ringlets around his head that hovered like foggy halos. She noticed that Constance had narrowed her eyes and lowered her face but kept her gaze on Annie.

"What's taken you so long anyway?" Sybil asked.

Annie held back the explosive news, news that would pack a wallop greater than a keg of gunpowder. Shrugging off the shock wave of despair, she stretched a smile across her face.

"Well, someone speak!"

"Sorry to worry you, Aunt Sybil. I shouldn't allow myself to fall into such distraction. So glad to see you, Doris. Tell me about Paris."

3
EMPTY-HANDED ORPHANS

Sydney, Australia 1850

Annie's fear that Abbot Dearborn would prosper in Australia as the Carraways sank further into poverty took deep root in her heart during their first difficult years in Sydney. For six long years, Annie had watched her young brothers reaching for manhood with nothing to show for it, no hope offered for their future. However hard she fought to hide her resentment, Annie couldn't help but blame herself, and Abbot even more so, for their struggles.

The sixth summer in New South Wales brought one last crop failure—a failure that had settled into Constance's life along with a fatal illness she had contracted. Annie had relived her mother's funeral so often, she had to remind herself that the grave was now five months old.

"We've only a few hours until sunset, Annie," Isabelle reminded her.

"Just one last thing to pack. What was that?" Annie whipped around, startled by the cry of the native birds. Even after six years of living in Australia, she still awoke expecting the trill of England's songbirds.

"Just a kookaburra," Isabelle said.

Annie had never grown accustomed to the call of the kookaburra in New South Wales, or the opposite seasons, the way the trees shed their bark, or the lack of winter snow. September would usher in a warmer climate instead of a colder one. By Christmas the temperatures would soar and summer would be upon them.

She looked around the empty Australian shanty they had called home for six years. As hard as they had all worked to make it into a home, it had never taken on the charm of their farm in Devonshire. She so missed the rich green hills of her beloved England.

"It's time to go, Annie." Isabelle tugged on her arm.

"I know."

"Drat!" Isabelle pulled the lavender ribbon of her bonnet too tightly and it caught the fingertip of her glove.

"Let me do it, Mussy." Her expression staid, Annie turned from the fireplace hearth where she stared at the garland of flowers around her mother's portrait. She untangled the bonnet cord from Isabelle's glove.

"When will you stop calling me Mussy?"

"Never."

"It sounds juvenile."

Annie ignored her, her attention focused on the task at hand. Stuck in the frame of Constance's portrait was a eulogy written in Clarisse's elementary handwriting: *Our dear mother died March 6, 1850.* Annie lifted the hand-scrawled paper from the frame and tucked it along with the picture into a box. She closed her eyes and kissed the picture.

"I miss her too, Annie."

"No more tears. You'll muss yourself."

"I suppose that's the last item," Isabelle said.

"None of us wanted to pack it." Annie wrapped the picture in newspaper. Before covering her mother's face, she stared at it again. A pity swept through her. She had watched with great pain the changes that had come into her mother's life. In the beginning, Constance had made an effort to see their farm succeed. She had hired two men—one to clear the garden plots and one to handle the plow. All of them, even young Clarisse, had worked to put out the first harvest.

"Remember our first crop?" Annie mused.

"Remember? How could I forget?" Isabelle helped secure the lid on the picture's box.

"I remember too. Clarisse came running into the house shrieking that the seeds had come to life."

"Clarisse lives in constant delirium." Isabelle laughed.

"To this day. We all went running out to find the newly sprouted potatoes. We must have looked foolish to the neighbors."

"Mother seemed so pleased."

"She was pleased. We all were. Here, let me tie that for you." Annie reached for Isabelle's bonnet ties.

"It's all such a pity. I know that God has His hand on us, and I don't want to question Him. But—"

"That was the crop destroyed by pestilence, wasn't it?"

"Yes," Isabelle agreed.

"The next year was the fire."

"Can we go now, Annie?" Isabelle took one last look around the empty room.

"Has Uncle Abbot's carriage arrived?"

"Just pulled up. His men have loaded our belongings into the wagon. The boys want to ride in the other wagon—to guard our belongings, they said. I thought it would be all right."

Annie nodded, only half listening to her sister. Putting away her mother's picture could not erase the memories of the last six years in New South Wales. Or the guilt.

"Want me to take the picture?"

"I will."

They waited in silence for a moment, a wordless tribute to their mother's memory.

"She never wanted to live here."

"Please don't start, Annie."

Annie allowed her sister's protest to pass without a response. She understood the truth much better than Isabelle, and it imbedded itself inside of her, far beyond the grasp of any trespasser. After the starvation years of crop failures, they had tried sheep farming. But they couldn't cope with the competition from the larger operations. Annie had blamed herself for that failure as well. Her mother never complained about the wilderness, but Annie could read the fear in her mother's eyes. Constance Carraway feared monetary failure worse than death. By February, she had fallen ill. Her fever had worsened in spite of the physician's belief in a fast recovery.

Isabelle lifted a small hand mirror to her face and applied a touch of cosmetic to her lips.

"Where did you get that?"

"Jones' Mercantile. Everyone's wearing it."

"You're only seventeen. Mother wouldn't have approved."

"I'm old enough to marry. This bonnet ribbon still doesn't look right."

"The ribbon's fine. And look at your dress."

"It's from Doris's closet. She says she never wears it."

"I wish you would stop dressing like that. Every day is not a ball." Annie didn't want to admit how much she hated any of them accepting charity from Doris.

"This is hardly a ball gown. If you cared anything about fashion, you would know the difference." Isabelle pulled out the bow that Annie had tied at her throat, fidgeting with it.

"I know the difference. But it's overtaken you. Let me tie it again. You know we've no money, and you've exhausted Aunt Sybil's generosity. Ever since that Hogan lad paid you a visit—" Annie tugged a little too hard on the bonnet string and caused it to pinch Isabelle's neck.

"Ouch! You hurt me." Isabelle rubbed her neck and jerked the bonnet ties from Annie's grasp. Her eyes narrowed, two smoldering violet hazes that threatened to ignite. She tied the bonnet herself.

"I apologize."

"I kindly remind you that my respect for fashion was kindled long before Thaddeus Hogan appeared on my doorstep! He's only a farmer, you know. What do farm boys know of fashion?"

"I don't know. But it would pay Thaddeus to take a few lessons in shrewdness if he expects to draw your attention."

"I'm not the shrewd one. Besides, you don't care what I wear at all. You're jealous every time a Dearborn extends a gift to one of us. Look. Now there's a red spot on my neck."

"If it were a gift and not a handout, I wouldn't mind at all. And I said that I was sorry!" She gently stroked Isabelle's neck. A hint of mirth formed a dimple in Annie's right cheek. Her face softened. Hiding a smile, she deliberated on what she should say next. Isabelle could act deeply childish and in the same breath sound so far beyond her years. Grasping her sister's wrists, she clasped them and held them next to her. She lifted her eyes in an apologetic fashion, her long lashes casting shadows on her face.

"All right. All is forgiven. But why are you so angry with me?"

"It isn't you. I'm not myself this week."

"So I've noticed. Rather surly, I would say."

"All right, I've admitted as much." Annie waited for Isabelle's gaze to lock with her own. Her sister always managed to deal out forgiveness in tiny measures. She finally evoked a faint smile from her.

"It's because we're being taken in by the Dearborns, isn't it?"

"I'm sickened by it. . . ." Annie's voice trailed off. Lowering her face, her blue eyes lifted to meet Isabelle's. She had taken full responsibility for her siblings long before Constance's death. Never would she admit that she needed Abbot's help or Sybil's pity. If she could have managed to keep the land, she knew in her heart she could turn down their offer. But without a home, they were forced to accept Dearborn charity. Beyond the parlor window, she could see her two brothers sitting atop the boxes on the wagon. Ahead of them, Clarisse clambered into the Dearborns' awaiting carriage, her long curling locks wrapped in bows of crepe and lace, another of Doris's influences.

"I know it's dreadful, but Mother left us nothing, Annie. She tried—we all tried to make the farm work. New South Wales is a wilderness. How could we have known?" Her words rang with a note of dismissal.

"Poor Mother." Rubbing her fingertips across her lips, Annie felt her eyes mist, but no real tears emerged. Her emotions all dried up, she couldn't cry anymore.

"The driver's here. Let us away. We've a fine practical room to share, as does Clarisse with the twins. We owe our dear aunt Sybil a world of gratitude." Isabelle mustered a cheery smile.

"It's all for pity's sake, though. They look upon us as a charity situation, Isabelle. To them, we're empty-handed orphans. I can't bear it." Recalling the heated conversation between Sybil and Abbot, Annie's emotions swelled with discomfort. She could see it in his eyes, hear it when he spoke to her. Abbot resented having his dead sister-in-law's penniless children forced upon him. Already, she had sensed the contempt when conversing with the twins and with Doris.

"We have to bear it," Isabelle went on. "All of us. Proper women cannot turn themselves out onto the streets. Like it or not, Uncle Abbot will provide for us. He paid off Mother's debts as well as purchasing our farm. I shouldn't doubt that it would become our dowry after all is said and done." Isabelle organized the inside of her purse and drew the cords shut.

"You've always been naïve, Isabelle."

"Ladies, we're ready to take our leave now." The driver stood in the doorway.

"Coming, sir." The August sunshine enveloped Isabelle as she stepped out and curtsied to the driver. Instead of answering Annie's last caustic remark, she walked away.

"I'm sorry again, Isabelle," Annie whispered. She watched her younger sister stroll gracefully toward the carriage. Annie could never hold her tongue, another source of her deepening pool of guilt. But Isabelle, blind to the faults of the Dearborns, was ever the optimist. She could find streams of sunlight at midnight. No matter how colorfully Isabelle embellished their future, however, Annie couldn't imagine anything pleasant about living with the Dearborns. Nor did she count on a dowry from Abbot. Worse than that, sharing a room with Doris would be akin to having her pride trampled upon at every waking moment.

Isabelle's disgruntled expression caught her eye. Annie shuffled past her sister, allowing her petticoats to brush against her with sassy innuendo. Isabelle on occasion had to be reminded about who was the oldest.

"We've kept them waiting long enough," Isabelle said.

"Isabelle, hush. Onward, driver! We've no time to dawdle." Annie forced an imperious tone, but she didn't feel imperious. Not today.

"Now bring your pen across like this. Young Farrell, I trust you'll bring some fresh ink tomorrow. Your well is nearly dry." Mason Hale, a successful Sydney architect, stood over his two apprentices.

"Yes, Master Hale. As you know, my father has met with some hard times." Rogan Farrell pulled his pen tip up diagonally, leaving a slight train of ink along the side of his straightedge.

"I know." Hale waved away the young man's comments. Farrell referred to the bush fire that had incinerated thirty years of the Farrells' work in a single day. Having had several thousand sheep with all of their grazing land destroyed, the Farrells had been forced to sell off much of their remaining flock just to buy more grazing land. "But if Donovan Farrell intends for his eldest son to become an architect, he surely realizes the necessity of a bottle of ink."

"Yes, sir. I've saved enough to purchase the ink myself, but it's nigh my mother's birthday. You know how birthdays are."

"Yes. I know all about birthdays." Hale turned away and marched nimbly into his small office. Returning with a box of coal, he shook some out into the embers of the stove.

"Thank you, sir. There's a bit of a nip in the evening air," Harry Winston, another apprentice, said as he began putting away his drawings.

Hale disappeared into his tidy office with the coal box.

Rogan watched as Winston tucked his drawings into an expensive leather case. He had trouble understanding Hale's patience with Winston. He arrived late in the morning and seldom finished one drawing before he had begun another. As for himself, Farrell wanted no hard words with him, although their first meeting had met with mild friction. Winston had a caustic presence that frayed Farrell's patience. Harry's father, Lord Reginald, was an earl; his kinsmen sprang from a long lineage of barons and baronesses. Young Winston had spent all of his years living in a superficial fashion, squandering his father's money on young, impressionable women, his taste for expensive wine as important to him as the air he breathed. Rumor had it that Harry's zeal for gambling would one day bring about his ruination.

"Finished for the day?" Farrell cut his eyes askance.

"None of your concern, Farrell," Winston rankled.

Rogan turned his eyes back to his own design. He would never allow Harry Winston to draw him into conflict in the presence of Mason Hale. Nor did he desire to make Hale aware of their silent war, although the tension between them could not be hidden. Rogan knew the truth about Harry, and his hidden satisfaction would have to suffice. Determined to settle his carousing son into a responsible role, Lord Reginald had easily secured for Harry the apprenticeship with architect Mason Hale. Rogan had waited for two years to be accepted into the apprenticeship, two years spent as a common laborer under a man Rogan detested. But Hale had wanted to see what Rogan was made of, to be sure of his commitment to the field.

Rogan detected Harry's stare boring through him, but he wouldn't give him the satisfaction of a blink.

Hale breezed into the room again.

"Interesting design, Farrell," Harry Winston muttered. Loose strands of auburn hair fell about his face, glinting like fool's gold in the glow of his candle.

"It isn't finished." Rogan Farrell's tone suggested his suspicion. He knew that when Hale was about, Harry poured on the flattery. Rogan turned his back on Harry. He worked another thirty minutes, truly wanting to squeeze another hour out of his pen. But weariness beset him. He had arisen at dawn to help his father feed the remaining flock. Saddling up the family mare, he had charged into the cold gray dawn, his mind full of his new house-plan design. He had set the rough outline to paper now, but his satisfaction had waned under the critical eye of Mason Hale.

"You'll soon be putting us all to shame, Mr. Farrell. Patience, young sir." Hale raised his heavy brows, his brown eyes assessing Farrell's dissatisfaction.

"With all due respect, patience doesn't feed us, sir." He couldn't tolerate himself being cast in a callow light.

"No, it doesn't. How well I know. But neither does money bring you the satisfaction you now seek. The earnest pursuit of nothing but wealth can bring a man's ruination."

"Let me take my share of '*dis*satisfaction', then, and I'll be the judge of my own 'ruination'." A smile curled into Farrell's cheeks, defining his elegant cheekbones.

"Here, here! Let us all fall into such gainful 'ruination'!" Harry Winston lifted his bottle of ink high into the air in a mock toast.

"Back to your labors, young squires. I shall teach you the finer craft of architecture and allow a more cruel master to teach you the ways of life."

"And who, pray tell, will be our cruel master?" Harry chuckled.

"Why, life itself, Mr. Winston. And this indomitable depression that settles itself upon New South Wales." Hale drew out his books and laid them on his desk before returning to his office.

Rogan penned his name at the bottom of the draft. Carefully blotting the ink, he lifted his candle and scanned the design once more, mentally reconstructing the flaws pointed out to him by Hale. The long shadows of late afternoon stretched across the wooden floor. He set about to straighten the drafting room while Hale met in another room with his banker.

"I'm taking my leave. Let Hale wait here until dawn if he must." Harry loosened his cravat.

"Shall I balance Master Hale's books today, Winston, or would you care to have a go at it?"

"No. You go on. I wouldn't want to deprive you of the joy." He turned to look at Farrell full in the face, his glacial blue eyes staring out from his ruddy countenance.

"You'll have to conquer the bookwork soon enough. Master Hale expects it of his students. It is one matter to become masters of our craft, but quite another to oversee our finances."

"You bore me, Farrell. But perhaps one day I'll hire you to keep my books. You seem to keep them well enough."

"I'll do well to manage my own affairs."

"Then manage your own, and I'll keep mine in my own way."

Rogan gripped the ends of the parchment and rolled the drawing into a tight tube.

"You don't think I should be here, do you, Farrell?"

"My opinion is worthless to you. Why ask?"

"You think you're better than I, more skilled, don't you?"

"I'll leave that decision to public opinion one day."

"Why wait? Your public deserves you now—today."

"I don't have the wealthy backing to support my architectural endeavors. Some of us poor souls must *work* for our keep." Instead of waiting for his response, Rogan stepped abruptly toward Mason Hale's large desk. Settling himself into the wooden chair, he lifted the quill, dipping it twice before proceeding.

He began the calculations, noting the payments and setting aside the retribution to be paid out. Hale had fared well in Sydney as an architect. Georgian architecture had finally arrived in the wilderness, and with painfully slow change, the temporary shanties that dotted the mud roadways had given way to permanent structures in both Sydney and Parrametta. While many colonists succumbed to the depression, Hale had kept up his living with commissions from the government. A blight had hit many crops and wiped out a great deal of the local commodities. The sudden reliance on imported produce had sent a blow to the fledgling economy. But unaffected by the farmers' market, Hale remained steady in his work.

With his usual swiftness, Rogan reconciled the books and reworked his calculations. Exercising patience, he found a suspicious entry and set to work proving the erroneous number.

"Problem, Farrell?" Winston whisked across a row of books with his fingers.

"An error on my part," Rogan said. "I thought I knew this entry, but I see now in Hale's own handwriting, the client's paid him in part. Not like Smithfield to offer partial pay, though." He glanced once more at the figures. The ink had faded, so he traced over the numbers again with his pen.

"I grow weary just watching you, Farrell. Good night." Harry yawned.

"At least it appears to be Hale's handwriting." Rogan was still pondering the entry.

"Ah! As our dear Mr. Mason Hale so adeptly pointed out, we've a depression with which to contend. A partial pay is well to be expected. You worry too much, Farrell."

At that moment, Mason Hale stepped out of his office with the banker at his side.

"Master Hale, we've attended to the chores."

Rogan shot Harry an accusing glance.

"If you will, I must away and see to a certain young woman," Harry went on, making haste to rearrange his cravat and shake loose the frill of his sleeve.

"Go on, then, Mr. Winston, if you must. And off with you, Mr. Farrell. It would do you well to chase a petticoat or two."

"In due time, sir." Allowing his face to drop in a droll manner, Rogan clasped his long fingers across his chest.

"Ah, don't tell me. Allow me to venture a guess. In due time, *after* you've earned your fortune?" Hale leaned toward his stubborn prodigy.

Rogan didn't reply, but he offered Mr. Hale a faint smile.

"Such a bore, Farrell. Good evening to you all!" Harry Winston donned his coat and hat and made fast for the door. He bowed in a cavalier fashion, his red queue falling across his shoulder. His patience spent, he shut the door behind him as he left.

"You may take your leave, sir. I'll lock the doors and put away the books," Farrell offered, as was his custom.

"I thank you, kind sir. How the company of Hale, Harding, and Biddle ever made progress before taking on young Farrell, I shall never know!" Hale handed the banker his coat and then put on his own. He strode over to Winston's desk. In a kind gesture, he blew out the apprentice's candle. Then he straightened up, his right brow lifted in a curious slant. Farrell watched with mild interest as the senior architect fished around in his pockets.

"I almost forgot. A birthday present for your dear mother."

Hale pulled out a small box wrapped in plain paper.

"Sir, I did not intend to imply—"

"I insist! We can't allow a little depression to blow out the promise of a birthday, now, can we? Open it, lad, and tell me if it's something you feel would please Mrs. Farrell." Hale popped a monocle into his left eye.

"You want me to open it?" Rogan asked.

Hale nodded, his lips pursed.

Rogan tore away the folds at one end and looked inside, his face filled with bewilderment.

"Well?" Hale asked.

"It's a bottle of ink, sir."

"She has need of it?"

"Not exactly, sir."

Hale put on a great show of disappointment in his choice of gifts.

"I'm sorry, sir, but—"

"Drat! I should have allowed my dear Anna to select the gift. Never good at such deeds." Drawing himself up, he buttoned his coat and opened the door to allow his banker friend to lead the way out.

"Coming, Hale?" the banker asked.

"After you, Mr. Higgins. Well, I've no need for more ink, Mr. Farrell. You keep it yourself. I'll ask Anna to find something more suitable for your mother."

"No, sir. With complete gratitude for all you do, I know what business you're about and I won't stand for it!"

"Good evening, Mr. Farrell. And my best wishes to your mother. You'd best take your leave soon if you're to find her a proper gift before the shops all close up." Hale slammed the door and left Farrell with nothing else but the sound of the bell that rang from the doorframe. Through the windowpane, the last rays of sun slid behind a bank of clouds.

Muttering to himself, Rogan Farrell closed up the books and put them away. With great resignation, he set the new bottle of ink on his desk. Old Hale was a stubborn soul and would never take back the ink, no matter how much he insisted. *Charity!* He slammed his hand against his desk top. *Has it come to this now?* He gathered up his drawings and shoved them all inside a hand-made cover to take home with him. He would work until midnight on the plans, if need be. The sooner he could begin to sell his own work, the sooner he could begin to pay back the generosity of old Mason Hale. He lifted the bottle of ink and gazed with misery upon it. He hated poverty. He would do his best to bury it in the deep pit of his past. He blew out his desk candle and prayed good fortune would soon be upon him. Matters could surely grow no worse.

4

THE SUSPECT

"Ouch! You're pulling my hair!" Doris Dearborn sat by the tall picture window in her bedroom. Behind her stood Isabelle. While she sat against a straight-back chair, Isabelle plaited silk flowers into her hair. She stared into a mirror at her own pale reflection, her brows pulled together in a pained expression.

"I'm sorry, Doris." Isabelle cast a playful glance toward Annie, who lay across the bed watching them.

Doris had been sick all morning, running to the washstand to splash water onto her face.

"Have you met this Charles Lafferty fellow?" Annie asked.

"No. I wish he weren't coming," Doris said.

"Why?" Annie saw that her cousin's hands trembled.

"Why can't I meet him casually, at a party, or while out riding? This formal arranged business, well, it makes me sick. Physically, literally sick."

"But don't you want to marry?" Isabelle pressed down the loose hair that stuck up along Doris's crown.

"Not like this," Doris said. "I feel like I'm being judged, like a hog at market."

Annie dropped onto the bed, laughing.

"It isn't funny!" Doris said.

"Forgive me, but you make me laugh." Annie wanted to sound apologetic. She had begun to feel a greater pity for her cousin.

"Help me cover these. I look dreadful, as though I have a fatal illness. Perhaps I do." Doris counted the freckles along her nose and lifted a pot of cosmetic from the vanity.

"Nothing's wrong with you." Annie pulled a pillow over her ears, weary of Doris's whining.

"Doris, I like your freckles. Don't cover them." Isabelle said, cupping her hands over the cosmetic jar in Doris's hand.

"You do?"

"If he doesn't like freckles, then he's not worth the bother. Who would want such a vain man? Not I," Annie said.

"Why do you care? You never freckle." Doris jerked the jar from Isabelle and rubbed the cosmetic into her cheeks.

"I tried to freckle once," Annie said.

"On purpose? That's why you never have suitors. You've no sense of style," Doris said.

"Doris, don't say things you'll regret," Isabelle said.

"You don't have to defend me, Mussy," Annie said. "I just don't tailor my looks to everyone else's liking." Annie was growing weary of the conversation. She wanted to be somewhere else.

Just then Sybil stuck her face through the doorway. "I'm off to Mrs. Hazelthrow's."

"Good-bye, Aunt Sybil." Annie offered a meager wave.

"Mother, don't leave!" Doris yanked a flower from her hair and hurled it down.

"Doris, we've had this discussion. If you need anything, Ada will see to it."

Annie could see the impatience in her aunt's eyes. Her eldest daughter's emotional spells drove her to distraction. But Annie felt that Sybil's solution—to leave her to her own devices—resulted in little benefit. Doris only grew worse after her mother's departure.

"Have a wonderful afternoon with Mr. Lafferty. Annie, do try to calm her." Sybil dismissed herself from sight.

Annie closed her eyes.

"You should dress now." Isabelle picked up a towel and wiped her hands. "Charles Lafferty will be here soon."

"Make him wait. How important can he be, after all?"

In Annie's estimation, the fellow sounded like a bland sort, but he already owned a large tract of land in Parrametta. His kinsmen had settled in New South Wales fifty years ago. He would one day inherit his parents' entire estate, one that had been passed on to them by their ancestors. His parents had expanded with livestock ten years ago. The Lafferty estate now boasted one of the largest farming operations in New South Wales. Aunt Sybil had called him a "suitable candidate." Numerous suitable candidates had paraded through the Dearborns' manor house to meet Doris. All of them sent Doris running to the washbasin.

Annie felt Doris should tell her mother the truth—that she didn't want her life organized and set in order by someone else. Every arranged courtship only pushed her further from believing herself worthy. The pressure to perform forced Doris further inside herself.

"I'm tired of all this talk of courtship and freckles and hair," Annie complained. "Why not just tuck it all under a bonnet and be done with it?" She lifted her book, scanned the pages, and closed her eyes to commit her study to memory.

"Charles Lafferty is courting her in the parlor," Isabelle said. "Doris can't wear a bonnet in the parlor." She tugged at a tangle in Doris's hair.

"I think I'm going to be ill again." Doris fanned her face. "Annie, ask Ada to fetch me some water. What if I faint?"

"I've the perfect cure—run and tell your mother that you don't want to meet this Lafferty fellow," Annie said.

"Isabelle, will *you* fetch Ada?" Doris closed her eyes and crossed her arms at her bodice. She then clasped her smallish fingers about her bare shoulders as though she had a chill.

Isabelle glanced at Annie, pleading with her eyes.

"All right, I'll do it." Annie slipped on her cloth shoes, strolled to the doorway, and glanced out. There were no servants about, so she strolled out into the hallway. She breathed out a sigh and muttered to herself. Finally she located one of the housemaids. "Have you seen Ada?"

"Downstairs, Miss Carraway."

Ada Towley had been with the Dearborns since before Doris was born. Whenever Doris was in need of emotional support, she called on the spinster maid, who doted on her without fail.

Annie turned around and walked away from their room. She descended the carpeted stairway, then padded across the roomy waiting area. She could hear the kitchen maids chattering and the clanging of pots and dishes as they prepared for the evening fare. Hearing snatches of conversation, it sounded to Annie as though they were gossiping about the Dearborn girl's suitor. Annie shook her head. "Ada!" Pity welled up inside of her, for she fully understood the truth—if Abbot had not offered such a handsome dowry on Doris's behalf, this young man would never give her a second glance. Doris always showed her worst side in front of strangers, a practice that ensured her isolation.

Before being drawn into a relationship, Annie would be certain her future was designed of her own making, and not at the hands of two greedy families who sought a perfect monetary match. As for herself, she would rather live alone than allow Abbot Dearborn to dictate her life.

She glanced around, trying to catch sight of Ada.

"Annie?"

"Yes?" Lost in her quiet preoccupation, Annie had not heard Isabelle descend the staircase.

"All finished now. Tell our cousin how lovely she looks." Isabelle stood behind her cousin on the steps, her delicate fingers clasped around Doris's thin upper arms.

Doris's eyes twitched nervously as she lifted her face and gave a wooden smile. Annie admired the costly dress she wore but struggled to not compare the two young women's faces. Isabelle, a demure beauty with her auburn locks, perfect ivory skin, and soft violet eyes, smiled easily, an elusive blush across her cheeks. Even after applying almost no cosmetics this morning, Isabelle's rosy face caused her cousin's painted features to pale next to her own. "You do look lovely, Doris. What elegant flowers." Annie nodded her approval. "And your dress is quite lovely."

Doris burst into tears.

The next hour lingered, an unmerciful period that stretched toward the hour of high tea like a countdown to the gallows. Annie tried to immerse herself in a history book, but she found it difficult to focus her attention. Doris had set the household staff into a frenzy, making manifold demands of them. Annie strolled through the downstairs, her nose in the book.

"Annie, could you come here?"

From outside the parlor, Annie could see Doris sitting on a settee with fear etched across her pale face. The fact that Doris had whispered her request made her curious. "Please, hurry and close the door behind you."

"I should be studying." Annie faced her, then walked inside, her book tucked beneath her arm.

"You read too much."

"What do you want?" Annie could see the sweat beading on Doris's forehead.

"I have an idea. It came to me clear, almost like a vision."

"Doris, you don't look well. I'll fetch Ada."

"No. Listen. We don't have much time."

"We?"

"I want you to wait here and pretend to be me. Make Charles Lafferty think you're me."

"You want me to lie? No."

"No. Not lie, exactly. Let him think that you're me. Don't tell him, just allow him to believe it."

"I can't. I'm busy—with studies." Annie tried to turn and leave, but Doris jumped up from the settee and ran to her.

"Annie, I can't do this anymore. Not like this, anyway. Please say you'll help me."

"Call it off, Doris!"

"Mother won't let me! She's too strong. And I'm too weak." A sob rose up, and tears filled Doris's eyes again.

"You don't have to be weak." Annie couldn't bear a second round of her tears.

"But I am. Meet Charles in my place, will you? You're charitable in your heart; I know you are."

"You've a twisted idea of charity. I won't lie for anyone."

"You're going to help me! Please, Annie, don't leave me in here. If Charles Lafferty sees me like this, they'll be talking about me all over Sydney and Parrametta." Doris grabbed her wrists.

"You shouldn't care what the gossips say." Annie pulled away.

"But I do! I can't bear humiliation!"

"You look a fright. Go back upstairs and ask Isabelle to help you." The more that Annie dabbed at Doris's tears, the more they streamed down her face, washing away the hour's worth of cosmetics.

"I can't find Isabelle!"

"I'll go and look for her."

"No! You've got to stay here and make believe you're me."

"I told you, I won't do that."

"What am I going to do?" Doris turned and looked at her father's liquor case. "Fetch me a glass."

"That would be a mistake, Doris."

"I'll fetch it myself, then."

"I'm going for Ada," Annie insisted, becoming worried over her cousin's increasingly erratic behavior.

"All right with me!" Doris shouted after her.

Annie ran out the door. She searched from room to room but couldn't find the maid. Finally she caught a glimpse of her entering the kitchen from the back garden. "Excuse me, Ada?"

"Yes, child." Preoccupied, the maid answered without glancing up.

"Doris isn't . . . well enough to meet Mr. Lafferty. Someone must stop all of this nonsense," she said. "When he arrives, will you send him away?"

"I can't do that, Miss Carraway. Mrs. Dearborn wants Doris to face up to 'er fears."

"But she'll never face them, not like this. Surely you see the folly of all this?"

"That I do. Don't give much thought for arranged marriages. I love young Doris and want the best for the girl, but I can't go against our mistress." Ada Towley, a portly woman with a round face and heavy brows, shook her head.

"Ada, you've got to help her."

"I wish I could, lass."

"If you don't, she'll be humiliated. I'm worried about her."

Ada gave Annie a compassionate look but shrugged her shoulders helplessly. "I don't want to see 'er 'urt again, poor girl. T'would be much the pity."

"Is there nothing you can do to help?"

"Young Miss Isabelle done up 'er hair an' made 'er look the queen. I don't rightly know what else we could do to help the poor bashful girl." Setting up the candlesticks, Ada pulled out the best china place settings for the courtship meeting.

"Will you at least delay him?"

"Delay 'im, how?"

"I could ask Doris to meet me in here if you could help Mr. Lafferty bide his time. Perhaps if I had more time to calm her. She's much too nervous for her own good."

"You're right, I vow." Ada untied her soiled apron and draped it over her forearm. Her eyes lit up. "I'll do it. You bring Miss Doris in 'ere and calm 'er nerves—a shot of brandy in 'er tea. Not more than a smidgen, mind you. And I'll invite Mr. Lafferty to take a stroll."

"Here's what—invite him into the garden," Annie said.

"I can send 'im out there, but I'm only a maid. Surely you don't expect me to detain 'im."

"You're right. I'll fetch Isabelle, ask her to meet him. She can talk until dawn."

"Would she do it?"

"She'll do anything if she thinks it's charitable."

"What a lovely idea. I like it."

"Once we've settled Doris, we'll escort her into the garden and make her look important, as though we're escorting a duchess."

"Splendid! Now you run and fetch Doris. I'll watch the front landin' and stop Mr. Lafferty before 'e 'as a chance to see 'er all anxious and the like."

Doris stood outside the kitchen listening to her cousin and Ada. She held up her father's flask of rum, pressed it to her lips, and tipped the remainder into her mouth. Tired of being used as a bartering tool for Abbot Dearborn's burgeoning empire, she determined to find courage in any way she could. She could no longer stand by, passive and compliant. With the back of her hand, she wiped the traces of rum from her lips, set aside the flask, and ran down the long corridor that led to the home's entrance. Before Ada could reach Charles Lafferty, Doris would set in motion a plan of her own.

Run, Doris! Poise, girl! Make him believe what you want him to believe. You can do it!

Her feet swift as she left the room, Annie felt somewhat relieved, but she didn't like the idea of putting brandy in Doris's tea. Perhaps some chamomile would settle her. She climbed the staircase and strolled with purpose toward their bedroom. From the corner of her eye, she saw Ada disappear below. She turned and ran down the hallway. Once inside the room, she saw that Isabelle had busied herself straightening up after having spent so much time aiding her cousin.

"Hello, Annie. How is our cousin?"

"Ada and I are trying to calm her. Would you mind very much if I asked you to meet Charles Lafferty in the garden? Delay him as long as possible until Doris has had time to make herself presentable."

"She's not presentable?"

"I'll explain later. Will you meet him?"

"What do I say to him?"

"Tell him nothing about Doris, her being nervous and the like. He might not be the understanding sort. Ask him about himself. Men love to talk about themselves."

"But what if he asks about Doris?"

"You simply assure Mr. Lafferty that she will be out to meet him soon. The anticipation alone should only add to the mystery."

"I do love mystery!"

"Good. Now change your dress and make yourself presentable. We need you in the rose garden as soon as possible."

"All right. Give me a few minutes to change."

"Thank you, Mussy." As Annie turned to leave, she heard her sister's voice.

"Annie?"

"Yes?"

"You're such a queer girl."

"Why do you say that?"

"You're helping Doris. Why?"

"If she's married off," Annie explained, "it will give us the bedroom to ourselves. That's all."

"Of course, you're right. But that isn't your real reason, is it?"

"It's my only reason." Before her sister could detect the blush upon her cheeks, Annie rushed from the room. She hated it when Mussy started prying into her feelings. As much as she refused to admit it, though, her sister's suspicions rang true. She wanted to help Doris because no one else would do it. She ran to find her. They would need to work fast if this new arrangement were to work.

She pushed open the tall oak door. It opened, slow and deliberate. The silence inside the parlor worried her. "Doris, I've come for you. Doris?"

Doris ran down the carriage path from the manor house, stumbling and muttering. Father's driver had left a fully hitched calash in the shade of a wattle. The two-wheeled open carriage would be the perfect means for heading off Charles Lafferty. His family's large estate being only four miles east of the Dearborn estate, he would most likely enter the property from the rear entrance. She pulled herself onto the seat of the calash and grabbed the reins, startling the horse. The whip snapped in her grasp, and the horse whinnied as her senses spun. Although she felt ill from the rum, she also felt driven. Her emotions pumped through her, propelling her over the threshold of her timidity. The carriage circled around to the rear of the home, then careened down the path that led to the rear of the far acreage. She spied a smart-looking black cabriolet ahead. "Mr. Lafferty is right on time." She slowed the horse, then made fast to smooth her unkempt hair and straighten her skirts. To test her breath, she cupped her hand to her mouth and blew. She winced, then decided that she must remain in the carriage so he wouldn't detect the rum.

The cabriolet drew near, and Doris could see a young man, dressed in an expensive wool suit, driving it himself. She wondered why he had no driver. She wiped the shine from her face and poised herself. Ada or another servant might appear at any moment, so she made haste to meet him. "Sir?" She flicked the reins, then approached with caution.

The young man tipped his hat as she approached. "Mademoiselle—"

"Mr. Charles Lafferty?"

"I am he."

"I've come to bring you a message."

"Who, pray tell, are you?"

"I am—that is, I represent Miss Doris Dearborn."

"You are her lady?"

Doris started to confirm that she was indeed a lady's maid, but remembering her expensive attire, thought better of it.

"Or her kinsman, perhaps?"

"Yes. That's it. I'm her cousin."

"I trust Miss Dearborn is well."

"She is. Quite fit. But she is, that is—" Doris drew her hand to her mouth and closed her eyes as nausea all but consumed her.

Her head slumped back against the seat.

"Are you all right?" the young man asked. "You look ill. May I help you?"

"No." She shook her head, righting herself.

"I'm taking you back. Allow me."

"I'm quite well, thank you. Begging your pardon, but the young lady whose company you seek is making herself ready. Her morning has been full of . . . studies."

"Studies?"

"The Scriptures. She's quite taken with the study of the Bible."

"Is she? So am I."

"What a coincidence."

"So she's a woman of faith?"

"Yes. Great faith. Strong convictions."

"I can't wait to meet her."

"She's looking forward to meeting you. But she so hates all this arranged business."

"Does she, now?"

"Her fear is that her parents will interfere with the hand of God."

"I, too, have feared that I would miss God's hand."

"But perhaps it's by His hand that you meet."

"I hadn't thought of that."

"So you understand her caution in this meeting?"

"I only respect her for her prudent thinking."

"Shall we go, then?"

"Let's."

"Oh, and Mr. Lafferty?"

"Yes?"

"Do call her Mussy. It's her pet name, you know."

"Really?"

"Her older sister called her Mercy, her middle name, when they were quite little. But it sounded like Mussy. Funny the way names like that will take hold."

"So true. I, too, have a pet name."

"Well, use it, then."

"All right, I will." He laughed.

"Remember. She likes to be called Mussy."

"All right, then. Mussy it is. I like it."

A young maid, doe-eyed and timid, peered into Annie's room. "Miss Carraway, Ada says to tell you that a visitor has appeared in your aunt's rose garden. She believes it's Mr. Lafferty. She wants you to run greet him."

"She wants *me* to greet him?" Isabelle had already gone downstairs, so Annie wondered why Ada had sent for her.

"Yes. She says he's alone out there, but she doesn't know why."

"All right." Annie slipped back into her cloth shoes, wondering why Isabelle hadn't met him. She ran downstairs, glanced around the entrance, strode through the parlor, and then made her way outside. She could see a young man just above the rose hedge. "Sir? Mr. Charles Lafferty?"

"Yes. That's me." He lifted his face and smiled.

"I'm the cousin of Miss Doris Dearborn."

"Ah. Seems our Miss Dearborn has no want of cousins."

"So you've met my sister?"

"Yes. She greeted me promptly and asked me to wait here in the rose garden for Miss Dearborn."

"I'm glad to hear it. So you don't mind waiting?"

"Not at all. From what your sister tells me, she's quite a wonderful person. I'm looking forward to our first meeting."

"I'm so relieved to hear you say such things, Mr. Lafferty. I will see that Doris is hastened along. You don't mind if I go and see to her now?"

"Please. I am most anxious." He dusted his trousers and straightened his cravat. Then he doffed his cap and took a confident stance, which emphasized his muscular frame.

Annie loved his warm smile and his captivating dark eyes. More handsome than she had imagined, she realized how wrong she had been about him. She only hoped that Doris would not disillusion him. It was evident that Isabelle had done her work in preparing him for her. She thought it a great pity that Doris would never appreciate their endeavors. But she wouldn't worry about that now. "We thought that by meeting out here, your first encounter would be less conventional. That is, this arranged meeting in the parlor—"she paused—"so formal."

"I understand. Miss Dearborn has some reservations."

"So you're not bothered by all that?"

"Not at all. She sounds like a young woman of great wisdom."

Annie wondered if perhaps Isabelle had taken matters too far.

"Please allay Miss Dearborn's fears by telling her that I too am of the same mind as she."

"You don't say? So you're satisfied with a less formal meeting in the garden?"

"I agree. Out here would be much better; that's for certain." Charles Lafferty slid his fingers down a rose stem. "May I?"

"Please. Take as many as you like."

"Just one, for now." He snapped off the stem and lifted it to his nose.

"For her?"

"Yes. I'm sure it will pale next to her lovely face."

Anxiety welled up inside of Annie.

"Please tell Miss Dearborn that I will wait for hours, if need be."

"You have such a generous and kind heart."

"Would you give this to my lady and tell her it's from me?" He tried to hand her the rose.

"No, no. You should give it to her. It would mean more to her that way."

"You're so wise to tell me such things. And who, might I ask, are you?"

"I am her cousin Annie, who . . . cares deeply that Doris is handled with delicacy."

"I swear you have placed her in friendly hands. I will treat her as though she were an angel in disguise."

"You're a good man, Mr. Lafferty. Perhaps God indeed has sent you."

"I trust He has."

Isabelle stood in front of her mirror. The hem of her skirt had several broken threads and needed to be mended at once. She had found a downstairs maid, a woman handy with a needle and thread. She mended it at once without Isabelle's having to disrobe. After straightening her bodice, Isabelle adjusted the ribbons on her dress and smoothed back the stray strands of auburn hair that tickled her cheek. Then she opened her Bible and committed another Scripture to memory. If nothing else, she could share her knowledge of God's Word with him. If he proved to be a man of little faith, she felt it her duty to warn Doris accordingly. A bottle of perfume in her grasp, she dabbed a touch of the fragrant ointment around her throat. She then left the room and made her way to the rose garden. She hoped that Charles Lafferty had not been waiting too long. With a great sigh, she decided that always coming to the aid of Doris could become a wearying task. However, if Annie could be so charitable, then so could she.

Mason Hale turned up the wick on his lantern. Having sent his two apprentices home, he now poured himself a glass of ale and stoked the fire. He would present a new plan to the governor of New South Wales the next day. He had met with several dignitaries and garnered their approval for a new government office. Since the recent abolition of the transporting of convicts from England, he had also heard talk of a prison. Unfortunately, England had no prisons the Australians cared to model. The rebellious Americans had founded two prisons, but the scorn for America ran too deep to emulate their penal institutions. He had designed his government complex with some modern designs he had studied in England. Now he had only to achieve Governor Gipps's approval. Wanting all of his papers finished down to the last detail, he had worked Farrell and Winston night and day for many days. Both men had performed to his satisfaction, but he was exceptionally approving of Farrell's work. At times, he could see sparks of genius arising from the young man's pen. Organizing the drafts into an impressive presentation, Farrell had brought out details that old Hale himself hadn't thought to add.

He plucked his monocle from his weary eye and rubbed his eyelids. Lifting his glass to his lips, he drew in another long drink of ale and prepared to go home to his good wife. She had seen little of him during the past fortnight. It would do her heart good to find him at the supper table with his appetite intact. After he set aside the original building designs, he covered them with a clean parchment and laid them carefully on the desk. Not noticing where Farrell had meticulously stacked his financial calculations, his stout hand accidentally knocked the papers aside, causing some to tumble onto the floor. Agitated by his own clumsy comportment, he blew out a sigh. He bent his heavy frame sideways. With a groan, he scooped up the papers and tried to determine Farrell's system of order. He soon found the names of his clients penned neatly and alphabetized within the pages of the books. He proceeded to shuffle the papers back into the same order and had started to put them away when an entry caught his eye. He wouldn't have noticed it otherwise, but the insertion had been altered.

He fumbled atop the desk until he found his monocle. His brow and cheek squeezed the glass into place as he held out the record book. With a mind for calculations, he remembered in distinct detail this client's payment. Mr. Smithfield had sold a load of livestock and paid off the bill, as was his custom. Now the amount had been changed. *Why would Farrell change the entry?* A twinge of worry trickled through his emotions, but he reasoned that there must be a good explanation. Farrell came from good hardworking stock. Albeit, he had his ambitions, but he would never stoop to embezzlement, would he? Hale shook away the thought. He had treated Farrell like a son. True, he and his now-deceased partners had always set up their accounts with a grain of mistrust to ward away temptation. Common sense dictated as much. *But Farrell? Not possible!*

Then reasoning arose in his thoughts. Perhaps the client had had a change of heart. Perhaps Mr. Smithfield needed the funds for other reasons. Times were hard. Perhaps he had not paid as much as Hale first thought he would pay after all. Farrell might not have thought to mention the change in his payment. Besides, his age had beset him now—how often his dear wife had told him! He often questioned the reliability of his own memory.

Hale felt better already. He would take the books home and have Anna go over them with her calculating eye. Fatigue had gotten the better of him. He and Farrell would discuss the matter at first light when the young man arrived. By midmorning, they would both be enjoying their cup of tea and thinking on other matters. The problem would resolve itself.

Hale gathered the books into his arms and turned down his lantern. He put on his coat, closed up the stove, and walked out into the chilly twilight, where he stood beneath a streetlight. Opening the book in question once more, he gazed down, his silhouette still and dark against the yellow haze of lantern light. He stared again, hoping he had misread the record, somehow had been mistaken about the entry. But the mistake glared at him even from the mantle of night; it accused him of allowing too careless a trust. He closed up the book and disappeared into his carriage, hopeful that answers would arise with the dawn.

5

MISTAKEN
LOVE

"What's happened? Where's Doris?" Annie ran from the upstairs out into the front parlor. She saw Ada Towley standing red-
faced outside of the parlor.

"In the parlor, well along in 'er cups!" Ada said.

The news horrified Annie, sending a wave of anxiety crashing
through her senses.

"I only told you to give 'er a drop in 'er tea, Annie. She's gone
and emptied 'er father's rum flask!"

"But surely you don't think that I—"

"Think? It's not what I think. Come see!" Ada took her by the
hand, then led her into the parlor, where they found Doris slumped
over the lace tablecloth, moaning.

"Doris, you didn't!" Annie rushed to her side.

"Jus'—a bit. Not much, mind you." Pulling herself upright,
Doris smiled feebly and held up her fingers, measuring the amount
with her finger and thumb.

"Ada, this is dreadful!" Annie cried. "Let's try hot coffee!
Quickly!" She turned to stop a maid who scurried past. "Go fetch
some coffee. Make it quick! On with you, now!"

"If the Lafferty heir sees Miss Dearborn like this—"

"He can't, Ada! We must send him away. I'll run tell him myself. But you take Doris upstairs and douse her face with water. Then give her the coffee. Don't allow her father to see this. He'll kill her."

"Judge Dearborn? He'll 'ave us all flogged!" Ada shrieked.

"Quiet! We must hurry! Take Doris upstairs now, Ada!"

Isabelle had waited in the garden now for half an hour but had yet to see the mysterious Charles Lafferty. In his place, however, another visitor to Dearborn Manor had kept her company.

"I like a pet name. I've told you mine," he said.

"Yes, I like the name Chase. But how did you know I'm called Mussy? Only my brothers and sisters call me that." A quiet laugh spilled from Isabelle's lips. She walked beside the handsome young man in the garden, calm and serene, the midday sun gilding the edges of her hair and face. She wouldn't have spoken to him at all, but his gentle mannerisms allayed her fears.

"It's supposed to be a secret, my lady. Besides, it suits you."

"Why do you say that?"

"Because when I look into your face, I see mercy and grace. As well as—" His voice broke off and he looked away.

"Come now. Finish what you mean to say, sir."

"When I look at you I see also—an inherent strength, yet you look so delicate."

"You needn't flatter me."

"I'm sorry, Mussy. I've embarrassed you."

She shook her head but still couldn't look at him. His knowledge of her baffled her. Perhaps Uncle Abbot had told him about her.

"But your family has kept your beauty such a secret from the world. How could I have known?"

"My family? Who are you, Chase? Why are you here?"

"Who and why? Ah. Your thoughts run deep. Is it possible, Mussy, that it's by God's hand I've come?"

"Now, there we have a clue. You're a Christian man."

"I am. I spend every moment away from the toil of our farm in the study of the Scriptures."

"As do I." Isabelle's face lit up at this confession.

"But seldom have I found a woman like you, one so adept in her theology."

"You know this about me?"

"I do."

"You're playing some sort of game with me, but for the life of me I don't know the rules. I know I should send you away, but something keeps me from it." A smile formed at the corners of her mouth. She felt mystified by this young man, yet drawn to him.

"Send me away and my heart shall flounder."

Isabelle could not contain her laughter.

"You find me humorous?"

"I find you rather charming, actually."

"I'm glad of it. Is Master Dearborn about the manor today?"

"He's out in the far pasture. But unless you know well his land, you'll be lost for certain. You're here to see him?"

"I feel I must. I have an answer for him. Will you accompany me?"

"Actually, Chase, I can't. I'm to deliver a message for my cousin." She glanced around, puzzled that Charles Lafferty had never made his appearance. Then the thought occurred to her that perhaps he had already met Doris in the parlor.

"Another cousin?"

"Yes, but I've waited long enough. My sister will surely understand. And if you've matters to tend to with Master Dearborn, then I suppose I should hasten you to him."

"We'll take my carriage, then?"

"Why not? And since you know so much about me, you can tell me all about yourself."

Annie shoved back the kitchen door and ran inside, her feet scarcely touching the worn wooden floor. She saw Elvie, a kitchen maid, watching the kettle boil.

"Afternoon, Miss Carraway."

"Elvie, we need the coffee at once. Can't you hurry?"

"Hurryin' as fast I can, miss."

"You know we need this for Doris?"

"I've heard. Done got into Mr. Dearborn's liquor case, I vow."

"Quiet!" Annie tried to silence the woman. "If you will, please run and fetch Mr. Charles Lafferty for me. Ask him to meet me in the parlor."

"The young man wot's met your sister out in Mrs. Dearborn's rose garden. That one?"

"Oh, so Isabelle did greet him?"

"Greeted, talked, laughed, and done rode away with 'im in 'is fancy black carriage. Drove over yonder 'ill."

"Isabelle's gone with Charles Lafferty?"

"Yes. I watched the whole thing from that far window. Looked like they was 'avin' a jolly time of it."

"I don't understand."

"They're gone now, miss."

"What was Isabelle thinking?"

"Not about Miss Doris Dearborn, that's for certain."

"I'll have to go find them. That's all."

"Want me to send for a liveryman?"

"Yes. Thank you, Elvie. If Mr. Lafferty returns without my knowledge, will you show him to the parlor? I'll not be gone long."

"Gladly, miss. Oh an', miss?"

"Yes?" Annie, impatient, kept her eyes toward the rose garden.

"I won't be sayin' nothin' to the Lafferty heir about Miss Doris bein' in 'er cups an' all."

"Of course not! And tell my sister Isabelle that . . . that I've need of her in our bedroom."

"Yes, miss!" Elvie curtsied and departed at once, her brow furrowed.

Annie watched Elvie stride across the lawn.

"Has anyone seen my Doris?"

Annie turned around, startled by the sound of a voice. "Ma'am?"

"I can't find her anywhere," Sybil said. "Is she out somewhere with Charles Lafferty?"

Annie, with a blank stare, turned ashen.

"I tell you, sir, that I would never do such a thing! To accuse me of such is folly! Mr. Hale, you know my life, you know me—"

"I do—at least, I felt I did, Mr. Farrell. But we've studied all the books since you've taken them over. In the last eight months, we cannot account for eight thousand pounds." Hale paced, his face toward the floor. Behind him stood the men who had aided in the investigation—two of his banker friends, a military officer, and two town officials, as well as the client who had given him the pay for his work.

"I ask you to give me more time, Mr. Hale. I know I can prove my innocence. Where is Winston?" Farrell could sense the tightening tension in the room.

"Oh, Winston knows nothing of the books! I've sent him home. The lad can scarcely keep up with his own studies, let alone figure calculations. Now I ask you again, will you please explain to me, Mr. Farrell, why our good client's records have been changed? Is this not your own handwriting, traced over the first entry?"

"I truly believed that you did it, sir. Not that you tampered with it, mind you, but that our client here, Mr. Smithfield, had not paid us as he agreed to do. I thought perhaps you had made a separate arrangement with the man." Rogan walked behind Hale to read over his shoulder. "I only traced what I thought was your correction to make it more legible."

"I paid you exactly as I agreed to, sir—in full!" Smithfield held out the paper with Farrell's own handwriting, indicating as such.

"And I know I recorded it exactly as it should be! I remember doing so. But originally I made no other corrections. *I* didn't make it," Farrell argued.

"Mr. Farrell, are you implying that I would change my own records? I've nothing to gain."

"And it looks as though I do? Not reason enough, Mr. Hale. I am innocent!"

The room grew silent. Each of the men turned and looked at one another. They shook their heads as Mason Hale walked from the room, his silence punctuating his pain.

"I'm afraid you'll have to come with us, Mr. Farrell. We are woefully sorry. I knew your grandfather." The military officer stepped up, his guard snapping to attention.

"Not to worry! I'll be free before nightfall, my good man!" Raking his hair back with his hands, Rogan Farrell submitted himself to the authorities present. *God help me, Harry Winston, you did this to me!*

"Would someone please tell me about Doris? Have you seen

her?" Sybil asked. She glanced around the kitchen, puzzled. None of the maids would look at her.

"She's . . . she was a bit nervous, so Ada took her upstairs to calm her nerves. She didn't want her to appear anxious in front of Mr. Lafferty," Annie said.

"So where is Mr. Lafferty? I understand he arrived some time ago and I've yet to make the young man's acquaintance."

Annie watched Sybil's gaze, how she looked with purpose at the undisturbed tea service.

"Someone better answer me, and soon!" Sybil rankled.

"Let's adjourn to the parlor, shall we?" Annie suggested. "I'm certain Mr. Lafferty will return soon. Elvie saw him take a carriage ride and—"

"Carriage ride? With whom? Not Doris."

"I had just commenced to go and find Mr. Lafferty, Aunt Sybil. Why don't I do that now?"

"No. I'd rather you stay here and wait with me."

"But why?"

"You seem to know the most about this situation, dear. Inform me."

Annie heard the veiled threat in her tone. As much as she pitied Doris, she couldn't allow herself to fall victim to the blame.

"Well?" Sybil demanded impatiently.

"I know no more than anyone else." Without lifting her eyes, Annie breezed past her aunt and turned to grasp the tea service. She placed the sugar and cream on the tray and fumbled with the pastries. An uncomfortable knot formed in the pit of her stomach. She would try to seat her aunt in the parlor and then run upstairs to help Ada with Doris.

"Pardon me, miss. Coming through!"

The maid, with the suspicious single coffee cup on her tray, brushed past. Annie stepped aside and stood next to Sybil. She wanted to avoid Sybil's curious stare, so she fell in line at once behind the maid before taking a fast detour toward the parlor. Her heart raced as she stepped into the parlor, the tea tray jittering in her nervous grasp. With thoughts swarming to figure out the swiftest escape from Sybil's inquiry, she glanced around to find a suitable table for the tea setting. Then the door opened wide and in stepped Sybil.

"Well? Are you going to tell me where Charles Lafferty's gone? You do know, don't you?"

"Please don't feel so responsible, Mussy. Perhaps Judge Dearborn's gone back to the manor house."

"I apologize, Chase. I feel I've led you on a wild goose chase," Isabelle said.

"I'm glad. It gave me more time to get to know you. But I should take you back. I wouldn't want to worry your family."

"Yes. My sister does tend to worry." His tender qualities affected her in a way she could not describe.

"You've a good sister, then."

"If somewhat doting."

"How many sisters have you?"

"Two."

"Of course. I remember now. I believe Judge Dearborn mentioned it."

"Chase, we really should return." Isabelle knew that she had looked for too long into his compelling eyes, but her strength to look away now waned. She hesitated, and for an instant in time she felt she could look at him forever.

"Wish granted." He nodded, flicked the reins, and the black carriage meandered toward the manor house.

"I'm going up to see my daughter," Sybil said.

"Allow me, Aunt Sybil. I'll go and fetch Doris." Annie tried to bustle past her but found her way blocked by Uncle Abbot.

"That won't be necessary. I've just come from my daughter's room." Abbot stepped into the parlor and stood beside his wife.

"Uncle Abbot, she's not feeling well. You must understand that Doris is under a weight she cannot bear." Annie read the anger in Abbot's face. It took all of her courage to look into his seething eyes.

"Not feeling well? Annie, step into my study. At once!"

"You must allow me to explain—"

Abbot cut her off with an impatient wave of his hand.

"Will someone please tell me?" Sybil asked. "What's wrong with Doris?"

"Our daughter"—Abbot whispered the reply—"is drunk!"

"What?"

Annie dropped her head in her hands. The matter had now become volatile, beyond her control.

"I know all about the little liaison in the garden too."

"What liaison?" Sybil grasped her throat.

"It was no liaison! My sister—"

"Your sister's run off with Charles Lafferty. The servants saw it all from the kitchen."

"They don't know what they saw!" Annie, red-faced now, swallowed hard and struggled to keep her head.

"Ada said you gave the rum to Doris, Annie."

"I didn't!"

Abbot grew visibly angry, marched to the doorway, and glanced down the hallway. Then he stepped back inside the parlor and slammed the door to assure privacy.

"You gave Doris rum?" Sybil asked. "I feel faint." She leaned against her husband's arm.

A rap resounded against the parlor door.

"I'll get it," Annie said.

"No. I'll get it." Abbot whirled around and flung open the door.

"Mr. Dearborn, is it?" Charles Lafferty stood with his hat in his hands.

"And who are you, young man?"

"I am Charles Lafferty. I'd like to request a word with you, sir."

"Mr. Lafferty. I apologize for the delay in meeting our daughter." Abbot's face yet pale with wrath, he extended his hand.

"Actually, I've had a delightful time. I was never told of your daughter's beauty—both inside and out. May I see her again?"

Abbot's uneasy gaze betrayed his bewilderment.

"You've met our Doris?" Sybil asked.

"Yes. And I want your permission to see her again. I've never met anyone like her."

"Really?" Pleased with what she heard, a broad smile lit up Sybil's face. Annie saw Abbot's dubious gaze, and she felt equally perplexed.

"Miss?" Elvie peered into the parlor and addressed Annie.

"Yes, Elvie."

"I've asked your sister Isabelle to meet you upstairs just like you asked me. Need anything else, Miss Carraway?"

"No, thank you, Elvie."

"Judge Dearborn, sir, can we have that talk?"

"I'm sorry, Mr. Lafferty. But we'll have to cut short our visit with you. We've a family crisis to deal with just now. I'll see you're taken to your horse, though." Abbot signaled Elvie.

"I've a carriage right outside. No need for a liveryman. But might I say good-bye to your daughter just once more? I want to assure her that I will return in a few days."

"No!" Abbot said.

"What my husband means is that she's . . . resting."

"All's the pity for me, then. But to know that I have your blessing to return, I'd be nothing less than overjoyed." Lafferty planted his hat atop his head.

"Would Friday be good for you?" Sybil said, then beamed.

"Excellent!"

Charles Lafferty's glowing smile worried Annie. She knew in her heart that he hadn't had the opportunity to meet Doris.

"Oh, hello." He smiled at Annie, causing her to curtsy, all the while keeping her hand over her face. "Thank you for the message, good miss. Your cousin was well worth the wait."

"So my niece here, Annie Carraway, arranged your meeting in the garden?" Abbot glared at her in a way that only she could detect.

"I suppose she did. All thanks to you, Miss Carraway. Miss Dearborn had been detained with her Bible study, so she asked me to wait for her in the garden. I so admire your daughter's faith. I admire everything about her, actually."

"I see," Abbot said.

"Why don't I take you to your horse, sir?" Annie started for the door, hoping he would follow her.

"I wouldn't hear of it. I can find my own way."

"See you on Friday, then?" Sybil asked.

"Until then." He bowed and departed from their sight.

Annie waited for the sound of Charles Lafferty's footsteps to diminish into the silence. She longed to run upstairs, to hear the truth from Isabelle's own lips.

"Did you hear that young man? He wants to see Doris again?" Sybil's ecstasy rose as a fiery blush upon her cheeks.

Abbot folded his arms, watching his wife effervesce over the handsome young Lafferty fellow. He closed the door again and bellowed, "Oh, for the love of—Sybil! Don't you see what's happened? He never met Doris!"

"But didn't you hear him, Abbot? It's love at first sight."

"Charles Lafferty's not spent one second with Doris. Annie can tell you where he's been—and with whom. Tell her, Annie."

"Sir?"

"After all, it was you who arranged all this for your *sister's* benefit, wasn't it?"

"Uncle Abbot, if you're accusing me of any malice, then please be plain about it."

"Doris never met Charles Lafferty, did she?"

"I don't believe so, but—"

"It is in fact your own sister Isabelle who's been with him. But for the life of me, I cannot fathom how you pulled off the charade—made Charles Lafferty believe that Isabelle was Doris."

"I do feel faint!" Sybil teetered, fanning her face.

Annie beheld her uncle's bright, mocking stare. A sickening panic swirled through her. She couldn't believe his accusations. She looked past Abbot, her words sounding wooden. "I should go check on Doris . . . and my sister."

"Yes, you do that. And then I want to see you in my study—at once!"

Nodding, Annie slid past, her face colorless. Abbot would never listen, had never listened. She trudged up the stairwell determined to piece together the chaos.

Annie found Doris sleeping as soundly as any person in her condition would be. Her head bound with a damp cloth, she muttered in her sleep. Ada had drawn the curtains about her bed and bid the household to leave the girl to lie in peace. Annie peered around the room but saw no sign of Isabelle. She crossed the hallway to the room where Clarisse and the twins slept. The younger children had gone down to the library to attend to their studies. She speculated that perhaps Isabelle had wandered into their room. Riddled with anxiety, she pushed open the door. She hesitated, standing halfway inside the doorway. Isabelle stood gazing through the window, her back to the door, her shining curls wound up with silk rosettes. Annie strode up to her, then sighed and said with a somber tone, "Mussy—"

"Annie. There you are. Elvie said you've been looking for me."

"The entire household saw you leave with him, Isabelle."

Holding her finger to her lips, Isabelle continued to gaze out, her eyes a soft violet haze. "Look yonder. I see him now. He's going home for now, but he'll be back."

Annie turned her face to stare also. Beyond the garden, Charles Lafferty whipped his horse, a dapple gray stallion with a beribboned mane. Annie clasped her hands in front of herself and dropped her head. "Have you an explanation for this, Isabelle?"

"Explanation? Oh, I've worried you, I see. I'm sorry, Annie. I should have told you. I know it looked improper and all, me riding away with a strange man. But he's so gentle and a friend of Uncle Abbot's. I never worried for a moment. I shall not sleep again until he returns."

"Mussy, you can't mean it!"

"Oh, but I do. This is real, Annie. I've heard of this happening before, but feeling it for the first time—"

"Feeling what?"

"Love, of course."

"I think I feel ill. I'll go lie down with Doris."

"No. Don't leave me. I want to tell you all about Chase."

"Chase? You think his name is Chase?"

"Oh, but here I am rattling on. He told me that he met you. What do you think of him?"

"He's a nice young man, but he's intended for Doris."

"Chase?"

"Charles Lafferty! Why do you call him Chase?"

"Oh, is that what you think?" Isabelle laughed. "That I've stolen Doris's beau?"

Seeing the innocence in Isabelle's eyes, Annie knew her sister had not yet fathomed the dilemma that centered around her.

"Dear me, no. I've met a young man who had business with Uncle Abbot. His name is Chase."

"Isabelle, his business was courtship. You've spent the afternoon with Charles Lafferty."

"I haven't!"

"I swear it! Did you tell him your name?"

"He knew my name! He called me Mussy! Didn't you tell him? Aren't you the one who told Chase my name?"

"No!"

A single tear trickled down Isabelle's cheek.

"You have to right this, Isabelle. Uncle Abbot believes I've sabotaged this courtship on your behalf."

"I'm confused, Annie! Please tell me none of this is true."

"I can't! It's the horrid truth. And now he's fallen for you—for the wrong woman."

Isabelle's face softened. "He's told you this . . . that he has feelings for me?"

"You've swept the poor man off his feet."

A wide smile broke across Isabelle's face. "Then it *is* love."

"I can't believe what I'm hearing."

"Don't you see, Annie? This was by God's hand. No one made this happen. It just happened, and now I'm in love. It's real."

"Stop saying that! I'm not entirely sure about it—that someone didn't make this all happen."

"I didn't cause it."

"No, but you said he knew your name."

"He called it my pet name. Not once did he call me Doris."

"Well, I didn't tell him your pet name. But I'll find out who did."

"We must go first and tell Uncle Abbot, tell him how sorry we are about the confusion."

"A part of me should be sorry, but to say such a thing would be a lie."

"Isabelle, he thinks you're Doris."

"But he fell in love with me, not Doris." She cast an oblique gaze Annie's way.

"We're ruined if you say all that to Uncle Abbot. He'll toss us out."

Charles Lafferty had disappeared into the early gray of twilight. Isabelle lifted her hands, revealing the rose that he had picked for her. Holding it to her nose, she closed her eyes. "I'll see you again soon, Chase. But until then, I'll look for you in my dreams."

"This is insane. What if the man's a rogue?"

"You know yourself that he isn't. Did he tell you that he would return?"

"Friday. Aunt Sybil set the date. But he's expecting to meet Doris Dearborn."

"I'll tell him what happened. I'll tell Uncle Abbot. Doris didn't want to meet him anyway. She said so herself. Uncle Abbot will have to understand when Chase asks to court me."

"No, Isabelle! Uncle Abbot won't tolerate it." Turning about, Annie lifted her yellow skirts and seated herself.

"He'll understand. I'll make him understand—"

"You can't! Don't you see? This courtship with Doris and Charles Lafferty—it's all been arranged. You cannot stop it."

"I can and will. Doris will find other suitors."

"This is unlike you, Isabelle. You're toying with me—say it's true." Annie stood once more and looked directly into Isabelle's face. But all she saw was the beginning of a smile and the softness of her sister's gaze.

Annie tore from the room. Uncle Abbot would be waiting in his study and she didn't want him to have to come looking for her. She would give Isabelle time to come to her senses. No matter what had just transpired between the two of them, it was all a mistake. Charles Lafferty could never see Isabelle again.

Rogan stood in line behind the other convicts, his hands and feet shackled. Having suffered such sudden humiliation, he had not been given ample time to send word to his family. He hoped his father would arrive soon, as much as it pained him to be seen in such a way. But Donovan Farrell had been a longtime opponent of the convict transportation system that had recently been toppled. The Farrell name had been widely spoken of in political circles around Sydney along with other anti-transportation patriots like Reverend John West. If ever he needed his father's aid, tonight was the night. He filed into the cold, damp hold behind the others. The barred window had been stuffed with cloth to keep out the chill, and so the cell was dark. Only the guard's lantern illumined the grim faces.

"Look, we got us a dandy!" One of the convicts eyed Farrell up and down.

"Shut up, you!" the guard barked, holding his lantern high to reveal his leather whip.

"You can't leave me in here!" Farrell looked all around while the other male convicts began to scramble for a place on the floor. A rat scurried past and he lurched toward the cell door. He shouted at the guard, but it only resulted in the man whirling about and returning to his post. Rogan's mind raced for answers. He would have his father send for Winston. The apprentice had been at his side every evening while he posted in Mr. Hale's books. Winston would never confess to the crime himself, but perhaps he would lay aside his cowardice long enough to at least vouch for Rogan.

The clanking of metal keys against the bars drew his eye. The outer gate squeaked open. "Father!" His heart filled with relief. "Thank heaven you've come!"

"Rogan! What have they done to you?" His mother, Meredith, ran past her husband.

"I'm all right, Mother. Has my brother come with you?"

"Frederick is on his way."

"I am here!" Frederick said. "What's all this? You've been down at the Boar's Head causing a row, no doubt?"

Seeing the humor in his brother's eyes, Rogan shook his head. "I only wish it were true. Someone's tampered with Mr. Hale's books. They believe I'm the culprit, but I am innocent."

"Of course you're innocent!" Meredith said.

"We will bring you the best defense, son," Donovan assured him. "I'll go visit a judge. You will be freed tonight."

"No, please!" Rogan insisted. "I want Mr. Hale to know that I am innocent—not that I was freed because I'm Donovan Farrell's son. But I will accept the aid of a lawyer."

"Have you any money?" Donovan's face reflected his frustration.

"Yes. I believe I've enough. Don't use any of your money, Father. You need it for Rose Hill." Rogan recalled his own small savings, which he had hoped he could use to help his family keep their estate at Rose Hill. The depression had hit them hard, and they were on the verge of losing everything. And now this!

Frederick surveyed the pitiable conditions inside the jail cell and spoke up. "I'll bring you someone tomorrow, Rogan. I know of a lawyer. He'll do it and wait for his money, if need be."

"Thank you, Frederick. And could you please go visit Harry Winston? He was with me when I kept the books. He can speak on my defense. I don't know why he hasn't done so sooner."

"You don't?" Frederick asked.

"No, and I can't prove my innocence from in here. I suspect Harry may have had something to do with this—but he can't know of my suspicions, mind you."

"Do you know what you're doing, brother?"

"Yes, Frederick. Just get me the lawyer."

The Farrells lingered as long as the guards allowed. After their parting, Rogan stood until his legs gave out. Then he found a place against the wall and seated himself. He knew that he would sleep little, so he sat up most of the night waiting for the sun to rise and mentally preparing his defense.

6

THE DOWRY

Annie sat in Abbot's study. He had sent word to her to wait until morning for their meeting. She had dreaded the time, wanting the confrontation to be behind her. But knowing Abbot Dearborn the way she did, she was certain it was another of his ploys to gain ground. He always had a strategy and invariably emerged the victor.

"Miss Carraway?" Ada appeared at the doorway, a pitcher of water in her hand.

"Oh, thank you, Ada," Annie said as the maid refreshed her water glass.

After Ada had left the study, Annie's mind replayed the scene in the dining room the previous evening. Annie had hated the silent pall that hung over the room. Doris sat sipping hot coffee and nursing her hangover. Aunt Sybil took every occasion to offer up a look of disappointment. Worst of all, Isabelle entered the dining room chattering and full of exuberance. Annie had sat miserable and nervous, her hands twirling her handkerchief, while a heaviness settled in her chest. She had tried once more to reason with Isabelle, but she could only manage to evoke one promise—that she would wait until Abbot fully understood the matter to be a complete mistake before admitting her feelings for Charles. Appealing to Isabelle's own natural common sense, Annie had reasoned that if her feelings for Charles Lafferty were true, she would feel just as strongly about him by week's end. Isabelle had agreed.

However, keeping the radiance out of Isabelle's eyes and the rosy glow from her cheeks would be an impossible chore. Now Annie faced Abbot's large desk. She could hear him down the hallway barking out orders to the servants, preparing the farm laborers for their long day. Then he was caught up in conversation in regard to a new building endeavor.

Annie knew she shouldn't listen but found herself leaning toward the partly opened door.

"Miss Carraway?" Ada's face appeared around the corner once more.

"Yes, Ada?"

"Mr. Dearborn says to let you know that he's on 'is way. He 'as a busy day an' wants you to know that your meetin' will be brief."

"Good enough. Thank you." Annie never looked her in the eye but kept her gaze straight ahead. She felt angry and humiliated at the same time.

Within moments, Abbot bristled into the room, his hat in one hand and his cane in the other. He closed the door and seated himself behind his desk. His dark brows shadowed his eyes.

Annie hated his aloof demeanor but was grateful that he hadn't taken to shouting at her, a trait that usually emerged whenever the man felt challenged.

"I'll start by saying that your aunt and I are disappointed in your behavior. As you know, we've taken great pains to find a fit suitor for our daughter. She is a sensitive girl. She's both disgraced and embarrassed by yesterday's fiasco. She believes that in order to face this young man again, she would need much time to recuperate. Suitors don't come along every day. And this one believes he's met Doris—when indeed he hasn't! A most unfortunate concern."

"Please believe me, Uncle, when I say I'm deeply sorry for all the confusion. I'm sorry that Doris feels embarrassed. But you should have seen her before—"

"I've seen all I wish to see."

"I'm sorry but—"

"Sorry will not repair the damage. What of your sister? She's set her sights on the Lafferty heir as well, eh?"

"My sister also needs time, just as Doris does. She was an innocent party in this matter. Please do not blame her."

"She realizes that she has no dowry, doesn't she? The Laffertys would never agree—"

"No dowry?" His words flew at Annie. The matter had never been discussed.

"The dowry offered to the Laffertys was intended for Doris, not your sister."

"Surely, Uncle, you would offer a dowry for my sisters. I care nothing for myself, but you cannot leave them without means."

"Much is the pity, my dear. But your parents' land cost me a small fortune to reclaim. It left you and your brothers and sisters penniless. For the sake of Thomas and Linus, I can arrange an apprenticeship for them. And once the matter with Doris and Charles Lafferty is settled, we can discuss a small dowry for you and your sisters. But—"

"Uncle Abbot! You cannot mean that you would blackmail my sister and me!"

Her words ignited his infamous temper.

"Don't you accuse me of blackmail!"

"What else, then? What do I call it?"

"It's a simple arrangement. You tell your sister to dismiss any ideas about Mr. Lafferty. I will offer a practical dowry for Isabelle as well as yourself and Clarisse. Every farmer's son in this impoverished land will stand in line to court your lovely sister. She has many assets for a colonist to consider."

"This is an outrage! You cannot barter with our lives as though we're cattle! And you know nothing of Isabelle. She would no more marry a farmer than—"

"I can't afford to dawdle over this silly affair. I've scarcely time to make it to court this morning."

"You're a horrible man!" Annie weighed her options. His words pierced her mind like red-hot coals. If she had harbored bitterness toward her uncle before, it now stretched into full-blown malice. Her voice quivered and she hated herself for it.

"You'll have a talk with your sister?"

"But you've no right." She couldn't risk sending either of her sisters into the colony without a dowry. She shook her head, the tears now spilling freely down her cheeks.

"One of us has to be reasonable. As you journey along life's way, you'll see that I made the best decision for you—for all of you. You'll be needing a suitor as well."

"I won't do this for myself," she said. "And I don't want your tainted money!"

"I know that as well. You wouldn't be the daughter of my dear late brother-in-law if you acted otherwise. But it was his stubborn ways that killed him. If you care at all about your sisters' futures, you'll accept my offer for them as well as yourself. Remember that fact, my dear, as you discuss this. Guard your words. I want the matter laid to rest—at once."

Her eyes boldly met his, but she could not overpower him. The scales, as usual, tipped his way. She turned on her heels and marched from the study. *He's a monster!* She glanced up the stairs. It appeared that no one in the entire household knew of her plight. But she couldn't bring herself to tear out Isabelle's heart all at once. She would give herself time to formulate the proper argument so that Isabelle would understand and the matter would be settled. Recalling her sister's radiant face, she suddenly felt sickened at the task before her. If only she could wrench herself free from Abbot's grasp. But for now, she would be forced to comply, and her bitterness for the man would grow. She turned to take a walk in the garden, silent and defeated.

"Harry Winston." Rogan Farrell stood slowly, pressing his way through a cluster of convicts. The fact that he had slept little, and had resorted to intimidation to keep the mob from stealing his coat and boots, only heated up his rancor all the more when he awakened to find Harry Winston staring at him through the bars.

"Morning, Farrell," Harry Winston said.

"Pardon my appearance. I wasn't expecting visitors."

Harry looked down at the floor.

"Why are you here, Winston?"

"Your brother Frederick asked me to come."

"He's always been the thoughtful sort. Why have you really come?"

"Frederick thinks I can help."

"Can you?"

"I can vouch for your character."

"Awfully big of you."

Harry looked annoyed at the rebuff. "I think I should leave."

"What's your hurry?"

"I . . . I shouldn't have come here."

"No, please stay. They'll come soon with dinner and you should see what the cook can do with gruel."

"I'm sorry I can't help you, Farrell."

"But you've helped already, good man. How else would I learn to appreciate the finer things of life if I hadn't experienced hell first?"

"I must take my leave—"

"Wait!" Rogan reached through the bars and grabbed Winston's collar, although he had intended to grab his throat.

"Turn me loose, or I'll call for the guard!"

"What's the hurry, Winston? We're just two good friends having a chat, eh?"

"Tell me what it is you want."

"Say you'll help me, Winston! Say you'll vouch for my innocence. You were with me every second of every evening. You know I wouldn't tamper with Mr. Hale's books."

"Not exactly true."

"What isn't true?" Rogan released him.

"That I was with you every second of every evening."

"It's most certainly true!"

"No. You have keys. I don't. You can return anytime without my knowledge."

"You mean to say that you don't have keys?"

"No. I turned them down. Didn't want the responsibility."

"What the devil are you trying to say? That I embezzled from a man I highly respect?"

"I've heard of worse crimes."

Rogan grabbed the bars and shook them.

"Temper, Mr. Farrell."

"You're a liar!"

"I'm not going to lie for you."

"I didn't ask you to lie."

"It was implied."

"This is madness! What, pray tell, would be my motive in all of this?"

"You needed the money, obviously."

"Drat it, Winston! You know I'm innocent! You listen to me—"

"Listen to you? I've listened to you for well nigh a year. You maligned me and patronized me with your superior airs."

"I've offered you respect that you never earned."

"You pompous egalitarian! You toss me an occasional bone and expect gratitude."

The words stunned Farrell. He had never realized that he sounded patronizing to Winston.

"Are you so blind to your own flaws, Rogan?"

"Flaws? Is that the topic of the day? Look at me! I'm locked up like an animal, you idiot!"

"I'm leaving! I don't care to be insulted any further."

"Winston, don't leave me like this! I'll—"

"You've no reason to threaten. And you've little recourse. How did you think I could help? I know nothing of the records you keep."

The words seeped into Rogan's emotions. *Why is Winston lying?* He could no more sustain a conciliatory tone than he could break through the iron bars that held him.

"Good luck, Rogan."

"I am innocent, Harry Winston! You of all people know it!"

"Use your father to get you out. He found you the apprenticeship in the beginning. Use Donovan Farrell's influence and leave me out of your schemes."

Farrell read the resignation in his face, heard the finality of his words.

"I pity you in your circumstances, Rogan, but I cannot aid your poor choices."

"Leave me, then!" Farrell exclaimed. "I never want to see your petulant face again, Harry Winston!" He could hear the muttering among the convicts, expressing their scorn for one above their ranks having been tossed in among them. Out of the corner of his eye he could see Winston turn and leave. He kicked aside his empty dish and slumped against the wall. The lawyer would surely arrive soon. Cupping his hand to his mouth, he closed his eyes and blew out a ponderous breath. *Pull yourself together, man!* He had to maintain his good reasoning, had to mentally prepare for his day in court. Insanity would not sit well with the judge.

Annie walked slowly among the symmetrical rows of hedges and roses. Looking down, her features hidden by her hood, she unbuttoned her blue walking coat, feeling too warm from the sun. She hadn't noticed that Isabelle had sauntered into the garden. "What are you doing, Annie?"

Annie's face lifted. But instead of her usual enthusiastic greeting, she offered no reply.

"Something's wrong," Isabelle said. "It's about me, isn't it?"

"How did you find me here?"

"I watched you from our window. I could see your mood stirring all the way from the house."

"I'm glad you met me here," Annie said. "I've something to share with you."

"Let's go inside. I'd like some tea while we talk." Isabelle turned away, but Annie laid her hand upon her sister's sleeve.

"Wait, please. I need to tell you something. It's about our uncle . . . and it's about Doris."

"I don't like the worry in your face. Mother used to carry the worry on her face like that."

"You know that our mother could leave us nothing. Our uncle wants to—" she struggled to spill the words that would cast Abbot in the best light—"to help us. All of us. He is prepared to offer a dowry for you and for Clarisse. Even for me . . ."

"A dowry?"

"Although I don't want it," Annie said.

"Annie, that's wonderful news."

"Wait. There's more. He wants to find you a proper suitor."

"But he doesn't have to find one. Charles Lafferty is—"

"Isabelle, you must hear me out. What I have to say is important. And you must listen."

Nodding once more, Isabelle's brow furrowed, her eyes riddled with anxiety.

"Charles Lafferty is . . . not your suitor. That unfortunate incident was all sheer accident. But as your eldest sister, it becomes my responsibility to find the solution."

"I didn't ask you for a solution."

Annie looked away, seeing that Isabelle's bottom lip quivered.

"Why are you doing this, Annie? I thought you would be on my side."

"It's not about taking sides, Mussy. It's about your future. You're much too beautiful. And too smart. You yourself said you would never marry a farmer. Mr. Lafferty's more suited to Doris."

"Uncle Abbot's making you do this."

"I want what's best for you—"

"I can't believe what I'm hearing. You, of all people, know that our uncle is a ruthless, mean-spirited man. With all due respect to him and Aunt Sybil for taking us in, we must not forget that—"

"No. That is, he and I have spoken and feel that it is in your best interests to—"

"I can't listen anymore. These aren't your words." Isabelle jerked away.

"Don't leave, Isabelle! Please, I can't bear your being angry." Annie ran to stop her.

"Then tell me the truth!"

Annie stared at her sister. A gust of wind blew through the garden, swaying the roses and loosening the red and yellow petals. The sky had turned an ashen gray, matching the color of their moods.

"Tell me in your words."

"I'm telling you the truth. Uncle Abbot will not allow you to see Charles Lafferty. If you try, he will offer no dowry on your behalf. The Laffertys would forbid such a thing."

"Does Charles Lafferty know any of these things?" Isabelle's eyes, sullen and brooding, studied her with suspicion.

"Uncle Abbot is going to pay a visit to the Laffertys late this afternoon. He's going to tell Charles that he did not meet Doris. He's going to offer his apologies and arrange another meeting for them both."

"What if Charles asks to see me again?"

"When Uncle Abbot paints you as a penniless orphan, I'm certain the Laffertys will pursue the issue no further." Annie answered in an even tone, muting the truth of her words with gentle honesty. She looked away.

"Paint me as penniless? Even Abbot wouldn't stoop to such levels."

"He would. But if you swear to him to lay aside the matter, I am certain he can cast you in the best light possible and yet direct Mr. Lafferty's attentions toward Doris."

"If I cooperate?"

"Unfortunately, yes."

"This sickens me."

Annie could only look at her, could only inwardly will her sister to do as she pleased. She wanted to tell her to defy Abbot Dearborn. But the end result would be disastrous. She could never say what she really wanted to say.

"I suppose it's decided for me, then."

"There is a good side to all of this bother."

"Such as?"

"If Doris marries, we can have her room to ourselves."

"I find little humor in this. I'm dying inside and you make jokes."

"Please don't hate me."

"I could never hate my sister."

"I did overhear some news this morning."

"Tell me. I could use some news."

"Aunt Sybil wants a new house."

"What? But this house is perfect. What would she do with another house?"

"She wants to build on our old homestead. She loves the stream that runs through our land. They plan to offer this house as part of Doris's dowry."

"Oh." Isabelle's lashes shadowed her cheeks.

"But it's good news really. We can move back to our land."

"I thought Sybil hated our land."

"She sees some potential now. But for us it will be like moving back home."

"I'm glad you see it as such. I'm glad for you, Annie."

Seeing that the pain still lingered in Isabelle's face, Annie kissed her on the cheek.

"Still, I can't help thinking about him."

"Time has a way of healing those wounds."

"Really?"

"You've only just met him, after all. Besides, I hope your suitor has ten times the money of the Laffertys."

"Don't say such things. I had no interest in Charles Lafferty's money. I had no idea who he was when we met. I thought he was here on business with some of Uncle Abbot's affairs."

"I know all of that, Isabelle. And I agree with your sentiments. It's for that reason that I know I shall marry a pauper. But happy we will be, and I'll have no part in a greedy man's world again."

"Marry a pauper? Annie, sometimes I feel you take your ideals much too far."

The two of them laughed and gathered a bouquet of roses, one that would brighten their room and remove the stench from the morning.

7
ROGAN'S REPRIEVE

"Order in the court." Judge Abbot Dearborn called the court-room to order, adjusting his powder white toupee. He settled himself against the tall wooden chair and muttered under his breath.

The bailiff walked in beside the sheriff and spoke to Judge Dearborn. "Got a pretty one for you today, your judgeship."

"What's that?" Dearborn caught the note of sarcasm in the bailiff's voice. He lifted his eyes, weary of the banal drudgery of Sydney's courtroom. He studied the defendant—a well-dressed young man. An older couple strode in behind him and took a seat. He thought he detected a spark of anxiety in both of their faces. The older gentleman's face struck him in a familiar way, but he couldn't place his name.

"Look's like a bloomin' dandy," the bailiff said.

"Name?"

"I am Rogan Farrell, Your Honor. And I've fallen prey to mischief."

"We'll see, won't we?"

"Judge Dearborn, Mr. Farrell is without representation." A be-wigged lawyer addressed Dearborn.

"I'm representing myself, Your Honor," Rogan explained.

"Very well." Dearborn waved the lawyer away and ordered the bailiff to proceed with the preliminaries. He offered a directive glance to signal the court official to be smooth and quick about his business. Listening to the charges, he sat forward, interested in the deviation from his usual morning of litigation.

"The court calls Mr. Mason Hale forward," the bailiff barked out.

"Mr. Hale, what is your charge against this man?"

Dearborn wanted the case settled and the day to find its swiftest end. He had matters to resolve with the Lafferty family.

"Your Honor, it pains me so to bring this charge before you." Hale's face reflected an inward sorrow.

"Why so?"

"Mr. Rogan Farrell is my apprentice—and a gifted architect, I might add."

"State your charges, please."

"Mr. Farrell has been the keeper of my records." Hale lifted his books for the magistrate to examine. The bailiff gathered the records into his arms and delivered them to the judge's bench.

"All of these?" Judge Dearborn glanced over his spectacles at Hale.

"Have him open the one on top, Your Honor. The place is marked inside." While the judge was examining the book, Hale's eyes scanned the courtroom. He quietly addressed the bailiff. "Have you yet noticed whether a Mr. Harry Winston has made his appearance?"

"You look dashing today, Harry." A young woman lounged across a tufted armchair in her parents' ballroom. She lifted her lashes in a coquettish fashion and made merry her conversation with several stylish young men and women who had come to call. She eyed Harry Winston's expensive tailored suit.

"Thank you, Cadence." Harry sipped on brandy and parried with the daughter of Javier Hamilton, one of Sydney's wealthiest merchants. He shook the frill of his sleeve and offered the girl a warm smile. Cadence Hamilton had flirted with him since the moment of his arrival. He took full advantage of her interests. He toyed with her, keeping a distant mien, yet knowing all the while he drew her in. "Ferris, old man, could I bother you for another brandy?"

"I was about to ask you the same." Ferris Bentley glanced over his shoulder. He turned his back on Harry while an acerbic smile creased his cheeks.

"Well, I suppose—" Harry's brow lifted.

"Allow me." Quick to respond, Cadence clapped her hands and summoned a maid. "Beda, pour Mr. Winston another brandy, please."

"Ah, you came to my rescue. I understand your parents are sending you away to study in France."

"It's much the fashion now, I suppose."

"You're not pleased?"

"Not displeased," she said. "But, no, not pleased either." She sighed, and her restlessness reminded Harry of a young foal looking beyond the pasture fence.

"What is it you wish to study?" he asked.

"Men."

"Cadence Hamilton!" One of the young women, Mary Lorimar, had overheard the conversation. She and a few of the other young women stood over Cadence, feigning their disapproval.

"All right, then. I'll study china painting. How's that for a lie?" Cadence replied, her green eyes exultant.

"A toast to our most gifted hostess. May all of France resound with the splendor of Cadence Hamilton's artistry." Harry laughed and lifted his second glass of brandy. His broad smile revealed his approval of her.

The Hamilton ballroom continued to fill with the early-afternoon revelers, all young men and women who attended the affair under the guise of attending a tea. But a Hamilton tea offered little in the way of light refreshment. The wine poured freely, loosening the tongues and the collars of some of Sydney's finest. The ballroom grew noisy, and the violins in the far corner of the room could scarcely be heard. Harry Winston downed the second drink and set aside his glass onto an already overfilled library table. "I need to take a walk." He stood and excused himself from the Hamilton girl. He found a group of his peers out on a flower-laden portico and rubbed his temple, feeling the power of the brandy saturating his senses.

"Isn't today the trial of Rogan Farrell?" one of the young men asked.

"Trial? Oh dear," he said. "Mr. Hale wanted me to be a witness." His mind groggy, Harry struggled to recall the events of the last few weeks.

"You're a bit late, Winston. Or am I telling you something that you already know?" The young man, Peter Hastings, held up his watch and winked at the others.

"It slipped my mind, is all. You would think my entire world would be occupied with the fate of Rogan Farrell."

"Well, if he *did* embezzle Hale's money, he should be locked up, I would think. Or hanged. Don't you think that's true, Harry?" Hastings asked.

"I believe he should be locked up. Of course! Why wouldn't I?" His eyes narrowed and he felt the impugning stares of the young men, some of whom he knew to be comrades of Rogan Farrell.

"Unless you know of another thief. You wouldn't know of one, would you, Winston?"

Hastings' comment kindled his ire, but he kept his tongue.

"Ah, look at the wheels turning. Perhaps he does know," another young man taunted.

"I know of no other thief."

"Listen all! Tonight old Masterson and his wife are away. His son's setting up the library for poker. Who's game?" Hastings asked.

While the company of bored young men vocalized their interest, Harry nodded but felt a hesitancy. He had lost a good deal of money while gambling over the last two weeks and wanted to hold on to the rest. He knew they baited him, awaiting his response. But he finally succumbed. "I'm in." He slid a glove through his fingers, then turned, trying to remember where he had left his glass. The room's atmosphere gave rise to few empty glasses, so his had to be among the obvious. A group of young women chatted near a mirrored sideboard while nibbling on pastries and tea. He knew some of them and esteemed this one clique to be rather priggish. But one young woman in particular caught his eye. She was slender, shapely, and attired in a beige glacé silk dress. When she spoke, the other women turned and listened. He tried to catch her eye, but she paid him no heed and returned her attention to her young friends.

"What catches your eye now, Winston?"

"Hello, Thomas," he said.

"Who is she?" Harry drew his friend aside by the sleeve.

"Who?" Thomas asked.

"That young woman there. Blond, very blond. Lovely." He straightened his cravat and tugged at his mulberry-colored waistcoat.

"Oh, that one," Thomas said. "She's an orphan." He shrugged and offered the comment with an air of distaste.

"Orphan?"

"She and her siblings have come to live with her uncle and aunt. Her parents died. First her father in England. Her mother died while over here."

"Pity." Harry tried to act disinterested. But her intriguing face and aloof manner drew him like a moth to a candle.

"Well, don't lose heart, Winston. Her uncle's a wealthy man. I'm sure he'll see she's provided for."

Thomas's words were all the encouragement Harry needed. He tugged once more at his waistcoat and strode toward her. Then whirling about, he asked, "What's her name?"

"Annie Carraway."

Rogan could no longer mask his pain. Anxiety fluttered in his chest, and he saw at once the color had drained from Hale's face. Mason Hale had been like his own father. Now they faced each other like opposing generals. He moved his shoulders around in an effort to quell the terrible tension he felt.

"What is it you want me to inspect, Mr. Hale?" Dearborn adjusted his gold spectacles. After having examined the book in question for several minutes, he looked down at him, his brows arched. He maintained an imperious demeanor.

"In the right-hand column of the right page, Your Honor. See the markings only five lines down?" Hale asked.

"Yes, I see." Dearborn's bottom lip protruded and his brows pinched together. He grunted and then his eyes widened with interest.

"That amount was altered, sir. Our client, Mr. Wesley Smithfield, paid a higher amount to us. The difference is—missing from our accounts."

"Mr. Smithfield is here in the courtroom?" Dearborn glanced around.

Hale nodded.

"The court calls Mr. Wesley Smithfield forward!"

"I'm present, Your Honor." Smithfield came forward, holding his hat in his hands.

While Smithfield gave his testimony, Rogan watched the magistrate's face. He could see the judge studying the honest demeanor of Mason Hale and scrutinizing the forthright testimony of Smithfield. The prosecuting lawyer, Arnold Matthews, questioned both men at length. But Rogan assessed that Judge Dearborn had already begun to formulate opinions of his own. Mustering his waning confidence, Farrell spoke up. "Your Honor, if I may speak on my own behalf."

Dearborn began to offer up a protest, but Rogan could no longer stand by voiceless while his fate was decided for him. "I am an honorable man, sir. It is true that I for one year have kept Mr. Mason Hale's records. As his apprentice, he afforded me every opportunity to learn the trade of his most responsible profession. So in order to teach me the finer skills of good business sense, he had me keep his records. But I ask you, sir, isn't it illogical that I would make such an obvious attempt at embezzlement, knowing full well that my master would check the records periodically? If I were such a cunning thief, wouldn't I be better off to hide my treachery?"

"I've witnessed such a thing," Dearborn said. "Some thieves make their schemes obvious in hopes that they would appear trapped, a victim, if you will. Have you anything else to say, Mr. Farrell, before I pronounce judgment?"

"I do, sir. While you and these fine gentlemen banter about my innocence or guilt this morning, the real thief is running free in this colony. This matter cannot be settled in such a way. Have you no means to investigate?"

"Who do you feel has committed the crime, Mr. Farrell?" Dearborn said.

Rogan hesitated. He had no proof of Harry Winston's guilt.

"Very well, then—"

"If I had more time, sir—"

"Your Honor?" Donovan Farrell spoke for the first time.

"What is it now?"

"I am Donovan Farrell. Rogan Farrell is my son."

"Go on," Dearborn said.

"Our son is innocent of these charges. He has shown nothing but commitment to Mr. Hale and his business. Mr. Hale, you know of Rogan's integrity. Why speak you so poorly of him today?"

"Donovan, I am only going on the evidence, not on Rogan Farrell's past. He's a good student and full of promise. But the temptation before him, I daresay, may have been too great." Hale defended himself now.

"Mason Hale! I am innocent, I say! It is by circumstance alone that you accuse me!"

"Your Honor, what the defendant says is just." Arnold Matthews spoke up on Rogan's behalf.

"Nonetheless, we cannot be blind to the facts before us," Dearborn said. "Mr. Farrell, you look the part of the innocent. But in your hands a trust was laid. Now that trust has been broken and you must pay the penalty." He sat forward, studied Rogan Farrell's countenance, and clasped his hands. He lifted the gavel and pounded the bench a resounding blow. "Stand before me please, Mr. Farrell."

"Sir." He stood erect, unflinching.

"You are guilty as charged. I hereby sentence you to hang at the gallows—"

The words fell on Rogan's ears like searing coals. Rogan could hear his mother's sobs behind him. He shook his head but couldn't form the words that flew at his mind. *This is insane! A nightmare . . .*

"May I get you a brandy? I know where they keep it." Harry spoke in a casual tone to the young woman but eyed her with strong interest.

"None for me, thank you," Annie said, resuming her discussion with her friends. "And Isabelle is quite put out about the matter. But I wanted to quell any scandal about her. She is hopeful of her own suitor, and I say . . ." She turned to glance toward Charles Lafferty, who stood in the corner laughing with his friends. "I say she is better off without him."

"You speak of the Lafferty heir?" Harry attempted once more to draw her attention. He gave a knowing glance toward Lafferty.

"Do you address me?" Annie threw back her shoulders, the ruched frills of her gown rustling as she moved.

"I only attempt, dear lady. I cannot address a deaf ear."

"Your name?" She addressed him in a voice both courteous and patronizing.

"Harry Winston."

"Good day, Harry Winston." Annie eyed the fashionable young man and then looked away.

"Annie, this is the son of Lord Reginald Winston—*the* Winstons of Sydney," one young woman gasped.

"My fond greetings, then, to your good kinsmen, Mr. Winston."

"And to yours. Would you be so kind as to lead me to the source of those dainties you leave uneaten upon your plate?" Unflappable, Harry continued to nurse his brandy.

"You may have these, if you wish." Annie glanced down at the delicate pastries and held out her plate to him, her eyes lit with a challenge.

"No, I couldn't take yours, but if you would be so kind as to show me . . ."

"All right, then. If you insist. Follow me." Resignation rose in Annie's face. Never had she met such a persistent man. She turned to make her way to the mirrored sideboard where many of the sweets had been placed. She felt all eyes upon her but cared little about the opinions of the other guests. She had only discussed Isabelle's plight because exaggerated rumors had already begun to circulate. Perhaps the matter would be satisfied in their minds and the vicious suppositions quelled. She held out her gloved hand and directed his eyes to the lace-topped sideboard. "All your heart desires."

"I agree." He kept his eyes planted on hers until she looked away, uncomfortable. Winston hesitated. His mouth curled on one side, and his eyes flickered with desire.

"Your Honor, Judge Dearborn?" Hale said.

"Sir? You wish to speak?" Dearborn asked.

"If I may interject, I feel that hanging is too severe a punishment for Mr. Farrell. He's a young man, sir. Young men make mistakes—"

"I am innocent, Hale! Why don't you investigate Harry Winston?" Rogan rankled.

"Winston? Which Winston?" Dearborn asked.

"The son of Reginald Winston," Hale answered.

"Have we another suspect, Mr. Hale?"

"His family's quite prominent, Your Honor, and I certainly haven't considered him at all as a suspect."

"I don't care if his father's the governor," Rogan interrupted. "He had as much opportunity as anyone to tamper with your records. And I wish to know, why is Mr. Winston not present in the courtroom today?" Farrell demanded.

"I don't know why he isn't here." Hale looked nervous. "I . . . I asked him to come."

"Is it true, Mr. Hale?" Dearborn asked. "Has Reginald Winston's son had access to your records?"

"Harry Winston knows nothing of my books. He's—not capable!"

A murmur rippled throughout the courtroom.

"And I am?" Farrell folded his arms across his chest.

"Yes! You were responsible for my books, sir! It was your sole duty. Harry Winston knows nothing of accounting." Hale's face grew red.

"Mr. Hale, are you certain?" Dearborn pressed him for an answer.

"I . . . I don't know! But someone's stolen from me, and it was Mr. Farrell's responsibility to see to it that it didn't happen." Hale fumbled for the words.

"You're certainly not here to send Mr. Farrell to the gallows for carelessness, are you, Mr. Hale?" Dearborn clasped his fingers atop his rotund frame. "I must ask you, Mr. Hale, is there a grain of doubt in your mind as to Mr. Farrell's guilt? Is it possible that another has embezzled from your books?"

"Anything is possible, Your Honor, but I swear to you—no other person to my knowledge has had the opportunities afforded Mr. Farrell."

"Mr. Rogan Farrell, it seems we have a grain of doubt as to your guilt or innocence. This matter must be deliberated further after a more thorough investigation. But I cannot release you knowing that you have every reason to flee the colony." Dearborn adjusted his robe and sat forward.

"Sir? I've every reason to stay and prove my innocence."

"Nonetheless, we cannot set an accused man free."

"What is it that you propose, sir? That I be returned to those rat-infested holds?"

"You shall remain in the court's custody—"

Hale blustered, "But, Your Honor—"

"You will serve this colony as architect until the day of your trial. This period will afford you the time you need to present your case—and find proper representation."

Donovan Farrell spoke up. "Judge Dearborn, may we please take our son home with us? I can assure you he will not run from this case."

"I cannot agree, sir. You are speaking from your heart and not your head. Rogan Farrell will remain in the custody of this court until the day of his trial."

"In jail?" Donovan grew incredulous.

"I have a private jail on my land," the judge went on. "You will remain there for a time, Mr. Farrell. But only as a matter of convenience as you carry forth your architectural duties. If I so much as see you near the stable or—"

"Judge Dearborn, if I must remain in custody, I would prefer the private jail you so kindly offer me. I swear to you, I will not leave the premises until my case is settled. And I most willingly submit my services as an architect to the colony, or to any service you so desire."

Dearborn's brows lifted with interest.

"I'm confident my innocence will be proven soon enough and my position with Mr. Mason Hale restored."

"So be it." Dearborn stood to take his leave, giving the bench a resounding whack with his gavel.

"Thank the good Lord." Meredith Farrell shook her head and embraced her son.

Rogan turned to Mason Hale. "I trust you'll find the good Mr. Winston well in his cups by now, sir. Perhaps he'll be an asset to you knowing he has free rein in my absence."

Hale stiffened, started to speak, but then turned and strode from the room.

"It would serve you well not to provoke Mr. Hale, son," Donovan said.

"I care little what Hale thinks of me at this point. Perhaps I'll find another architect under whom I can apprentice—once I'm free."

"He's the best in the colony, Rogan. You've already learned so much from him." Donovan persisted in trying to reason with him.

"Or, better yet, I'll find new means for seeking my way in this world. Try to do your best, make an honest wage, and see where it lands you—in jail or dancing the hornpipe at the gallows." Rogan's voice held a bitter, cynical edge. He stared into the distance as though he had disappeared inside himself.

"Stop, Rogan. You're just angry, is all." Meredith tried to console her son, but he pulled away.

"Yes, I'm angry. But wiser too." He fell in line behind the two guards who tarried on his behalf. He heard his mother call out to him and he looked back toward her.

"Be grateful, as I am, that you're safe for now, Rogan."

Rogan could think of no response. As he stood waiting to receive the shackles upon his wrists and ankles, he turned away from his parents, knowing they would despise his thoughts if they could hear them. They were good Christian people who never had thoughts like he now had. But he had fallen into a deep well, and he was determined to fight his way out of it—no matter what it took. He would save goodness for a simpler time, a quieter moment when life would not demand such drastic measures.

"We're praying for you, son. Grandmother Katy's in prayer right now," Meredith said.

Rogan nodded and turned away. Just as he was sure that God had turned away from him.

8

COURTING A
ROGUE

"Aunt Sybil, I don't want Uncle Abbot to arrange a courtship for me." Annie stared out the window of her uncle's study. Several weeks had passed since the incident with her sister and Doris. Abbot had said little since then about courtship, so in her mind the matter had been laid to rest. She had vowed to cooperate in regard to her sisters, but she felt she had made herself understood in regard to her own future. She didn't want Abbot controlling her life.

"Have you any idea how fortunate you are?" Sybil demanded as Annie continued to stare out of the window. "The Winstons are a fine family."

"I've no interest in Harry Winston. He's a rogue."

"You challenge us at every turn."

"I mean no disrespect."

"You make no plans for your future, and when your uncle attempts to intervene on your behalf, you fly off on impulse and defy our wishes."

Pressing her fingertips against the cold glass, Annie felt frustration rising. She wanted to make plans for her future. But with her limited resources, she could hardly go sailing off to Paris like Doris. Yet she wouldn't be forced into a marriage of convenience, a promise she had made to herself as a girl.

"Don't you understand, Annie? Without our help, you're destitute. You've no recourse. The Winstons are one of the finest families in the colony. When they approached Abbot in regard to their son, Harry, we couldn't believe your good fortune. Can't you see what's fallen right into your lap?"

"And how does this courtship benefit Uncle Abbot?" Annie bristled.

"What are you saying?"

"I've stated it clearly, I believe."

"Then you're a hopeless cause."

"I'm only trying to understand motives. Abbot knows that I've no use for prestige. I want to know if he stands to gain through this arrangement—if only Annie will cooperate."

"You and your pious airs! You toy with this young man's affections and then act shocked when he responds in kind."

"I did nothing of the sort!"

"You, my dear, are as manipulating as—I see you spinning your little web! If you had come to me with this young man's offer, well, it would all be in your hands. It's a game with you. You want control!"

"Then let's give the girl control, Sybil."

Surprised, Annie saw Abbot out of the corner of her eye and wondered how long he had been listening.

"You and your siblings can find another situation—"

"Abbot!" Sybil said, her face flushed.

"Sybil, allow me to deal with the girl in my own way!"

"She's not just a girl. She's our family, Abbot. What are you saying? That you want her to leave?"

"I don't want to stay!" Annie's heart pounded against her chest. Hurt now mixed with the anger, and she couldn't control her emotions. She stood paralyzed by her own words. Her aunt and uncle stared dumbfounded at her.

"Don't be foolish! Where would you go?" Sybil asked.

"Hear me out. What I mean to say is that I can leave, Aunt Sybil. But, please, allow my brothers and sisters to remain."

"You'll do no such thing! Abbot, you can't send her out into this colony alone. You know what would happen to her."

"Sybil, you will leave now!" he said. "Allow me to deal with her—"

"Uncle Abbot, please! I don't want you two quarreling on my account."

"Quiet!" Abbot shouted.

"Mr. Dearborn, sir." Ada had stepped into the room.

"Not now, Ada," Abbot said.

"But, sir, you said I should tell you when Mr. Winston arrives. He's 'ere now, sir."

"He's here?" Annie whispered. Realization burgeoned in her mind. Abbot had no intention of asking her to leave. He had only been trying to force her to resolve the matter, push her into a decision in order to bring her into compliance with his own selfish motives. The decision had already been made. Her eyes narrowed and she saw the look that passed between Abbot and Sybil. "You invited him without telling me?"

"Annie, your uncle and I thought you would be delighted. How could we have known that Mr. Winston's courtship offer would upset you?"

"I won't see him," she said. "I'm going upstairs. I'll have my things packed by tomorrow morning."

"You're the most stubborn woman I've ever met!" Abbot fumed.

"Abbot! Leave us, please."

"What did you say?"

"Give her some time. Give us both some time."

"I'll give you a quarter-hour to speak sense to this girl. Then she can tell Harry Winston herself, let him know what a fool she is! I wash my hands of it!"

"Why wait?" Annie asked. "I can speak to him now."

Rogan pulled the cloak about himself. In spite of the favor the judge had shown him, he still received the same treatment as any Sydney convict. The scratchy prison uniform had begun to smell, and he needed a bath. He had been spared the humiliation of wearing the canary yellow of desperate criminals, but he did still have to wear a gray jail uniform with a black number stamped on the back. Although being Dearborn's prisoner offered him little in the way of luxury, spending days locked inside the private jail on the Dearborn estate had, in the beginning, been a welcome respite.

The Sydney jails were cramped, full of vermin and sleazy convicts. In here he at least had some time to himself, time to think. After a week in the jail, the guard who stood vigil spent less and less time watching him, and Rogan was allowed out in the afternoon to walk the far eastern grounds of the estate. But the solitary hold had taken its toll on his senses. The longer he tarried in Dearborn's block jailhouse, the sooner he wanted a private confrontation with the man who had set him up. He wanted out—and soon.

Rogan had grown up hearing of the private jails built on the manor estates. Rich landowners and politicians often used convict labor to tend their fields, care for their flocks, and sometimes to look after their offspring. Convict labor was Australia's own private brand of slavery. But convicts being lawbreakers, they would eventually step over the boundaries and commit a crime against the owner. Instead of sending a convict back into the military penal system, the landowners would inflict their own kind of punishment—the whip and confinement in their private jails.

He stopped from his labors to take a mental rest from his drafting work. A sunny day beckoned his attentions, drawing him to stare out the small window. The rear of the manor was partially visible, and on some days he could see family members and servants strolling back and forth from the stable to the house. He looked forward to their strolls. It offered a diversion, however small, in his solitude. He had noticed three young women at different times but had never met any of them because the daily meals had been delivered by a stableboy. They seldom took an outing without their summer wrappings, so he could only daydream about their feminine forms moving blithely beneath the cashmere.

Rogan finally slammed his fist against the wood and cursed. *How long until I'm free?* He could go insane waiting for his trial date. Surely his brother, Frederick, had news about his case's investigation.

He studied his calendar once more. Frederick would arrive for a visit within the hour, another diversion he anticipated. Just days ago, Frederick had brought news of their father's involvement in a local labor movement. Donovan Farrell had been at the forefront of any reform movements in Sydney. He had joined forces with John West and a small handful of emancipists' offspring to topple the transportation system in Sydney, although the transportation of convicts from Britain still prevailed in other New South Wales colonies. Since then, other problems threatened them as well.

Local citizens were struggling to gain employment. Instead of hiring the local citizenry for labor, the manor lords, or graziers, had taken to hiring less expensive Chinese workmen and using free convict laborers to ward off bankruptcy.

The Farrells had hailed from convict stock themselves. Rogan's grandmother had followed her convicted and transported parents, George and Amelia Prentice, from England as a girl. After fulfilling their jail sentences, the Prentices had struggled to make a farm work. Eventually their children had carved out a successful sheep operation, naming it Rose Hill. But with Rose Hill now staring at financial failure, the tide had turned for the Farrells. Finding work had grown paramount. Transported convicts were taking up all the positions that the local labor force needed to survive. Rogan had grown up knowing that the Farrells despised the transportation system. His grandmother, Katy Gabriel, had told him all the stories. Growing up in the wilderness colony, she had met with much peril and watched her parents suffer greatly as emancipists. Eventually, she had met an emancipist, Dwight Farrell, and they soon married and had children. Rogan's father, Donovan, was the son of Dwight and Katy Farrell. Dwight had died from a snakebite when Donovan was a mere lad. Eventually, Rogan's grandmother remarried a sea captain she had known since her childhood.

Rogan forced himself back into his work. He bent over the desk, pulled out a measuring device, and dragged his attention into the present task. Dearborn had wanted a new judicial office square designed. He had mentioned that he had more ideas about some designs he would need—more personal work. Unsure of his intentions, Rogan had merely set himself to the current task for now.

He could hear a horse approaching. Anxious, he arose and ran to the window. His view a partial one, he could see a rider dismount.

"What hail, brother!"

"Frederick!"

Rogan watched the door as the guard opened it and saw Frederick remove his hat. Then he saw the hesitation in his eyes, always uneasy about stepping into the dank jail. Under his arm he had tucked a copy of the *Sydney Morning Herald*. He pulled it out, fast to wave it in front of him, and handed it to Rogan. "I've something I want you to read."

"All right. They never want to deliver the newspaper here for some reason. Horrible service here. 'Depression Settles in New South Wales.' This is news?" Rogan asked.

"No. Not there." Frederick pulled the newspaper from Rogan's grasp and flipped the four-page periodical over to the back page. "Here. Right here." He pointed to a small column, nearly hidden by the advertisements of goods brought in by the latest ships.

Rogan scanned the paper until the small column caught his eye. " 'Gold in California,' " he read, then muttered, "Foolish whims."

"Why do you say that?"

"What if they're wrong?"

"Dear brother, I don't believe they're wrong."

"Well, let's pack up and go, then."

"I *am* going."

"What?"

"I haven't told our father yet. I want to study the matter more. But this could be our one opportunity. This could be our fortune, the thing to salvage Rose Hill—"

"Frederick, you talk nonsense!"

"Listen to me!" Frederick said. "We're about to lose it all, Rogan. Everything! Rose Hill is near bankruptcy."

"Easy, old man! We've heard of gold strikes, even here in New South Wales. I don't believe those stories. Until now, you didn't either. They're invented to send foolhardy lunatics off on a tangent in order to sell them goods."

"And that's exactly what I intend to do. Men are flocking from all over the world to California. They'll be needing goods, food, camping supplies—"

"Well, at least you sound a little more shrewd now. You might do well with that strategy."

"Not just me, Rogan. I want you to come with me."

"Sorry, old chap. I do have a problem." Rogan eyed the guard who waited at the door. The brothers stepped toward the rear of the jail.

"You're innocent, and Judge Dearborn knows it. He's using you to build his new estate."

"What's this you say, mate?"

"I heard some of the blokes down at the pub blathering about it while in their cups. Do you mean to say that Dearborn's not mentioned your drafting him a new house plan?"

"Not exactly. Not yet, anyway."

"You'll awaken soon enough. Meanwhile, you're being kept here under a gentleman's oath. You're not being fully guarded. We could leave in a fortnight."

"No. Not until I'm pronounced innocent."

"But what if you're not?"

"I will be. They've no real proof that I embezzled from Mason Hale."

"They'll want a conviction. If they can't find the real crook, you'll do in their eyes."

"Freddy, going off to some mining camp will only worsen your situation."

"No worse than standing idly by while the ship sinks."

"Don't go, Freddy!"

"Are you coming with me or not?"

Rogan stared at his brother. The silence between them conveyed his answer clearly enough.

"Well enough—"

"Wait. Give me more time, will you? Think of what you're asking of me—to break out of jail, for one thing." Rogan couldn't bear the thought of Frederick leaving without him. As foolish as Frederick's plan sounded, the idea of running off to California intrigued him.

"Just say it, Rogan. Say you'll go."

"Give me more time. Can you not wait until I'm tried?"

"You'll not be tried until Dearborn's finished with you. Wait and see if I'm right. Then when he's got what he wants from you, you'll be hanged. Do you truly think they're going to accuse Lord Reginald's son of embezzlement? He owns half of Sydney."

The two brothers sat in silence for a moment before Rogan spoke again. "I want to speak to Dearborn myself. If he so much as mentions a personal drafting job, I'll reconsider. No, if he so much as mentions it, then I'll not wait a fortnight. We'll away at once."

"To California we go, then. I'll pack your things."

"Miss Carraway." Harry Winston bowed and grasped Annie's hand.

But Annie, in no mood for Winston's courtly affectations, slipped her hand out of his. She had led the way to the parlor but only to set matters in order at once.

"Harry, how you've grown. It seems we just saw you running up the church steps to Mass," Sybil said.

"Good morning, Mr. Winston." Annie faced him fully.

"Annie Carraway. Still lovely as when I saw you last."

"Uncle Abbot, Aunt Sybil, I want to speak to him alone."

Sybil turned and left through the parlor door, but Abbot lingered, his gaze planted on hers.

"She's in good hands, Judge Dearborn," Harry said.

"I'll leave the door open." Abbot gave Annie a threatening look.

"Good day to you, sir." Harry nodded to the departing magistrate.

"Please be seated." Annie offered a settee to him. She took her place across from him and forced a polite smile. He had a dashing appearance, she admitted, but she couldn't forget this arrangement was being forced upon her. "Mr. Winston—"

"Please call me Harry. No formalities. I tire of them, as I'm sure you do as well."

"I'll make fast my point. I understand you wish to court me."

"Me and a thousand others." Winston unbuttoned his waistcoat and leaned casually against the tapestried settee.

Annie disregarded his statement, knowing of his reputation for flattering young women.

" 'Courtship' is so provincial. Mind if we call it something else?"

"I'll leave that up to you."

"I'll have to mull it over."

"Harry, you know of my situation. My father and mother have passed on."

"Yes. I've been told."

"I've four siblings for which I feel responsible."

"But why? Your uncle and aunt provide well for them. You're fortunate to have such an uncle, I'm sure."

"Surely I am fortunate. But your offer of courtship comes so swiftly. After all, we've only just met." Annie kept to herself her opinions about Abbot.

"Annie, allow me to tell you about myself." Harry stood and walked over to face her. Then he extended his hand.

She scrutinized his gallant mannerisms. Seeing the sincerity of his gaze, she haltingly placed her hand in his. He pulled her to her feet at once.

"I want you to know some things about me. I know what I want.

In the past, I've met many women, but none like you. You're different. You see, we didn't meet by mere coincidence at Cadence Hamilton's party. I watched you across the room. I wanted to meet you. *Chose* to meet you."

"Did you?"

"Look." He led Annie toward the window.

"Look at what?"

"Beyond those Dearborn hills is another estate. It is to be mine upon the day I marry."

"I see. You need a bride as soon as possible."

"Not just any bride." Harry wouldn't allow her to turn away. He gripped her wrist once more. Lifting her hand to his lips, he kissed it softly.

"I can't allow it, Harry." Annie continued to move away in spite of his advances.

"Why not?"

Annie heard a sound that disturbed her, the sound of someone crying. She walked away from him and stood at the door.

"What's wrong, Annie?"

"Someone's crying. *Isabelle?*" she called out, then strode into the waiting area and stood at the foot of the stairs.

Ada ran down the hallway, her face flushed; then she too stood at the foot of the staircase.

"Ada?"

"I wouldn't go up just yet, miss. Your sister's in a bad way. Seems your uncle's asked 'er to leave. Says she's caused trouble in regard to Doris's beau, Charles Lafferty."

"Uncle Abbot!"

"He's gone now, Miss Carraway. Gone off to town and already about 'is business. He said he'd find a room and a new situation for Isabelle before candlelight tonight. Says 'e knows a woman wot needs a maid."

Just then Linus ran down the stairs followed by his older brother, Thomas. "Annie, why is Isabelle crying?"

"Into the kitchen with both of you," Ada said. "You'll find some fresh scones with your tea."

"I want to talk to my sister!" Thomas exclaimed, red-faced.

"It's all right, Thomas. I'll see to Isabelle," Annie said.

Linus ran off in search of hot scones, but Thomas trailed behind, gazing up the stairs.

"Off with you!" Ada persisted until the boy had joined his brother.

"Ada, where's my aunt? Where's Sybil?" Panic rioted through Annie.

"Gone too. Had a bridge game and tea today."

"How convenient!"

"Mrs. Dearborn's just gone off to 'er usual Tuesday affairs. She can't ever fix it when Judge Dearborn's got 'isself in such a way. It's best she go on about 'er business. Let 'im simmer."

"Abbot Dearborn's a horrible man!"

"Don't say such things about 'im, miss. I vow that somethin's happened. Somethin' that made 'im behave like this. You know of somethin', Miss Carraway?"

Annie didn't answer the maid.

"Something wrong, Annie?" Harry Winston stuck his head through the doorway.

"I should go to my sister."

"I'll go with you," Harry said.

"No. It's best I go alone."

"No, miss, allow me to go. You stay with your visitor," Ada said. "Things need to cool off, is all. Surely the judge will see clear to let 'er stay." Ada lifted her skirts and began ambling up the staircase.

"Please tell her that I'll be up shortly." Annie walked past Winston, her cheeks bright red. She couldn't allow Isabelle to be forced out. She knew of only one thing that would change Uncle Abbot's mind. If nothing else, she had to buy her sister more time.

"Don't worry yourself, Annie. These things have a way of working themselves out."

"Yes, they do, Harry."

"On our other little matter, I realize this all seems so sudden, but—"

"Harry, you will think me fickle, but I've reconsidered your offer."

"Why?"

"Isn't that what you want?" Keeping her voice low, Annie's gaze fell just beyond the parlor doorway where Ada stood vigil.

"First you turn me down without blinking. Now you've had a sudden change of heart?"

"I . . . I've reconsidered, is all."

"I hope it's because you've a great fondness for me." Harry

reached for her hand again, but she pulled away.

"I shall grow fond of you. Who wouldn't?" Her smile wooden, she turned and tried to look straight into his eyes. But she could read his face. He stared dubiously at her.

"I'm going to close the door," Harry said.

"It's of no consequence to me, Harry."

"I want you to feel free to speak candidly. I want honesty. Will you give me that?"

"I will," Annie nodded. Once the door had closed, she saw that Harry Winston's stare took on a calculating light.

"I want you to tell me the truth." He poured himself a glass of brandy and then offered a glass to her.

Annie waved aside the offer of the drink. She could not bring herself to look up at him.

"The truth. Your uncle and my father were more than pleased at my offer. I had hoped that you would be amply as pleased. But you aren't tempted with my fortune, are you?"

"Not in the least."

"You realize, I find that trait in you attractive? That, among many other things. But I don't want you forced into my bed—"

Annie tried to step away again, but he stopped her.

"Would you please stop walking away from me? What are you running from? Not me?"

"No, not you."

"Who, then?"

"My uncle insists that I cooperate."

"And if you don't?"

"He's asked my sister Isabelle to leave. It's all a matter of what he wants."

"So if our courtship is announced today . . ."

"He'll allow Isabelle to stay." She wondered if she should trust him with this information.

"What if I say that we've both decided to give our courtship more time to cultivate?"

"Then Abbot will accuse me of malice, of undermining this arrangement between himself and your father."

"Why is it so important to him?"

"I had hoped that you could answer that question."

"I'll try to find out. Until then, we shall be forced to play it out, but only for a time. When you feel we've satisfied your uncle, we shall have a horrible row. You will find me with another young lady, and your uncle will understand why you must absolve your-self of the arrangement."

"That's deceptive."

"It's cooperative. Your uncle wants you to accept the courtship. You've complied, is all."

"Why are you doing this for me?" she asked, skeptical.

"After all, this is all of my own doing." Winston raked his hand through his hair and smoothed his silky red locks.

"I'll have to give it some thought. If you'll excuse me, I must send a messenger at once to my uncle to tell him that I want to see him. He can't do this to Isabelle."

"He'll want to know about us."

"I know."

"Will he allow Isabelle to stay if you're undecided about the courtship?" Winston asked.

"I'm not certain."

"He's a shrewd man. Yes?"

"Yes. All right, then. I accept your courtship. But only for a lit-tle while."

"I'll see to it that my father knows right away as well."

"You do that, Harry. Good day to you." Annie ran from the room.

Harry followed her with his eyes, his gaze examining her shapely form. "I couldn't have planned it better myself," he chuck-led. A furtive smile curved his face and he downed another glass of brandy. He had another lady friend to visit, one who would be glad to keep him company.

9
GOLD IN CALIFORNIA

Rogan glanced up and saw that his breakfast was being delivered. He laid aside his pen, straightened his back, and cleared off the table. But the young woman hefting the large tray and a tea service surprised him.

"Thought perhaps you had tired of the bland gruel. We had more than enough for breakfast and it's wasteful to throw it away."

"Thank you. I usually eat here on the drafting table." He patted the tabletop in front of him.

"Certainly. I trust you'll find it all quite delicious."

"You're not the stableboy, are you?" He shot an admiring glance at the attractive young woman.

"No," she said. "I'm the Dearborns' niece, Isabelle. My siblings and I are living with them now because of our mother's death last March."

"My condolences."

"You're not like most of the convicts, are you? Condolences?" Her nose wrinkled.

"I'm an architect, actually. I've been, well, there's no use in offering up a story. No one wants to believe a man behind bars."

Isabelle unrolled the utensils from the cloth napkin and placed them carefully beside the hot dish of food. Rogan noticed the manner in which she prepared the table, obviously a young woman well versed in etiquette and decorum. "I'm willing to listen. I know how it feels to be misjudged, if that counts."

"I suppose that's true of everyone," Rogan said, taken in by the girl's sincerity.

"Are you going to tell me?"

"Oh yes. I believe that I was framed, although I can't prove anything right now. Working as an apprentice for an architect, I was given the responsibility of calculating the firm's books. Now a large sum of money is missing, and they suspect me."

"Surely you'll have a chance to prove your innocence?"

"I hope to have a chance. I'm representing myself. My father's lost much of his sheep business, and I daresay he cannot afford to hire a lawyer on my behalf."

"Well, I know who can help, if I can't." Isabelle poured fresh water into a decanter.

His interest piqued, Rogan asked, "Who?"

"God. I'll pray for you."

Rogan's face fell. "Oh . . . I thought you meant—"

"Wait. I know how it sounds to you. But without the help of my Savior, I would be lost. What have you to lose if I offer prayers on your behalf?"

"Nothing, I guess. That would be all right," Rogan surrendered.

"Thank you."

"And I apologize for my skepticism. I appreciate your concern, uh . . ."

"Isabelle." She reached into her pocket. "I've something else for you."

"For me?"

"It's old. I'm certain you have one at home, but you can borrow this one while you're here." She set a Bible on the table.

"Thank you . . . Isabelle." Rogan had hoped for a bottle of wine, or at the very least a half-bottle. He disguised his disappointment behind a cordial tone.

"If you don't want it—"

"Oh no, really. It's thoughtful of you to go to the bother. After all, I'm a complete stranger and you had every reason to be fearful of coming here today. By the way, why *did* you come here today?" He placed both palms on his knees and leaned forward. A part of him wondered if she hadn't been sent by his grandmother, Katy.

"The entire household's talking about Judge Dearborn's new convict." Isabelle lifted the cloth from the bread basket and then brushed the crumbs from her hands.

"Truly?" Rogan's face reddened slightly.

"I hoped to cast some light your way, to share some kindness. . . ."

"You wish to convert me?" Rogan nodded in a knowing manner without looking up.

"Well, I . . ."

"You felt that by offering me a shred of human kindness, I would fall to my knees and—"

"Stop! You're not at all as I imagined. You're . . ." She hesitated. "Rather impertinent."

"I'm not a lowly, ignorant, groveling convict, if that's what you mean."

"I'm sorry if I've insulted you. It was not my intent." Isabelle backed toward the door, her face flushed.

"Isabelle, forgive me, for I have sinned."

"You mock me."

"I don't intend to mock you. But surely you admit—"

"Good day to you, sir. So sorry to have bothered you."

The door slammed shut. Rogan stood and watched her all but running back to the manor house, mincing her steps as she went. He hadn't had time for religion in years. It would probably surprise Isabelle to know that when he was a boy his grandmother had encouraged him to memorize many Scriptures. But he couldn't piece one together now if he tried. He had set his sights on digging his way out of poverty, and to do so, he had to lay aside every distraction. The payoff had been a room of his own and a convict number. Being falsely accused now festered inside of him. God had a strange way of paying him back for all of his hard work.

He picked up the Bible but couldn't bring himself to open it. It would be a sacrilege, he decided, to be so mad at God and try to act otherwise.

Isabelle had jumbled his concentration. It would take his full attention to focus himself on the plans again. He saw her disappear toward the manor house, lifting her skirts and sashaying away from the jail as though she had been scalded. He laughed in a puzzled way and returned to his solitude. But the mischief he had just committed continued to nag at him. Then, slowly, realization set in: He had just smitten the first person to have shown him kindness in weeks. *And a beauty, at that. Idiot!*

Annie watched Isabelle from Clarisse's window, saw her weave in and out of the yellow myrtles until she disappeared through the rear portico. Since Abbot's reversal of his decision to allow Isabelle to stay, she had grown somewhat distant and had taken to disappearing on several afternoons, sometimes afoot and sometimes on horseback. Annie didn't tell her the real reason for Abbot's change of heart, fearing that Isabelle would take drastic measures on her behalf. Instead, she had painted a happy picture of bliss for her sister, making her believe the courtship with Harry Winston was one of her own making. But the fact that she dug herself deeper into deceit pricked at her conscience. It had become harder to pray, more difficult to ask God's help in the matter. But soon the charade would be behind her, and she would make her peace. She had introduced Harry to Isabelle only last night and felt they had been convincing. If Isabelle didn't see through her masquerade, then neither would Abbot.

Soon their bedroom door opened. Isabelle entered, out of breath.

"Mussy, there you are," Annie said. "Please tell me where you've been going."

"I've been taking Uncle Abbot's convict his dinner, is all."

"Every day?"

Isabelle didn't answer.

"What's he like? Uncle Abbot's convict, that is."

"He's dreadfully ungrateful. And a heathen." Isabelle stretched out across her bed and slipped her feet out of her shoes.

"Why do you say that?"

"I took him a Bible and he mocked me."

"You shouldn't have gone out there, Isabelle. The man's a convict. What if he had hurt you?"

"He's not at all as any of us would think. He's a . . ." Isabelle's voice drifted away.

"He's a what, Isabelle?"

"A gentleman."

"Uncle Abbot's convict is a gentleman? The devil, you say!"

"Part devil. Part gentleman. He's quite the . . ."

Annie saw that her sister had drifted into a quiet slumber. They had both had a trying week. And now she had to make herself ready once more. Harry Winston wished to take her out to see "their" land. She dreaded the theatrics, the show that she would have to put on for her uncle and for Harry's family. Harry had warned her that to unfold their scheme too soon might draw suspicious questions from Abbot. So she stripped herself of her simple house dress and slipped into a carriage dress. She stood in front of the mirror, adjusting the white muslin skirt and the four flounces. Then while she touched up her cosmetic, she felt a pang of guilt. For whatever her noble causes, she also realized she was becoming too skilled at deception. Her mother and father would both have been disappointed. But knowing she had saved her sister from an uncertain future, perhaps they would have forgiven her. In order to live with herself, she had to believe that to be true, even though she had trouble forgiving herself.

"Close the door, son." Lord Reginald Winston, a stout middle-aged man, stood in his study. Once he had dismissed the maid, he poured two glasses of wine.

"I've done everything you've asked of me. What now?" Harry asked his father. He studied his father's countenance and saw the resignation rising.

"Your grandmother has some concerns. She's hearing gossip during those bridge games of hers."

"I don't give a hang about some old biddy's gossip circle!"

"Ferris Bentley's great-aunt told her that some gossip is circulating about you and Hale's missing funds."

"You defended me, didn't you?"

"As best I could. It all looks suspicious. I told you that from the start."

"If I didn't know better, I'd think you suspected me as well." Harry sipped the wine and then held it in his mouth.

"I told you I don't know anything for certain. It's your gambling habits I question at this instant. I hope that justice has rightly been served and the culprit apprehended."

"I'm sorry that Rogan Farrell was accused. I never would have believed it of him either, but I can't have the blame laid on me just to satisfy the Farrells."

"All that aside, your grandmother has asked me to warn you about your standing in this colony, about our family's standing. As you know, she's promised you land if you marry well."

"How well I know. It was at her insistence, not mine that—"

"She's pleased with your selection of the Dearborns' niece, but she wants this gossip to stop at once. The sooner you marry and settle into the colony as Mr. and Mrs. Harrison Chambers Winston, the happier she'll be."

"You realize that Annie Carraway doesn't love me?" Harry gazed into the cold fireplace.

"Infatuations are better saved for the poor. For now, it's your reputation that's in danger."

"I'm taking Miss Carraway for a carriage ride today. Tell Grandmother Chambers that I'm showing her our land. We can start the building of the estate at once, if that pleases her."

"It will please her to no end."

"Good. We can't have her worried, her and her six hundred thousand."

"Don't be so crass."

"Just joking. I must be off, Father." Harry pardoned himself from his father's study. After he had called for his driver, he stood out on the front landing to gather his thoughts. He had been relieved that Annie Carraway had settled for a temporary arrangement. Marriage didn't suit him, but he couldn't afford to lose his wealthy grandmother's trust. The lifestyle he had grown accustomed to would never hear of it. So Annie Carraway would need to be plied, would need to be lured. She would see things his way sooner or later. She would make a lovely bride, he decided, and a biased judge would make a more than suitable father-in-law. Dearborn had wavered somewhat on the dowry, but he would come around on that account sooner or later. Marriage need not be any different for him than bachelorhood, he decided. Deeper pockets would always be in his favor, and more than enough women would avail him of their time if the need arose. He hailed his driver. "Henry, my good man. Let's not keep our lady waiting, shall we?"

"Annie?" Groggy from her nap, Isabelle arose and began to dress herself.

"You're awake." Annie tucked pins into her hair with one hand while holding the newspaper with the other.

"Yes. I've been awake for a while and I've been thinking."

"About what?"

"You, mostly."

"Why?"

"You've changed a lot since we've moved here."

"We all have." Annie set aside the paper.

"I'm just . . . well, concerned, is all."

"Concerned?"

"Perhaps I'm wrong, but I haven't seen you pray as often lately. Not like before, anyway."

"How do you know whether or not I'm praying? Isn't prayer something that's between God and myself?"

"I sound intrusive." Isabelle began buttoning up her lilac dress.

"Only slightly," Annie said. "But just because you don't see me on my knees at sunrise doesn't mean that—"

"I know. I apologize." Isabelle walked to the mirror and stood in front of it.

"No need. But not everyone wears their religion so boldly as you, Mussy."

"I'm not speaking of anyone but you for now."

"What do you want me to say? That I'm as good as I should be every day? That I pray often and study the Scriptures? I can't be like you."

"You're not supposed to be like me, Annie. I'm terribly flawed."

"I've yet to find a single blemish on your soul." Annie noticed an inward pain etched on Isabelle's face.

"My faults are legion. It would do you a great injustice to imitate me. It is Christ Jesus alone whom we should imitate."

"Isabelle, I'm afraid I shall greatly disappoint you if you wish for me to emulate Christ himself. I should do better to live up to your standards and at least accomplish in part what you do in whole."

"If it is for me that you strive spiritually at all, then you've failed at the start."

"I know what you're saying. But I—" She looked away.

"Go on."

"I was about to say that I practice my faith in quiet ways, but if the truth be known, I should say that I practice my faith in seasons." She lifted her gloves from the table and found her Bible beneath them.

"You want to explain?"

"I waver and then I soar."

"Why do you waver?"

"I don't know."

"Is this Harry Winston a man of faith, Annie?"

"No, he isn't."

"You didn't even hesitate. You don't love him, do you?"

Annie glanced up and saw the Winstons' carriage approaching from a distant hill.

"Annie?"

"He's coming, Isabelle. Will you fasten my dress for me?"

"You didn't answer me."

"If you'll answer my question about where you've been going at noon, I shall answer you."

"I can't tell you." Isabelle stood behind her and began fastening the hooks on Annie's dress.

"Why not?"

"It would make you a party to my villainy."

"Now you *must* tell me," Annie said. "What is it, Mussy? I know you and know that whatever you do, it must be for a noble cause."

"Turn about and let me finish your hooks."

Annie complied but couldn't help glancing at her over her shoulder. She saw how Isabelle forced her gaze to the floor, how she could no longer look at her.

The door opened and a maid peered into the room. "Miss Carraway, your gentleman caller approaches."

"Thank you. I'll be down shortly." Feeling Isabelle's slender fingers lift from her bodice, Annie turned around and offered a sympathetic gaze. She looked at Isabelle fully, then saw that a tear slipped down her cheek like a thin, transparent ribbon. Annie wiped her sister's cheek with a handkerchief and kissed her gently on the side of her face.

"I know I look foolish," Isabelle said.

"Don't say such things. I can see this is a matter you don't take lightly. When you're ready to tell me, I'm willing to listen. Until then, I won't ask you any further questions."

Annie could smell the stench of cigars before she entered the parlor. She waited outside the doorway for a moment listening to

Uncle Abbot conversing with Harry.

"So you've already begun house plans. Splendid! I've an architect designing Sybil's next house. She's already decided this house is too cramped. My advice—don't build too small."

"Naturally, it's my own design. It's a manor house, a gabled affair with lots of windows. Annie seems so taken with her aunt's garden that I've planned a surprise for her—a splendid English garden in the rear of the property. It will have a hedged walkway all the way out to the pond."

Annie cupped her hand to her mouth. She had known Harry to embellish, but his house plans might sound just a bit farfetched to her suspicious uncle. She would interrupt their talk at once before Harry had stretched their little lie beyond belief. She entered the room as casually as she could manage.

"Annie, my dear!" Harry exclaimed. "Ready for our ride?"

"Ready when you are, Harry." Annie pulled on her gloves, nodded, and pressed her lips together while keeping her eyes to the floor. She didn't want Abbot to notice any anxiety.

"Oh, there's one change in plans."

"Oh?" Abbot held out his glass while his butler filled it with more wine.

"What change?" Annie didn't trust Harry's bent for the unpredictable. She also noticed his look of apology.

"My grandmother insisted upon joining us today. She's yet to meet you and—"

"Why, that *is* a surprise." The thought unnerved Annie. She could never maintain a convincing interest in Harry during an hours-long carriage ride. Nervous, she fidgeted with her bonnet and then finally allowed the ties to hang loosely. "Where is she?"

"She has trouble with her right knee—rheumatism—so she stayed in the carriage. We should keep her no longer."

"Of course. Good day, Uncle Abbot."

"I shall return your niece before the supper hour, if that's satisfactory." Harry offered his arm to Annie.

"Stay as long as you like," Abbot offered cheerily, although Annie detected the derisiveness of his tone. She trudged past Harry's waiting arm without so much as an acknowledgment.

PART TWO

A good man out of the good treasure of his heart
bringeth forth that which is good; and an evil man out
of the evil treasure of his heart bringeth forth that
which is evil: for of the abundance of the heart his
mouth speaketh.

Luke 6:45

10

A PRAYER FOR ROGAN

Annie peered into the Winstons' expensive coach, where she observed Harry's maternal grandmother, Hertha Chambers, sitting with her plump, rounded shoulders pressed against the carriage seat. Attired in an abundance of dark berry taffeta and soft netting draped around her shoulders, her pale countenance and long cadaverous fingers gave her a corpselike appearance. Annie ducked slightly to enter the double-brougham carriage, a handsome affair painted in gleaming black and embellished with gold trim.

"Greetings, Mrs. Chambers. I'm Annie Carraway." She cocked her head slightly, partly to offer a gesture of respect and partly to keep the feathers of her embroidered bonnet from bending against the cushioned ceiling.

"Afternoon." The grand matron eyed Annie with a sweeping glance, her scrutiny evident. She answered in a low tone, her face without hint of a smile.

"Sorry to keep you waiting, Grandmother." Harry seated himself next to Annie and removed his hat at once.

"I expected as much."

Annie felt another sigh escape her lips. She hadn't counted on a chaperone today, although she decided that taking such a long carriage ride alone with the notorious Harry Winston might be unwise after all. But she had wanted to discuss the plans with him to call off their engagement, a plan that arose inside of her like a brush fire. Now they would have to speak at a later time, and she would be forced to suffer in silence under the scrutiny of an agitated woman.

"Lovely day for a ride, eh, Grandmother?"

Hertha Chambers only shrugged.

"Nice weather," Annie said.

Hertha Chambers grunted, indifferent to anything they said.

Annie closed her eyes and prayed for the day to be over. It was not the type of prayer that Isabelle would have had in mind, but it was heartfelt, nonetheless.

Rogan stared incredulously at Sybil Dearborn and the young private who accompanied her into the jail. She pored over lists and lists of specifications for the house she wanted him to design. He could see right away that the plan would take weeks. He had hoped to be free soon.

"Our first home is far too small. I want this one to be splendid. Do you know how to design splendor?"

"Judge Dearborn knows of this?" Rogan queried, hoping the woman's wishes would not have to be carried out.

"Why, of course? Didn't he tell you?" She made another notation with a steel pen.

"He must have forgotten."

"I want the master bedroom to be twice the size of our present *boudoir*. And see here? These large French doors open out onto a balcony. That's where I'll have my tea, when the mood strikes." Her voice rose with a swell of material satisfaction. She had scrawled out a rudimentary drawing of her own.

A sickening realization began to boil inside of him. His brother, Frederick, had been right after all. Dearborn had only brought him to his private jail to design his home and then send him quietly off to the gallows. *Perhaps this plan will take longer than even Dearborn imagines.* "Mrs. Dearborn, you realize that this house plan is quite elaborate. I would need much time—"

"Take all the time you need. I want it to be perfect." She drew out the words, making the matter sound of grave importance. "This is the house I want all of my grandchildren to remember me by. Besides, I've my nieces and nephews living with me now—five in all, besides our girls still living at home. We're too cramped, all of us in one place like this."

"How dreadful for you."

"I'm hiring a nanny as soon as the new house is complete. My sister's children take up a lot of time. And when their oldest sister marries, I'll have no help at all."

"That would be a shame, madam. Do you speak of, what was her name—ah, yes! Isabelle, is it?"

"No, not Isabelle, although she *should* soon settle on a suitor. The oldest is Annie. Now, as I was saying about the house . . ."

While she prattled on, Rogan recalled the other sister he had only seen from a distance. If she was as pious and troublesome as her sister Isabelle, better for everyone that she should quickly marry off.

"Pardon me, Mrs. Dearborn, but I do have a request."

"Request?"

"Yes. For such an elaborate undertaking, I will be needing my better drafting equipment," he lied. "Can you send a messenger to deliver a letter to my brother, Frederick?"

"You say you have need of better equipment?"

"You deserve only the best for your new manor house."

"Private, can you handle the matter?"

"Of course, Mrs. Dearborn," the private said.

"The sooner the better, my good man." Rogan pondered about how the weather would be this time of year in California.

"Are you a Catholic, my dear?"

"No, ma'am. I'm Protestant." Annie was growing tired of Hertha Chambers' unceasing questions.

"How will this be? A Protestant mother and a Catholic father? What of the children?"

"Well, all Winstons are christened Catholic, of course. Isn't that right, Annie?" Harry lifted his right brow and tossed a nervous glance her way.

Rubbing her right thumb atop her left one, Annie gathered her thoughts and prepared to suffer through yet another of Harry's falsehoods. They would wed in February. She would have six wedding attendants, and after a month's stay in London, where they would visit the Winston relatives, they would return and make their home in Sydney. They wanted many children, he had further lied. It was all so much fiction, she wondered if she should keep it in a journal just to remember what lies Harry had told and to whom.

"Annie dear?"

"Christen our children Catholic?" She looked at the carriage floor and forced herself to nod.

"Well, is there any matter on which you two don't agree?"

Annie studied her dubious gaze. The silence in the carriage grew uncomfortable.

"Yes. As a matter of fact . . ." Harry hesitated, but Annie could see the wheels turning in his thoughts. "I would much prefer the parlor be painted white, but Annie insists upon a pale rose."

She looked away, biting her bottom lip.

"Well, I must side with your fiancée on that matter, Harrison. I know you're studying architecture, but leave the colors for the woman to decide. After all, it is she who will be home all day minding the home fires."

Annie felt nauseous.

Rogan lay face up on the cot, his anger coming to a roaring boil. All that Frederick had predicted about Dearborn's intentions had come to fruition within a matter of minutes. Abbot Dearborn's wife had appeared at the door, her head full of ideas about how she could become the mistress of the largest mansion in Australia. Judge Dearborn had achieved his purpose after all, or so he thought. Rogan conceived a plan. He would have to begin the drawings right away and pretend that Frederick was assisting him in order to shroud his frequent visits. Above all, they could not arouse suspicion.

Dearborn had yet to settle on a court date, a point that Frederick had used as proof of his suspicions. The realization ignited more anger. Rogan stood and began to pace. Dearborn's niece Isabelle might be able to dig up more facts. He would have to befriend the girl in order to find out if she had access to information.

A thousand ideas tumbled about his mind, but more than anything else he realized he might have to flee the jail soon.

Then a new form of guilt raised its head, sloshing his emotions around and unnerving him. If he escaped from Dearborn's jail and fled for California, he could never return. His escape would be highly publicized in the newspapers. His mother and father would be shamed, and all would believe him to be guilty. The news might even stretch as far as California. If so, he would be hunted like an animal. He cursed. How he longed to be free in order to unearth the truth about Hale's embezzled funds. But freedom at any cost would bring him even more bondage. He would never see his family again, and his brother would be wanted for abetting a criminal.

Rogan gripped the bars on the small window and laid his head against the stone windowsill. His eyes misted, and he longed for the sanctuary of his own small room at Rose Hill. His feet shuffled against an object, causing him to look down. The black binding of Isabelle's Bible caught his eye. He had stepped on it and left behind a dusty footprint. He raked his hand through his dark hair, stooped to recover the Bible, dusted it off, and set it on the table. But the anxiety that clouded his thoughts prevailed. He returned to the window where the daylight streamed in and warmed his face and hands. He longed for the light, for the life it brought forth. He had taken the light for granted, its merciful disbursement on every living being whether bond or free. He lifted his face, thankful for the cloudless day. He would bask in it momentarily and then begin the house plans for Sybil Dearborn. Perhaps the tedious new work would help clear his thoughts for a better plan for himself.

"Take a look, will you? It's a lovely piece of land. A stream runs through it." Harry Winston assisted Annie from the carriage.

The one thing about Harry that made her most uncomfortable was his ability to lie. He could make anyone believe anything. If she didn't know better herself, she would almost believe that he thought their engagement was a genuine arrangement. But with his grandmother watching their every move, she could say nothing at all. She pulled off her gloves. The sun appeared, driving away the few clouds that had dared to linger. Weary of Harry's bantering, she walked away feigning interest in her inspection of the land. In the distance, the Blue Mountains bordered the Australian horizon with a sparse scattering of trees nestled in its spreading lap. The Winstons' cattle grazed along a flat expanse that disappeared over a green slope. Just above the slope, she could see the stream meandering slowly into a thicket of trees. She had to admit that Harry had been handed a treasure, one she knew he took for granted.

"Now, the house should go over here," she heard Harry say loudly.

"Where, Harry?" She hoped the dreariness of her mood was not reflected in her tone.

"Over here, dearest." He stood with his hands in his pockets but gestured with a nod of his head. He wanted her to join them, she could tell. So Annie lifted her skirts, trudged toward them both, and followed his eyes to the point he indicated. The spot he had chosen was much farther away from the slope.

"See what I mean?"

"But I see a much better place. See where the cattle are grazing? It has a lovely view of the stream." She felt silly for saying so.

"Is that right?" Harry smiled and laid a finger thoughtfully aside his face. His brows lifted with interest.

"Don't look at me like that," Annie said to Harry under her breath.

"Annie prefers the slope, Grandmother. What do you think?"

"I like it. She has a good eye."

"Thank you." Annie saw that the older woman smiled for the first time. She felt Harry slip his hand into hers. He drew her slightly against himself, and she felt his breath against her neck.

"You've exquisite taste, my dear."

"What are you doing?"

"I'm enjoying myself."

"Well, please stop."

"Why? Aren't you enjoying yourself too?"

"No." She stiffened, but he persisted, refusing to take his gaze from her. She felt him drawing her in, his eyes full of silent expectation.

"Admit it, Annie. You like it out here."

"I think we should leave now, Harry," Annie spoke up. "Your grandmother is growing tired. We should take her home."

"Thank you, my dear. Yes, I am tired."

Annie made assisting Harry's grandmother into the coach a

task of great importance. The old woman's eyes shone with her approval of Annie. Once Hertha Chambers had settled into the seat, Annie immediately seated herself next to her and engaged the woman in conversation. Harry took his place alone and across from them, his eyes never leaving Annie. But she scarcely acknowledged him, making great show of her sudden interest in his elderly grandmother. Upon their arrival at Dearborn Manor, she prepared to alight. She would have no choice but to allow Harry Winston to escort her to the door. Her brisk pace nearly left him behind, but he soon found his way to her side. She detected a spark of anger in his tone.

"What are you doing?" Harry asked.

"I would ask you the same question. We both know this engagement is a charade. And I know you wish to convince our families that it's true, but you've carried it too far, Harry."

"I apologize," he said. "But you've confused me. You're quite the actress yourself. I could've sworn that you had feelings for me. I thought I felt something between us. Was I mistaken?"

"Yes, you were mistaken. Of *course* you were mistaken, Harry. You've known all along that our engagement is temporary. You've no intention of marrying me or anyone else." The way he studied her worried Annie. He had a hesitation in his face that bewildered her.

"It could all change, Annie. I'm not incapable of love. Is that what you believe about me?" He stepped toward her and, with care, gripped her shoulders.

Annie read beyond his handsome smile, his dapper airs. Her mistrust for him multiplied.

"I want you to trust me, Annie."

"I don't know you, Harry Winston. And you don't know me. But I do know this—you're up to something."

"That is unfair."

"But I'm right, am I not?"

"You have my word. I shall honor our original agreement. But you realize that if we break it off too abruptly—"

"I know," Annie said. "Just a little while longer, then?"

Harry nodded, a faint tinge of pink rising on his cheeks.

"Good."

"I had only hoped that our friendship could grow."

Annie felt ashamed for having ever made the agreement. She now realized she had forced them both into an uncomfortable situation. Seeing him stand before her looking so guileless caused a flutter of guilt to arise. She hesitated and still could not look into his eyes. For a moment she wished she could with honesty make matters better.

"What are you thinking?" He looked hopeful.

"Are you saying you really wish to court me?"

"Would it be so awful?"

She allowed a nervous smile to play around the corners of her mouth. Harry kissed her cheek and softly brushed her face with the back of his hand. She wondered if the anxiety fluttering around her stomach might be a warning.

"Grandmother?" Rogan had looked up from the rudimentary desk in full expectation of seeing his brother march through the jail doorway. But Frederick being nowhere in sight, he laid down his pen, his head cocked to the side. He stood at once. The last person he expected to pay him a visit today was his grandmother, Katy Farrell Gabriel. An original colonist who had arrived in Australia on the First Fleet, her role as the young housemaid to Australia's first governor, Captain Arthur Phillip, had been the salvation for her convicted parents.

Rogan had always admired the way his grandmother, as a young woman, had taken charge of Rose Hill, assisted by her brother, Caleb. The two of them together had doubled their flock and their earnings in only a few short years.

"My dear Rogan, look what they've done to you."

"What brings you here, Grandmother?"

"My Rogan!" Her eyes misted and she held her feeble arms out to him.

"I'm all right, really, Grandmother." He embraced the aging matron. He had insisted that his family not inform her of his plight, hoping to have found his freedom before now.

"They didn't want me to know, but I'm not a fool."

"I didn't want you to see me like this. I didn't want to make you ashamed."

"Ashamed? Of you? Never, Rogan. I knew when I heard the story that you were innocent. How could anyone accuse you, much less Mason Hale? He, of all people, knows better."

"I'm equally surprised that Hale would think such a thing, but

I'll prove my innocence. I've my own ideas about the culprit. Time will reveal the source. I'm sure of it." He attempted to sound hopeful but could already see her reading straight through him as she always did.

"I know you will."

"How is Robert today?"

"Resting. Husbands grow old much faster than wives, I believe."

"Mother always said it was the sea that took the years away from Robert Gabriel."

"Could be," Katy said. "But he's home now and I believe he's glad of it. Let someone else take the helm, is what he says."

"I'm glad you came by today, even if it means your seeing me like this. I get lonely in here most days." Rogan led her to a chair.

"I'm glad you like my company, Grandson, but I'm here on business."

"Business?" Rogan observed the glint in her deep blue eyes. In spite of her years, her eyes still effervesced with her personal zeal for life. He couldn't hide his amusement at the humor he found in her words.

"Yes. You think an old woman can't carry on business? I'm old—not dead."

"I didn't say that you—"

"I've no time for bantering about with you, Rogan. Listen to me. I've got some money, and I want you—"

"No. I can't let you do that."

"Don't interrupt me!"

"I'm sorry, but Rose Hill needs all the financial backing that all of us can muster. I won't drain what's left on legal fees."

"Families are supposed to sacrifice for one another. We could always buy more land later. Rose Hill is dirt and grass and trees. You're my flesh and blood."

"No," Rogan said. "Rose Hill is more to you than a plot of dirt. You know that to be true more than I do, Grandmother. Rose Hill is you. It is Katy Prentice, and Katy Farrell, and Katy Gabriel. It is you. And I won't allow it to die. Rose Hill is our legacy."

"You are my legacy, Rogan." She pulled out a small purse and opened it at once. Shaking out a few gold coins, she held them out to him.

"I can outlast your stubborn ways. I'm just like you, you know."

"You could never wake up early enough to outlast me." Katy shoved the coins into his hand.

"Now, what do you expect me to do with the money?"

"Hire a good lawyer. Not one from around here, mind you. Send for one, if you must, but get a good one and get yourself out of here."

"I should give this money to Father. He needs this worse than I do."

"He'll work out the problems. Just give him time, Rogan. He wants to hold on to Rose Hill as badly as you do. The Farrells have confronted worse monsters than this blasted depression."

Rogan kissed her good-bye, hating to see her go. He labored over his work for another hour. Then, his attentions spent, he began his afternoon habit of staring out the window. He now hoped the Dearborns' niece would return, if for nothing else than the pure enjoyment of hearing her rattle on about her religion.

Katy stood a good distance from the jail. She could see her grandson pacing, which tore at her heart and brought tears to the surface. She had her doubts about the judge who had sent him here, having known of Abbot Dearborn since his arrival some years back. She did not trust the judicial system any more than she trusted the devil himself. She knew that in the blink of an eye, the courts would hang an innocent man just to free another jail cell. With her head bowed, she prayed in silence. *Heavenly Father, please keep your hand on Rogan. He needs you now, although he'll be the last to admit it. Send those into his path who will pave the way for his freedom—freedom from wrongful accusations, and freedom from the sin that blinds him. Help him to come to know you, Lord, as I know you. In the name of your Son, Christ Jesus, I pray. . . .*

11

ABBOT'S CONVICT

Annie watched Isabelle heft the large dinner tray into her arms. In spite of her warnings, Isabelle insisted upon delivering the evening meal to Uncle Abbot's convict. She would have to hurry before the sun disappeared at day's end. While Isabelle meandered across the kitchen threshold, Annie strode to meet her.

"I'm taking Uncle's convict his meal, is all."

"If I didn't know better, I'd say you've taken a fancy to the man."

"Don't ever say such things, Annie."

"I'm teasing. Can't I do that anymore, or have you completely lost your sense of humor?"

"Walk with me, please." Isabelle adjusted some things on the tray.

Annie saw her take long, purposeful strides toward the rear exit of the house. She shrugged and then followed at once, her curiosity piqued. Once she had caught up with her sister, she could see the determined set of Isabelle's jaw, her eyes fixed on some distant point.

"Are we alone?" Isabelle asked.

"You're acting peculiar again. I know I've promised not to ask, but—"

"You're right. You promised not to ask."

"This is all so unfair, Mussy. Why won't you trust me?" Annie said. "And why the hurry?"

"I'm late."

"More's the pity. The convict might have you dismissed."

"Annie, I need your help, but I can't tell you why."

"Mussy, are you in some sort of trouble? Because if you are—"

"No, but I've no time to explain. No time at all. Will you—would you mind taking Mr. Farrell his supper?"

"Me?" she asked. "Yes, I would mind."

"Please, Annie. You've no idea how much your help would mean to me."

"But I don't know how to deal with a criminal. I lack your talent with the less fortunates and—"

"Please?"

"You are up to something, aren't you?" She saw Isabelle's large, pleading eyes, the warmth of her smile, and suddenly Annie's resistance wavered. She felt her will bending to Isabelle's appeals.

Isabelle bit her lip and turned her face eastward, no longer able to look at Annie.

"But knowing you, Mussy, it's surely something of merit." Annie could see that her words had a strange effect on Isabelle, whose face filled with unexplainable sorrow.

"I only wish that I could be as full of goodness as you think I am."

"You're ten times as good as anyone I know." Annie took the tray from her hands, scarcely noticing that Isabelle had donned her best pair of gloves.

"I must away, Annie." Lifting her skirts in an uncharacteristic fashion, Isabelle kissed her sister upon the cheek and ran until she disappeared behind the stable.

"Mussy, please—" Annie watched her go. No longer able to bear the mystery, Annie decided she would deliver the convict his meal and then at least take a walk in the same direction. Not to eavesdrop but to protect her younger sister's interest. *If I don't look out for you, no one will.*

She glanced down at the tray. Next to the covered dish lay a brass key. After she had set the tray atop a barrel, she lifted the key and tried it in the lock on the jail door. The rusted lock groaned, then clicked. Annie dropped the key into her pocket and retrieved the tray. Her first meeting with the man, and she was already filled with dread. She made a mental note to avoid any conversation with him. Her promise to her sister then fulfilled, with the meal delivered, she would excuse herself right away. She heard him speak as the door opened.

"Good evening."

"Your supper." She lifted one knee to shove open the door but found that he had stood and opened it for her. While the door swung open, she prepared to face an unkempt sight. Her eyes widened as she beheld the handsome man dressed in practical yet stylish attire.

Equally surprised, Rogan Farrell bowed at once. His mouth turned up on one side and he gazed at her through smiling eyes.

"I'm here in place of my sister."

"Isabelle?"

"Yes. I'll be out of your way soon and—"

"I don't believe we've met." He held out his hand.

"No." Annie flew past, prepared to place his tray upon the table but found it cluttered with architectural drafts.

"I'm Rogan Farrell."

"My sister Isabelle has made it her duty to see your evening meal is delivered. But she had an errand and asked if I would do the honors. . . ." Her voice trailed off. She felt awkward, which made her blush all the more.

"I thank you. You must be the Dearborns' daughter."

"Actually, no. I'm Abbot's niece." She hesitated, having already broken her promise to herself to leave at once.

"Have you a name?"

"I'm Annie," she said. "Isabelle and I live with our aunt and uncle. Along with our siblings."

"I see. You've lost both of your parents, then?"

She nodded, then glanced down at the tray.

"Isabelle's told me some of your plight. You're actually from England?"

"My father died while we lived in England. Mother died here in Australia. My aunt insisted that we come and live with them here." Annie hated her breathless chattering but felt powerless to stop herself. The way he instantly drew her in also surprised her.

"So you must be the niece who's soon to be married?"

"That's right," she said. "That is, well—"

"A hearty congratulations, then, to a lucky groom."

"Did Isabelle tell you? That I'm getting married, that is."

"Actually your aunt told me. One of those things that comes out in conversation. That's all."

"My aunt . . . spoke with you?"

"You see, I'm acting as architect for the Dearborns." He shuffled through the papers on his desk and pulled out a sketchy draft.

"You're an architect?"

"That surprises you, I see. I'm designing their new home, along with some other government designs. Isabelle's told you nothing about me, I suppose."

"Not really."

"Oh."

"So your services to Uncle Abbot are . . . he's not . . ."

"Paying me? No. Without commission. You're perceptive, I see."

"I know my uncle."

"But at least they now allow me to wear my own clothes. And I can continue working until I've proven my innocence. Better than Sydney's jail."

Annie studied the drawings that he held up. She shook her head, not at all surprised at Abbot's strategy.

"In case you're wondering, I've been charged with embezzlement."

Not knowing how to respond, Annie held out the tray.

"I'm innocent."

"This is getting cold. Where would you like it?"

"You can put it here on the desk."

Annie glanced down at the clutter while he, with some difficulty, tried to organize it. She willed away a smile. His awkward haste to clear the desk for her amused her. She put the tray on the desk and was about to depart when her eye fell on a Bible. It lay under his cot, shoved against the wall.

"Something wrong?" Farrell asked.

"Pardon my noticing, but that Bible, it looks familiar."

"Your sister left it here."

"By accident or on purpose?"

"She is trying to convert me, I believe."

"Has she . . . converted you?"

He didn't answer.

"I'll take it out of your way, if you prefer. It belonged to my father, actually."

"Be my guest," Rogan said. "But then . . ."

"What is it?"

"I wouldn't want to hurt her feelings. That is, perhaps we should—"

"Say no more, Mr. Farrell. I believe you're right. If Mussy

wanted you to have it, then we'll leave it here for now. But once you leave here, could you—would you mind leaving it behind? Sentimental reasons, you know."

"Oh, of course. I wouldn't have any need for it. Since you mention it, would it be possible . . . I'm sorry. I shouldn't be asking anything of you in my position."

"You can ask. If I can't do it, then I'm certain you're a reasonable man. You seem as such anyway."

"You see, your uncle, Abbot Dearborn, has the power to lock me up and throw away the key. I don't want to anger the man."

She waited, unsure of what he would say next.

"I'm working on these plans for him, but he's yet to give me a trial date. Could you try to find out if my trial has even been set? It is my right as a prisoner to know."

"You mean to say that you've been locked up without promise of trial? I'm sure that's not legal."

"And I've yet to secure a lawyer. I have a family member who's trying to find one for me—one I can afford."

"I'll see what I can find out. My uncle's work is a private affair. He seldom discusses such things with me. But if the matter arises, I'll bring it to his attention."

"Oh no. Please don't tell him I've discussed my trial with you."

"All right, then. But only if I happen to find out what you need to know will I tell you, Mr. Farrell. I don't make a practice of prying into Uncle Abbot's work." Noticing that his face filled with relief, she felt all the better for having agreed. A pity swept through her for the man. Part of her wondered if indeed this Rogan Farrell had been wrongly accused. However, she had other matters to worry about. Isabelle could be far away by now, and she would never figure out the reason for her sister's unusual behavior. She stood at the door, tipping her head in farewell.

"Good evening to you."

"Good evening to you, Mr. Farrell."

"Call me Rogan."

"I doubt you'll see me again."

"All's the pity."

"But good luck on your trial and all . . . Mr. Farrell."

She allowed herself one brief smile and departed, hopeful of catching up with Isabelle before nightfall.

"Clarisse, where are your sisters?" Sybil took her place at the end of the long dining table. Pointing to a candle that smoked without flame, she waited while the servant girl relit it.

"I don't know." Clarisse, now eleven, fidgeted with the large sash on the back of her dress.

"They didn't tell you anything at all—why they might be late?"

"No, but I can go and ask Mrs. Gunneysax." Clarisse finally pulled apart the ends of the sash and allowed them to drape over the sides of her chair.

"I've told you to stop the make-believe, Clarisse. You're too old for it, and it will ruin your mind."

"It isn't make-believe."

"Doris, have you spoken to them?"

"I didn't speak to either of them." Doris rested her cheek against her right hand, elbow atop the table.

"Posture, Doris," Sybil said. "Does anyone know what has happened to my nieces?"

Abbot appeared in the doorway, adjusting his collar and buttoning up his coat.

"Abbot, we don't know where Annie and Isabelle have gone."

"I'll send a man out to look for them," he said. "It's getting dark. Not safe in this colony for two young women to be out flitting around like gadflies."

"I do remember something, though. Isabelle likes to take your convict his dinner, Father," Doris said.

"My convict? What business has she with a convict?" Abbot yanked his napkin from the table and dropped it into his lap.

"Isabelle wants to convert him." Thomas didn't succeed at veiling his cynicism.

"Your sister's always been serious about her faith, Thomas. Something you could use more of, no doubt." Sybil clasped her hands in front of her and waited while all the others bowed their heads.

Thomas stared straight ahead.

"As a matter of fact, Thomas, you may ask God's blessing on our meal tonight."

"I feel I should go out to the jail," Abbot said before Thomas could begin to pray. "Something's amiss, I believe, and I'm going to find out what it is." Abbot gripped the arm of his chair, prepared to stand.

The sound of girlish talk drew all their eyes. Annie and Isabelle strolled into the room, both looking rather sheepish.

"Where on earth have you two been?" Abbot asked.

"Outside, actually. We took a stroll in the rose garden." Annie found her place at the table.

"In my garden after dark? Absurd! Why, you're not wearing your shoes!"

"The ground was quite damp and muddied our slippers," Annie said. "We didn't want to muss the rug, and we knew the dinner hour to be upon us, so we left our slippers at the door." She took her chair but not before lifting her skirts again to reveal her bare feet. Even Doris laughed.

"Go find another pair of shoes at once. How vulgar!"

"I apologize for our tardiness, Aunt Sybil." Isabelle spoke in her usual poised fashion, then broke into laughter when Annie cupped her hand to her mouth to stifle her own mirth.

"Stop at once!" Sybil grew terse.

"Aunt Sybil's right, Annie. We don't want to be vulgar."

"Don't mock me, Isabelle. Besides, it hasn't rained. How could you muddy your shoes in the garden?"

"The liveryman had emptied the trough to clean it, which soaked the dirt. We didn't see it in the dark, is all," Annie said.

"Liveryman? You were out at the stables? I thought you were in the garden," Sybil said.

"We were in both places." Annie spoke the truth, but she hadn't intended to speak of the stables.

"That will be enough from both of you. Thomas, I believe I asked you to say grace."

After Thomas had mumbled a prayer, Annie made haste to finish her meal and hoped that Isabelle would do the same. When she had found her sister earlier standing on a knoll behind the stable, she also saw what Isabelle had been hiding all along. Mussy hadn't yet explained anything to her when they both stumbled into the muddy trough water in the dark, but Annie had her presumptions. Their cloth shoes ruined, Annie had led them to the rear portico in haste. Since the dinner hour was upon them, Annie was afraid Sybil would send a servant after them if they didn't hurry.

Annie didn't understand why Isabelle would be so secretive about her actions, but she felt a need to protect her until all had been fully explained. And Isabelle certainly had much to explain about the young man whose carriage took off when Annie had appeared so unexpectedly.

12
ANNIE'S FITTING

"Just tell me if I know the man. That's the least you could do for your own sister." Annie braided Isabelle's hair into two long strands that hung past her waist.

"You didn't see him then, did you?"

"No, I told you that already."

"I can't answer. You know I would, but—"

"But you won't, is all. You've no good reason, Mussy. I tell you everything."

"If I could tell you, I would. But for you to know would . . ."

"Would what?"

"It could involve you in the matter. I don't want to see you involved. I want your hands clean of the situation."

"As though I care that my hands are clean. They already believe that I sabotaged Doris."

"You don't care, but I do. Trust me, Annie. You don't want to know."

"Then I think I know already." Annie smiled, feeling the power of her knowledge.

"Please don't say, if you do."

"I would love to imagine it's that Lafferty chap. Charles, or whatever his name is." Annie stared off as though caught up in the dream herself.

"I asked you not to guess."

"Allow me a guess. He comes by to court Doris and then sneaks out to meet you, his secret true love. You've stolen him right from under Abbot's nose with no one the wiser."

"Stop, please."

"Worse than that, you've planned to run away and marry him." Annie was so caught up in her levity that she didn't notice Isabelle's anxiety.

"Annie, please!"

"But Uncle Abbot steps in and the next thing you know, if you marry Lafferty, he will lose his inheritance. But he doesn't care, so away you both run, into the Australian sunrise before the Dearborns awaken and find you gone!"

"How could you possibly know?" Isabelle asked.

"Mussy, I'm only playing—"

"I swear I can't keep a thing from you, Annie Carraway! Not one blessed secret."

Stunned by her sister's confession, Annie stared at her without a word.

Saturday morning brought another warm dawn. With Christmas only weeks away, Sydney's hot summer would soon be upon them. Annie made haste to dress and run down to breakfast. She had planned to join her brothers, Thomas and Linus, on a horseback ride. She could see Sybil waiting at the foot of the stairs.

"Good. You've dressed already," Sybil said. "We've much to do today."

"Such as?" Annie stopped only halfway down. She offered a dubious stare.

"Dear me, have you already forgotten? Your engagement party is only weeks away. All of Sydney is coming and you've nothing proper to wear."

"More's the pity, Aunt Sybil. But I promised Thomas a jaunt on horseback this morning. Can I join you later?"

"I've an appointment with the best seamstress in town. We've only an hour to finish our meal and meet her. She's worked us in."

Annie stood silent, her brows tilted in pain.

"We can't be late."

"You should've asked me," Annie said. "Shouldn't I be making some of the decisions?" A flutter of anxiety rose within her. The time of wedding preparations was fast approaching, and she would be forced to carry the charade into deeper waters of deception if Harry didn't act soon.

"If you would take the reins, my dear, I'd gladly hand them to you. But you never give the matter a thought, or so it seems. And since your mother's not alive to oversee a proper engagement, I'll have to do it. I refuse to be embarrassed by an ill-planned affair."

At breakfast, Annie picked at her food, eating little of her morning victuals. When Isabelle sat down next to her, she had to force a polite greeting. Deep in her own troubled thoughts, Annie recalled that Harry Winston would be joining them for church in the morning and then for Sunday dinner. After dinner, she would invite him for a stroll out-of-doors. She would insist that their engagement be brought to a close as soon as possible—before the engagement party ever arrived. If Abbot went to the expense of an elaborate party, he would likely insist that she and Harry follow through with their promise, no matter what her feelings. Besides, the guilt of it all had begun to eat at her. She decided she had to speak with Harry about his plan to stage a horrendous love affair in order to end their engagement. She couldn't go through with this charade, she realized—feigning outrage over his unfaithfulness. Perhaps he could live with such deceit, but she couldn't.

The false engagement had become a battle inside of her. By day, she managed to keep her mind occupied with other things and thought little of it until Harry called. But at night, when she had no distractions, Annie had to face herself and the lie she was living. Her dishonesty loomed large, making her feel as though she had become two persons—the one who lived according to Abbot's rules by day, and the other who faced the truth about herself at night.

If Harry didn't act soon, she would have to do something about it herself. Out of her agony she had prayed, had asked God to make a better way for her, had asked His forgiveness. She could no longer live with such wretchedness inside.

She felt certain that Aunt Sybil, in the end, would be in agreement that the engagement be called off. Once Annie made it plain to her how wrong it would be, appealed to her sense of right and wrong, Sybil would understand and would make things clear to Abbot. A spark of relief caused her to relax—until she remembered this morning's dreaded errand. However much she hated it, she still had to suffer through the miserable chore of being fitted for a dress. She would go to Sybil after her talk with Harry tomorrow, though. Together, they would cancel their plans and make it right with both families.

"What's wrong with you?" Isabelle whispered.

"Nothing."

"Now who's hiding something?" The two sisters offered a simultaneous nod at their aunt and continued picking at their food. "You're angry with me. I know you are," Isabelle said.

"Aunt Sybil, where is our uncle this morning?" Annie asked.

"Don't answer me, then," Isabelle continued to whisper.

"Your uncle Abbot is meeting with your future father-in-law, Lord Reginald. You know how these men can be—ironing out all the financial questions, the arrangements for your home. I'd much prefer to be left out of such matters myself." Sybil held up her silver knife and gazed at herself.

Annie could still hear Isabelle muttering in her ear.

"You've no right to be angry with me," she was saying.

"I'm not angry, I swear. I'm happy for you." Annie smiled through clenched teeth.

"Do you mean it?"

"Does she mean what?" Sybil laid down her knife and fork and waited for the answer.

Isabelle, her face flushed, fell silent.

Annie spoke up. "I was just wondering if my sister could come with us to the fitting?" She knew better than to look at Isabelle now.

"Of course, Isabelle. This is your sister's biggest affair ever. You should be at her side."

"I wouldn't want to intrude."

"No intrusion, but we should be off soon. I'll summon the driver." Sybil excused herself from the table and left the room.

"Annie, we're supposed to meet Thomas and Linus in the stable. They're already dressed and waiting for us."

"If I have to suffer through this indignity, then I can't bear the thought of you off on a jaunt without me."

"You act as though you've no intention of marrying Harry Winston."

"Why do you say that?"

"Are we ready, ladies?" Sybil glanced into the dining room, snugging her gloves against her fingers.

"*Please* come," Annie said. With her eyes, she begged in a language that only Isabelle could understand.

"Yes, Aunt Sybil," Isabelle said. "We're coming."

"This entire affair makes me nervous, Winston. You know that, don't you?" Abbot Dearborn paced in front of Reginald Winston's desk.

"Which is why I want the matter settled at once. When I discovered you had moved the Farrell lad to your jail, well, it caused me some alarm."

"His services were needed by the colony. You know how costly an architect is these days."

"I know your dear, sweet Sybil is thrilled to have a personal architect on the premises to render the drawings for her new estate."

"An afterthought, I can assure you."

"Nonetheless, a conflict of interests, and one that might surely be questioned at a later date."

"Are you suggesting I send him back to the colony prisons, to be thrown in with the rabble? Have some mercy on his soul, man!"

"You know that he's accusing my son, the fiancé of your niece, of embezzling Hale's funds."

"And so are others accusing Harry of the crime. A matter that's old gossip, Reginald. Have you discussed the crime with your son? What has he to say of his predicament?"

"He's anxious to see Rogan Farrell tried and sentenced to hang at once. He doesn't understand the delay. Nor do I."

"For one who's so concerned, he certainly paid no heed the day of the trial. His presence might have enlightened us on the matter, persuaded us to settle. But we lacked evidence. Rogan Farrell appeared as pure as newly fallen snow. I had to delay, or arouse suspicion."

"When is his new trial?"

"I've yet to set it. I had hoped your son would appear with proof. Perhaps he's witnessed something, anything that casts aspersions toward Farrell. Has he no testimony to offer?"

"What are you suggesting? That Harry lie in order to bring the matter to a close?"

"I'm suggesting nothing of the sort. But I and others feel that Harry worked side by side with Farrell every day. There's talk that he's helping Farrell cover up."

"Absurd! I've heard nothing of the sort."

"You're his father, Reginald. Who would say such things to you?

"Then I shall talk to him. But the trial date must be fixed and his sentence swiftly delivered."

"You realize that embezzlement carries a high penalty—death?"

"And well it should. Rogan Farrell's crime will be a lesson to others so tempted."

"What shall I tell Sybil? She's counting on those house plans."

"Harry can finish them. What do you think the lad is studying, after all?"

"I've often wondered, actually."

"This marriage will settle him, I believe. Your niece is a strong girl. She can help Harry find his place in society. A girl like Annie can bring a young wandering man back to reality."

"I just hope she can keep him at home."

"Just as Sybil has done for you?"

The men chuckled, shook hands, and held out their cups for the butler to refill.

"This fabric is stunning. Wine, is it?" Sybil inspected the shimmering satin.

"More of a cranberry, actually. It will set off her eyes, I believe." The seamstress beamed at Sybil's approval.

Annie stood quiet and still, holding to the bed frame while a girl refastened her corset. As another girl carefully measured her, a third stood holding up fabrics for Sybil to approve or disapprove.

"I don't need to see anything else. I love the cranberry satin." Sybil took a seat next to a large oval mirror.

"Excellent choice, ma'am," the seamstress said.

"Now about the style, what have you in mind, Mrs. Plenty?"

"Look through these books and tell me what suits your fancy."

The frail woman handed Sybil a magazine.

"*Godey's Lady's Book*. I haven't laid eyes on one of these since we departed England. Annie, you should be looking at this book, not me."

Her back to Sybil, Annie continued staring straight ahead. She wanted to disappear from sight or for the floor to swallow her. Her conscience began nagging at her. She couldn't allow Aunt Sybil to pay for the dress.

"Here's a lovely design," Sybil said.

"Aunt Sybil, how much will all of this cost?" Annie asked.

"What is your price, Mrs. Dearborn?" Mrs. Plenty again addressed Sybil instead of Annie.

"Price is no issue, Mrs. Plenty. We want our niece dressed in the most fashionable style of the day. What is all the rage this time of year for Paris?"

"Paris is chilly this time of year, madam. You should dress her as one would dress in the summertime in Paris. Sydney is dreadfully warm in December."

"Of course," Sybil answered, reflective, her eyes still planted on the magazine pictures. She held up another picture for all to see.

"Ah, but see the *robe princesse*? The lace overskirt is a costly garment. The overskirt could cost up to several hundred crowns. The dress—a thousand."

Sybil's eyes grew wide, and Annie felt relieved at the shock that registered in her aunt's face. "We're much too practical for that, aren't we, Aunt Sybil?" Annie hoped her aunt would agree, but Sybil gazed at the picture again with longing.

"Engagements of this magnitude are costly, Miss Carraway. We can use some designs from a few years back, though. Less lace, less fabric—we can find a more frugal pattern." Mrs. Plenty turned to dig through her stack of books.

"Wait. What of Mary Hastings' engagement party? Didn't you do all of her sewing? Her tastes were exquisite."

"Her mother, Lady Charles Hastings, selected her design from the book you hold in your hands. But her father is a duke and—"

"That's quite enough. We wouldn't want Annie wearing a gown of inferior quality," Sybil said. "Isabelle, what say you about this gown? We've heard nothing from you."

"It's stunning. Annie would look beautiful."

A sickening swell erupted inside of Annie. She could see the pang of sorrow in her sister's face. She knew her sister's thoughts as though they were her own. Isabelle would love to be the object of the family's attention right now, the recipient of a wedding with all the trimmings. But she could neither discuss the love that burned inside her nor entertain thoughts of the Laffertys' approval of her. For Isabelle, there could be no grand engagement party, no stylish gowns, and no costly wedding dress. However, Annie could never divulge to her sister how unfair she thought their situation. Her silent misery offered no hope of relief. Isabelle had found something that she herself might never know. If indeed Isabelle had truly found love and captured the heart of a man who adored her, then Annie could never express her secret envy. Mentally, she recalled the memory the previous evening of the two of them perched atop the grassy berm in the moonlight. He had embraced her gently and kissed her. If the sight hadn't so shocked Annie, they might have lingered together under the moon's spell. But without thinking, she had called out to Isabelle, an act that had sent him dashing for his carriage.

Once Isabelle had divulged the truth to Annie, they had both laughed at how foolish they must have looked—Isabelle stealing away to meet her secret beau, and Annie, the suspicious sister, spying on them.

"Annie? Annie?" Sybil now stood next to her, arms akimbo.

Shaking free from her quiet reverie, Annie's lashes flew up in surprise.

"What on earth have you been daydreaming about?" Sybil asked.

"Nothing." She turned to face the women as Mrs. Plenty draped the cranberry fabric around her waist.

"Do you like it?" Sybil stepped away to look at the fabric once more.

"Do I like what?" Annie's brows pinched together, her confusion evident.

"Why, the satin, of course. Where is your mind today?"

Annie's eyes locked with her sister's. She saw the mist rise in the rims of Isabelle's eyes, and it caused her own to tear. Her own silent pain she could face, but she hated to see it mirrored in Mussy's soft violet eyes.

Isabelle kissed her own fingertip, then delivered it to Annie's cheek in a comforting gesture.

"This is all so . . . it's just so much change coming into my life right now, Aunt Sybil. I . . ." Annie struggled to choke down the lump that rose in her throat.

"Oh dear, let's give them some time. I believe our Miss Carraway needs a moment alone with her family." Mrs. Plenty directed the other seamstresses from the room.

"It's all right, ma'am," an assistant said to Sybil. "Just wedding jitters."

The two assistants scurried ahead of Mrs. Plenty, and they all three disappeared behind the door into the parlor. Annie stepped toward Isabelle and the two embraced, then fell into quiet sobs.

"What's all this? Tears?" Sybil visibly masked her own feelings with impatience.

"I apologize, Aunt Sybil. I hope I haven't embarrassed you." Annie wiped away her tears, but they were only replaced by more.

"I only wish that . . . I wish that my dear sister were here to see to you girls. I don't know what to say. I just feel so . . . inadequate." Sybil's lip trembled.

For some reason, Aunt Sybil's unexpected display of sympathy had the opposite effect on Annie and Isabelle. The sight of them all standing in this stranger's house weeping struck a note of humor in Annie. She began to chuckle, a contagious act. She, of course, knew why she wept, and why Mussy wept. Sybil didn't know but thought she did. Annie's mirth grew in intensity, so much so that it sent Mrs. Plenty scurrying into the room.

"Whatever's going on?" The seamstress stared, wide-eyed.

Isabelle found her composure while Annie held her sister close once more. She wanted to wrap the fabric around Isabelle, hold it up to her face, and select the most expensively vulgar fashion for her in *Godey's*. "I love you, Mussy" was all she could think to say.

"I love you too, Annie."

"I believe we can continue with the fitting." Sybil took her seat once more, dabbing at her eyes while the seamstress and her assistants attended to Annie.

13
FROM THIS
TIME FORTH

Annie stepped out onto the porch of the small church. She had been the first to slip out when the vicar had dismissed the morning service. She had absorbed little from the minister's message, but she blamed herself for it. Her prayers had been reduced to brief snatches of requests where she asked God to mend her failing hopes, ease her conscience. Neither could she find comfort in Isabelle's list of do's and don'ts. The Sunday message had offered, if nothing else, a time of reflection for her. However, even reflection lost its appeal when she felt so far from God. While she sat between Isabelle and Harry Winston, she had noticed such a contrast between the two—Isabelle, so fully committed to doing what was outwardly right, her attention hanging onto the parson's every word, yet racked by the guilt of her secret obsession. Harry sat, eyes glazed with tedium, biding his time until he could slip away for a drink. Annie felt it fitting that she should sit between them, riding her whitewashed fence of spiritual apathy.

Then there was Aunt Sybil, whose blindness to Harry's hedonism baffled her. Slow realization had manifested the truth to Annie that Sybil and women like her, her affluent friends, had placed their faith on a separate plane from their other priorities. Sybil's faith lay neatly wrapped in a tidy box where she could pull it out on Sundays—a sort of convenient piety—whereas her ambitions for prestige and wealth loomed larger than any other priority, driving her decisions, her future, and the fate of her family.

Every conclusion Annie drew wound a tightening noose around her soul until she felt exhausted, unsure of how she fit into God's picture, or if indeed she ever would. Yet for the first time in years, she wanted to know. The pages of her Bible fluttered open as she searched for some grain of truth. She stopped at the book of Philippians and randomly selected a verse: *But made himself of no reputation, and took upon him the form of a servant, and was made in the likeness of men: And being found in fashion as a man, he humbled himself, and became obedient unto death, even the death of the cross.*

"You are so deep in thought today." Harry stood beside her, glancing at his pocket watch.

"I need to talk to you, Harry. Privately." She closed up her Bible and held it next to her.

"We shall, I swear it. After dinner?"

She nodded but continued to stare straight ahead, absorbed and pensive.

While Harry engaged himself in chitchat, Annie returned to the carriage. Her desire to be alone, to pose her questions in private and not under the glass of someone's scrutiny, kindled something new inside of her. It was as though she stood close to some invisible bridge, one her heart desired to cross over. Once she reached the other side, she knew instinctively that an answer would emerge. Isabelle, she felt, teetered on the edge of spirituality. Surely something deeper than a stone tablet of rights and wrongs could be found by which to live one's life. Annie did not close her eyes or kneel. Formality felt senseless. Her silent prayer had more meaning to her than any religious ceremony she could recall. She simply talked and directed her prayers to the Man on the cross. Enveloped at once by a sweet peace, she knew that He listened.

The fact that she brought up the past, admitted feeling angry about her parents' death, didn't cause the sky to rumble in angry retaliation. So she continued, and with every confession, she felt a weight lift from her. Her resentment of Doris lost its fervor, and Annie wondered why she had ever felt jealous at all. It was as though she could breathe for the first time, or see a little farther, although she had no answer for her quandary with Harry. But for now, she felt like a colt wandering onto a fresh new pasture. The fodder looked a little more savory to her. God had answered in more ways than she thought possible. No loud voice from heaven, no angel chorus—none that she could hear, anyway. Just answers borne on a silent voice that pointed her back to what she had just read, the death on the cross.

Annie sensed that she herself died with that realization. Her desires, her condemning thoughts, her worries, all dissolved into a heap of mental ash. Then, without hesitation, her heart came alive, kindled by a faith she could understand. One driven by mercy and love.

"There you are, Annie." Sybil stepped into the carriage, followed by all of the children.

"I'm here." Annie closed her eyes and felt the carriage shake as each family member scrambled to find seating.

Dinner with the Winstons took on an obligatory air, all of the talk surrounding the engagement party festivities. Annie made small talk with Harry's mother and father, but felt as though she needed to stand and make a declaration. She glanced up at Harry, who sat engaged in lively conversation. He appeared to enjoy the attention, to revel in the plans. As she looked at him, he turned about and faced her.

"Would it trouble you all if I took my lovely bride-to-be for a stroll?" Harry asked.

The women winked at one another and the men chuckled. "You two go on and take your walk," Abbot nodded.

"But mind you return quickly. We've a scrumptious dessert," Sybil said.

"We won't be long, Aunt Sybil. But I'm much too full for dessert." Annie stood and smiled for the first time in days.

"Watching your figure. That's a good lass," Harry's mother said. "Enjoy it now while there's time." Mrs. Winston and Sybil shared a knowing laugh as they engaged in more wedding conversation.

"My, Annie, how you beam," Isabelle said. "If I didn't know better, I'd say you're in love."

"In a manner of speaking." Annie said it into her ear, then saw her curious gaze.

Annie turned from her sister and walked as fast as she could from the dining room, hearing the chattering of the ladies as she went. Harry strode equally as swift and took her arm in a gentlemanly fashion.

"Harry, I can no longer live a lie," she said, feeling buoyed by the truth, determined to right the wrongs in her life.

"Quiet, young lady," he said. "Wait until we're outside." He took her hand.

"Where are you taking me?"

"Let's stroll through your aunt's rose garden. We can talk where no one will hear."

Annie walked ahead of him, speeding them both past the green arbor and around to the garden settee. She felt as though she would take flight before they rounded the hedge that led to the rose arbor. As she was about to seat herself, Harry took her arm and turned her around to face him.

"Will you listen to me, please?"

She nodded. Unsure of his intentions, she tried to read past his enigmatic smile.

"I'll speak first if you don't mind," Harry said, "then I want to hear your feelings." He clasped both of her arms and placed his hands to the sides of her slender forearms. His fingers grasped her silk sleeve, toying with it.

"Speak, then. For I've much to say to you, Harry."

"I know we've botched this relationship from the beginning, but I want to make matters right with you, Annie. I've never met anyone like you."

His words surprised her.

"I want to know you better, Annie, but on your terms. I've made a mess of my life. You could help turn me around."

"You're asking me to reform you?"

"They're all wanting a wedding date from us today. But it's our decision, after all, isn't it? We could plan a long engagement. And what if our feelings—*your* feelings for me began to change? It could happen."

"You're sincere?"

"I know this was supposed to be a charade, Annie, but I can't conceal that I have feelings for you. I want to make a life with you, but I don't want to allow anyone to rush you or me. Let's have a splendid romance—on our own terms. I want to give you the chance to fall in love with me."

"I want to believe you—"

"You can now."

His words stirred her. For the first time she felt as though he truly needed her.

"Allow me the chance to court you, to woo you, to win you." He pulled an ornate box from his coat pocket and held it out to her.

"This isn't—"

"No, it's not a ring, a fact that greatly disappoints my mother. I want to give you something I thought you might really want. I want to spoil you."

"That's not necessary."

"Isn't it?" He leaned toward her and brushed her cheek with a kiss.

"All right." Annie looked first at the gold-braided box and then at Harry.

"Open it," he urged.

"This seems a little insane, doesn't it?"

"Be insane with me."

Gingerly she untied the purple satin ribbon and looped it over her small finger. Then the tiny lid lifted in her grasp and she peered inside.

"I've found you a lawyer, Rogan. He's an honest man and has no ties with the politicians. He'll be by in a few days to see you, to hear your case." Frederick stood before Rogan's drafting table in the jail.

"Frederick, I knew you'd come through!"

"It's Grandmother you should thank. She's a determined woman. She's even spoken to Dearborn's wife at one of her teas. She's absolutely relentless. Perhaps we should've asked *her* to represent you."

"She's spoken to Sybil Dearborn! I pity the poor woman. You know for certain?"

"I swear she did. And put the grand lady to shame in front of the other ladies for what her husband's done to you. Katy Gabriel's afraid of no one."

"The devil himself runs when he sees her coming. What's in the bag?" Rogan pointed to the heavy cloth sack.

"Mother sends her best to you, some roasted game and a whole pie. And this from me." Frederick reached into the sack and pulled out a bottle.

"Red wine. I kiss your feet, Frederick. Good man, good show!" Rogan cradled the bottle beneath his arm and grasped the sack with the other.

"And the name of your lawyer." Frederick handed him a document.

"Who is he? Is he any good?"

"His name is Richard Barclay. He's a man to be reckoned with. He'll turn the courtroom upside down if need be."

"I'll never forget this, brother. Please give our grandmother a kiss from me and tell her I'll see her soon, on the outside of this jail, no less."

"I believe you, Rogan. And I trust we'll be headed for the hills of gold before you know it."

"While you mention it, I've considered your offer, old man. No harm in two lads finding their fortune in the bottom of a streambed. Two lucky blokes we'll be."

"Thought you'd see the light."

"It's so elaborate, Harry." Annie held up the heavy piece of jewelry. The sunlight trickled over the precious gems, slipping over and into the facets and setting the brooch afire with light. She didn't want to voice her full approval, in spite of the jewelry's remarkable qualities.

"But you like it?"

"In an odd sort of way. I like old things. Not priceless, necessarily, but things with something of a history."

"I knew that about you. You're not cut from the same cloth as other women."

"It looks priceless, Harry. You're certain you should give this to me?" She turned it over, examined the back, saw it was made of gold.

"I have no doubt. See the diamonds? A few rubies . . . sapphires. It reminded me of you."

"You didn't steal it, did you?" A quiet laugh broke through her otherwise sober face.

"Don't be droll," he said. "I inherited it, actually. My father's mother, Selina Winston, left it to me."

"Harry, I can't. It's too costly."

"I want you to wear it to our engagement party. The women will be filled with jealousy."

"That's important to you, isn't it? That others are jealous of you?" Annie slipped the brooch back into the box.

"Not fair, dear, dear Miss Carraway. You've misjudged me all along."

"Perhaps. I've misjudged many."

"Not so fast to agree, now. Something's different about you."

"I'm not the same. At least, I hope I'm not."

"I like you just as I found you, a flower of gentility with a fiery center of cynicism."

"Fires can be destructive, Harry. That's what I wanted to tell you. I want my marriage to be stable. You and I need more time." When she held the box out to him, he shook his head.

"I won't take it back. My mind's made up. You can't usurp the world's entire supply of stubbornness, you know."

"I'll take it for now, as long as we both agree that we should ask our families to give us more time."

"It dulls next to your eyes."

"Thank you, Harry. It is stunning." She opened the fastener and slid the pin into her bodice.

"Let me help."

"It's so heavy. I'll have to take care I don't damage the dress."

"You'll wear it as it should be worn. A genuine article worn by a genuine article."

"I don't deserve that kind of flattery."

"No flattery intended. I, Harry Winston, do forthrightly swear that I will speak the truth and only the truth when referring to the fair lady Annie." He placed his right hand beneath her chin, cupped it, then brushed her face with the back of his hand.

"Harry, when will we know that this is the right thing to do? I've made up my mind; I want to make all the right decisions from this time forth."

"If my words fail to convince you, let my deeds speak." He drew her close and pressed his lips against hers.

Rogan watched Frederick leave the jail. A bank of dark clouds had rumbled its distant threat of rain, and Frederick made his farewell brief, then departed. Rogan hated to see him go but never indicated as such. He and Frederick had an understanding as brothers: Never place too much emphasis on sentiment. He watched the horse and rider grow distant while the life ebbed from him, leaving him aching inside and feeling hollow. He had all but decided to return to his drafts for Sybil Dearborn, but he allowed his gaze to linger on the handsome couple standing just beyond the hedgerow. He recognized the young woman at once as Dearborn's niece, Annie. She had brought him his dinner on only the one occasion, but the memory of her lingered, nonetheless. Her sister had returned faithfully every evening, offered a Scripture recitation when she could muster the courage, and then without ceremony left him to eat alone.

The couple stood in the rose garden for some time, engaged in conversation. But the red-haired gentleman had handed her something and then made his move. Rogan found in Annie's fiancé a hint of the familiar, and the thought entered his mind that perhaps he knew the man. Being too far off, though, he couldn't determine for certain. He felt certain of only one thing—that the man had a way with the ladies. He plied her skillfully, taking his time with her, making no sudden moves. He could see the man's hard-sought-after prize lured doelike into his waiting grasp. His chicanery in full sight, Rogan felt for certain that this intelligent woman would see through his ploy. But perhaps she desired to be lured, he decided. After all, the Carraways had been orphaned. No doubt Abbot Dearborn had arranged this courtship with some wealthy family.

He stood speculating but knew nothing for certain. For the girl had told him nothing about the arrangement. He imagined at one point that he detected a hint of pain in her face when he had brought up the subject. Miss Annie Carraway had offered him no personal details, though, and showed no desire to divulge anything about herself or her life. She remained a mystery, one that offered the greatest degree of frustration to Rogan. He would most likely never cross paths with her again. Perhaps all of this together was the reason she had begun to occupy his thoughts—her elusiveness. He could only hope that the request he had made of her would come to mind and she would return with the news he needed to hear, that a trial date had been set. The attorney would insist upon knowing, of course. But if his request ferried the Carraway girl back here to the jail—the not-so-pious Carraway—her fair company might at least liven up his cheerless day and offer his eyes a feast more palatable than the rock-and-mortar confines of Dearborn's jail.

"Stop, Harry!" Annie pulled away and turned from him.

"What have I done now?"

"I want to go back to the manor house."

"But I thought—"

"You thought wrong."

"I've made it clear that I need you. What can I do to make you trust me?"

"You said you'd give me time."

"Time is all we have. You want me to feel guilty for wanting to be near you?"

"I don't know. I feel so confused. I thought I knew what I wanted, that we should call it all off until—"

"That would be foolish, Annie. Your uncle would never agree. Nor would my family. And they do know how to make life difficult for us."

"Difficult in what way?"

"What of your sister? Your other siblings? Don't they all stand to lose everything if you throw away this proposal?"

"Harry, when I said we needed more time, this is what I meant. We always seem to say the wrong things to each other."

"I want to court you in the proper way. To say it more clearly would take a genius."

Annie thought she detected sincerity, could see his desire to capture her affections in a natural way. Yet when they kissed, she could only feel discomfort and the pressure of Abbot's stubborn vigil over her life.

"Let's call it off, then, Annie. I'll not have a bride living under my roof who hates me."

"I don't hate you."

"Don't you? If I couldn't see the contempt in your lovely eyes, then I sensed it in your kiss," he said. "I'll tell them all now." He turned and began to walk away.

Annie could make no immediate reply. Her breathing quickened and a helplessness swam through her. She watched him storm from the garden, but felt torn between running after him or staying behind while he bore the impact of their families' disapproval. Her thoughts raced ahead to what Abbot would say to her and the decisions he would make in regard to Isabelle and the others. She had asked God for wisdom, but it had escaped her. Isabelle and Clarisse would have no dowry, and her brothers no education. Annie felt a burst of wind and heard the thunder hammer the skies of Sydney. She could no more allow Harry to dissolve their engagement than she could sentence her family to hang.

While the wind tore at her clothes, she ran, and reality buffeted her mind, her emotions. She could see his tall, masculine form disappear into the rear of the manor house. She stumbled past the hedgerow, but gaining her balance, lifted her skirts and made fast for the house. She had to stop Harry from doing the one thing she secretly longed for him to do—release her from a life of social obligation. The sky let go of its watery burden, and the rain began to fall like hard, angry tears upon Annie's crown. She threw open the rear door and ran into the parlor. Her personal desires crumbled. For the sake of her family, she would surrender her life and her dreams. "Harry! Wait, please!"

"I thought you might be coming soon. Dreadful weather we're having." Harry sat alone next to the fireplace, sipping brandy.

"You didn't tell them, did you?" Annie ran toward him, breathless and wiping the rain from her face.

"Dear me, no. I'll allow you to do the honors."

"Annie Carraway, you're drenched!" Aunt Sybil stood in the doorway. Harry's mother peered over her shoulder, her brow lifted with interest.

"We were caught in a shower, Harry and I."

"Here, I poured one for you as well." Harry lifted a second glass.

"Ada, please bring some towels for Annie." Sybil turned from them and walked down the hallway.

"Have you and Annie had a lovely visit, Harry?" Mrs. Winston's eyes glistened, her anticipation of an announcement evident.

"Quite lovely, Mother," Harry said. He ignored the way she looked at him, expectant of some news.

"Oh, Harry, you're teasing me. Have you something to tell us?"

"You'll have to excuse my mother, Annie. She's the impatient sort." He downed his brandy and smiled up at her.

"Harry Winston, you'll tell me now!"

"I'll let Annie tell you, Mother."

"But, Harry, we've—"

"You may as well get it out. I'll never have a moment's peace at home if you don't." Harry persisted, his eyes assessing her sharply while he yet maintained a gentle tone.

"Oh, I can't bear it! Harry can be cruel, you know," Mrs. Winston said. "Please tell me. I promise I'll act surprised when you tell the others."

"We cannot decide on a wedding date, Mrs. Winston." Annie felt surprised at her own words.

"Harry, why not?"

"Would you like to explain, Annie dearest?" He stood and poured himself another brandy. He stepped toward her, and when the maid appeared, he took the towel and wrapped it with gentle attention around Annie's shoulders. So only she could see, his eyes widened with surprise.

Annie didn't like his pampering her, but she stood still and allowed it.

"Can't have you catching your death, can we?"

Annie felt a shiver run through her but thought it to be as much her circumstances as it was the chill from the rain.

"There you are! I heard the thunder and hoped you both had sense to come inside." Abbot strode in, an unlit cigar poised between his fingers.

Harry pulled a reed from the small woodpile and lit it with a match. Then he held it toward Abbot in a gentlemanly gesture.

"Thank you, Harrison." Abbot winked.

"You wouldn't have two of those, would you?"

"All you want. Now, don't let me interrupt." Abbot inhaled on his cigar, a look of satisfaction resting in his eyes.

Tension rose in Annie's stomach. An arranged marriage had never been her intention. Yet numerous friends had married under the same circumstances. Her plight would surprise none of them. She realized Harry had offered her their only solution for now— to put them all off for as long as possible. She glanced at Harry, saw his eyes widen with interest. But he only continued to nurse his drink.

"You've something to say, Annie?" Abbot asked.

"We've not decided on a wedding date. But later—perhaps closer to the winter—"

"A winter wedding!" Mrs. Winston clapped her hands together and bounced with glee. "It won't be so awfully hot then."

Sybil entered, saw the levity, and demanded to know the news.

"Sybil, they want to marry in the winter," Abbot said.

"How about June?" Sybil took Mrs. Winston's hand.

"Splendid!" Abbot shook Harry's hand. Reginald Winston joined them, and congratulations were delivered all around while the mothers speculated on the June wedding and then marveled over the brooch.

"Annie, you're so wise. Now we've plenty of time to make the proper arrangements," Mrs. Winston said.

"Why don't you gentlemen join me in the study for a cigar? We'll let the ladies make their plans." Abbot held up two more cigars. Harry kissed his bride-to-be upon the forehead and followed the men out of the room. His father stopped him just outside Abbot's study. "How did you manage a commitment so soon from Annie? I must admit, I had little faith."

"Just give her some time, Father. Annie will soon be more in love with me than she ever realized."

"I trust you have the same affection for her?"

"In due time." Harry's confident gaze settled into a brooding and distant stare.

"I look a fright. I'll go and change and return at once. You all don't mind, do you?" To Annie's relief, the women understood her plight. She all but ran from the parlor, past the smoky haze of the study, and toward the staircase. She wanted to tell Isabelle the news before the rumors spread throughout the household. Annie knew that Isabelle would express happiness for her, but it was Isabelle's regret for her own situation that troubled her. Once Doris realized that Charles Lafferty's visits had begun to diminish, suspicions would arise. She must encourage Isabelle to stop his visits. Plans for a winter wedding would now be thrust upon her. But June was more than half a year away. It would give her time to pray and ask God to help her, to help Harry. She could fall in love with him, she decided, if God willed it. But she had to be certain of his sincerity, certain that he truly wanted to change. *There's hope*, she assured herself.

Annie rapped on the door and slipped inside. She would tell Isabelle first about herself, then gently explain the prudence of never seeing Charles again.

"Annie, what's going on? You're wet. . . ."

"I've much to tell you, Mussy. Promise me you'll listen."

14
THE
ENGAGEMENT

Annie stood at the doorway of her bedroom, dressed in pink. She could hear the guests already arriving downstairs. She had watched with hidden dread as the calendar days fell away, pulling her closer to the day when her engagement to Harry Winston would be made public to the society of Sydney. Harry had come to call several times in the last week to affirm his affections for her and to assure her of his confidence in her in making public their decision to marry. He had brought her more gifts and more jewelry than she could ever wear in one night. Most of it sat untouched in a jewelry box on her vanity. Nervous, she toyed with the heirloom brooch that glistened near her shoulder, then she examined her gown. She had returned alone to the home of the seamstress and changed every decision made by her aunt. She had chosen a coral pink grosgrain fabric for the skirt, trimmed with three pinked flounces of the same material.

"If they're going to put me on display, then let it be in something of my own choosing," she had said to Isabelle. Looking once more into the mirror, she adjusted the wreath of pink roses and leaves in her hair. Around her throat and her wrists she wore the jewelry tastefully handpicked by Harry's mother—pearl beads, a pink coral medallion, and pink coral and pearl bracelets.

Isabelle walked up, stood behind her, then fluffed Annie's overskirt of point lace.

"Thank you, Mussy."

"You look nervous. Are you?"

"It's obvious, is it?"

"Only to me. You're so lovely, Annie. I only wish Mother could see you this way. And our father. You'll be the envy of every woman in Sydney tonight."

"That's not exactly what I want to hear right now—"

"It's true."

"Do you know, have you heard?"

"What, Annie?"

"Is Charles Lafferty coming tonight?"

"He doesn't want to come at all unless he can be with me. But his father forbids it."

"The Laffertys know?"

"They wouldn't dare tell Uncle. They want his engagement with Doris too badly. Abbot's offered a tremendously large dowry."

"If Doris would realize that she's being traded like a sealskin, she'd call off this entire affair."

"Would she, or is she smarter than both of us realize? Charles Lafferty's a wonderful man. He would make the best husband and father and—" Isabelle's voice broke, and by instinct, her hand flew to her mouth. She rested her other gloved hand on the back of the small vanity chair. Her eyes moistened, but she batted back the tears.

"You're tormenting yourself again, Mussy. I won't have it! I still say that Lafferty's a cad for stringing you along like this."

"He says he loves me. I believe him. I know he's sincere, Annie. Charles is not a liar like—"

Annie saw the sudden anxious gaze of her sister.

"I'm sorry. Please forgive me. I've no right."

"You mean like Harry Winston?"

Isabelle wrapped her arms around Annie in apology.

"You needn't apologize."

"I still don't understand this entire affair, Annie. Why won't you just admit to me and to everyone else that you don't love him? Surely he's smart enough to see it."

"He's mending his ways. You'll see." Annie could no longer bear to look into Isabelle's probing eyes.

Ada's flushed face appeared in the doorway. She had been running and said breathlessly, "Mr. Harry Winston has arrived, miss. You'd best go on down now. Good time to make your entrance."

"Coming, Ada," Annie said.

"If you both ain't the prettiest two in the land, I don't know who is!"

Both girls smiled at the maid, then kissed her face.

"And the two sweetest. Have to run. Must find Doris." Ada turned from them to go find Doris, who had been pale and nauseated for hours.

"She's in her mother's bedroom, I believe," Annie said. "Losing her dinner." She then grasped her sister's hand.

"Ready?" Isabelle asked.

"Walk with me. I need your support."

"All right. But just to the top of the stairs. It's your night, Annie. I could stay up here all night and no one would notice. That's how it should be."

"Not true. You're my maid of honor. I want you at my side all night."

"You'll change your mind. *Harry* will change your mind."

The violins' strains began at once when Annie began her descent of the staircase. The early arrivals stopped and gazed up at her, making her feel more uncomfortable than ever. She took a deep breath and planted her eyes on Harry, who waited, devilishly handsome as ever, at the foot of the ornate staircase. She smiled and took his arm, her stomach roiling and her senses spinning.

Isabelle made her polite greetings, the perfect maid-in-waiting to her older sister. Accepting a glass of punch from one of the maids, her eyes scanned the room with cautious longing. As much as she hated to see Doris hanging on the arm of the man she so foolishly loved, his absence would raise far too many questions in the minds of the Dearborns. Besides, if all she could do was catch an occasional glimpse, it would at least satisfy her burning desire to see him, if not be near him. Annie's insistence that she keep away from him had become her only strength.

"A gentleman asked me to give you this, miss." One of the women hired to serve at the party stood with her arms outstretched, holding a silver platter.

"All right. Thank you." Isabelle glanced down, nervous. She saw the folded piece of paper and quickly grasped it. Her gaze darted about the room. Finally, she spied him standing near the piano with a glass of punch. She acknowledged the maid with a nod. The bright lights of the chandelier revealed too much. So she hid herself in the next room, into which few of the guests had yet wandered. Her fingers curled around the note, she glanced right, then left, and opened it, anxious. *Oh, no, dear sweet Charles!* Discreet, she would catch his eye, and somehow indicate her disapproval of his request. She could never agree to meet him on such a night as this one. After she had torn the note into small pieces, she found a container the maids used for disposal and scattered the evidence into the remains of the evening.

Her cheeks felt flushed, but she hoped no one would detect her anxiety. She stepped out onto the floor where the guests had commenced to dance. The path she took through the throng led her toward the piano. She prepared her words. He would understand. In the past he had always agreed with the voice of wisdom when she had reluctantly denied his requests to meet. But Charles no longer stood next to the piano. Nor could she find him anywhere. *Please be here!* She searched frantically, but soon realized that he had most likely already gone to their hill beyond the barn to wait for her. If she tried to send a message through one of the servants, she would most certainly arouse suspicions among the gossiping house staff. She would have to go herself—and quickly.

Annie's smile felt frozen. She had greeted so many dignitaries and politicians she could never hope to keep their names straight. Faithfully at her side, Harry, who knew everyone, prompted her. His gift for remembering names offered a strange sort of comfort.

"My throat is so dry, Harry. Can we stop all this nonsense for a few minutes?"

"If you'll all excuse me, I wish to have my fair lady to myself, if only for a brief moment." He bowed and planted a kiss upon the hand of another politician's wife, then took Annie's hand in his own and gazed longingly at her. The women cooed admiringly at his chivalry.

Annie could see the envy in all the women's eyes as they strolled past the parade of feathers and glitz. Harry had won everyone's hearts. If ever he had stained his reputation among the elite families of Sydney, tonight would wash away the memory for good. He was now, in their eyes, the epitome of faithfulness and the full-blown personification of every woman's devout fantasy. Annie accepted the plate of delicacies that Harry handed to her. From the corner of her eye, she saw a group of her friends in the corner and longed for the simplicity of their womanly chatter. Her mind returned to those brief days of freedom, but she dismissed those thoughts, believing them to be childish daydreams. She scarcely tasted the crusty dessert and only half listened to Harry. All evening, his conversations with her had consisted of nothing but the house plans. Such talk made her restless.

"Have you heard anything I've said, dearest?"

Annie's brows lifted and her eyes widened.

"I know just what you need."

"What, Harry?"

He pulled a small black box from his coat pocket.

"No more gifts." She swallowed the bite of pastry.

"This one's a necessity."

She felt him grasp her left hand and slide the diamond-studded gold band onto her finger. Then he bowed and kissed it.

"It's lovely."

"It's a little large. Look at your tiny fingers. But wear it tonight, for me."

Annie stared at it for a long time. She could think of nothing to say. Her eyes roamed the dance floor in search of diversion. Immediately, Isabelle bustled past her, offering the escape she so desperately needed. She handed her plate back to Harry. "I'll return shortly. I should show this to Isabelle."

Her eyes followed Isabelle as she meandered through the crowd toward the back of the manor house, bearing two over-loaded plates of food.

"Mussy, wait!" Annie called out, but her sister didn't so much as acknowledge her. "I'm going with you, Mussy." She ran to her side.

Isabelle hesitated briefly, but only flung her a confused glance. "No, Annie. I'm taking Uncle's convict some food." She glanced around nervously.

"You can't mean it! He's waiting for you, isn't he?"

"Walk with me, Annie. I've got to talk to someone."

The two of them ran out into the night, the moon reflecting gold and brazen against their glistening gowns and nervous faces.

Rogan tossed restlessly on his flimsy cot. He could hear the sounds of laughter and music. Instead of lightening his heart with the sounds of gaiety, it only served to drive the stake of frustration further into his emotions. His lawyer had not appeared today as promised, but instead sent word of his delay. Rogan had frittered away the day, half attentive to his drafting task while traces of worry began to settle in his mind. The attorney was a new arrival from England, and Rogan realized the man would need time to establish himself in his new home and set up his practice. But as each day passed without the least hint of progress, Rogan's confidence in his future ebbed from him, leaving him worried and fretful about the trial.

The sound of women's voices caused him to sit up. He raked a hand through his hair. In the dark, he struggled to remember his own face. He gave little thought anymore to his appearance. A torch glowed just a few feet from the jail window.

"Who goes there?" the guard said.

The sound of clanking metal against the door brought him instantly to his feet. The door opened slowly, but from the corner of his eye he saw a woman running past the window.

"Mr. Farrell?"

"Miss Annie Carraway?" He recognized her voice at once. It sounded good to him. Her lovely presence had warmed his worried heart the first and last time she had come. Now, standing before him in a glittering coral-colored gown, he thought the sight of her would take his breath away.

"My sister wanted you to know that, in spite of your unfortunate situation, she was yet mindful of you tonight and felt you might need some . . ."

He glanced at the two plates in her grasp.

"Some evening refreshment." She held out the heavy platters.

"Your sister is most kind. She sent you in her place?"

"She's indisposed."

"Call me when you're ready, Miss Carraway." The guard fastened the door.

"I see. Or most likely she has run up to hide behind your uncle's barn with that gentleman friend of hers." He took the platters and placed them on his tabletop.

"Gentleman friend?"

"That was your sister I saw running past just now, eh? You two are a curious lot. Young Isabelle hides behind barns to kiss men and you run after to cover up her trail."

"My sister does not run around kissing men behind barns, as you so rudely put it! She is—well, Isabelle has more integrity than you or I will ever possess," Annie said. "And I ask that you please lower your voice. Such conversation could cast aspersions unnecessarily. She does not deserve such a thing."

"I apologize, then." Rogan lifted the warm towels from the food and examined his spice-laden bounty in the dim torchlight.

She acknowledged his apology with a nod. "But whatever your reasons for appearing so suddenly with your offerings, I am grateful, if not for the nibbles, then at least for the presence of your most delightful company." Rogan meant what he said. His waning hope had left him desperate for any human contact, as well as making him a bit more humble, but her sudden presence offered much more than he could have dreamed of having.

"Your gratefulness is acknowledged."

"Please express my gratitude to your sister." He rubbed his unkempt beard that had grown while he was imprisoned.

"I shall pass along your message in a sincere manner, however impertinent you may appear to me." She turned to leave.

"I apologize for any impertinence, Miss Carraway. But before you leave, I must know—"

"Know what?"

"Has your uncle mentioned my trial date to you?"

"My uncle does not share his business affairs or affairs of the court with me or any other family member. I'd dare to say that even Aunt Sybil knows nothing of his business in the colony."

"I believe you when you say that your uncle doesn't share his business with you. Why would he? But you're a willful sort, I'd say. If you determined to know something, I'd imagine that nothing in heaven or hell could stop you from finding out."

"You know nothing about me, Mr. Farrell, and I'd thank you to keep your personal assessment of me or any family member to yourself. Perhaps you're skilled with manipulating lesser minds."

This woman, Rogan determined, could find a quarrel with any topic he could name. His ire sparked, he marched toward her, determined to make her understand his desperation.

"I'd ask you to keep your distance, sir."

"Woman, I want you to understand this is my life, not something to be trifled with! Now, I'm an innocent man, and it would appear that you could find in your heart a spark of sympathy." Too late, he realized that he had spoken overly loud and harsh.

"Miss Carraway? Are you all right?" the guard asked.

"I don't know. Am I all right?" She glared at Rogan.

"I apologize for my anger, Miss Carraway, but you've no idea of the hell I'm in. You only know about your parties, your expensive gowns—"

"I don't have to listen to this, to have you make statements about me when you know nothing about me. You think I was born with a silver spoon?" she asked. "I've known as much pain as anyone and have my own prisons with which to contend."

"Yes, I see you sashaying past the windows of your palace prison every day!" He turned away from her and seated himself on his cot.

"It's not your business, sir, to interfere in my private affairs, or my comings and goings."

"Why not? I've nothing better to do." Rogan stretched out across the cot, his fingers clasped behind his head.

Annie's face took on a soft light. A faint smile caused a dimple to appear. She turned to seat herself in Rogan's drafting chair. "Neither do I."

Rogan shook his head, his mirth quickened by her mettle. Soon he found himself immersed in conversation with this elegant vision. The more she told him about her past, the more he began to leave behind the worries of the day and allow himself to be captivated by her presence.

"So does your aunt always have such an elaborate party just before Christmas?"

"She has elaborate parties at the drop of a hat. But this one actually has meaning. It's my engagement party."

He noticed the flat way she said "engagement party" but reserved his comment. "Your engagement party? So how does one escape the party if one is the guest of honor?" He saw the worry in her gaze and regretted having brought up the subject.

"Dear me, I've forgotten the time! His mother will be calling the guests together for our announcement at any minute!" She looked down at her ring, gathered up the front of her dress, and ran to pound against the jail door.

"I wish you wouldn't go."

"Guard, open at once!"

"What's the hurry? They'll keep eating and drinking without you."

She turned and smiled at him.

"I'm glad you came, Miss Carraway."

"Thank you, Mr. Farrell, for such a lovely evening."

He noticed her cynical tone but loved it all the more. Standing, he bowed his head slightly. She disappeared from his grateful presence in a flurry of lace and silk and hypnotic perfume.

Before he could sit down to the elaborate spread, a shadow crossed his window. *That will be the sister returning from her evening rendezvous.*

"Mr. Farrell."

"Hello again." Surprised instead to see Annie Carraway peering at him through the bars, he smiled broadly.

"Mr. Farrell, I will try to find out about your court date from Uncle."

He noticed the delicate way in which she whispered his name.

"What could be the harm?" she asked.

"I'd be most grateful."

"But you must never say that I'm the one who told you. It could be dreadful for me, as well as for you."

He made a cross over his lips, swearing his vow in as gentlemanly a gesture as he could muster. When she disappeared from sight, he blew her a kiss.

Annie ran like the wind, all the while praying that Sybil or Mrs. Winston had not already made a huge scandal of her missing presence. Ahead, she could see the lone figure of a woman standing outside the door. Just before she reached the rear portico, she recognized the young woman and stopped to straighten her gown and tuck in the loose strands of her hair. She felt her cheeks grow flushed but hoped the darkness would mask her anxiety.

"Annie?"

"Hello, Doris. What brings you out-of-doors?"

"I was wondering the same about you. Your future mother-in-law has all of the servants on a mad hunt to find you."

"I feared as much! I only took a walk to clear my thoughts. Then I took the convict some food. I pity him. Don't you?"

"You'd best go inside. Your dearest Harry is anxious to make your announcement."

Annie saw the way Doris glanced out into the night, a questioning look on her face. Before her cousin could ask any further questions, Annie turned to go inside. As she spied Harry up on the staircase making inquiry with Ada, her mind raced ahead to the months that would soon be upon her, faster than any engagement party. But her decision held firm in her mind.

"Annie, have you seen Charles? I seem to have misplaced him."

"Misplaced Charles?" Annie laughed, glancing back at Doris. Her comment had struck a humorous chord. Doris, however, failed to see the humor in her comment and turned away to continue her hunt.

"Hurry up, dear. Mother wants to call the guests to attention." Harry gestured for her to join him upstairs.

Dread seized Annie with more force than at any other time she could remember. But she closed her eyes and asked God to strengthen her.

"I couldn't find you," Harry said.

"Harry, I took a walk outdoors with my sister, and I'm afraid I've mussed my hair." She pulled out a loose strand.

"You look lovely, dear. We've kept our guests waiting long enough."

The force of his tone annoyed her. "I'll only be a moment." She bristled past with all the verve of a cat teasing a dog. Just before she turned to go to her room, her attentions were drawn to the doorway opposite the one she had just entered. Charles Lafferty marched through it with Isabelle in tow. Annie could see the anxiety in her sister's face. They appeared to be arguing, and Isabelle pulled him back toward her as though she pleaded with him. On the other side of the room, Doris continued her search, going from guest to guest. Within minutes, she would, without fail, find them together. The chance that she might fall into one of her emotional spells in plain sight of all nagged at Annie. Uncle Abbot would be in a fury with Isabelle and Charles. He wouldn't understand how hard Isabelle had struggled to keep her distance. *He'll kill them both. I've got to stop them, create a diversion!*

"Harry, I'm ready!" Breathless, Annie grabbed his arm.

"What? But you said—"

"I know what I said, but you're right after all. We shouldn't make our guests wait any longer. I'm ready now." She tucked the loose strand of hair back into her coif.

"You're a strange young woman." Harry shook his head and then allowed his eyes to rake over her boldly. "And irresistibly beautiful."

His admiring glance should have flattered her, but she felt nothing.

"And who am I to argue with such beauty? Judge Dearborn, Annie and I are ready." He took her arm and placed it over his own. He lifted his chin and lowered his eyes, taken in by her stunning presence.

Annie pressed her lips together as Harry offered another of his adoring smiles. Judge Dearborn mounted the staircase to announce the engagement of his niece, the lovely young woman who buried her face in the sleeve of her fiancé—the woman so overcome with joy that she wept. Then, being surrounded by the throng of her young women friends, she was escorted to her room upstairs while the men all retired to smoke and drink and boast of how they never understood women.

15
No Secret Wedding

"Wake up, Mussy," Annie said. The pale yellow light of predawn cast its net across Isabelle's slumbering visage.

Isabelle moaned, stirred, pulling the sheet up to her chin. Her face a still, cherubic portrait of blissful slumber, Annie hated to wake her.

"What time is it?" Isabelle didn't open her eyes.

"Time to wake up. We need to talk."

"Even the rooster's not crowed. I want to sleep."

Annie heard the frailty of her tone and knew why she would prefer to sleep. But while Annie had bid farewell to the well-wishers, Isabelle had crept to bed and fallen to sleep without explaining what had happened between herself and Charles. She shook her again.

"Please, Annie—"

"We need to talk. Before Doris awakens." Annie said it in her ear.

"But the sun's not up yet. Wait until after breakfast."

"The sun is up. I have to go to some ridiculous tea brunch." Annie recalled the sudden inundation of social gatherings that honored her engagement to Harry.

"Have a wonderful time."

"You're going with me, and we'll not have any privacy at all."

Isabelle rolled onto her back. Her eyes opened slowly and she stared momentarily at the ceiling.

"Awake now?"

"Who's giving you a tea?"

"Harry's grandmother. It will be dreadful and I'm not going without you."

"You're so lucky. It's as though all of Sydney's been forced to stop and take notice of you."

"Quiet, you. I don't give a quid for all of Sydney's opinions of me. Now, sit up, please."

"All right." Isabelle pressed her pillow up against the tall walnut headboard.

"Keep your voice down. If Doris hears us, we'll be hanged tomorrow at high noon."

"Oh, is that what we're talking about?"

"Tell me what happened with Charles. I saw you arguing. Everyone would've seen you arguing if I hadn't drawn their attention."

"You looked like a queen, all of your adoring subjects drooling at your feet."

"I'm losing patience."

"First of all, it wasn't an argument. Not really, anyway. Charles . . ."

"Go on."

"Let's go into the upstairs library. What if Doris wakes up?"

"She won't. I'll know if she does, I promise."

"Charles wanted to make an announcement of his own. He asked me, Annie."

"He asked you? You mean . . ."

"He tried to have me run away with him last night—to find some other judge or a vicar to marry us. Can you imagine the scandal?" she asked. "But I refused to ruin your evening. Such a thing would have ravaged the entire party, you know—Uncle Abbot sending men out to search, the Laffertys frantic to find their son, Doris crouched over the hedgerow, ill—"

Both girls sat silent, their hands cupped to their mouths as they stifled laughter.

"You've grown wickedly funny, Mussy. But if you had done it,

I wouldn't have thought the night ruined."

"No?"

"I would have been happy for you. You're in love and I'm envious."

"Annie, I know you don't love Harry."

Annie gazed into her sister's eyes, which now looked deep into her soul, two bright lanterns searching for truth.

"Tell me the truth; I have a right to know. Is it the Winston money?" Isabelle gripped the soft laced sleeve of Annie's dressing sacque.

"You know me better than that," Annie answered.

"Have you feelings for him?"

"Sometimes love takes time. Aunt Sybil says—"

"She doesn't know, Annie, that it's supposed to be wonderful and painful all at once. At least, that's the way it's been with me. I don't see that with you and Harry. Or am I mistaken? I know I've never been as smart as you."

"You're ten times as smart. Fate has dealt me many hands, and wisdom has seldom been mine to call for keeps. But in this case, I've prayed for God's wisdom."

"I'm glad you're praying."

"I've prayed for you as well. I don't want to see you hurt by this Lafferty matter."

"But what about you? I want to see you happy. For now, all that I can have are snatches of happiness, the moments when I'm with him and the lonely hours when he occupies my mind. But I'm not so certain your marriage to Harry Winston will bring you that kind of happiness."

"I've found happiness now in my faith. People will always disappoint us, Mussy."

"True . . . how could I argue with that? I've seen you awake some nights on your knees. Don't think I haven't questioned myself as I've watched you of late."

"It's the one thing I'm sure of."

"But why marry a man you don't love?"

"It's my way of providing for you . . . and Thomas and Linus and Clarisse."

"Then don't do it!"

Doris stirred.

"You'll have to keep your voice down," Annie whispered.

"None of us have asked you to make such sacrifices on our behalf, Annie."

"You needn't ask. I promised our mother that somehow, some way, you'd all be cared for."

"But Uncle Abbot will offer a dowry for both Clarisse and myself. He's told you that himself."

Mentally weary from the party, Annie had not reasoned ahead in offering her excuse to Isabelle. Isabelle circled too close to things she wouldn't discuss. "He will keep his promise, won't he, Annie? This has nothing to do with you and Harry, right?"

Annie swallowed hard. She now wished that she had allowed her sister to remain in her innocent state of slumber.

"Right, Annie?"

The rain continued to blow outside the jail window, but Rogan had fashioned a canvas shutter for such occasions to protect his work and keep the cell as dry as possible. He pulled out the extra blankets that Isabelle Carraway had left him on one occasion. A blanket pulled up to his chin, he shifted on the narrow cot and tried once more to relax, to think about catching an extra hour of sleep and nothing else. But his mind kept roaming back to that other Carraway sister. He wished, in part, that she had never entered the jail only a few hours ago, for now he couldn't keep her from entering his mind. Every time he would begin to drift, he would imagine he smelled her perfume.

His eyes opened once more. Beyond him on the floor, two soft white objects drew his attention. Too weary to get up, he tried again to fall asleep, but his curiosity soon sent him reeling out of bed. With one hand he held them while he twisted the brass handle on his lantern with the other. He chuckled to himself and now understood why the perfume scent wafted through his room. *She dropped her gloves.* He held the gloves to his nose just to be certain. But, as he had suspected, the soft essence of her perfume permeated the fabric, leaving behind a haunting reminder of her visit.

Once he had folded them together, he tucked them into his bag of drafting materials for safekeeping. He would of course return them to her personally. She had, after all, promised to find out about his trial date. He would invite her in and tell her he had something for her. She would be grateful, he imagined.

He returned to his cot and closed his eyes, pleased for the lovely image he held captive in his mind's eye.

"We should never have depended on Uncle Abbot for our dowry," Isabelle said.

"I know how you feel. I've felt the same way many times. I can't go to sleep in this bed or place my feet under his dinner table without being reminded of the fact that this isn't really our home. I'm no fool," she said. "I realize we're here only at Sybil's insistence. But the fact remains that we are family to the Dearborns. If Abbot will pay our dowry, yours and Clarisse's anyhow, then I say, let him. It will more than make up for the tyranny we've lived under here at the manor house."

"But if, in fact, we give up our dreams for the sake of security, haven't we lost a part of ourselves?" Isabelle asked.

Stunned by Isabelle's perceptiveness, Annie clasped her hands in front of her, hoping that she appeared to ruminate upon her words. But in truth, she once again felt at a loss to speak.

"If you're marrying Harry Winston for me or the others, lay aside your foolish obligation. We will make our way through by some other means. God will see to it, won't He?"

"What if this is God's way?"

"What if it isn't?"

The two sisters stared at each other for several moments.

"But what of your future, Isabelle? You've declined one offer of marriage already today."

"Did I say that? That was not my intent—to mislead you, I mean. I didn't turn down Charles Lafferty's offer of marriage."

"What's that you say?"

"I only told him that I wouldn't run away with him last night. You think I could stand by and watch you lavished with parties and elegant gowns, while I cower away, hiding my marriage to the man I love?"

"Well then? What did you tell him?"

"I accepted."

Once more at a loss for words, Annie's eyes misted. She wanted to wrap her arms around her, wish her well. But the consequences frightened her.

"I want a proper wedding, though, with a proper dress. I want you to attend me as I'm doing for you."

Annie sat back, startled by her words. She beheld her trusting, innocent countenance. With all the wisdom of her years, Isabelle had yet to learn the ways of the world.

"Are you listening to me?"

"Doris has been promised to Charles Lafferty. Don't you see that what you're saying is impossible? The Dearborns and the Laffertys are two powerful families. If you attempted in the least to come between them, to make them accept you and your wishes—oh, Mussy . . ." Annie said no more, just kissed her forehead, feeling protective of her.

"What could happen? What's the worst they could do?"

"They would destroy you, Mussy. They would destroy all of us."

"I am not afraid."

"Don't draw your sword yet, little knight, until you've sized up the dragon."

Isabelle drew up her knees and pressed her chin against them. Annie read her thoughts, saw the spark in her eyes. Her little sister had just discovered what she wanted in life, and Annie felt somewhat envious.

"What do we do now?" Isabelle asked.

"I'm suddenly tired. Let's go back to sleep. We'll think more clearly if we're rested. They'll wake us in an hour anyway," Annie said.

"I'm not certain I could fall asleep now."

"Will you try?" She grasped Isabelle's shoulder and waited for her affirming, if reluctant, nod.

Instead of returning to her own bed, Annie curled up next to her sister, pulled the coverlet over them, and waited as a sudden flurry of rain rocked Isabelle to sleep. Too caring to assault her impressionable determination at this early hour, she would try to reason with her later on. Isabelle had no idea of the monster she was up against. Abbot Dearborn, to her knowledge, had never lost a battle. Nor did she feel he would lose this one—not with his honor, his reputation, his own daughter at risk of embarrassment. *She's tired. She'll be more apt to listen after she's rested.* She breathed a silent prayer, knowing that God would hear, just uncertain that she had yet gotten His answer.

16

MELANCHOLY AND LACE

In spite of the early-morning conversation that followed an evening of pomp and feasting, Annie reawoke with only one thought. It struck her as strange that her first thoughts of the morning would center on the man locked up in Abbot's jail. Perhaps the pity she felt for him had also piqued her interest in him. But whatever the reason, she would casually bring up the subject over breakfast to test Abbot's response.

"I can't believe you're still in bed," Ada said. She shook Doris and stared at the two sisters curled up in one bed.

"I was awake earlier. I fell asleep again." Annie yawned and nudged her sister. She gazed up, pulled back the heavy sage-colored curtains, and realized that the sun now shone brightly over the horizon, gold as citrus and stoking itself for the day. Christmas had almost arrived, she realized. All of Sydney had dragged out the garlands of eucalyptus and adorned the shop windows with gay ornaments, toys from England and France, and tempting delectables, in spite of the depression. While distant family celebrated the holiday on the other side of the globe tucked under a blanket of cold, Sydneyites bustled through the town square with nothing on their heels but the taint of Australian Christmas dust. But Annie loved Christmas in Australia, the candlelight carolers, the merry well-wishers.

Prompt to shed her night sacque, she donned a plain-surfaced cotton dress, metallic blue-and-cream plaid. It felt good on and she liked the simplicity of it compared to her elaborate gown of the prior evening.

Isabelle stretched and rubbed her eyes.

"We have to attend the tea today. Remember? I want to buy some gifts this morning before we go. Hurry!" She applied some cosmetic and then turned to leave. "Perhaps we should take some breakfast to your convict this morning. He seemed so appreciative of the food last night."

"The cooks see to him on Saturday." Isabelle pulled her feet from under the coverlet. "Actually, they see to him every day, I suppose. I only take his evening meal as a charitable gesture."

"Oh. Well, then, meet me at breakfast, will you?" She dismissed herself and made her way downstairs. The household already bustled with the flurry of servants. Annie could hear the menservants standing beneath the staircase engaged in excited discussion.

"They say that a man with a dray can make a hundred dollars a day there and that horses is sellin' for twice and three times the goin' rate."

"Even if you don't strike gold, you'll be rich just from the services that's needed!"

She knew at once their choice of topic. *The California Gold Rush. We don't even know if it's real or not, and here perfectly sane men are losing their minds and heading off in packs.*

She glanced up and down the long dining table. Thomas and Linus had already seated themselves next to Doris and Aunt Sybil. They both yawned, sleepy from the late evening.

"Good morning, Annie. You need to hurry. We're going to market with Aunt Sybil and Doris." Clarisse adjusted her large crepe hair bow.

Annie tried to hide her displeasure. She futilely had hoped to have a morning alone with her sister. She lifted one brow, preparing a mental defense.

"We've so much to do before your wedding, I could hardly sleep last night," Sybil said.

"Actually, Isabelle and I have already discussed the need to buy some gifts this morning and we would—"

"Splendid!" Sybil said. "We're all thinking alike this morning." She shook out her napkin.

Annie tried to contain an inward sigh as she took her place across the table from Thomas.

"Annie, dear, you're not wearing your ring," Sybil chided.

"It's a bit large, so Harry's having it sized to fit me."

"Sleep well?" Thomas asked.

"I managed to. Is Uncle joining us for breakfast?" She eyed Abbot's empty chair and remembered her vow to Rogan Farrell.

"Not this morning." Sybil's mouth drew up in a speculative way.

The news dissatisfied Annie. She truly wanted to find out about the Farrell trial, had even rehearsed the conversation mentally. No need to arouse suspicion.

"Oddly enough, he's already eaten and gone off to some meeting. Something about California, but who cares anything about California? Where is California anyway—Spain?"

Thomas and Linus laughed. "It's in America."

Annie shot a look of warning at her unruly brothers.

"Well, I don't really care where it is." Sybil buttered her scone.

"Uncle has an interest in the gold rush?" Annie asked. The thought struck her as odd and uncharacteristic of Abbot, but only because his strong financial interests had centered on New South Wales.

"Another scone, please, Annie." Linus held up his plate.

"You've heard of the gold rush, haven't you, Aunt Sybil?" Annie passed the bread basket to Linus.

"It's a myth, I'm certain."

After breakfast, Annie reluctantly climbed into the Dearborns' handsome black double-brougham. It struck her as odd that the carriage gleamed unusually bright, as though just polished. She then observed that her aunt and Doris had dressed in their best finery for outings, all the way down to their petticoats. She slid to the far side and waited for Isabelle to join her.

"What sport!" Doris said as she climbed in next and seated herself beside Annie. "The entire town will be buzzing about the Dearborn party."

Now the sudden trip into town made sense to Annie. Sybil had no interest in buying Christmas gifts. She only wanted to insert herself right smack into the center of town so that she could boast about her evening's guest list and bask in the jealousy. A cloud settled over Annie's thoughts, and she wished she could have stayed home.

"Annie, we must begin to collect more laces for you. The Parker girl has three trunks of laces and you've only a sampling." Sybil pulled aside her skirts to make room for Isabelle and Clarisse.

"I've all the laces I need." Annie thought of the three overskirts in her traveling trunk. She wore them on occasion but gave little thought to them. The carriage lurched forward. She pulled aside the black curtain and glanced out across the property. The jail had been discreetly tucked behind a row of trees and was not visible to the casual observer. But Annie could see the rock base and pitied the man forced to use his architectural skills in such a slavelike manner. She knew he must have a family, and she worried that his confinement would dampen their holidays.

"Is that what you plan to wear to your tea today?" Sybil's face reflected her discontent.

"I like it. It's practical. Aunt Sybil? Do you know who the man is that's locked in the jail? Do you know his family?"

"He's embezzled a great deal of money from a prominent architect. And yes, I've had dealings with his family. They, of course, believe him to be innocent," she said. "But families are like that, aren't they?"

"I've an idea; it's been on my mind all morning. Why not invite him to join us for our Christmas dinner? We never eat half what's served and—"

"That's scarcely the point." Sybil stiffened. "We can't ask a common criminal to seat himself at our table. Especially not at Christmas. Besides, your fiancé will be there and he—well, let's just say it would be highly improper." Her disapproval evident, Sybil clasped her hands in front of her.

Her comment raised more questions in Annie's mind. "Why would Harry—"

"I think Annie has a wonderful idea," Isabelle interrupted. "Is charity, Aunt Sybil, only giving so that others may observe and applaud? Is it not Christian to aid the widow, the orphan, and the prisoner? To do such a thing would be like washing the feet of Christ himself."

Sybil flung a sidelong glance at Isabelle. Her face drawn and sullen, she shook her head and fell silent.

"Come with me, please." The guard stood before Rogan, who

sat sipping a lukewarm cup of coffee.

"May I ask where we're going?" Rogan gulped down the brew, then scowled.

"Someone 'ere to see you. To your feet."

"Well, then, good man, invite them into my fair abode." Resistive to the guard's pressure, Rogan turned back to finish the last bite of his bland-tasting breakfast.

"He wants to meet you elsewhere, in 'is carriage."

"You trust me that much?" Rogan set aside the empty cup. Secretly he felt glad to be invited out of the jail. He'd spent so long inside that the full sunlight shot sharp pangs into his sensitive eyes.

"He's your lawyer, fool. And I've something to ensure your return." He patted his rifle. "Now, to your feet or I'll send 'im on 'is way!"

Rogan raked his hands through his oily hair and buttoned his vest. Stepping out into the unfettered light of day refreshed him. The thunderstorm the night before had greened up the grass and left the trees glistening, diamondlike. His worn boots pressed against the soft, pliable ground. Ahead, on the manor road, he spied the carriage, a cobalt blue clarence. *A man of means*. He neared the coach, and a driver alighted and opened the door.

"Step inside, sir."

Grateful for the respect, Rogan offered a nod of appreciation.

"Mr. Farrell, please have a seat." Lawyer Richard Barclay doffed his coal black hat and set it next to him. He gestured with his hand, offering the seat that faced him.

Rogan accepted and joined him.

"Your grandmother, Katherine Gabriel, has told me something of your dilemma. Why don't you give me your version?"

Rogan shared his entire story, leaving no details to the imagination. While he spoke, he observed Barclay's confident mien, the way he conscientiously checked his gold pocket watch from time to time, as well as the way he kept careful notes inside a cloth-bound journal. Outfitted in a claret frock coat and long black trousers, he had loosened his cravat at the throat and unfastened his collar button—because of the heat, Rogan assumed. He had an interesting angular face with a daring mustache and a smile presumably reserved for only the purest of humor.

"I'm curious," Barclay said. "Why is it that Judge Dearborn keeps you here rather than in the Sydney jail? Has he indicated his reason to you?"

"I presume he found me to be less of a commoner than the other prisoners. Oh, and my employer—former employer, Mr. Mason Hale—found a grain of pity in his heart for me," he said through clenched teeth, his tone cynical.

"Am I to understand that Hale's been a friend of your family, actually a friend to you?"

"Was."

The lawyer continued to make notes.

"He requested that the magistrate exercise a bit of mercy on my behalf until my trial date. Have you been able to unearth this elusive bit of information, by any chance?" Rogan sighed.

"You mean to say they've yet to set your trial?"

"I've made inquiry; I've sent messengers. Nothing so far."

"You see the folly of trying to represent yourself, Mr. Farrell?"

"Yes, Mr. Barclay, but my intent is honorable. All for the sake of my family's financial plight, you understand."

"The depression. Yes, I understand fully. But once you're proven innocent and pursue your most respectable vocation, you should more than make up for the temporary setback," Barclay said. "You are a young man, after all. Don't have such a bleak outlook."

Rogan liked the man already, admired the way he spurred him on.

Barclay made more notes.

"I admit I'm struggling with my outlook. I'm so isolated here, although the alternative would be insufferable," Rogan said. "I feel I've lost the human side of myself, let alone my manhood. Seldom have I been given a chance to bathe."

"You're allowed to wear your own clothes. I daresay that's unusual."

"Mrs. Dearborn insisted. In case one of her guests saw me on my brief walk that I'm allowed from time to time."

Barclay scrutinized his appearance, obviously gazing at the growth of beard and his unkempt hair.

"I know I look a fright."

"I'll insist that the days leading up to your trial will allow you better essentials for bathing and grooming. Anything else?"

"How soon until I'm free?"

"I can't know that yet. Not until I secure your trial date."

"Do you believe me, Mr. Barclay, that I'm telling the truth?"

"I've no doubt, Mr. Farrell. But what I fear is why the real criminal has not been revealed. You truly believe this Harry Winston committed the crime?"

"I do. And that his family's influence has helped to shroud his guilt. Reginald Winston's connections are far-reaching. The Dearborn and Winston friendship is no secret."

"The politics are corrupt here, as I'm sure you know. Military rule is waning, and transportation's all but dead. But the politicians are all dregs tossed over from England's greasy plate. The Sydney government is bound to be a cauldron of frauds and degenerates," Barclay said. "Proving your innocence would be easier if the man you suspected hailed from the lower side of Sydney town. But I'm not here to prove Harry Winston's guilt. My business is to prove your innocence."

"I want justice served, Mr. Barclay."

"In due time," he said. "Well, I must take my leave. Give me a week to conduct a more detailed investigation. I'll return next Saturday, if that will satisfy you." He picked up his hat.

"I'll anxiously await your return."

"But be careful what you say to family members, guards, and the like. If you're here for a dishonorable reason, it could be that someone's trying to keep you out of harm's way. Mind you don't offer any personal details to anyone. They could use it against us in court." He closed up his journal and tucked away his pen.

Rogan hesitated long enough for Barclay to detect his unease. "You haven't spoken to anyone out here, have you?"

"Only Dearborn's two nieces. Just casual talk, mind you."

"That could be a mistake. What if Dearborn has sent them to you to ply you for information?"

Rogan tried to recall his conversations with the two young women. Neither of them had ever made personal inquiries or even so much as asked why he had been locked in the jail. "I assure you, Mr. Barclay, these girls are as pure as snow."

"They unwittingly could be used, however. Don't discuss your trial or your case with either of them. Understood?"

He considered the request that he had made of Annie Carraway but decided to keep the matter to himself for now. "I understand."

"Look, Annie," Isabelle said. "There's Uncle Abbot." She pointed ahead to the newspaper office.

"Where, Mussy?" Annie walked across the bustling town square with her sister, saw the groups of impoverished men, the cabbage-tree-hat boys wearing their poorer version of a gentleman's top hat. They bantered back and forth, scratching at their moleskin trousers. Merchants stood out in the light of day, most of them gathered in front of their shops discussing Sydney's labor crisis.

Isabelle pointed to David Jones's large store across from the post office. The Jones mercantile specialized in supplies for graziers, well-to-do stockmen who lived in manorial fashion. Men like Abbot.

Annie saw the cluster of men but tried to act disinterested.

The two of them had managed to shake free from Sybil and Doris, leaving them behind to gossip in the square. Doris had been immediately set upon by several older women who wanted to know when she would be announcing her own engagement party. Annie sensed Isabelle's discomfort and quickly excused them both, expressing her need to examine some new laces for her trousseau. Clarisse had watched them go, her aunt's arm carefully crooked in her own while her face displayed her agony. She had called after them, begged to go with them, but Annie and Isabelle made fast their escape.

"Abbot's business meeting must have been held somewhere in the square," Isabelle said.

"Who cares? Let's go down to the harbor and see who's heading off for California."

"California? Since when did you find an interest in the gold rush?" Isabelle spotted some frocks in a shop window.

"I didn't, necessarily. But don't you love the excitement of it all—men leaving behind all that they call secure for lands unknown?"

"It's foolhardy."

"Yes, but it's so unconventional." Annie had found herself growing more and more restless of late. News of finding gold in faraway America drew her troubled thoughts away from her personal dilemma.

"Let's go see what Jones has today. I've heard a new shipment of goods arrived from England." Isabelle tugged on her arm.

"Look, a newspaper boy. Let's buy a paper. You there! Boy!" She handed the sooty-faced lad a coin and immersed herself at once in the front-page article. She felt Isabelle give another yank on her arm.

"You can read the newspaper later! Let's go before Aunt Sybil finds us and pulls us into one of her dreadful hens' meetings." Isabelle dragged her down the rain-streaked thoroughfare, discreet in lifting her skirt above the boot-trampled cobblestone while giddy laughter spilled from her lips.

"It says here that the local citizens should not foolishly head for California, but rather they should engage in the trade and commerce generated by the California starvation districts. Speculators interested in trade should stock up on goods such as tinned meats . . ." Annie's voice faded as she read in silence.

"Well, go on, Annie. Don't stop midsentence."

She was so absorbed that she scarcely heard her sister's strong complaints.

"Read on!"

"Oh, it says that the gold fields are full of degenerates and robbers, that good men should stay home and tend to their own affairs. That's strange, isn't it?"

"I think it's sound advice."

"But why do the journalists care if Australians go to the California gold fields?"

"I don't know and I don't care," Isabelle said. "Look in that window at those dresses. I adore the mint green one, the laced ready-made. I do love ready-mades."

"You didn't really believe that I wanted to go and look at laces and dresses, did you?"

"You're usually the truthful sort."

"I changed my mind." Annie looked up from the newspaper. Curious, she observed the way the newspaper editor, John Fairfax, and the shop merchants clustered about her uncle.

"I'm going inside, Annie."

"All right. Go on in and look around for me. I'll join you soon; I promise." She waited for Isabelle, too suspicious to go inside the dry-goods shop. Annie made her way with caution toward the group of men. With the newspaper in front of her, she hid her face but also finished reading the article.

What Class ought to go to the Diggings? Persons who have nothing to lose except their lives. Things you should not take with you to the Diggings. A love of comforts, a taste for civilization, a respect for other people's throats, and value for your own. Things you will find useful in the Diggings. A revolving pistol, some knowledge of treating gunshot wounds, a toleration of strange bedfellows. What is the best thing to do when you get to the Diggings? Go back home. What will be the ultimate effect of the discovery of the Diggings? To raise prices, to ruin fools, to demoralize a new country first, and to settle it afterward.

Annie could hear Abbot's voice above the others. Stepping around three pigtailed coolies, she positioned herself beneath a streetlamp, her back to the men.

"The local laborers are restless," the editor, Fairfax, said. "They see the Chinese taking their jobs, the convicts working for slave wages. They can't compete. The diggings are a temptation for them."

"But if all our laborers load up on boats and leave, then who will do the menial tasks?" Abbot yanked out his cigar and spat.

"It's a dilemma. If we raise wages, then we cut into local profit," Fairfax said.

The other graziers nodded and muttered among themselves.

"I want to commend you for the job you've done, Fairfax. Those reprints from that American magazine should put some starch in their plans. You're a genius at propaganda." Abbot relit his cigar. The smoke covered his head in a haze.

While the group of wealthy men began to disperse and file into the Jones mercantile, Abbot remained behind. Annie stayed hidden behind the streetlamp but watched him as he gathered a group of Chinese laborers together. He obviously cared little that the locals threatened a strike and his own house staff talked of hopping a boat for California. He only cared how it all appeared to his affluent circle of friends. Most of all, he seized every opportunity as he saw fit to squeeze what little profit remained from a staggering economy.

She folded up the front page of the newspaper and tossed away the rest. Isabelle was waiting inside. She would go in and make her purchases for Christmas. Not forgetful of Rogan Farrell, she would buy some soap for him and an inexpensive shirt. Isabelle's speech at breakfast had rung true, she reasoned. The man was their prisoner, and they had some obligation to treat him with Christian compassion. But she couldn't allow herself to be completely distracted. She had a wedding to plan. She sighed at the thought, but a night's sleep had given her the time to reckon with any residual doubts. Harry had convinced her of his sincerity, and she owed him a chance. She had already heard that Abbot had made plans to interest Aunt Sybil in a private school in England for her brothers. Thomas and Linus would protest at first. But if they could be sent away, far from Abbot's control, then she wouldn't worry about them as much when she married and left them all behind. Harry would surely not mind Clarisse coming to live with them, and, of course, Isabelle and Charles Lafferty would certainly realize the futility of their thinking.

She snapped open the newspaper and perused the article again, but this time reading it with new insight gained from the editor's own lips. She mused inwardly. Gold diggers and treasure seekers all had their place in the world. But she had hers and it would be faithfully at the side of Harry Winston. Her brow furrowed as her eyes misted uncharacteristically. *Must be the dust rising from the streets. The rain caused it.* While stepping into the dry-goods store, she called out to Isabelle. She quickly dabbed her eyes with a handkerchief and tucked it away in her purse.

"Mussy, I want to look at the laces."

Isabelle offered a look of surprise.

"I've changed my mind again. Let's make it a grand wedding, why don't we?" Three eager shopkeepers gathered around her, holding up their wares. She stepped into a fitting room, where a young woman assisted her with fastening the undergarments and cinching her waist. Yet as each cloud of lace surrounded her, she felt herself also wrapped in a strange melancholy.

"Annie, are you all right?" Isabelle fluffed out a large petticoat.

"I'm quite all right. Aren't all brides happy?"

Two more women entered the room, their hands clasped onto a long veil that floated behind them as they walked. They fitted her head with the veil's crown of silk rosettes. The soft netting enwrapped her, seemed to whisper as it fell across her shoulders and down her back. She hadn't counted on selecting her bridal veil today. But she hadn't counted on many things of late, so she felt it proper to begin making her journey toward the day in June when her life would change forever. The more she faced reality, the closer she would find herself to accepting Harry's sincere efforts at love. She shook the anxiety from her thoughts and allowed the women to dress her like a doll.

"I like this one," she said. "It covers my face better than some of the others."

Isabelle glanced up sharply, her young violet eyes startled, searching, unable to fully grasp all that they beheld.

17

CANDLE
CAROLERS

"Judge Dearborn, you've a letter from England," the butler said.

Abbot took the letter and turned it over. After he'd studied the handwriting for a moment, he shoved it into his coat pocket.

"News from England," Sybil said. "Let me read it."

"It's for me, Sybil. Nothing of interest to you, just judicial matters, is all."

"All right, then." Sybil fidgeted with her collar, her face pensive.

"You've seemed fretful this morning. Something wrong, Sybil?"

"There's something wrong all right. Abbot, I want that man off our property!" Sybil rearranged sprigs of greenery along the parlor hearth, then turned to face her husband, an angry pang in her eyes.

"I've set his trial date for mid-February. It won't be much longer and this entire ordeal will be finished." Abbot adjusted a pair of reading glasses on his nose and studied a law book, which angered her all the more.

"You're not listening to me. That Katy Gabriel's telling everyone that we've illegally locked up her grandson in our jail. I'm embarrassed, Abbot. Don't you care about me, what our friends think?"

"I care a great deal, Sybil. Why else would I have him design your house? But you know we need to keep an eye on Farrell. He's accused Winston's son of the embezzlement, and we can't have accusations like that one floating around the colony," he said. "If you would weigh the matter, you'd see I'm right."

"Well, throw him in a Sydney jail with the other convicts. He'll be spreading no rumors in there."

"He's spreading no rumors from *our* jail. And what of your cherished new house plans?"

"Can't Harry Winston finish them?"

"He's no architect, Sybil. Not yet, at any rate. Even his father has turned his own plans over to Mason Hale. Harry's trouble is, he can't settle his thoughts long enough to finish anything."

"And we want him marrying our niece?"

"She's not our daughter and until now has only been a liability. This marriage will be good for her, for Harry, and for us."

"I know what you say is true. The extra burden of Constance's children has almost been the death of me. I swear it's aged me."

"I've some thoughts on that matter, if you're willing to hear me out." He closed up the book and laid it in his lap. Sybil seated herself next to Abbot in a tufted chair, her brows raised in an inquiring way.

"There's a boys' boarding school in London. Not the expensive one, mind you. I'd like to send Thomas and Linus away to it. They're almost grown now."

"Annie knows about this?"

"She wants what's best for them. She's deliberating the matter now. She can't take them all with her into this marriage. I daresay Harry Winston could never manage them."

Sybil rested herself against the chair back and closed her eyes.

"This meets with your approval, or no?"

"I feel relieved already."

"I'm glad to hear it. Then we'll find a suitor for Isabelle, some farmer, and all will be settled."

"Now, there's another matter, Abbot. How could Isabelle think that Charles Lafferty would be interested in her instead of our Doris?"

"I've not heard mention of it since the unfortunate day he first came courting. I wouldn't worry, my dear."

Ada stepped into the room. "We've cleared away the Christmas breakfast, ma'am. The children want to know if they may open their gifts."

"Tell them to exercise patience, Ada. We'll be in shortly," Abbot said.

"They'll be in the parlor waitin', then, sir." She excused herself.

"Sybil, I've no doubt this Farrell man will be found guilty. Once he is, he'll be hanged, and this matter with Harry Winston will be settled once and for all. We can't risk sending him to a public jail. It serves us better to keep him here. Once he's finished your drafts, you'll see that I'm right."

Annie stopped outside the door. Abbot hadn't noticed that Ada had left the door ajar. His mentioning Rogan Farrell's name drew Annie to the partially opened entry. Not at all comfortable with eavesdropping, she turned to leave. But Abbot's words both alarmed and confused her. The fact that Abbot wanted Rogan so swiftly sentenced and executed caused her to ponder his guilt or innocence. Nor could she understand why Harry Winston would be involved. Not once had Harry mentioned Rogan Farrell's name. Abbot's voice grew louder, so Annie moved away farther down the hall, her aunt's Christmas gift still in her grasp. She ran behind the staircase and waited.

"I don't want anyone in the household to know of Farrell's case or Harry's involvement, Sybil. Not Doris, nor anyone who might casually break the news to Annie. She mustn't know anything."

Annie stood with her back to the servants' door. She now understood why Sybil had been so upset when she had suggested inviting Abbot's convict to tonight's Christmas dinner. Harry would be present. Something horrible had happened between Rogan Farrell and Harry Winston. Rogan had accused Harry but instead had been arrested himself. Before dinner tonight, Annie determined to visit the jail once more and exact the truth from Rogan Farrell. If Harry had committed a crime, she had a right to know. She stepped out from behind the staircase after Sybil and Abbot had passed.

"Looks as though they're all awaiting us, Sybil." Abbot gestured for his wife to enter.

"I see everyone except Annie," Sybil said.

"Oh, there you are, Aunt Sybil," Annie said innocently. "I've just wrapped your gift. Let's all go in together, shall we?"

"What a surprise! I can't wait to open it."

Annie hoped her aunt did not detect her unsteady gaze.

Rogan floated in a restless slumber. While he slept, his dreams attacked him with accusations. Yet, distantly, he heard a song that softened his cruel realities with yuletide harmony.

Silent night, holy night, all is calm, all is bright. Round yon virgin, Mother and Child . . .

He felt himself struggle to run toward the song, to feel the warmth of its message, and behold the light it shed on his dark nightmares. He tossed violently on the cot. The rickety bed finally gave way and collapsed. He sprawled onto the floor, dressed only in his undergarments. Anger shot through him. He had wearied of the jail, its cramped conditions and its rickety, lice-ridden bed. Richard Barclay had forced the court to give him a speedy trial in February. But still eight weeks away, he had to find a way to manage some uninterrupted sleep. By the time his trial date arrived, he would need to at least appear sane. His thoughts now bordered on mania, and surely he looked the part of a madman. He turned to fumble with the tattered rags that formed his mattress. Then the sound of singing caught his ear, and he sat silent on the dirt floor while melancholy swept through him. *Have I died?* The angelic strains began as a whispered prayer, then echoed against the stone walls. He stood with a deliberateness and made his way to the window. He saw before him the familiar faces, the joyous smiles intended for him, and he felt for a moment as though he had been swept up into a heavenly realm.

"It's Christmas, Rogan! Merry Christmas!"

"Hello, all!" He waved wildly at the Farrell clan and friends gathered out front. With his face pressed against the bars, his eyes brimmed with hot tears.

"Join us in song!" a young cousin said.

"I can't sing." Rogan shook his head.

"Neither can we!" Frederick said.

"Joy to the world, the Lord is come, let earth receive her king. . . ." His voice hoarse, he lifted it to join the others. It felt awkward, but the feeling grew better the longer he sang.

"Repeat, repeat the sounding joy. . . ."

"Oh, Mother, it's ready-made, isn't it?" Doris held up the costly gown in front of her.

Isabelle rested her head against Annie's shoulder and emitted a sigh. Annie grasped her hand and said quietly, "Don't say a word. How could Aunt Sybil have known that you've been looking at that dress?"

"Because," Isabelle said, "I showed it to her."

"You're certain?"

"That day we all went into town to finish our shopping, Aunt Sybil met us in the dry-goods store and she saw me admiring it. I had no idea that she returned to buy it."

"Don't say anything." Annie turned to help Linus untie the ribbon on his small gift. She laid the ribbon across her bright red gown.

"I wouldn't give them the satisfaction."

"After all, Doris is her daughter. When you're a mother, you'll want the best for your children." Annie hoped she sounded reasonable. As angry as she felt, she didn't want Isabelle to know. It wouldn't help the matter, she resolved.

"When I'm a mother . . ." Isabelle's voice drifted. She stood and walked over to the window. Annie allowed her to go. She had every right to brood. Soon Harry Winston and Charles Lafferty would arrive and the tension would begin again. Charles would dutifully take his place at the evening meal next to Doris while Harry stayed close to her side. She seemed to have finally succeeded in helping Isabelle understand the vainness of her love for Charles. But when she saw them across the room from each other, saw the pain of their separation, she was filled with self-loathing. She felt like another of Abbot's pawns. As much as she had wanted to help her sister, perhaps she had only hurt her worse.

Sybil sat in a chair close to Doris, admiring the gifts surrounding her oldest daughter. The twins showed off their store-bought gifts to Thomas and Linus. The sight of it all sickened Annie. If they didn't live here, she realized, the boys, Isabelle, and Clarisse wouldn't feel the effects of the comparison. As much as they all appreciated the comfort of their uncle's home, the difference in their station as orphans had always become evident at Christmas. Annie had taken on sewing and tutoring assignments, had made her own gift money. But she could not bestow on her siblings the kind of gifts that Abbot and Sybil lavished on their girls.

"Aunt Sybil, you haven't opened my gift for you," Annie said.

Sybil pushed away the opened boxes strewn around her feet. She found the thin, rectangular box that Annie had given her. She pulled away the ribbon and lifted the lid. Her eyes lit up, her glee evident.

Annie knew she would be surprised. The lace gloves had cost her a week's wages. But she had wanted to show her gratitude for all Sybil had done for them, even though Abbot's resentment toward them nagged at her. She decided it best to divert Isabelle's attention from the gifts altogether, so she joined her at the window and invited her to light the candles.

"Clarisse, you've not opened your gifts," Ada said.

"My head hurts, Ada. Make it stop." Clarisse held her head.

"I told you not to stuff yourself, child. It will make you swell so that your clothes don't fit."

"Look! Candle carolers! They've come to sing." Isabelle pointed to the area of lawn outside the window. She and Annie made haste to light the last candle in the window.

The children jumped to their feet at once. Annie ran ahead of them all, being first to the front door. She opened it wide and saw the faces of the singers. She returned their smiles but noticed one caroler who did not smile. One older woman dabbed at her eyes but then joined the others in song.

"Aunt Sybil, look! Come see!" Clarisse exclaimed.

The children crowded around the door, which prevented Sybil from viewing the twenty or more carolers. She could hear the Christmas songs, though, and it caused her line-etched face to form a faint smile.

"Dear me!" Ada said. She had just walked in. "Where are our manners? We should invite them in for rum punch."

"Yes, let's!" Isabelle said.

"Who are they? Do we know them?" Sybil pressed in between the twins, her eyes narrowed with caution.

"They look familiar." Annie looked at her aunt, hopeful she would invite them inside. Then she stepped aside to allow Sybil to see.

"Why! They're emancipists, some of them. Shut the door!" Sybil's face grew grim and her cheeks turned ashen.

"Sybil, what's the meaning!" Abbot said. "After all, it's Christmas—"

"I said, shut the door." Her hands trembling, Sybil walked past him as though she had seen a ghost.

Abbot gestured for the children to back away. Annie stood next to him, puzzled by her aunt's rash behavior. She saw the carolers' merry countenances and felt ashamed at what her aunt had asked of her.

"Abbot, it's that Katy Gabriel trying to embarrass me, is all!" Sybil fidgeted with her collar.

Annie saw her uncle draw a protective arm around Sybil.

"Who is Katy Gabriel?" Isabelle asked.

"Never you mind!" Sybil rankled.

Abbot chased the children from the door, then gazed out himself.

"Can we at least offer them some pastries to take with them?" Annie said it so only Abbot would hear. She stood quietly by as he observed the scene for himself.

"Annie, please take the children back to the study at once," he said. "That woman's only come to cause us trouble."

The last face that Annie saw, the old woman with her red-rimmed eyes, haunted her for the remainder of the day.

Rogan held up a shard of broken mirror to his face. His grandmother had slipped it to him through the window. No wonder his mother had looked so shocked when he peered through the bars at her. She vowed she would ask Barclay to get permission for her to return one day this week with Frederick to help with his grooming. If they wouldn't allow him a razor, perhaps under close guard they would allow his brother to transform him back to his former human appearance. Rogan mused at how women could be such funny creatures. In the face of strife, a woman's vanity could yet raise its willful head.

With haste, he had dressed himself when he had seen so many ladies present. With their songs yet lingering in his mind, he began to undress again. The heat of Christmas day penetrated the jail in spite of his primitive window dressing. Sliding off his shirt and then his trousers, he seated himself on the collapsed cot and began to pull off his stockings. Without warning, the door lock jangled. He grabbed for his trousers, but the door flew open without restraint. Having only one leg in his pants, he stumbled forward on one foot, then caught himself on his drafting table. He began to protest but stopped in midsentence.

Annie Carraway stood before him, a small box in one hand, a longer box in the other, and the blush of red across her cheeks.

"Dear me, I'm so sorry! I—why aren't you dressed?" she asked.

"I wasn't expecting company."

"Surely you know better than to sit around in your unmentionables!" She turned her back to him.

"Did it occur to you that you could knock first?"

"It's the middle of the day! It never occurred to me. Should it have?" Annie's voice still fresh with embarrassment, she stood with her left hand covering her eyes.

"It's the polite thing to do, one would think." Rogan cursed and then jumped around putting his other foot into his trousers' leg.

"Have you hidden yourself now? Or should I leave?"

"Hidden myself? What sort of pretentious tripe is that?"

She offered no reply but stiffened instead.

"Patience, my dear." He buttoned his trousers and then reached for his shirt.

She relaxed her hands at her side but kept her back to him.

"Decent enough now, I suppose."

Annie turned around, but not with the same swiftness with which she had first entered. She did not lift her face at once, but kept her eyes fixed on the packed loam floor.

Rogan threw on the shirt and then yanked up his stockings. He saw how she observed him sprawled on the collapsed cot.

"Nice bed."

"It broke with me, Miss Carraway. You might mention that to your uncle. Needed: one new bed for jailed architect."

"I can't stay long." She swept her long tresses from her face.

He looked at the boxes she snugged under her right arm.

"But I—that is, we have something for you, what with it being Christmas and all."

Rogan had never noticed a hint of awkwardness in her tone before, so to see her struggling for words amused him. Tossing aside his boot, he crossed his legs in front of him and smiled up at her, his eyes guileless and lit with amusement.

"It's nothing really. Just . . ." She handed the boxes to him but still had not made eye contact.

"You didn't have to do this, Annie."

"It's the Christian thing to do."

"Whatever your reason, I'm grateful."

She turned away, folding her arms at her waist. He watched her for several moments. Beyond her prim nature, she had some charm that seemed touchable.

"What a surprising day. First my family comes to see me, now this. What more could a convict ask for?"

"Your family was here?"

"Yes, they caroled for me right outside the window," he answered matter-of-factly. He laid the longer box down and fumbled with the frivolous-looking ribbon on the smaller one.

"The candle carolers? You mean that group of carolers—"

"They're my family."

"I saw them. They came to the manor house, I believe."

He laughed.

"I fail to see the humor."

"My grandmother caroled for your aunt? She's a feisty sort, that Katy Gabriel."

"So that older woman is your grandmother?"

Rogan didn't answer her. He was examining the contents of the box, a look of bafflement on his face. He stroked his scruffy beard, then cocked his head.

"You need soap, don't you?"

"I don't know, do I?"

She eyed his disheveled appearance, then blushed once more.

"Here's what, ask that maid of yours to bring me some hot water and clean towels, and I promise at least a partial transformation."

"I've taken care of that already."

"Aren't you the remarkable one."

He could see that her thoughts drifted toward the door.

"Guess I should open the other one." He held up the longer box.

She folded her arms in front of her and hesitated.

Annie didn't sprint for the door, a matter that continued to amaze him. So he set aside the soap and the box of toiletries that she had given him, opened the other box, and pulled out the new shirt. He again caught the scent of her perfume and hoped she would at least linger long enough to leave behind her womanly fragrance. He stepped aside to offer her the only chair in the room.

"No, I should take my leave."

"I know you must think . . ." He struggled to find any reason to draw her into a conversation.

"Go on." She stopped, her eyes suddenly conveying some interest in him.

"I know you must think that I'm a common criminal. But I am—was a gentleman. I have been wrongly accused of something, and no man in my circumstance could maintain his . . . comely appearance." He opened the palm of his hand and saw how soiled it had become.

"I've made no judgments, as such," she said. "I hope you realize that I've never pried into your affairs. But I've often wondered— only because you've brought up the matter—if you didn't embezzle from your employer, have you any idea who might have? Or is it rude of me to inquire?" She stepped forward, her bright holiday attire rustling around her satin slippers.

"I don't mind, really." Rogan read the caution in her eyes. He stopped and remembered Barclay's warning. What if Dearborn, upon hearing of his lawyer's involvement, had sent her to find out information? He would only offer a minimum of detail, he decided. Just enough to cause her to linger here with him in this lonely jail. Barclay couldn't deny him this one sweet luxury.

"Have they any other suspects?"

"You wouldn't know the scoundrel, I'm certain."

Annie finally took the seat, lifted her shimmering red skirts from the dirt floor, and folded them around her calves.

"Sorry, the maid hasn't cleaned up lately." He couldn't help but notice her tiny feet gracefully joined to her shapely, slender ankles. He observed how her long ivory fingers intertwined around one another. Her eyes widened and she had the look of an anxious doe. Perhaps Dearborn had sent her after all.

"No one you know," he said. "I'm really not supposed to discuss my case. My lawyer's advised against it."

"I understand." She lifted her hair away from her face and began to pull it back to where it hung in long clusters of curls from her fingers. She retied a ribbon round the cluster and allowed it to fall again around her shoulders. Rogan longed to touch just one of those curls, but to do so would surely cost him his head.

"I really must be on my way, Mr. Farrell."

"No hurry, is there? What I mean to say is that I feel rather poorly about your bringing me a gift. I've nothing to give you in return."

"In light of your circumstances, I certainly expected nothing." She clasped the door handle.

"A merry Christmas to you, then," he said, wondering if she detected how anxious he sounded. He loathed himself right now, hated the fact that this lovely young creature found him in such a humiliating condition. She made no attempt to hide the pity she felt for him. He could see it in her eyes, sense it in her every gesture. Had he met her last year at a ball or even at the market, he would surely have lacked no words to approach her. Now he stumbled around like a fool, only convincing her more that he belonged in this cage.

"Merry Christmas to you, sir." She walked away from him and he watched her go, watched her glide across the estate in her gown of crimson and disappear into the manor house where she belonged with her wealthy family, her loving fiancé, and her padded world of security.

18

A Sad Silence

"I don't want to go away. You've agreed to this?" Thomas paced in front of Annie. The sunlight glinted off his tousled auburn locks. He stopped in front of her, his hands in his pockets.

"I don't want you to go away either, but I think it's best for you and Linus." She hated the misery she saw in his gaze. He and Linus had found a certain degree of happiness at the manor house. They loved hunting and horseback riding. But the school in Sydney offered so little in the way of higher training, unless a boy desired to be a carpenter or a blacksmith.

"How long have you known?"

"For certain? Uncle Abbot and Sybil told me the night of Christmas."

"You've known for two days and didn't tell me?"

"I was afraid it might spoil your Christmas. I've struggled with how to tell you. This is difficult, Thom—"

"When will you tell Linus?"

"I'm telling him tonight. But since you're older, I had hoped that you would help me, could offer comfort to him. If you're anything less than enthusiastic, this could frighten him, I'm afraid."

"This was Uncle Abbot's idea, I presume." Thomas scooped up a loose rock and hurled it into a far eucalyptus tree.

"Yes, initially, but, Thomas, if I marry Harry Winston—"

"If?"

"Did I say 'if'? *When* I marry Harry Winston, I don't want you to be here in the manor house without me. Uncle Abbot is a . . . he's a shrewd man. I don't want you or Linus to take on his ways. I want you to be more like our father." Since hearing of Abbot's plan to hang Rogan Farrell, she had been consumed with getting the boys away from the manor house, out of harm's way. To witness such a thing would be too harsh for her brothers.

"Our father left us nothing. That's why we're so dependent on relatives. Perhaps I should be more like Abbot, and so should you." He stood with his arms folded, his face sullen.

"Don't say such things. We can rise above all this without greed." She hadn't noticed the bitterness in his voice until now.

"I don't want greed, I just want money. Lots of it." His mouth curled into a faint smile.

Annie knew she should chasten him, but all she could feel for her sibling was pity.

"There's talk of a gold strike," Thomas said.

"I've heard, in California."

"No, I mean here in Australia. Just north of Parrametta in the unsettled territory. Speculators have gone in to see about it."

"Here in Australia?" Annie was surprised.

"Yes, and I've a good mind to run off and strike it rich for us," he said. "For you, Annie." His eyes softened.

"Thomas, why for me?" In spite of his churlish adolescent ways, she had begun to see traces of manhood emerging in him.

"So you wouldn't have to marry that Harry Winston."

"I've chosen to marry him."

"You're meant to do other things in life."

"Like what?"

"I don't know. Just other things besides marry a drunken lout."

Annie grew silent and she felt a heaviness sink into the pit of her stomach.

"You don't love him, do you?"

"Harry has changed, Thomas."

"That's what all drunken louts are supposed to say, eh?"

"Where do you get such things?"

"I got eyes."

She looked into them and saw the same fathomless blue she once saw in her father's eyes.

"And I got feet. And I say these feet need to go north and strike it rich. That's what I say."

"I would never let you go." Annie grew more serious, and the fact that he persisted in this dangerous dream gave rise to worry.

"Why not?"

"You're still a boy. Besides, this school will help you be as rich as you want, Thomas. What do you want to be? A banker? A physician? You can become anything, you know."

"Know what I want? I want me a piece of land—a large spread, mind you. The biggest flock of sheep that Sydney ever saw. A pretty wife, prettier even than you," he said. "And I want gold, so much that no one'll call Thomas Carraway an orphan again." He hesitated, then turned and looked toward the mountains.

She wanted to argue with him, but if she allowed herself to be honest, she felt the same fire of desire within herself that she saw blazing in his own young eyes. She knew some of the families who looked down on them all with pity, and she hated it. "I want to talk about your journey," she said. "What will London be like this time of year, do you think? Rather cold, I'm certain."

"Dear me! Sweet Jesus, help us!" Ada Towley ran through the house wringing her hands.

"What is it, Ada?" Drawn by the maid's alarm, Sybil, who still wandered about in her morning jacket, set aside her coffee.

"It's young Miss Carraway! She's fell ill and I can't get 'er awake. She's 'ot with fever and pale as death, ma'am!"

"Which Carraway?"

"Young Clarisse, the baby!"

"We should find her sister at once. Where's Annie?"

"Out on the portico with 'er brother, Mister Thomas. I'll fetch her straightway."

Ada streaked through the parlor, shouting all the way, which drew out the household servants who were toiling about in their morning business. *"Miss Carraway, Miss Carraway!"*

Annie sat with pen and paper drawing out the journey from Australia to England for her brother.

"What are you doing now?" Thomas asked.

"I want you to see it for yourself. It would be like an adventure, Thomas. You wouldn't go alone. Uncle Abbot would send an escort—"

"Miss Carraway!"

Alarmed by the fright in Ada's tone, Annie stood at once, which sent the pen skittering across the stone porch.

"It's your youngest sister, Miss Clarisse!"

"Clarisse? What's wrong?"

"She's come down with fever. And you know what 'appened to the Hanson girl down the road just two weeks last. I see death on 'er face."

"Stop it, Ada! You'll frighten the entire household carrying on so. Now run and fetch some cold water and rags. Then send for Dr. Haines. I want him here at once. No delays, mind you."

Annie raced toward the staircase, followed by Thomas. Guilt pricked at her emotions. She had awakened early to only one urgent thought—discuss the matter of the school with Thomas. She hadn't looked in on Clarisse or bothered to wake her. Fully expecting a reply, she called out and bolted for her room.

The door to Clarisse's room stood partially open, but she heard not a single sound.

Annie flew in and saw that one maid hovered over Clarisse while Aunt Sybil stood stroking her hair from her face.

"The child's burning up with fever." Sybil glanced up at Annie, her face grave.

"Have Ada bring up more wet towels!" Annie shouted to the young maid.

"I've sent the twins from the room. I'll send for a doctor," Sybil said.

"Ada's doing that now." Annie ran to her side. "Clarisse, wake up." She shook her. Panic swept through her.

"Do you know, Annie, if she has complained of anything?" Sybil asked.

"She was fine yesterday. I don't understand."

Ada came running in with a bowl of water and cloths. "Fetch me that stand over there," she ordered the young maid who trailed on her heels.

Annie met her on the opposite side of the bed. At once, she and

Ada began administering the wet cloths to Clarisse's face and arms. Sheer fright swept through her. She had never felt a fever so high.

"What's wrong?" Isabelle entered and saw the entire household in a frenzy.

"It's Clarisse, she's hot with fever!" Annie said.

"It's that family down the road. They've brought this on," Sybil said with cold dignity. She turned and headed for the door.

"What can we do?" Isabelle asked.

"I'll go down and wait for the doctor." Sybil bolted away.

Annie's mind raced for answers. She tried to recall what her mother once did for fever. She pulled up Clarisse's gown and began rubbing down her feet and ankles with the cool, wet cloth.

"That's the ticket!" Ada said. "What else can we do? I feel so helpless 'til the doctor can come."

"Laudanum, Ada. She'll be needing it."

Ada rushed from the room.

Two hours passed before the physician arrived. He appeared in the doorway with Sybil standing behind him.

"Dr. Haines, it's my sister!" Annie ran to him.

"Hello, Miss Carraway. Sorry to be so long. A woman in the borough had a horrible time delivering her baby." He pulled off his coat and set to work examining Clarisse.

"What do you think she might have?"

"Could be typhus. There's an outbreak in the colony."

"Jail fever?" Ada's face grew ashen. "That's not possible, is it? Not 'ere at the manor house."

"It's that jail," Sybil fretted. "I'm going to insist that Abbot tear it down."

"You've a jail on the property?" The doctor checked Clarisse's pulse.

"It only has a single prisoner and he's never been ill," Annie assured him.

"Has he complained of lice?"

"He has," Isabelle nodded.

Annie stared at her, incredulous.

"Isabelle, you should have informed someone," Sybil said.

"You'll need to have the jail bedding thrown out and burned. Scrub it all out, walls, everything, with creosote and swab it all with quicklime." Dr. Haines directed his attention to Sybil. "Have the convict's clothing burned and issue him new ones. He should be examined for lice."

"I never should have allowed you girls to go out there." Sybil paced.

"But, Aunt Sybil, the Farrell man's not fallen ill and neither have we." Annie didn't know why she felt the need to defend him.

"I understand," Dr. Haines said. "It's all a precaution. The family down the road's been stricken with typhus as well. It's highly infectious. We'll need to isolate it here. Do you have a place where you can take the younger children?"

"I'm sure the Winstons would take them in for now," Ada said.

"Annie, send for Harry at once," Sybil ordered. She gazed up at Ada, who nodded in agreement.

"The Hanson girl died, didn't she?" Annie asked, lifting her face to meet the doctor's weary gaze.

"Have you administered any medicine to Clarisse?" he asked.

"Laudanum. Not two hours ago, we did." Ada wrung another towel over the washbasin.

"Good. Administer laudanum every few hours or so, giving her two spoonfuls at a time."

"Has she complained of a headache?" He pulled the coverlet up around Clarisse's chest, which heaved with her heavy breathing.

"I believe, sir, she did mention a headache this week. Christmas Day, it was," Ada said. "But you know children, how they complain. How could I have known?"

"Ada, why didn't you tell someone?" Angered, Annie's frustration spilled over.

"Annie, Ada's right," Isabelle said. "How often do we have a small headache and then it passes? It's all right, Ada. I believe Clarisse mentioned to me that her head hurt. None of us could have known." She turned to comfort the maid.

Annie felt her cheeks redden.

Visibly hurt by Annie's accusation, Ada hoisted the large bowl into her arms.

"Ada, I—" Annie moved toward the maid.

Ada diverted her eyes and started for the door. "I'll go for some fresh water again. If you'll all excuse me."

Her emotions pricked by guilt, Annie swore she would apologize to Ada at once.

"Will my girls catch it?" Sybil asked.

"You should take every precaution," Haines said.

"Her fever's raging. Clarisse, please talk to me!" Annie placed her hand on Clarisse's forehead again. To manage one rational thought right now would take more strength than she had. She closed her eyes and prayed.

"Join me in the hallway, will you?" The doctor took Sybil by the sleeve.

"I'm coming as well." Annie followed them. The way he spoke to her aunt—the hushed tones, his urgent manner—disturbed her.

"Join us, then." The physician gestured with a nod, his eyes and face etched with exhaustion.

Disheartened by his solemn expression, Annie almost wished she had stayed at Clarisse's bedside. She followed them out into the hallway and, with pained caution, closed the door.

"I'm disturbed that Clarisse has fallen into delirium so soon. This would indicate the disease has entered its final stages, but we won't know for certain for another day. More than likely, she's been ill all week. The early symptoms are easily ignored, which is unfortunate." He pulled on his dark overcoat and donned his hat.

"What are you saying?" Sybil asked. "That you can do no more for the child?"

"I'm sorry, Mrs. Dearborn. I'll return again in the morning, but if she worsens, send for me right away."

"Thank you, doctor," Sybil said. She dabbed at her eyes.

Annie stood in stunned silence for a moment.

"I'm so sorry, Annie." Sybil tried to embrace her, but Annie pulled away.

"But she's going to get better, isn't she?" She called after Dr. Haines, catching up to him at the top of the staircase. Once again she tried to speak, but the words caught in her throat. A tear trickled down her cheek, a thin, translucent ribbon that exposed her inner anguish.

"Actually, I've seen children pull through typhus much more often than adults," he said. "But I want you to know the truth of the matter. You deserve as much." The physician's face welled with sympathy. He turned and disappeared down the staircase.

The morning dragged on longer than usual. Rogan rubbed his now-smooth jaw, still somewhat sensitive from the sorely needed shave he'd gotten the day before from his brother, Frederick. He had taken a bath as well, using the soaps and toiletries given to him by Annie Carraway on Christmas Day. His stomach growled, the only indicator that the dinner hour approached. He held out his new shirt, slipped it on, and buttoned the cuffs and collar, enjoying the feel of new cloth. Since he had heard nothing from the Carraway sisters for two days, he hoped that Annie would bring his meal today. He would surprise her with his clean-shaven look.

"Your tastes are impeccable, Miss Carraway." The mirror on the windowsill showed him a more civilized image than the days prior. He practiced a smile.

Rogan felt a well of self-satisfaction. The Dearborn plans now nearly complete, he examined the drafts one by one, stacking them in an organized fashion. He tucked the drawings into a leather case to keep them safe until their completion. Sybil Dearborn had been more demanding of late, insisting that the construction of the new manor house should begin soon, even though she had yet to select the exact site. He stood, stretched, and decided to request a brief stroll. He had seen no family members about and felt the exercise might make him more visible to Annie. He walked to the window and peered out. The cook at least should be sending the noon meal soon. Distant voices drew his gaze. He heard someone draw near, could see a group of servants headed for the jail.

The lock banged against the wooden door, and the light of noonday washed across the dank floor. He started to speak, but before he could manage a single word, he was shoved outside. While two male servants held him on either side, the older servant woman stripped him down bare. "I beg your pardon, madam! This shirt is new and a gift from the lady—"

"Strip out everythin' inside, gents!" She ordered the servants into the jail.

The menservants bustled around inside the jail, and soon the bedding, the broken bed, and even the windowshade had all been hurled out onto the ground.

"Burn it all and bring in the creosote!" one of the men barked.

"I demand to know the meaning of this!" His clothing stripped right off of him, Rogan raged as they tossed it all onto a heap.

"Pipe down, mister!" The older woman tossed smelly, soapy water onto his skin.

"Am I some beast that you would treat me as such?"

"We've a sick child inside, come down with typhus, she 'as.

Doctor says it could've come from 'ere."

"Someone has typhus?"

"Mrs. Dearborn's young niece. She's burnin' with fever. Now, 'old still!"

"I'll take my own bath, thank you kindly." Rogan yanked the pail from her, then the scrub brush.

"Suit yourself." The maid took his trousers, his shirt, all of his toiletries, and tossed them onto a newly stacked brush pile.

"I trust you've brought me something else to wear?" He glanced down at his bare self and then made no attempt to disguise his annoyance.

The younger servant girl turned her face from him and blushed.

"Go on," the older maid said. "Give the man 'is new clothes."

"Try these on, Mr. Farrell. It's all we 'ad on such short notice," the young maid said.

"Now who has typhus—not Annie Carraway?" He felt a strange sense of worry but didn't want to show it.

"No, not 'er. It's the youngest girl, Miss Clarisse Carraway, that's up and come down with the fever. Poor child's delirious."

Rogan had heard of typhus, or jail fever, around the Sydney jail. Seldom had it been heard of out in the boroughs and around the manorial estates.

"I'm supposed to ask, 'ave you 'ad any 'eadaches of late? Any fever to speak of?" the maid queried while handing him a towel.

"I'm fine!"

"Good. All's the better, then." She held out the clothes for him, a yellowed shirt and a worn pair of brown trousers.

"I'd rather you give me back the new one." He pointed to his new shirt that lay on the heap, but she only shook her head at him. He stepped into the pants but found the fastener wouldn't come together around his waist.

"They're a bit small," she said. "Didn't know you was such a big man."

"You'll be so kind as to complain to my tailor?" Rogan folded his arms across his bare chest.

"No need to be so snappish. That's all we could find until Mr. Dearborn's arrival. He should be 'ome early. Mrs. Dearborn's sent a man for 'im to come 'ome at once. But I ain't one to be diggin' around in Mr. Dearborn's room. You'll just have to be satisfied with these until later, I s'pose." The older maid stood arms akimbo and shrugged.

"Burn all this?" A servant ran past with the leather case.

"Not if you want to live." Rogan stepped toward him and yanked the case from his hands.

"What's that you've got there?" the maid asked.

"Mrs. Dearborn's new house plans. Almost finished house plans, I might add. She'd kill for much less, I'm certain."

"Just check the case for vermin and give them back to 'im." The elder servant growled, then began handing out mops and pails.

"I want my boots." Rogan saw them loading his clothing and boots onto the heap.

"You'll be fitted for a pair later. Now leave us to our work. Here!" she said. "Get busy yourself." She handed him a mop.

Annie gazed out her own window. She had paced beside Clarisse's bedside for so long that her feet ached. Clarisse had stirred a few times but never came fully conscious. Annie could now hear the children bounding back and forth, scurrying to gather up their few belongings before the Winstons' carriage arrived.

She watched the distant melee as the servants torched the bedding that had been taken from Clarisse's room, as well as the items they had stripped from the jail. A pity swept through her when they had begun to strip Rogan Farrell. She had looked away, although little of him now remained a mystery to her. Then the light of humor came into her face when she saw that he had stood up to them. *He's no convict*. She watched him carefully, the assured way he stood, his confident manner. When the maid had handed him the mop, he gave it back to her at once, even under threat of the lash. She then realized something had changed about his appearance. A gentle rap at her door caused her to whirl about.

"Miss Carraway, I'm supposed to tell you that Mr. Harry Winston's come for all of you. Mr. and Mrs. Dearborn are leavin' as well," Ada said. "I'll be seein' to your sister, Clarisse, until 'er fever breaks."

"I'll not be leaving with them. I'm going to take care of Clarisse myself."

"I've seen to typhus patients before, miss. You wouldn't do no good 'ere, and I promise to send for you as soon as there's any change."

"No, Ada. You go on, if you want. I'm not leaving."

"I understand. But I'm stayin' with you." A sympathetic smile creased the maid's aging face.

"Thank you, Ada. But how could Doris do without you—" Annie's voice broke. She burst into tears. The maid ran to her and threw her arms around her.

"I'm so sorry, Ada! I've been so awful to you and, well, Clarisse—"

"It'll be all right, miss. Now, don't fret. I can't take no more tears today."

"Please say you forgive me."

"Child, I 'ave no ought against you. Look at all you've gone through, losing both your mum and your father."

"It hurts so much, Ada."

"Ada knows. Lost my folks years ago. Still 'urts."

"If only Mother were here. Look at Clarisse lying there, and what use am I?" Annie sobbed.

"Hush yourself. Can't wish 'em back now. You're a strong girl; you'll make it through."

Annie waited for Ada to leave the room. She then bent at Clarisse's side and prayed until two maids came and led her from the room to bid her family farewell. Silence had never fallen so sadly on Dearborn Manor.

19
THE INVITATION

Several days passed with no change in Clarisse. Annie had read all of her own books twice and had now resorted to pilfering from Abbot's personal library. She laid aside a legal text and stretched her legs from the settee placed next to her sister's bedside. Again she felt Clarisse's forehead and assured herself that her fever had subsided, if only a little.

Dr. Haines had visited this morning. Surprised to find Clarisse still clinging to life, it had encouraged him. He had passed on the encouragement to Annie.

She breathed a silent prayer, a practice that had become more a part of her now than ever before. Ada had gone off to the kitchen to prepare a simple meal for them both. If it hadn't been for their dire circumstances, she would almost enjoy the solace she found in the nearly empty house. Annie trudged downstairs and made her way into the kitchen. Across the room, she saw Ada pulling a pan of hot bread from the stove.

"Dinner's almost ready."

"Join me tonight, Ada. I'm lonely."

"That wouldn't be proper, miss. Besides, I've already eaten my dinner. Once I've finished with servin' you, I'm off for an early evenin' in my room," she said. "What with everyone gone, I've finally the time to read one of those novels I've 'eard so much about." She hesitated, then pulled the book from her pocket.

"Which novel?"

"*Jane Eyre*. You won't tell anyone, will you?"

"No, I swear not to tell. When you've finished with it, you'll loan it to me?"

"You, miss?"

"Isabelle won't return until Saturday. I feel restless." The isolation had already begun to take its toll. She reached into the cabinet to retrieve her own china plate.

"May as well relax. Bein' miserable won't 'elp your sister t'all."

"I know. You go on to your room, then. I'll finish up here. No need to wait on me."

"But you look so tired. Did you sleep any last night?"

"I tried but awoke on several occasions. I suppose that would suggest that I've slept."

"Poor child. I'll not 'ave you waitin' on yourself. You go on into the dinin' room. I'll only be a minute. I'll fetch you some of Mr. Dearborn's wine. He'll never know." Ada's eyes glinted with mischief.

"Thank you, but none for me." Annie stretched, pulled the pins from her hair, and allowed the long strands to tumble about her shoulders. Just beyond the kitchen window she spied the jail.

"I'll see that the convict gets 'is grub as well."

"Poor Mr. Farrell. I'd all but forgotten about him."

" 'Poor man' is right. He's such a grateful sort and quite the gentleman."

"I've noticed the same to be true." She turned and started to make her way back to the dining room when an odd thought struck her senses.

"Anythin' else?"

"I've an idea, Ada. It would be a diversion, at any rate."

The maid nodded while spooning garlic potatoes into a dish.

"Mr. Farrell's already finished Aunt Sybil's house plans. And he's been left with no one to see to his exercise."

"He is, after all, a mere convict. A guard comes out to check on 'im, though, miss. He's not entirely without aid."

"Ask him to join me for dinner."

"No, miss!"

"I insist. And I'm in charge."

"But, Miss Carraway, 'e's a convict. We can't bring 'im into the 'ouse. And what of the typhus? He could be carrying it, you know."

"How ridiculous! He's fit as can be and I refuse to dine alone. Now run fetch him," Annie said. "He could use the change in scenery, and I could use the distraction."

Annie strode to the dining room, full of purpose. Ada watched her go, distressed at what she'd been asked to do.

Rogan saw the twilight spread its blanket across the horizon. It irritated him. For three consecutive nights, no guards or servants had walked the property to light the lanterns. The stern woman who brought him his meals handed them off abruptly and offered him no explanation. After dark, an occasional candle could be seen in the upstairs window. But for the most part, the manor house appeared abandoned.

He hated the pitch blackness of night. Although the jail had been kept free from rodents, he seldom retired at candlelight and found himself sitting for hours with nothing else to do but memorize the constellations and behold the waning moon. He breathed out a sigh and hoped his evening meal offered more diversity than yesterday's cold meat pie.

Richard Barclay had visited once this week, but his investigation of the matter had neither resolved nor absolved the crime. The locals had a keen sensitivity for newcomers. Barclay, in spite of his experience, had already come up against a fortress of suspicion. Rogan now felt the days swimming past with little hope.

"Mr. Farrell?"

The sound of the woman's voice stunned him, but he recognized her.

"Are you awake, sir?"

"Wide awake. Here with my supper, I trust?"

"No, Mr. Farrell. I've come to ask you to dress yourself, sir. You've been summoned to dine in the manor 'ouse." The woman pried the rusted lock open after some difficulty. She peered in, her large wide eyes tinged with fear.

"Dress myself?" He noticed how her voice rose scarcely above a whisper, and even in the lantern light her nervousness could be easily detected. He gazed down at the ill-fitting clothes that he had been given only three days ago, then directed her eyes to his obvious dilemma.

"Dear, that is a problem, ain't it?"

"I don't understand any of this."

"I'll explain. You see, our Miss Carraway 'as remained behind to care for 'er sister, the girl wot's been struck with typhus."

"Go on." Rogan's eyes glistened with interest.

"She doesn't wish to dine alone. You'll need to dress at once, and then I'll take you to the dining 'all."

"Your staff has burned every piece of clothing I had. I've nothing else to wear." He drummed his fingers against the tabletop, lowered his face, and gazed up at the maid with a cynical smile. He examined her weary face and saw the frustration that rose in her eyes.

"I understand, but we can settle that all inside. Guard, will you follow us to the manor 'ouse?" She opened the door to let the guard see her face, her lantern swinging on her arm.

Rogan followed her, intrigued but cautious.

The longer Annie sat at the end of the dining table, the more nervous she grew. She had sent Ada out to retrieve this convict against the maid's better wishes. She had watched as Ada, her evident frustration defining her worry, set a second place at the opposite end of the table. The extra table setting, the empty chair, all fixed glaringly in Annie's mind. She fully regretted her decision. Perhaps she should make short her conversation with the ill-kempt man. However sympathetic she felt toward him, her friends would find her actions not only improper but scandalous. She would make Ada swear to keep her foolish deeds private, and she in kind would swear never to request such a thing again.

She glanced up at the large clock. Ada had been gone for a good half hour. She wondered if the man had given her any problems. After all, she reasoned, with his criminal background, he could be capable of anything. Now woeful, she buried her face in her hands.

"Miss Carraway, your guest 'as arrived."

Upon hearing Ada's voice, Annie stood at once and then felt foolish for having done so. She turned to force a polite acknowledgment. But she stopped just short of making her brief speech. The man who stood before her looked nothing like an outlaw.

Annie leaned against the chair, her mouth agape.

Rogan stood tall, outfitted handsomely in perfect dinner attire. He offered a friendly smile and bowed politely, his frilled cuff fluttering as he brought his arm across his waist. His gleaming auburn hair had been swept back into a stylish queue, and he had shaven.

"Good evening, Miss Carraway." Rogan Farrell spoke in a cavalier fashion, his deep voice startling her.

"And to you, Mr. Farrell."

"And might I say, your hair is stunning all let down like that."

Annie moistened her lips and pushed a long strand of hair from her face. She had neither dressed for dinner nor bothered putting up her hair. Suddenly self-conscious of her appearance, she pushed her hair behind both ears, then, just as swiftly, pulled it around her face. Realizing that she was staring at him, she turned to make her way to her chair.

"This is quite a surprise," he said.

"Thank you, sir, for coming on such short notice." Every word she spoke sounded foolish considering his circumstances. She reached for her chair, but before she could pull it out, he had met her in her place and stood with fingers poised on her chair back. Under his watchful gaze, he offered her the seat. She glanced back at Ada, who stood with a wooden smile, then her eyes narrowed.

"My pleasure, Annie," Rogan said.

She aimed her gaze in the direction of the tabletop. Ada wouldn't understand that she had allowed him to call her by her first name. It had only been a gesture of her sympathy for him, but now the foolishness of it glared at her.

"It smells delicious, Miss Towley." Rogan clasped his hands in anticipation of the meal.

"I'll serve you now." Ada curtsied and left to fret her way into the kitchen.

Annie shifted in her chair, struggling to find her voice again.

"This is a beautiful home," Rogan said. "My family's home is nice too, but not this grand."

"You've—you look different. That is, you look well, sir."

"A proper shave will do a man good." He released her chair, then strode to the other end of the table.

Annie hoped the heat in her face could not be detected in the candlelight, a single candle centered on the table being the only thing between them.

Ada carried in the first serving dish.

"Must I sit so far away, Miss Towley?" He grasped his plate but awaited Ada's approval.

"It's not up to me, sir." The maid cast her wary eyes toward her mistress.

Annie sat making circles in her china plate with her finger. She glanced up, aware that they both awaited some sort of answer.

"The gentleman wants to move down by you, miss. What is your wish?"

"You may sit where you like." Her answer too abrupt, Annie chastened herself for not standing her ground with him.

Rogan lifted the plate while Ada scurried to gather the remainder of the place setting. Annie saw the maid's worried face and looked away when she shook her head at her. Rogan strode right up next to her. "Now we won't have to shout."

The two of them sat in silence while Ada filled their plates.

"Going out?" Reginald Winston lit his cigar and seated himself in an oversized chair in his study. He spoke to Harry, having noticed that he had donned his gray summer coat and hat.

"The household's grown rather noisy of late." As Harry spoke, the Dearborn twins ran past, followed by their cousins. He pulled out a small box and opened it.

"Is that Annie's ring?"

"It was too large, but it should fit now. I wanted it to be just right. No woman in Sydney has such a ring." He admired it, then closed the lid with a snap.

"You're going there now?"

"I want to surprise her with it."

"The Dearborns know you're calling on her, I trust?"

"No, but I'll return with news of Clarisse, which should appease them. I want our evening to be special, and I'll have no chaperones underfoot spoiling it all for us."

"If they find out, you'll never hear the end of it, you know. And you've no more need for scandal." Lord Reginald blew out a circle of smoke.

"How could they find out? I want time alone with her, and this is the only way I'll ever get it."

"All right. I am glad you're finding out about the child. I would like to know how soon the Dearborns might be allowed to return to their home."

Harry cast a nod his father's way and strode off. He stopped in the hallway and pulled several fresh flowers out of the large ornamental vase. With the ring box and the flowers in hand, he made fast for the door.

"Miss Towley, you're quite the cook," Rogan said.

"Ada's not really our cook, you know." Annie sat with her spoon poised above the bowl.

"You'd never know it. My compliments."

The maid blushed under his approval.

"Please, I must know, how is your sister?" Rogan's face somber, he lowered his voice.

"Clarisse is neither better nor worse." Annie set aside her utensils, her eyes full of a deep unspoken sorrow.

"I'm so sorry."

"But the doctor came by this morning and says that we will have to wait for a few days. I'm to keep an eye on her. I don't know what I would've done without Ada's help."

"I understand that the jail I'm locked up in could be the culprit. I feel responsible somehow."

"You shouldn't. All jails have that potential—of causing typhus, that is. But it's hard to really determine the source," she said. "The family down the lane has a jail, and their child died of typhus. My aunt wants to have the jail burned down."

"If they commence to do so, you'll please alert me."

A smile spread across her face, and quiet laughter spilled from her lips.

"I knew it."

"What? You knew what?"

"That you could laugh."

She looked down at her plate and lifted her fork once more.

The way he savored every bite of food and sipped slowly from his glass gave Annie great satisfaction. She felt herself relax with him and enjoyed their lively conversation. Never had she known that such a learned man had been locked up in Abbot's jail. But now even that saddened her. If she told him the truth, it could destroy what remained of his indomitable spirit.

"So how does it feel to be out of those cramped quarters?"

"I'm indebted to you. Once my case is settled, you name the place, and I will host the finest dinner for you."

"My fiancé would never approve."

"Who is your fiancé, by the way? You've never told me his name."

"More peas, sir?" Ada appeared once more bearing two large serving dishes.

"Yes, please." He sat back to allow her to serve him.

"Ada, would you prefer I finish with dinner tonight?" Annie asked. "Remember, your novel?"

"Dear me, no," Ada said. "I'm enjoying the company myself. Coffee?"

"We'd love coffee. But could you serve it in the parlor along with some of those pastries? I believe that I feel my appetite returning." Annie set aside her napkin.

"That's good news, miss," Ada said. "Mr. Farrell, you take your time with your supper, though. It'll take me a few minutes to make the coffee for you both."

"Do you have family here in Sydney?" Annie asked Rogan. "Oh, how silly of me. Of course you do." She remembered the carolers.

"Yes, you saw them all on Christmas Day. I'm native to the colony. My grandmother arrived as a girl on the First Fleet. She worked as a personal maid to Governor Phillip."

"Not *the* first governor?"

"One and the same." Rogan set aside his napkin.

"So your family doesn't truly hail from convict stock?" She remembered Sybil's accusations on Christmas Day.

"Only in part. My grandmother, Katherine Prentice, met an emancipist named Dwight Farrell. They married and had children. But he, being bitten by a snake in the outback, died and left her a widow. She didn't remarry for years. Wound up later married to a sea captain."

"She's still alive, isn't she? That was her I saw on Christmas Day, an older woman with sad blue eyes."

"Sad blue eyes?"

"Perhaps I'm mistaken on that count. Would you like to adjourn to the parlor for our coffee?"

He stood and allowed her to pass.

"You do justice to my uncle's wardrobe. Those *are* his clothes, aren't they?"

"I hope he doesn't mind."

A smile stretched across Annie's face as she showed him the parlor entry.

"Got our coffee all ready now!" Ada ran between them.

Annie watched how merrily Ada led them into the parlor. She found it amusing in light of her prior opinions.

"Here's your coffee, sir, and your cup, miss. And 'ere's mine." Ada took a chair next to them.

Annie bit her lip, lifting her brows in a questioning way at the maid.

"Did I forget something, miss?"

"Your novel?"

Ada put her hand to her mouth, blushed, then excused herself at once.

Annie conversed with Rogan for another hour. The longer they spoke, the more interested she grew in his life. He explained to her how he had been studying as an apprentice under the architect, Mason Hale. He also told her how his family, his father especially, had taken a principal role in toppling the old convict transportation system. Their sheep farm, named Rose Hill, had thrived for two generations until the depression had struck in Australia.

"Well, I'm off to bed now," Ada said. "Too old to be stayin' up so late." The maid stood holding her coffee cup in one hand and her copy of *Jane Eyre* in the other. She had donned her dressing gown and cap.

"You needn't bother trying," Annie said. "Now off to bed with you."

Ada hesitated and gazed toward the guard posted outside the parlor.

"I really should retire as well." Rogan caught the intent of Ada's gaze.

"Oh no, Ada. I'm not tired yet. I swear I won't keep him much longer. Do stay a few minutes more, Rogan. Will you?" She offered a genuine smile and hoped he would comply.

"If Ada feels that I should leave, then—"

"Ada, you don't mind, do you?" Annie pleaded with her eyes.

"If Mr. Dearborn got wind o' this, it'd be the end of me."

"He won't, I swear it."

"Not more than another half hour, then. You do swear it?"

Annie stood and kissed the maid. She cocked her head slightly and awaited Rogan's affirmation.

"On my honor." Rogan smiled, then looked away when a distant rap sounded.

"Dear me. Who'd come callin' at this hour?" Ada muttered.

"Don't answer the door, Ada. Go on upstairs, and if they persist, I'll send them away myself." Annie considered who indeed it might be.

"You're certain?"

"Absolutely."

"Annie, I believe my presence here could place you in a compromising situation." Rogan stood, his eyes filled with concern.

"You worry needlessly. Now, you stay here and I'll run and see who's at the door. I won't be a minute."

He smiled as he often did, but this time, his smile landed a hook in her heart.

It struck Annie as odd that she felt a swell of unexplainable exhilaration. She assured herself that to admire his driving intelligence and his knowledge of the colony's history was justifiable. But more than that, she enjoyed the unhurried way that he conversed with her. He made her feel as though every word she spoke was of utmost importance. She wanted to know more about him. With caution, she would ask him about his trial.

After she had walked through the parlor doorway, she looked back at him one more time. Once again his smiling gaze stirred her in an unexplainable way. Sympathy, she assured herself, had many engaging facets.

The knocking grew louder. "I'm coming!" She fretted as she walked toward the door. After she had lifted the bar, she clasped the large brass handle and pulled it open. Then her heart froze, startled by the sight of the late-night caller.

"Annie, I hope I've not called too late." Harry embraced her, pressed a lingering kiss upon her cheek, and offered her a fresh bouquet.

She felt the color drain from her face, then accepted the flowers without a word.

"I apologize for the hour, but I simply had to see you tonight. I hope my surprise visit doesn't upset you." He stepped back, allowing his eyes to study her.

"It is late—"

"I love your hair down like that, Annie. Promise me you'll wear it that way whenever we're alone." He lifted a gloved hand and ran his fingers down a long blond strand.

"You know that we really shouldn't be alone." She struggled for excuses and knew that she had to make him leave somehow. If Rogan Farrell wandered out from the parlor, it would be disastrous.

"I can't lie. I wanted to find you alone."

"It isn't proper, Harry—"

"Hang propriety!" he said. "You're soon to be my bride, and it's no one's business if I choose to spend time alone with you."

She felt his arm go around her waist, and he pulled her close to him. Her words were smothered against his lips as he crushed her next to him. She wanted him to stop but knew if she cried out, it could bring Rogan Farrell from the parlor. How she wished Ada would appear or that anyone would appear to quell his attentions.

"Is Ada gone off to bed?" Harry said, still holding her in his arms.

"She's still about." His anxious face unnerved her. She had never found him to be so forward, at least not with her.

"Have her bring out the wine and let's have a toast in the parlor. I've something for you."

"Harry, I told you I didn't need any more of your gifts. I'm beginning to loan them all to Isabelle as it stands now." A nervous laugh preceded her words.

"Not that sort of surprise."

"Besides, the parlor's not ready for guests at so late an hour."

"Then let's go upstairs." He walked toward the staircase and she saw the fire of his gaze.

"You don't mean what you say." His words sparked frustration in her.

"Don't I?"

"My sister's upstairs, quite ill, or have you forgotten?"

"No, I haven't forgotten."

"Then leave me to tend to her!"

"Blast all your correctness, Annie! How can I make you want to be with me?"

"It isn't something that can be forced." She could see that her words had stunned him into reality.

"Take this, then!" He tossed down the box.

"Harry, don't—"

"It matches the fire in your stubborn eyes."

"Is that . . . the ring?" Guilt pricked at her conscience, making her words sound staid and lifeless.

"Isn't it about time? I thought tonight would be special for us. Memorable." He lifted her hand and kissed her gently on her bare ring finger.

She forced herself to look at him.

"Isn't it time we started acting as though we're in love?"

"I don't like what you're saying."

"We'll never have this chance again, Annie. We've the house to ourselves."

"Harry, you promised not to pressure."

"Gentle persuasion, my dear, not pressure."

Harry brought her fingertips to his mouth and began to kiss each finger. Before she could react, he lifted her into his arms.

Annie struggled to break free, but he held her more tightly.

"What is wrong with you tonight, dearest? You're not yourself." He studied her face as she imagined he had often studied a poker hand.

"Please put me down, Harry."

"Soon enough. I'm taking you upstairs so you can rest." He kissed her again.

"I don't find this humorous!"

Harry stood at the foot of the stairs, held her for a moment longer, then set her down.

"Don't ever do that again!"

"You don't think I was serious?"

"I don't know. Were you?"

"I need a drink."

Annie saw him head straight for the parlor.

"Abbot keeps it in here, right?"

"I thought you'd stopped drinking."

"I did. Only drink now when I'm thirsty."

Her mind swarmed with excuses for keeping him from the parlor. But not sure that Ada had completely cleared away all traces of dinner, she hesitated to take him to the dining hall.

"Coming, Annie?"

"Not in the parlor."

"Where then, upstairs?"

Her shoulders tightened; she felt at a complete loss for words. She looked first at Harry, then toward the parlor.

"Look at you, little nervous mouse. You're hiding something from me, aren't you? I'm going to find out what it is." He smiled in a devilish way, made fast for the parlor, and pulled her along with him.

"What do I have to hide?" Panic rioted through her. She grasped his arm with both hands.

"I wonder."

"Harry, please come back another night!"

"Now I'm sure of it." He stopped outside the parlor door.

Her breathing labored, she stepped back and released his arm. While he twisted the latch, she closed her eyes. Instead of following him into the parlor, she waited, her fingers curled into fists at her side.

"Annie—" Harry said.

"I can explain."

"Step in here, please."

Annie smoothed her rumpled skirt and pulled her hair away from her face. Her mind raced with possible explanations but none that would cast her in a good light or even be believable. She felt her shoulders grow rigid as she strode into the room fully expecting to hear two men come to blows.

"Did you have company tonight?" Harry stood gazing at the two empty chairs and the two coffee cups on the table.

Her eyes darted around the room but found it void of any traces of Rogan Farrell. The guard had disappeared as well. Before she could answer, a voice spoke from behind her.

"She had coffee and invited me to join 'er."

"Ada?" Annie whirled around.

Wrapped in a blanket with a nightcap pulled tight around her crown, Ada peered with caution into the room.

Startled, Harry raked his fingers through his hair and straightened his back.

"She invited me to sup with 'er, Mr. Winston, sir. I know it ain't proper, but me and Miss Carraway, we're findin' it 'orribly lonesome out 'ere. As a matter o' fact, Miss Carraway's been sayin' all day 'ow she wished someone would come out to see about us."

Harry stood with his elbow poised on his folded arm. His left brow lifted in a cynical arch.

"But o' course without proper escort, we never expected you at this late hour."

Relief flooded Annie's mind, although she hated the fact that Ada had lied on her behalf. She started to speak, to tell the maid that she didn't have to offer excuses.

"But I never finished coffee with Miss Carraway. Just went off to bed with me novel. You 'eard o' novels, sir?" Ada's nose wrinkled and she leaned toward him.

"I've heard of them, yes."

Annie, relieved that Ada had in fact told the truth, turned to see the satisfaction on Harry's face.

"No need to explain any more," Harry said. "What was I thinking, that you would have callers so late?"

Ada laughed first, then Annie joined her.

"I should have never come out here unannounced," Harry apologized.

"Well, if you'll excuse me, I'll be back to me novel. Miss Carraway, 'ere, she'll be needin' 'er rest, too, Mr. Winston, with all due respect." She turned away from them to head back to her quarters.

"I am sorry, Annie. I must appear so foolish."

"No harm done at all."

"I can see you're tired." He shuffled and glanced down at the floor.

Annie stifled a genuine yawn.

"Perhaps I should leave now."

"I'll see you to the door. Why don't I summon you an escort? The hour is late."

"No, I'd rather return on my own."

Without any hesitation, Annie turned to lead him to the front entrance while curiosity played out a speculative scene in her head—the one averted by an old maid's cunning.

20
DOG AND PEACOCK

"I've missed you, Mussy." Annie gripped her sister's hand while they both stood vigil over Clarisse's bed. Isabelle's hand felt small, and she realized she had never noticed before how small.

"And I you." Isabelle bent over Clarisse's frail frame. She held a rose-colored poke bonnet, shirred on the inside and slightly worn around the rose plumes. It did not match her attire.

Annie knew that Isabelle had dressed hurriedly, could sense her worry.

"She looks so pale."

"She spoke to me last night."

"What did she say?" Isabelle smiled.

"She wanted some water and asked about you. Then she fell back to sleep."

"I think she's getting better."

Annie wanted to sound as hopeful as Isabelle. She returned her sister's smile.

They stood, arms locked, smiling down at their youngest sister.

"How's Aunt Sybil?" Annie asked.

"She could be better. The Winstons' house is cramped with all of us there. I want to stay here."

"No, I'd rather err on the side of caution." Annie knew that steering Isabelle out of harm's way would be difficult. With gentle nudging, she placed both her hands on her shoulders and pushed her away from the bedside.

"Where are we going?"

"We'll finish our talk downstairs."

They descended the stairs and crossed over into Abbot's library. Isabelle ran a finger across the smooth mahogany of the bookcase, noting the dust that had collected on it.

"Ada and I can't keep it all clean."

"Better that way. More to keep Aunt Sybil busy when she returns. Dr. Haines hasn't given you any indication, I suppose?"

"Not yet. I'm still hopeful, though," Annie said. "I've gotten brave of late. Let me show you some of Abbot's books. It's an astounding collection."

"I'm not as brave as you. I'd rather go to the parlor."

"Come on. What's the harm?" Annie selected two books and held them up for Isabelle to see.

"What's so astounding about them?"

"The story. This one's called *Frankenstein* by Mary Shelley. The other one's called *The Last of the Mohicans* by James Fenimore Cooper."

"I've heard they're ghastly stories. Are they un-Christian?"

"Not un-Christian or Christian, but interesting. And exciting," Annie said. "I'll put them both away." She watched her sister staring at them as though they had tentacles.

"No. I'll take a look. So this is how you've made use of your week? You've been reading every night."

"I've read some." Annie clasped her hands behind herself, her fingers fidgeting the frayed brown braid on her peplum. Her eyes glistened and her mouth turned up on one side.

"What else is there to do?"

"I've entertained, but just a smidgen." She pinched together two fingers and then walked from the library, her smile now taking on more meaning than she had intended.

Behind her, Isabelle's heels clicked in rapid succession against the wooden floor.

"I trust you've stayed busy with your studies, Mussy."

"Never mind my studies, how could you entertain? You and Ada have the house to yourselves."

"Not entirely."

"You're keeping something from me."

"It's no secret we harbor a certain architect."

"You've entertained Uncle Abbot's convict?"

Annie smiled.

"You are wicked," Isabelle said. "How often?" She stared at her, disbelief evident in her face.

"Every night. Swear you won't breathe a word to anyone."

"I want to stay here. You're here in the throes of danger while I'm chasing after Sybil's twins."

"I won't let you stay, Isabelle. Just a few more days. Surely Clarisse's fever will break. Promise you'll stay away until then?"

"It isn't fair! Is he—dangerous?" Isabelle slumped into a chair, her eyes wide.

"Somewhat. Remember, he is a convict."

"I think I shall faint with envy!"

"He's told me his worst secrets. Things I will take with me to my grave." She sat on the arm of the chair next to her, craving Isabelle's approval.

"What else? At least give me a grain of excitement to carry back home."

"He's coming tonight again, I think."

"He looked so frightening the last time. Aren't you afraid?"

"No, he wears Abbot's clothes and I keep a guard on him. I don't feel frightened in the least." Annie recalled his dark hair hanging in slight turns around his rugged jawline. She watched him comb it wet after telling Ada to give him soap and hot water. With the weight of water, it hung well past his shoulders. She had thought of offering to cut it for him but had grown to like it.

"You've given him Uncle Abbot's clothes? That's more dangerous than anything I could imagine."

"Surely you can understand why? They burned his clothes and I couldn't allow him to come to dinner dressed like a beggar." He had filled out the finely stitched seams of Abbot's clothes better than the old man, she recalled. With the cotton shirt fabric stretched taut against his shoulders and down to the wrist, the buttons strained to contain him.

"I'm staying for dinner, Annie."

"You can't. Aunt Sybil's expecting you, and I don't want her sending for you. Then everyone would know I've been keeping company with an outlaw. Pure gossip like that can ruin you."

"I'm jealous."

"But you're braver than me. After all, you saw him first."

"I didn't bring him into the house and plant him square at Abbot's dinner table!" Isabelle shoved the bonnet onto her head, adjusting it on her braided coif, but left the ties hanging loose.

"If you had been here instead of me, you'd have thought of it."

"I never would've done it. I'm really a coward."

"You visited him in the jail."

"I was only being charitable. But you, Annie, you're dangerous."

Heaving a deliberate sigh, Annie gazed down, her lashes shadowing her cheeks, and smiled.

It grew so quiet that Rogan could hear the two bay horses whinnying to each other across the stable doors. He saw the guard light a cigarette, amble by to take a gander at him, and then stroll away for his usual Saturday afternoon drink. Rogan's body sank into the thin mattress folds, his bare back curved against the wall. Last night he had been summoned again to the manor house. He had figured that Annie Carraway would have never invited him back after Tuesday's near fiasco. As Wednesday passed, he was somnolent and indifferent to his isolation. But Thursday had brought her maid back rapping at the door, handing him Dearborn's pilfered wardrobe. He had shrugged, dressed himself, and followed Ada, but felt like a stray pup being led through the back door.

Friday night's invitation surprised him even more, but he returned to the jail with the same sour taste in his mouth. Annie had intrigued him; she knew a lot about law and legal matters. But he found in her a thread of naïveté in spite of her learning. While she recited English law, he perceived the unsullied wall she had fashioned around herself, a wall that kept anyone from knowing her. He doubted that she even knew herself. At any rate, he realized, she knew nothing about men. She had painted a prim image of herself in his mind, a marble statue bound in high collars and propriety, cold and forbidden. When she had him return again last night, the exploitation rose evident in his mind. He was there only for her amusement, to keep her company while the family awaited her sister's recovery. Yet after three conversations, she had wound her way into his personal life and told him nothing about her own.

Particularly interested in Harry Winston's involvement in the case, she had delved into the secret corners of his life, and he had slowly told her everything. *Farrell, you idiot! Barclay warned you and you wouldn't listen!*

"Mr. Farrell?" The sound of Ada's voice and her familiar rapping brought him to his feet.

"Go away!" he shouted.

First one dress drew her eye, then another. Annie studied her reflection in the tall oval mirror. Inevitably, she realized the choice of dress didn't matter. She didn't have to dress to please anyone but herself. But her brief emancipation had stirred a mixed bag of emotions. Her life had been lived according to the whims of others. Having almost sole responsibility for Clarisse of late had made her realize her capabilities. Not being so dependent on the Dearborns had whetted her taste for independence. Annie liked the tang of it.

She also liked rummaging through Doris Dearborn's mostly untouched wardrobe. Freely she delved into her cousin's chifforobe, selected the green ready-made dress, the Christmas gift that had all but sent Isabelle into a riot. She smiled and held it up, a toilette of green French faille, with a daring front of cream satin richly embroidered and fringed with gold. Nervous about the off-the-shoulder sleeves, Doris had never worn it. Before she could talk herself out it, Annie pulled it over her head, careful of her hairstyle and the white aigrette with its soft, tufted plumes that lifted from a shimmering base of semiprecious stones. She had found the hair ornament in one of Sybil's personal trunks. Flaxen strands of her hair circled the crown of her head and fashioned a soft cushion for the jeweled ornament.

Annie took a second glance. She found that her shapely frame filled out the faille to her satisfaction. She paraded for a moment to straighten out the skirt panels that draped behind and trailed her steps. Harry Winston would certainly approve, but she found glad satisfaction in knowing the night would not be under his dictates. Given the facts she had accumulated from Rogan Farrell, she knew more than anyone now, more than Harry, perhaps even more than Abbot. But she would not immediately divulge her knowledge of the matter. Possibly, this Rogan Farrell had given her false information. Watchful, cautious, she would not make her judgment in haste.

Annie stood at the top of the staircase feeling regal. She took the steps in a slow, gradual descent before making her way to the dining room. Once there, she found the two place settings arranged at the end of the table. She sat in her chair and mused while watching the clock. While she waited, some questions arose about the prior evening. Dinner being at its all-time best, she had felt pleased and assumed the same was true for Rogan Farrell. However, as last evening's meal had progressed, she found herself more given to conversation than he. At times, she realized, he'd fallen silent. Instead of devouring the meal in his usual way, he ate just enough to satisfy her watchful gaze, then turned down Ada's dessert altogether. Perhaps she had asked too many questions. Her talk of nothing but the upcoming trial may have thrown the man into discouragement. Whatever the reason, his interest in her had taken a detour. His veering mood had left her uncertain. Tonight she would exercise caution. *I still know so little about him. I'll ask more about his family.*

"Miss Carraway?"

Startled, Annie turned to face Ada, who stood in the doorway, arms folded. She lifted her brows, a faint smile and the light in her eyes offering a questioning glance.

"He's not comin' tonight, miss."

Annie struck a fingertip in repetitive succession against the gleaming china plate, then rose from her place.

"Where you goin', miss? Not out there, I vow. Miss Carraway! Miss Annie . . ."

Self-satisfaction reeled through Rogan. With his sturdy arms crossed behind his head, he stretched out on his cot and rested. Ada Towley had looked so surprised, had bundled the clothing into her arms, and, mouth agape, slammed the door. If his anger had not sparked such a fire within him, he could almost laugh about it, but Annie Carraway would get the message soon enough. *I'm not your pet, little girl.*

After he'd confessed his concerns to Barclay today, he was met with stern reproof. He knew he deserved a good swift kick in the posterior for allowing himself to be so taken in. Barclay provided just the tonic he needed to send this gullible young spider reeling back on her proverbial web. *Blast you, woman!*

The padlock fell open with a loud clank. Rogan could already hear her angry muttering, so he closed his eyes and turned his back to the door.

"Mr. Farrell, are we having a problem?" Annie bristled.

Rogan didn't stir. Annie's voice all but echoed against the hard stone walls. He lay soundless, his own silence daring her to venture close.

"I'm speaking to you, sir! Have you an ear?"

"Two good ones, last I checked." He could tell that she stood over him now.

"Are you so filled with engagements that you would decline my perfectly good one?"

"As a matter of fact—"

"Ridiculous! Turn and face me!"

Now incensed beyond words, he sat bolt upright. After he'd taken a brief assessment of her bold attire, he stood. Only a sheath of paper would have slid between their faces.

"Don't you touch me!"

"You want me? Here I am, Miss Carraway!" Rogan threw open his arms. He could feel her breath against his face, see her chest heaving, the hint of fear in her eyes.

"You're impertinent and a fool!"

She backed away, but he took two steps closer.

"I'll call for the guard!" she threatened.

"Go ahead. But get this fixed in your silly little head, I'm not your *boy*—!"

"Back away, I say!"

"Or what, you'll scream? There's no guard out here." He could see the confidence slipping from her soft blue eyes. If recollections proved right, he knew that the guard had never returned and most likely wouldn't until later Sunday.

"You don't frighten me!" But her tone proved otherwise.

"I should. After all, I'm a *convict*, Annie, and a commoner. You want me lapping up your attentions like a cur dog, don't you? And that's another thing! Why do you call for me every evening? You're supposed to be engaged." He pulled her left hand up, holding it right up to her face. "Take off your ring! Does this mystery man of yours know what you're up to?" He could see his breath blowing against the feathered plume on her head.

"I said don't touch me!"

"Is this for me?" He fingered the tufts of her headpiece. She jerked away from him, but he grabbed her, forced his hands against her bare shoulders, and ran them down her sleeves.

"Ada!"

"She can't hear you. This dress for me too? Are you coming after me, Annie? Because if you are, I want to know in advance, so I can know just how to talk to you!" Angry, he gripped her arms.

"How dare you! You know I've no interest in you!" Her lashes fluttered and her eyes misted.

"Well, what about me? I'm a man, Annie! You think you can parade around under my nose like some overdressed peacock and not get chased?" He released her and she ran for the door. He watched her reach for the latch, all the while keeping her terrified eyes riveted to his.

"I should never have trusted you!" she said.

"Don't worry, you never did!"

"You're a horrid man!"

"Run, Annie! Run to that loser whose money can't keep you on a leash—"

"Quiet, I say!" She trembled in front of him, her pomp draining into a pool of tears.

And with every soft tear that slipped from her sapphire eyes, a part of him ebbed with it, feeling wretched, worthless.

Her hand trembled on the latch, but she didn't turn it.

He refused to be fooled by her again. He stomped toward her and placed his hand atop hers, just to be certain she found her way out.

She looked up at him, stiffening her back.

"Go on! You said you were leaving. Aren't you going to leave?"

But she just kept her eyes on him, eyes that danced with more life than he'd ever had inside that cold ambition of his. He told himself that he would toss her out, make her leave. She wouldn't make a fool of him again. Then he felt her fingers tremble beneath his grasp on the latch. He started to pull away, but she didn't. So why should he?

"I . . . I'm sorry if I've angered you, Rogan."

Her words, soft whispers that breathed life into him, startled him with their transparency.

"You're right. I've acted like an idiot," she confessed. "Look at me!"

"I'm looking."

"No, I mean, this isn't me. I . . . I don't know who I am. God forgive me. . . ."

"Don't cry, Annie." Hesitantly, he slipped his arm around her.

Annie buried her face in his chest. She felt like heaven against him, like something precious he wanted to protect. Rogan put his other arm around her, allowed her to cry, to let out whatever it was that was trying to force her to be someone she wasn't. Barclay wouldn't approve, but having her this close even for a brief moment was almost worth a hanging. He stroked her hair, pushing the damp strands from her face.

"I don't know what to say, Rogan. I—"

"You don't have to say anything. Just don't wake me right now. I've been needing this for a long time."

A rose-colored haze had formed on the morning horizon that washed the trees gray and paled the grassy hills as fine as a watercolor. The liveryman had opened the pasture gate, allowing the horses to run and graze. Annie loved watching them gallop and romp. Horses, like children, had an unfettered enjoyment of the universe, knew their place in it, and found contentment in small snatches of freedom.

Annie, wearing the simplest plaid frock in her closet, sat out under the rear portico. Breakfast would be served soon. Her request to have it out-of-doors had surprised Ada. But an outdoor breakfast hadn't been her own idea.

Rogan had surprised her by suggesting it. Her foolish behavior had brought out the best in him somehow. No matter how much she had apologized, he sympathized all the more, told her she had every right to feel emotional. Then he had proposed the breakfast.

The fact that she could recall every word of his, and had awakened that morning thinking about him, both disturbed and stirred her. Isabelle had called her behavior "dangerous." But Annie felt drawn to him in other ways—ways that could best be described as friendship. She had cultivated several friendships within the Dearborn social circle, but none had satisfied her, nor been genuine. Isabelle had pulled away almost entirely from the wealthy class they had been forced into because of what she called the "orphan taint." No matter how friendly the individual, behind their animated gaze lay the judgment that the Carraways had no money of their own. Annie kept telling herself that she could rise above it, but until now she hadn't realized her desire for a genuine relationship, one unblemished by the knowledge of her impoverished past.

She could see Ada's portly frame ambling over the hill. Anticipation lit up inside her, but she also felt a hint of anxiety, fearing he might not come again. Then his head bobbed just above the hill's crest.

"Good morning!" Rogan waved freely.

Annie nodded and allowed herself a broad smile that felt natural to her. She saw he had donned the clothes she had sent to him—the fine white shirt, the roan-colored trousers. The morning sun played off his dark hair in violet hues that complemented his tanned face.

"Hurry, I'm famished!" she said.

"Don't rush me, I'm enjoying the landscape."

"It is a beautiful morning."

Rogan hesitated, looking at her in a way that told her he wasn't referring to the day.

"Ada's made a wonderful breakfast, haven't you, Ada?" Annie fixed her sights on the maid.

"I didn't want to serve it cold, so you'd best give me a few minutes," Ada said.

Rogan stood behind the chair next to Annie's. He had a pensive gaze, one that reflected his inward thoughts.

"Would you have a seat, Rogan?"

"Surely. How's your sister this morning?"

"She's scarcely stirred at all. But thank you for asking."

"Clarisse is fortunate to have you for a sister."

"I feel that way about her."

"What's she like?"

"Before this—young, full of life. She has this doll that she converses with. Calls her 'Mrs. Gunneysax.' Aunt Sybil's worried that her fantasies will damage her mind, but I love her imagination. It's what makes her—" Annie's voice broke. She brought her hand to her mouth.

"I'm sorry this is hard for you. I shouldn't have—"

"No, I should talk about it. About her. She remembers little about our life in England, so she makes it up and it makes us all sound so—grand. I love seeing the world through Clarisse's eyes."

"Maybe we should go up and see her."

"No, we don't have to do that."

"But it would be good for her, I feel. For me, anyway."

Still feeling him to be unpredictable, Annie simply awaited his next comment.

"I'll be careful," he assured her.

"All right. Ada's in no hurry to feed us." Annie stood and led the way.

When she had looked in on Clarisse earlier, she had looked so pale, lifeless. Annie opened the door to her room and allowed Rogan to step inside.

"I love this room, the way the sun comes in on her bed every morning," Annie said. "I keep hoping she'll awaken to it."

"Has the girl said nothing at all since she fell ill?"

"She spoke once, said she was thirsty. But then she fell asleep again."

Rogan bent over her.

Annie felt her brow, stroked the hair from her face.

Clarisse stirred, her small fingers curled and uncurled atop the coverlet.

The maid had brought in a fresh basin of water. Annie soaked a clean cloth, cooled her brow with it, washed her limbs. "We should go now, Rogan."

"Thank you for bringing me up here," Rogan said.

They had just turned to leave when Clarisse gasped, coughed.

Annie whirled around, thinking she had heard her call out.

Rogan hesitated, waiting in silence.

"Annie . . ." Clarisse whispered in a low voice, as quiet as a kitten's purr.

"Clarisse, are you awake?"

The child opened her eyes and blinked several times.

"Try to talk, Clarisse. Can you understand me?" A tear spilled down Annie's face.

Weak from the fever, Clarisse nodded. "My head hurts."

"I know, Clarisse. We're trying to make you well."

"Who is he?" Clarisse asked.

"He's Mr. Farrell, a friend."

Rogan moved in closer, smiling at the little girl.

"Hello, Mr. Farrell."

"Very nice to meet you, Clarisse."

Annie continued to blot her own tears. The weakness in her sister's voice discouraged her.

"Mr. Farrell, have you ever seen God?" Clarisse turned her eyes on Rogan.

Annie could see the distress on Rogan's face, knew that he didn't know how to answer. She nodded at him, encouraging him to answer in any way he could.

"I don't believe I've ever seen Him," Rogan said.

"He's very pretty," Clarisse said. "Like a Christmas star." She coughed again.

"Clarisse, I love you. . . ." Annie wept openly.

"So tired." Clarisse closed her eyes again and fell asleep.

Annie held on to the bedpost until she could regain her composure. Rogan stood behind her, his hands clasped, his head bowed.

She regretted now that she had brought him up, had involved him in her sorrow, but she felt glad that her sister had spoken again. Before she left, Annie placed another kiss upon her feverish brow, then invited Rogan to join her downstairs. They walked in silence until they reached the top of the staircase. She saw him blink, then press his lips together as though he wanted to speak. Annie waited.

"I've always wanted to know what God looks like," he said.

She agreed but couldn't manage an answer, didn't want to think that deeply for now. That's where she usually found the pain was wedged—deep inside.

21
THY WILL BE DONE

Rogan kept his face close to the bars so that he could see sideways. Annie Carraway's lithe movement now familiar to him, he watched her walking ahead of a group of people. The quiet, summery days, the private ones spent with the lonely mistress of Dearborn Manor, had vanished, replaced by the sudden activity at the manor house. The group of women dressed in black troubled him, but having no word today from any of the household servants, he could only wait.

He first saw the strands of her honey blond hair glinting beneath her veiled hat, the hair he had touched, held in his grasp. She had surprised him the other night and the next morning at breakfast. Most women like her seldom revealed that much of themselves in so honest a way. As much as it pained him to see her agonize beside her sister's sick bed, he hadn't regretted going. The night he saw her in the jail, she had revealed some other things about herself. One thing she had divulged—her doubts about this heir she was engaged to—proved that she really wanted nothing to do with an arranged marriage. She never told him the lout's name. But just in hearing her speak, he had drawn a picture of the philanderer—a card-addicted carouser whose silver spoon and wandering eye had been a magnet for gullible young women. The senseless side of it baffled him—why her uncle would agree to such an arrangement.

At one point, her brow had furrowed while she spoke. Rogan answered only in brief affirmation. He didn't want to spoil the moment, wanted to hear what she had to say. It had been obvious to him she needed to air her woes, so he had offered her the chair at the drafting table and kept silent. Then came a deeper confession. Her mother's death troubled her. With the tragedy now some years past, he yet had detected the fresh trace of pain in her eyes. As she had spoken, her guilt over losing both parents, and having to take refuge with her aunt and uncle, had spilled over more than once. Yet he knew she held back some of her thoughts, a few of her troubles. For he could see the wall more clearly now than in the past. And yet she herself chipped away at it, from the foundation up, if for no other reason than to catch a glimpse of what awaited her on the other side.

With a close eye on the processional, he watched as one woman moved forward, ahead of the others. Almost certain he recognized her as Sybil Dearborn, he saw her leave her husband's side and bolt for the girls. While Annie and her sister walked arm in arm, taking the soft green berm in slow, steady steps, he watched them climb the hill with caution, but also with strength, as though they approached a mountain. Two lads, their limbs still awkward with the dew of pre-adolescence, trudged behind with their hands shoved into their pockets and their heads down. Then, out of a dense copse of trees, six men, long in body and clothed in black summer suits, plodded behind them bearing a small wooden coffin.

After the funeral, everyone sensed that the two sisters wanted to be alone. Harry and his family excused themselves while the girls ascended the stairs. Annie whispered Clarisse's name all morning. She had first spoken it as the sun emerged to rouse the rest of the world. After having spoken it, it took on life, and so the more she said her name, the more alive Clarisse seemed to her. Even the room where she had slept lifelessly for so many days now breathed as Annie had wanted Clarisse to breathe the morning she found her lying still against her white linen pillowcase. And if the walls breathed, then the swaying boughs outside her window were the heartbeat, and the birds took on her childlike songs. But none of it comforted Annie.

Not even the dress they had laid her to rest in—her favorite color, April blue—had brought Annie the comfort she sought. Everything, every personal item, her doll—all of it looked like Clarisse, but none of it would ever bring her back.

Even the pencil drawings Clarisse had pressed into the walls with hat pins mocked her now. She yanked them down, every penciled reminder of the life that had been extinguished for no good reason.

"What are you doing?" Isabelle, her face wan, stood behind her.

"I'm putting these away." Annie stacked the tattered drawings in a heap.

"Could you not leave them up for a day? I find comfort in them somehow."

"Comfort?" Opening a table drawer, Annie hid the pictures from her sight. She lifted Mrs. Gunneysax from the traveling trunk, then opened the lid to hide the doll away.

"Don't, Annie."

"Why didn't we think to bury that doll with her, so she—"

"Annie!"

"So she wouldn't be alone!"

"Stop, I can't bear it!"

"And all these things. We've got to get them out of sight, have to—"

"I'm hurting too, Annie! It's not just you; we all are." Isabelle tugged at the fingertips of her black gloves.

"Clarisse was improving, Isabelle. I watched her improve. Then I woke up and she had left me. She didn't say good-bye or tell me she was leaving."

"Not everyone gets the chance to say good-bye."

"Well, someone forgot to tell me! Tell God for me, will you? Dear God, please allow sick children to say good-bye to their loved ones!"

"I wish you'd stop." Isabelle dabbed at her dewy eyes.

"God allows our questions, Isabelle. I have to believe that, or else I'd go insane."

"God's taken Clarisse to heaven. I don't question why, Annie. I just know that I trust Him completely with her."

"But He should have taken me. I've no reason to be here."

"I won't let you say such things. Besides, you do have a purpose, Annie. You're going to marry and have a family. You're smarter than anyone—"

"You always say that, but there's no evidence it's true. And what if I don't want a family, don't want children? Not any born to a drunken father, at any rate."

"Harry's changed. You've said so yourself."

"He's changing, but only outwardly to please his family. I know that now. I've had time to think it all through."

"You don't know his heart. Only God knows his heart."

"I know that Harry Winston has much at stake. He's a gambler, but he won't risk his entire future. He'll go through with this marriage. Then he'll go back to his old ways."

"Call it off, then!"

Isabelle seldom lost her temper. Annie sensed the sudden change in her, realized she'd gone too far. She grasped for words, words of comfort and assurance that wouldn't sound at all as wooden as they felt to her.

"Isabelle, I—"

"I'm sorry. I shouldn't shout at you right now. Not ever."

"I deserved it. I shouldn't be rambling on about my problems, Mussy. We're going to feel better soon. If not in a few days, then perhaps in a few weeks." She kissed her and they hugged until the sun set.

Sybil sat in the parlor, draped in her mourning frock and still wearing the long veil indicating the deepest of mourning that fashion dictated. Around her clustered women from the colony, friends who had lingered to offer comfort and to leave behind food offerings for the family. Her face sullen, she sat dry-eyed for the first time all day. While some of the women spoke in whispers, others relaxed and began to speak of other matters, smatterings of gossip.

Ada, her face red and raw from crying, busied herself taking their dishes of food to the kitchen. She set out tea and prepared some of the food on platters to offer to the guests. Another knock at the front door caused her to excuse herself again.

Sybil turned down an offer of food but accepted the tea from a friend. She had just stirred in a pinch of sugar when Ada reappeared, hovering in the parlor entrance.

"Ada? Have we more guests?"

"Yes, Mrs. Dearborn. We've one more guest."

"Show her in, please."

But the maid lingered, her eyes gazing to the side.

"Ada?"

"Yes. Right away, Mrs. Dearborn." She disappeared.

Annie and Isabelle entered instead. Sybil shifted in the lounge chair, shrugged, and drew her attention back to her visitors.

"Mrs. Katy Gabriel here, to pay her respects." Ada made the announcement and took one step back.

Silence skittered across the parlor. Sybil set aside her teacup and scowled at Ada but could say nothing.

"Hello, Sybil." Katy stood statuesque in spite of her years. Dressed in simple day attire and a feathered hat, she strolled toward Sybil, her gloved hands still gripped around a covered dish.

"Hello, Katy." Sybil sounded hollow.

"We were grieved to hear about your young niece. My family wishes to offer our condolences."

"Thank you." Sybil stiffened her back, resting her hands in her lap, a prim portrait of veiled emotion.

The chatter resumed around the parlor.

"Ada, please take our guest's food to the kitchen. Katy, would you have some tea?" No smile accompanied her offer.

"Thank you, no. But know that my prayers go with you, Sybil."

Annie felt complete admiration for the woman. If Katy Gabriel had noticed Sybil's cold reception, she did not show it in her calm comportment. She nodded at Annie and then at Isabelle, then turned away from the impertinent stares that had followed her into the room.

"I'll . . . I'll walk you to the door, Mrs. Gabriel." Annie moved toward her but also acknowledged her aunt with a caring nod.

Katy Gabriel accepted Annie's arm. They walked solemn faced to the entry. "It was good of you to come, Mrs. Gabriel, but you surprise me. You know that your grandson is locked here in our jail, yet you offer gestures of Christian charity."

"I can't worry about my own feelings. It's God whom I answer to, not myself."

"You've given us all an example to follow. I only wish I could find such humility."

"It's simple when you understand the principles."

"Such as?"

"Once I asked God to establish His throne in my heart, I also asked Him to command from there as well."

Annie felt stunned by her words.

"You know that prayer, don't you? 'Thy will be done on earth as it is in heaven.'"

"I do, but I've never heard it put that way before."

"I'm praying for you, Annie. For your family."

"I need it, Mrs. Gabriel. My heart feels completely trampled. I miss her." A tear spilled down and splashed onto her collar.

"Poor child. You know your Clarisse is with the angels, don't you?"

Annie nodded.

"God sharpens us in the strangest ways. You won't see it now. But later, you'll look back and realize what He's been doing in you all along."

"You've greater insight than I. Shall I summon your driver, Mrs. Gabriel?"

They waited while the butler opened the door.

"Yes. See him there?" Katy asked. "He's my grandson. One of my grandsons, but they're all as handsome as Frederick here."

"Frederick? Rogan Farrell's brother." Annie recalled the name.

"Why, that's right. Rogan's told me about your visits."

"He has?" She glanced behind her.

"I should thank you. He's in need of kindness right now. He told me that your sister left him a Bible. She's rather direct, that one."

"She is at that. Isabelle should be a missionary."

"I don't think he's read it, though—the Bible."

"No, I suppose you're right. Rogan's not the Bible-reading sort."

"You've noticed that about him too. Are you, child?"

"I am, Mrs. Gabriel. More now than in the past. I find comfort in it, though I'm undeserving."

"But you have Christ all over you. Did you know that about yourself?"

"No one's ever said that about me."

"You've a good heart. Your charity comes without a price tag. That's what will speak to my grandson's heart."

"Here's your carriage, Mrs. Gabriel." Annie stepped back to allow Frederick's assistance, offering him a polite smile.

"Thank you, Annie, for all you've done for Rogan." Katy settled herself in the open carriage.

Her cheeks tinged red, Annie curtsied and then turned away,

hoping no one had heard Katy Gabriel.

"Ada's prepared dinner for us." Isabelle waited at the parlor door.
"Are you hungry yet?" Annie folded her arms across her stomach.
"No, but you know Ada."
"That I do."
"Let's offer our thanks to Sybil's visitors and then slip away."
In full agreement, Annie followed her into the parlor. A strange
mood had settled over the room, one she attributed to the sudden,
awkward appearance of Katy Gabriel. Clustered around Sybil, she
heard the women engaged in quiet discourse.

"She doesn't bother me," Sybil said. "We must accept her visit
at this time. It's our Christian duty. But that doesn't mean that I'll
accept her attacks on my husband and me. We cannot be blamed
for her grandson's problems."

Distressed at her aunt's words and feeling them inappropriate,
Annie started to leave, but Isabelle bade her stay.

Of course, the ladies voiced their agreement with Sybil, which
stoked her ire all the more. "She's a fine one to be worrying about
our affairs when she should set her sights on her own."

Annie recalled Rogan's concerns about his father's sheep business. Ignoring the women who were engaged in such gossip, she
offered her thanks to those who stood in quiet groups engaging in
proper dialogue, then excused herself from the room, whether or
not Isabelle thought she should.

The bounty-laden serving tables in the dining room remained
scarcely touched at the end of the meal. Only her brothers and Isabelle joined her. Clarisse's chair stood empty, adorned on one
post with one of her favorite crepe hair ribbons.

Isabelle saw Annie's observance of it. "I'll put it away."

"No, please leave it. I'd never noticed before that all her ribbons
are made of crepe."

"By the saints, you're right, Annie," Ada said.

"Meaning what?" Isabelle asked.

"Crepe is usually reserved for those in mourning, dear." Ada
smoothed the long ribbon that hung from the bow.

The three of them gazed at the crepe bow for a moment.

Thomas spent most of the meal staring at his plate, while Linus
fidgeted and, more than once, asked to be excused.

"I think we all should remember that Clarisse is now with our mother and father. Think of them all there in heaven waiting for us." Isabelle's hands trembled.

"No! I don't want to think about it anymore," Thomas said. "I don't need any more reminders." He tore the ribbon from the chair.

"Thomas!" Annie laid aside her utensils.

"I hate it here, hate that everyone dies and leaves us! I hate being told what I'm going to do today and tomorrow. We live in an asylum."

"Master Thomas, please seat yourself and finish your food," Ada pleaded.

"I don't want to. I'm not hungry. Does it make sense to eat today? I want to go back a few days. I want to see my sister alive again."

"We all do, but we can't bring her back." Annie's eyes teared.

"Why did I have to leave here in the first place? Clarisse needed us here all around her. If we'd been here—"

"Then you'd have gotten up on Wednesday morning and found her gone as I did. I couldn't stop it. God knows how much I wanted to make her wake up. I would have changed it all if I had the power." Annie reached across the table, placing her hand atop his.

The chair underneath swallowed him up as he slumped into it.

Ada retrieved the bow and tied it back onto Clarisse's chair. Her hands trembled.

"Ada, I'm not hungry either. Why don't you put away the food? Perhaps our appetites will return later. We know how to fix our own plates if that happens," Annie said.

"Yes, Miss Carraway, I understand, I do." Ada burst into tears and ran from the room.

Not able to muster another shred of comfort, Annie returned to the parlor. She would bid her aunt and uncle good night in hopes that she could offer a more civil side of herself the next day.

Hot, sultry night air radiated through the open front door. Sybil stood in it, waving to the last carriage full of mourners. She folded her arms and turned, causing her veil to fill with air and billow behind her. The butler closed the door and, weary faced, dismissed himself to his quarters beneath the stairs. Sybil started upstairs. But she stopped, a glint of something indefinable sparking in her eyes.

Making fast her path to Abbot's study, she presented herself to him in a becoming way. "Abbot dearest?"

"I thought you'd retired. You've something on your mind?"

"I've had a thought. Mind you, not very well thought out. Perhaps you could offer your views."

"I know that Gabriel woman showed up today." He put away his bottle.

"You know?"

He nodded.

"Then you know how dreadful she's becoming. She only dropped in to embarrass me."

"Ada said she brought us a dish of food. Quite neighborly of her."

"Neighborly? Or does she enjoy making sport of me in the midst of my trials? I wasn't the only one who saw through her. Everyone agreed with me."

"You discussed your dislike of her openly?"

"I only agreed with our guests. Katy Gabriel's got to be stopped."

"Have a seat, dear. You obviously need to talk."

She took the chair facing his desk and wrung her handkerchief.

"I've never seen you so distraught. This goes beyond the death of your niece, doesn't it?"

"Think of all that land being wasted in Parrametta by those— ruffians."

Abbot's brow lifted with interest.

"You know it's taken so long to have that man finish my house plans. Now when I study them, they won't look right out here at all. This house needs a special place. A bigger landscape."

"You're something else, Sybil."

"They're about to lose a perfectly good piece of property, all because of their mismanagement."

"I wouldn't say that the Farrells have mismanaged their sheep operation. They've been dealt the same depression as everyone else. We've been fortunate."

"We've used common sense and taken care of what we have. Now Katy Gabriel's squandering what little she has on that expensive London lawyer, that Richard Barclay."

"Rogan Farrell has a right to honest counsel."

"He has a pauper's right and no more."

"Go ahead and say what you're meaning to say, Sybil."

"I want Rose Hill."

"Not ambitious, are you?"

"No more than you. Don't you suddenly act righteous on me.

We could give our manor house to Doris when she weds Charles Lafferty. I wouldn't mind living in the old Farrell house until our own is finished."

"You always were the practical one, Sybil."

"You think I'm demented."

"No, on the contrary, you're as sober as sin. You realize the stir we would create in Sydney over this? Farrell's a popular man—helped to topple the transportation system."

"I don't care!" she bristled. "None of our friends would give him the time of day. He's still common, and his mother's meddled for the last time."

"You're certain that her intent was evil?" Abbot asked.

"What I think is of little consequence, but one fact is now more clear to me than anything else. We should have thought of it sooner. Rose Hill is prime land and should be developed by people of means."

Standing outside of Abbot's study, Annie felt her breathing quicken, felt her heart skip a beat. She had heard more through the door than she had intended. Needing to absorb the still quiet mood of a household in mourning, she turned to disappear onto the portico. The heavy scent of roses hung on the silent air. She stood outside until the moon cast its pale light, lining her figure in its pure silvery touch. A yellow glow, soft as a firefly, emanated from outside the jail, inviting her to come near. A part of her knew she should run and spill the horrid truth. But instead she stiffened her back and seated herself on a bench. Rogan would be forced to tell his family at once if she breathed a word of it.

She recalled what Katy Gabriel had said to her, and the words slapped against her senses in turbulent waves. Annie closed her eyes.

"Our Father which art in heaven . . ."

PART THREE

But we have this treasure in earthen vessels, that the
excellency of the power may be of God, and not of us.
2 Corinthians 4:7

22
MOONLIGHT NUPTIALS

"How much are you asking?" Abbot Dearborn's desk top reflected the man's face who sat across from him. He drummed his fingers against the mahogany, awaiting the man's reply.

"Did I say I was asking for anything, your judgeship?" the man asked, his face drained of color.

"Blackmailers usually do."

"Your Honor, I'm not a blackmailer. I've only told you the truth as it was told to me by Harry Winston."

"Harry told you all of this? I find that hard to believe."

"As I said, sir, he was well in his cups that night. We had all gone broke but one, and Harry was taking it hard, pouring his drinks down like they was water."

"So Harry got drunk and told you all that he embezzled the money?"

"No, nothing like that. He was only threatening something drastic, though not in earshot of anyone but myself. I saw he was in his misery, so I walked him to his carriage. Seemed the charitable thing at the time," he said. "He was babbling about being broke, said if his father got wind o' this game that he'd be disinherited for sure. That's when he made up his mind, so to speak."

"So he hadn't actually done anything yet?"

"Not yet." The man turned the brim of his hat nervously in his grasp and shook his head.

"Go on."

"I told Harry he just needed to go home and forget his losses, but he had spent something that wasn't his. He never said it was Mason Hale's money. He called it a loan and said that he had no way to repay."

"But he didn't say who he had borrowed from?"

"Said it was another apprentice."

"The devil you say! Do you remember, did he ever mention Rogan Farrell's name?"

"Not that I recall, Judge Dearborn. But I was well in me cups too. It's all a little blurry, but I could remember things or forget them just as quickly . . . with a little motivation."

"I wouldn't doubt it. I wonder why Farrell never said anything."

"What's that, sir? You mean the other apprentice? I hear he's smart as a whip, that one."

"He must have realized that it was his word against Harry Winston's." He bent over and began fingering the safe next to his desk.

"If it weren't for it being such hard times and all, sir, I wouldn't even consider—"

"As I said earlier, how much?"

"I've need of some new carriage wheels an'—"

"Shut up, man! How much?"

Rogan woke up early and set to work straightening the jail. He bundled the linens for his makeshift bed and shoved it all against the wall. His grandmother had sent him a new suit of clothes through Frederick. After he'd buttoned up the tan vest, he felt a bit of his manhood restored. He pulled his trousers over the tops of his brown leather boots. New shoes were a welcome relief. He wiggled his stocking-clad feet around in them and took an extra swipe at them with a cloth. Barclay had scheduled a preliminary meeting this morning, so he felt an urge to have all of his things in order and to present himself as he would on the day of his trial.

A rap at the door brought him to his feet. Allowed in by the guard, a face appeared, but it wasn't Barclay's. "Frederick? I didn't expect to see you."

"Rogan, I need to talk to you."

Frederick's urgent tone disturbed Rogan. But seeing he held his finger to his lips, he offered no response.

"Guard, I wish to take a stroll with my brother. May we?" Frederick asked.

The inevitable wait while the guard responded irritated them both; however, they had little choice but to humor him with veiled respect.

"You kin take 'im as far as that there garden. See yonder?" He shouldered his rifle.

Rogan directed his brother's eyes to the rose garden.

"We see it," Frederick nodded. The door squeaked open once more.

"Why the hurry?" Rogan had to quicken his steps to keep up with him.

"Something's awry, I fear."

"Tell me now. Best to spill it all out at once."

"Someone's trying to buy Rose Hill out from under us."

"Tell me who it is." Rogan saw the sweat beading across Frederick's brow.

"None of us know. It's the mystery that has our father worried. Hear this—he had worked out a deal to purchase several hundred sheep, but the man backed out, said he'd had a better offer. Wouldn't sell us the sheep. Now another man's appeared at our door, says his man is willing to help us out of our dilemma. Wouldn't give us a name, but the offer is for half of what the land is worth."

"Father would never agree."

"He can't hold on without more sheep," Frederick said.

"Who would want to run us off our land?"

"I don't know. It's got me baffled."

A breeze stirred through the rose garden, the only sound for the space of a few minutes.

"I know that if Grandmother offers the money needed to pay the higher price for the sheep, she can't pay Barclay." Frederick pulled off his coat and wiped his brow.

"But the trial's in only two weeks—"

"I know, the fifteenth. We've been forced into a gauntlet where you're concerned."

"I should make Dearborn pay me for those house plans. He owes me."

"He *owns* you, is more like!"

A rage swam through Rogan. He wanted to pound someone but couldn't fight a ghost.

"Father's thinking of selling part of Rose Hill to make up the difference."

"He can't do that!"

"We don't know who we're fighting, Rogan."

"Insist on knowing the man's name. The next time this lout shows up, mind you, make him give you a name or there's no deal."

"There's no deal anyway."

"Get his name. Understand?"

Frederick offered a meager nod, but Rogan could see the surrender in his eyes.

"What about California, Rogan?" He pulled out a newspaper clipping and handed it to him.

"I'm fighting this thing, Freddy! Someone's getting off free while I take the blame, so I have to win. Someone else will lose, but not me!" He snapped the article out of his hand and pocketed it.

"The guard's flagging our attention."

Rogan sighed inwardly.

"I just can't see any way clear," Frederick said. "If Father sells Rose Hill, he can start again."

"He knows the land, knows how to make it turn a profit. He needs time."

"Time's up, Rogan."

"We're almost to the top of the hill, Freddy. Don't give up on me now." While they trudged back toward the jail, he struggled to offer assurance to his brother.

"I'm trying, Rogan. I swear it. But I'm not seeing a light ahead, except the one shining its beam from California."

"Good-bye, Freddy." Rogan stepped into the jail, keeping his back to the door. He didn't want to watch the door close behind him or see the defeat again in Frederick's face. It was all too much weight at once, and he needed to save his strength for the upcoming fight.

"I want to put off the wedding, Uncle Abbot." Annie paced in front of her uncle. She had offered to run Sybil's errands for her, and the ride into Sydney allowed the courage to build inside of her, the courage she needed to stand up to Abbot. Insistent that the driver take her to the government building, she had waited outside of Abbot's office for an hour before being admitted.

"The wedding's not until June," he said. "I know you've suffered a great loss with Clarisse's death. But in a few months, you'll see. The cloud always lifts."

"Waiting until spring would offer me more time to plan— maybe in October. I can't concentrate on anything right now."

"Allow Sybil to plan for you. She loves weddings."

"I would rather plan it myself. Aunt Sybil has—well, her ideas are not so modern."

"Modern? Have you mentioned any of this to Harry Winston? To anyone, for that matter?"

"No. I plan to share all of this with him tonight. He's taking me to a party at the Hamiltons'."

"I'm against this delay, but I'll leave the decision up to you and your fiancé."

"Thank you, Uncle Abbot. This will honor my sister's memory in a fitting way." Annie departed Abbot's office more swiftly than she had arrived. Never would she have believed that he would have given in so easily. As sad as the circumstances were, she knew that Clarisse's death had surely softened the man. A change had swept over the entire household.

Sydney's streets bustled with carriages and street vendors. She would lose herself in the noise and hope to gather her thoughts before tonight. In regard to her grief, she had spoken the truth to Abbot. Not a day had passed since Clarisse's funeral that she hadn't thrust her head into the room to find it inhabited only by the twins. Seeing the space once filled by her small bed now replaced by a traveling trunk caused a deep swell of anguish to rise in her, black as the Atlantic and just as cold.

As Annie stood in the town square, an image formed in her mind. She could see Clarisse holding Sybil's hand, her eyes pleading not to be left behind. She should have taken her with her the day they had bought her veil, but in her zeal to be rid of Doris and Sybil, she and Isabelle had seized the opportunity to slip away. If she could buy back a day, it would be that one. She would live it for Clarisse instead of herself.

The veil hung in her wardrobe, a hovering reminder of the wedding. Annie determined that she would reason with Harry, and he would have to understand why she needed more time. His desire to have the wedding date moved forward would become secondary to Annie's need to mourn. Then the matter of the embezzlement charges loomed. With more time to investigate, Annie could at least settle the issue in her own mind. Even more troubling, she worried over Sybil's decision to buy Rose Hill. No matter how hard they fought to muzzle the facts, she had to at least attempt to unearth the truth about them. If Rogan Farrell proved to be nothing but a liar, then he deserved to hang. But it was the probability of his innocence that gave her hope.

Annie remembered how he had settled her down, calmed her the night he had turned down her offer of dinner. Rogan had held her, expecting nothing in return. Not too many men would have done that without wanting something more. In those few minutes with her face buried against his chest, she felt her life connect again as though she had found the bridge back home. Since her mother's death, Annie's emotions had wandered in search of a place to nest.

With the memory of Rogan's touch still fresh, only sheer determination had kept her away from the jail. She had to understand why she wanted to go back. It had to be an important reason, something beyond charity, beyond her yearning to do good. Perhaps her desire to fly back to him was just her heart's way of telling her that she shouldn't settle for a world washed void of color. If her feelings for Harry had taken on shape, they would appear as bleached seashells, some broken, some whole, but all washed ashore like skeletal remains. Before she could decide what she truly wanted in life, she first had to know what she didn't want. Annie didn't want barren love.

In the past, her mistrust of anyone had been the force that kept her a step ahead of trouble, had kept her skirts from the fire, so to speak. As a child, she had learned to mistrust men. She thought that mistrust empowered her, kept her afloat, would keep her heart from sinking into the same mire that almost destroyed her mother. She still had night fears about Jock Carver, although she never mentioned his name to anyone. In that way, he remained invisible and benign. But keeping the world at bay since then had not kept her from feeling the pain.

It occurred to her why she had treated Rogan in such a cavalier way. She had compared him to Jock without realizing it. Annie remembered how powerful she had felt summoning him, telling him when he should leave. It had been no wonder that he accused her of treating him like a dog. By keeping him within her own restraints, she had protected herself—but from what, she wasn't certain.

Annie stepped into the dry-goods shop. The boys would be leaving soon for England and needed extra trousers for the journey. After going through her own bureau this morning, she also realized her gloves were missing, and she needed a pair for tonight's party. She dreaded the party, hated confronting Harry with the delay in the wedding. More than that, she hated his arguments. But after tonight, life would be simpler, would offer her the time she needed to pull together all the missing pieces in her life.

"Where are those nice soaps?" Annie asked the clerk.

"I'll show you, miss."

She would allow herself another trip to the jail. Rogan had been stripped of all his personals, and no one would see to him if she didn't. She grasped another white shirt from the men's clothing shelf, lifted it to her face, and tried to remember how it looked in the candlelight.

"Thanks for coming by, Harry." Abbot offered a cigar.

"None for me, sir." Harry refused Abbot's offer of a chair and a drink as well.

"What's your hurry?"

"I'm escorting Annie to a party tonight and I'm short on time."

"She's whom we need to discuss. This unfortunate matter with her sister. It's gotten her all confused in the head. You know how women can be so easily set off."

"Go on."

"She wants to put off the wedding."

"Indefinitely?"

"She says until the spring. She's not mentioned it to you?"

"Not a word. I've done as you've asked and tried to move up the date. She says she wouldn't have time—"

"The spring's not convenient for us, Harry. It would be much more convenient to do it even earlier—this fall. April's good— March would be even better. We'll have her married, then we can concentrate on Sybil's new house."

"More convenient for you, but what about Annie?"

"I know my niece. The longer you wait, the more time she has to cancel the plans altogether."

"I don't mind if Annie wants to wait until the spring. Right now this Farrell trial has my insides in knots. The sooner it's settled, the sooner I can think more clearly myself."

"You're worried about the Farrell trial?" Abbot asked. "You know with whom you're speaking?"

"Yes, but Farrell's hired an expensive attorney. Barclay," Harry brooded. "He's been making frequent visits to Hale's office. He's spent hours behind closed doors with Mason Hale. Neither of them are asking me any questions."

"Has you worried, eh? Have you offered them any help?"

"Of course not."

"Perhaps you should reconsider. Your memory's been a bit fuzzy. It could all come back to you now."

"Yes, my father's told me of your suggestions."

"I've suggested nothing, Winston, and you keep that in mind tonight after you've had a few too many at the Hamiltons' estate!"

"I don't plan on drinking at all tonight."

"Excellent, but I don't believe you."

"I'm not a fool."

"Well, if this trial's accomplished anything of value, scaring the devil out of you is one good thing."

"If this is why you summoned me here—"

"No, it isn't, and you'd best listen. I had a talk with one of your gambling buddies today. Seems you mentioned a debt to him one night when you'd had a few too many. Did you borrow money from Rogan Farrell?"

"He told you that?"

"Just give me an answer. Did you?"

"I paid him back. I don't owe Farrell anything."

"Good." Abbot twisted his cigar to the other side of his mouth. "How'd you pay him back?"

"With my winnings."

"Don't lie to me, Harry!"

"I'm going to be late tonight to pick up your niece if—"

"She can wait."

"I paid him with the winnings from the game that night."

"You never win."

"I got lucky."

"I've heard otherwise."

"What do you want me to say?"

"I just paid dearly for the silence of a witness—a witness that could free Rogan Farrell and put you in with the rats. You want to tell me the truth, or do I need to investigate this matter as presiding magistrate?"

"I had to pay Farrell back. He would talk; he has too many friends. I couldn't allow my father to find out that—"

"How much did you lose?"

Harry's hands trembled and he reached for a handkerchief.

"So you stole from Mason Hale to pay back Farrell?"

"I never said that!"

"You never will." Dearborn pushed himself away from the desk and stood. He strolled to his window, closed the curtains, and turned to face Harry. "But you will do as I ask."

"What else do you want? I've done everything you've asked."

"I want you to sweet-talk that niece of mine. Convince her that delaying the wedding won't accomplish anything. Assure her of your love, make her feel secure. Women want security, man! They'll put up with any tomfoolery if you can promise them that."

Harry studied Abbot but didn't reply.

"I've moved heaven and hell for you, Winston! It's high time for paybacks. We understand each other?" Abbot's eyes bored into Harry's with a cold threat.

"Yes. I believe we do. We'll have our April wedding." He waited, expectant of Abbot's reply.

"And you'll testify that you caught Rogan Farrell tampering with Hale's books?"

"I will," Harry nodded.

Abbot extended his hand and the two of them shook on it.

"I'm in no mood for this," Annie complained.

"You shouldn't go, then. Cadence Hamilton's parties are no place for people of conscience."

Isabelle braided silk rosettes into Annie's hair.

"I've gone before."

"Yes, and look at the results. That's where you met Harry Winston."

"You're so full of cheer tonight, Mussy. Must you try so hard to lighten my load?"

"I don't mean to sound negative, but all Harry needs is another excuse to drink."

"I can't keep him from that if that's what he's determined to do."

"You sound as though you expect him to fail."

"I want to know the truth about him."

"All finished." Isabelle strung a few beaded baubles around her crown.

"He's 'ere!" Ada called from the downstairs.

"All set?" Isabelle pressed down the stray strands of hair at the nape of her neck.

"I am." She offered a gentle hug, then peered toward the door to find that Ada had remained at the foot of the stairs.

"What's in that bag?" Isabelle asked.

"I bought a few things for Rogan Farrell. Soap, a new shirt."

"So kind of you to think of him. I'll take them to him."

"No, I'll do it."

"All right."

"You haven't mentioned Charles Lafferty of late. I'm glad you've finally gotten over him, Mussy."

Isabelle kept her gaze down on the vanity top.

"You have gotten over him, haven't you?" Annie asked.

"Hurry, can't keep Harry waiting."

"Don't wait up for me. I've some things to discuss with Harry and I'll most likely be late."

"I won't wait up." She righted herself, gazing fully into Annie's blue eyes.

Ada called up again, her voice reflecting impatience.

"Isabelle Mercy Carraway, are you all right?" Annie asked.

"I'm perfectly fine. Really I am."

"Miss Annie Carraway!" Ada stood in the doorway, red-faced, her lips pursed and her brows lifted.

"Oh, Ada, you'll ruin your complexion!" Annie laughed, causing Isabelle to laugh as well.

"Mr. Harry Winston's waited long enough, don't we think?" Ada bristled.

"Have a wonderful time," Isabelle said.

"I'm off to bed. You need anythin'?" Ada asked Isabelle.

Isabelle shook her head while Ada tapped impatiently on the door.

"One more thing—are the boys all packed?" Annie scooped her purse off the bureau. She awaited Isabelle's nod, then lingered for just a moment, taking in her sister's pure countenance.

"They're as packed as they'll ever be," Isabelle said.

"Well enough. Say a prayer for me, then. I've a difficult night ahead."

"I will."

Isabelle watched her go, even ran to the front library to watch the carriage pull away. She loved her sister and so longed to have her be a part of all of her plans. But because of her deep devotion to her, she couldn't tell her everything—how her own bags had been packed all day; why she couldn't wait up for her tonight. How she would steal into the boys' room momentarily and kiss their sleeping faces for the last night as Isabelle Carraway. Charles would come for her soon. By midnight she would be Mrs. Charles Lafferty, bride without fanfare, without trousseau or trunks of laces. But she would be in his arms once and for all and would remain so—"Until my last breath," she whispered. *Please forgive me, Annie. I know you'll understand later. I'm not completely mad, as some will imagine. Just a little driven.*

Hurriedly, she scrawled a nervous letter and stuffed it into Annie's pillowcase along with a newspaper clipping. She hoped that Annie could figure out its meaning. Drawing down the lantern wick, she waited by the windowsill for an hour while the household grew quiet. She watched for the distant flicker that would forever change her life, forever change things between herself and Annie. *The light! I see you, love. I'm coming. . . .*

23
A PLACE TO
PRAY

The sunrise met Annie wide awake. After a restless night, she could recall every ticking of the clock and knew when the youngest child had bounded down the hallway at daybreak. She saw Doris arise and leave the bedroom in her drowsy state to send for her morning basin of water. She glanced numerous times at Isabelle's empty bed.

Last evening's events had fallen across her life like small black dominoes that beat her down against her will. Harry Winston had never left her side the entire evening, even when Cadence Hamilton, appealingly drunk, had tried to coax him away. Under the moon's guarded watch, he had informed her on the ride home that their wedding date must be moved ahead. This had caused her great anxiety. He offered her little reason for this sudden change in plans; he only mentioned their responsibility to her uncle and aunt. Abbot and Sybil needed to move ahead with their house plans and with plans for their own children, he explained. He even used Clarisse's death as an excuse, stating that Annie had a responsibility to herself to move on with her life as soon as possible, to leave tragedy behind and embrace her future. His proposed

April wedding date had startled her. She had bid him a fast good-night, having never acknowledged his request at all.

She would never agree to it. But his urgency alarmed her, making her feel as though circumstances were moving her life invisibly beyond her control. Sybil and Abbot would be expecting a new wedding date from her this morning. She had hoped to tell them that Harry had agreed to September or perhaps October. She realized that they would ask her over breakfast and would press her for an answer. But she would have to convince them to lay the matter aside. She had worse news to share now.

Under the coverlet, she found Isabelle's letter still close to her bosom along with a newspaper clipping. The article spoke of a new Australian territory, saying it would be called Victoria. In spite of her wishes for Isabelle's happiness, she never thought that her sister would hide such an event from her. True, she had hinted that she would marry Charles when he had asked for her hand at the engagement party, but she had never mentioned his name again. Annie thought it all a ruse. Anger wedged itself in her throat so tightly that when Ada rapped at her door, she couldn't manage a single word.

"Everythin' all right, miss?" The door opened gradually.

Annie attempted to force a nod, but soon Ada's eyes met her own.

"Whatever's wrong, Miss Annie? You're pale. Are you come down with somethin'? Please say you ain't got fever." Ada shut the door fast behind her.

"No, Ada." Annie's voice was hoarse; she tried to clear it and begin again. Before she could slide the letter beneath her pillow, Ada saw it.

"What's that? And where on earth's Miss Isabelle? Is she already dressed?"

"Ada, Isabelle's gone."

"Gone? Gone where?"

"That, I don't know."

"What's wrong?" Doris appeared in the doorway, her hair tousled over her eyes, her gown rumpled from a sound sleep. She stepped in beside Ada, yawned, and laid her cheek against the maid's plump shoulder.

Unable to look her cousin in the eyes, Annie glanced away.

"Where's Isabelle?" Doris asked.

"Doris, I'd best tell you all at breakfast. Could you leave me now? Ada, please help the boys along. They've only a few hours until—" Sorrow rose up in her and she now regretted the decision to send Thomas and Linus away. Realization eroded what remained of her composure. Tears coursed down her pale cheeks. Then a sob arose, an act that sent Doris shrieking for her mother.

"Please, Ada, stop her," Annie pleaded. "She'll only make things worse."

Ada offered an abrupt nod and left to chase down her frenzied charge.

Meanwhile, Annie slipped into a gray linen dress, one she could wear to the harbor. She pinned up her hair with little care, listening to the commotion out in the hallway. After she had wiped her eyes, she stood to wait for the furor to hit her.

Sybil entered the room. "Annie? Doris says you're crying. Where is your sister?"

Standing behind Sybil, Ada sighed, her eyes full of apology.

"Aunt Sybil, she's gone. When I arrived home last night, I fell into bed exhausted; I didn't even change my clothes," she said. "Later, before daybreak, I awoke and realized what I'd done. I turned up the wick, and that's when I realized that—Mussy's left us."

"In this wilderness?" Sybil asked, worried.

"She's not alone," Annie said.

Doris stepped in, wearing the freshly pressed dress that Ada had given her. From behind her mother, she reached with one hand and gripped Sybil's forearm, her fingers trembling. "She's with Charles."

"Doris, what makes you say that?" Sybil whirled around and addressed her daughter.

"Charles Lafferty has never loved me."

Annie noticed how Doris spoke with such clarity, so even in tone, so emotionless.

"He loves Isabelle," Doris said.

"He's told you this?" her mother persisted.

"He didn't have to tell me. I've seen it in his eyes. I think all of you knew. Even you, Mother. You can't make two people fall in love." Her voice quavered.

"Time brings love, Doris, and patience. I didn't love Abbot before—"

"Aunt Sybil, Doris is right. Charles is in love with Isabelle. They ran off last night and told no one." Annie stiffened her back and held out the letter. When she saw Isabelle again, she would scold her for leaving her to contend with the confusion.

Doris stood silent while her mother scrutinized the letter.

"The Laffertys won't tolerate it. They'll have it annulled!" Sybil flew into her usual hysteria.

"No, I don't want to marry Charles Lafferty. I want to fall in love like Isabelle." Doris stretched a trembling smile across her face. "And like Annie."

Abbot poked his head into the room. "Is this a private meeting or is everyone invited?"

"Abbot, your niece has something to tell you," Sybil said.

"Annie, you want to tell me what this is all about?" he asked.

With all of the worried faces in the room, it annoyed Annie that her aunt expected her to clarify the problem.

Doris spoke up. "I'll tell you, Father."

"Doris, I want you to go to your room and wait for me." Sybil stepped away from the door.

"No, I want to tell Father myself."

"Don't you dare defy me!"

"Let the girl speak, Sybil." Abbot heaved an impatient sigh.

"Charles and Isabelle have gone off to be married."

Numb to all emotion, Annie turned to collect her things into her reticule. As Doris explained, Abbot naturally erupted.

"There's something else I want you to know," Doris went on, "especially you, Annie."

Annie looked up at her cousin in surprise.

"The day that Isabelle met Charles in the garden, it was all my doing."

"Hush yourself, Doris!" Sybil exclaimed.

"No, I won't hush. No one gave me the liquor from Father's cabinet. I got it out myself, because I . . . I'm a coward. At least I was. . . ."

"Thank you for telling me, Doris," Annie said.

"None of this can be true. Doris, you don't have to cover up for your cousins—"

"Mother, please accept the truth for once in your life." Doris faced her, even when Sybil slapped her across the face.

"Aunt Sybil, don't!" Annie ran to her cousin's aid.

"You've embarrassed me in front of our family! For years you've done nothing but embarrass—"

"Have I, Mother? Well, accept one more embarrassment. I won't marry Charles Lafferty, even if you bring him back."

Annie turned away from them and left the room. She knew she had to get her brothers to the ship before Abbot came to his senses and stopped them. Without explanation, she awakened Linus and Thomas and hurried them to dress themselves. Then she returned to gather a few things, to see that the sack of goods was taken to Rogan.

She could hear Abbot storming the halls occasionally as he hitched up his trousers and searched for his coat and hat, overcome with anger. Isabelle had defied the great magistrate, Abbot Dearborn. Justice would prevail. Annie felt a small part of herself separate from the situation, a sort of self-preservation. The part of her that pulled away was calmer and felt no anxiety over the matter. But that part of her warred with the side that took the blame for everything. If she hadn't been so caught up in her own worries, she would have noticed the changes in Isabelle, would have seen this coming. When Abbot glared at her, she could see he blamed her too.

She reminded herself that she could leave soon with the boys and at least have a few hours to think on all that had transpired, with every matter put into proper perspective. She wanted Thomas, especially, to understand about a few things, to prepare his heart and mind for independence and for manhood. She laced up her boots, but as she finished dressing, a thought shot across her mind. She told herself that it was a panicked thought, one to which she should pay no heed. Thoughts like this could instigate drastic changes to life—as drastic as the choice just made by Isabelle. And wouldn't that be a shame, to be as miserable as Isabelle right now?

Thomas and Linus stood at the front door, holding their hats in their hands and looking more like men than even Annie could imagine. She talked in private to both of them while they awaited the carriage. Sybil had backed out of the trip altogether, too distraught to manage a sensible thought. For that, Annie felt grateful. She would have them all to herself for their momentous send off, albeit a painful one.

"Miss Carraway, your uncle requests a word with you before your departure." The butler stood in the hallway and awaited her response.

"Fine. I'll be right there," she said. "I'll bet he has some money for you both. Thomas, you see that your escort takes care of all your money. Unscrupulous men board these ships looking for prey—"

"I know, I know," Thomas sighed.

"Coming, sir." She lifted her skirt to step away and follow Abbot's butler to the study. Somewhat surprised to know that Abbot had not already departed for his duties of the day, she shrugged and entered the study. "Uncle Abbot?"

"Please sit down."

Fully prepared, she knew that his anger over Isabelle's elopement would still be fresh. She responded at once and took the chair.

"My calendar's needing a date from you, dear."

"Date? You mean the wedding?"

"Precisely."

Fully expecting this request, an unsettled feeling stirred inside her. She felt as though his eyes bore into her, scrutinizing her every thought. She swallowed hard. "We're at odds with the dates."

His brows lifted at her response, but she couldn't tell if it were from surprise or gladness.

"Which date has Harry chosen?"

She didn't want to say.

"Come now, out with it. I'm very busy today."

"April, sir."

"Splendid, then we'll—"

"I've not agreed to April."

"You'll consider the date, then, while you're out today? Sybil must know—arrangements to make and all that."

"Yes, sir, I'll consider it."

"Allow me to inform your aunt. She has enough troubling her today." He scrawled a memo indicating they would meet again later in the day.

Anxiety swirled through Annie. "I told Charles that April might not offer enough time—"

"Tut, tut! More than enough time, if this is what pleases the two of you."

She wanted to say that the date didn't please her at all, that she wanted to call off the entire affair, that she didn't love Harry Winston. But instead she stood, wordless. Abbot had already been handed too many reasons to change everything.

"You realize that your brothers are being offered a rare opportunity for two boys in their situation?"

"Yes, Uncle Abbot, I do."

"I've some money for them." He held up a small case and handed it to her. "See that their escort, my good man Henry, oversees their finances. He can set up a trust for them; he has the letter from me.

They will be provided for until their education is complete."

"I'm grateful to you. Is that all, sir?"

"One more matter. I feel you should know that we've sent out men to search for Isabelle and Charles. His father's furious and is on his way here now. If indeed they've wed, we will quietly undo the mistake and begin anew. Tell no one of this, and the mistake will be laid aside, although your sister has forced me to deal with her."

"You're having their marriage annulled?"

"Charles is a grown man, far more mature than your sister. He's simply allowed his emotions to get in the way. He'll agree to having the marriage annulled once he's been made to understand the gravity of the matter."

"I understand," she said. "I should take my leave now. My brothers and I covet our last few hours together, you understand."

He nodded and a smile appeared, but it did not mask the threat in his dark eyes.

"Good day, Uncle." As Annie all but ran to join Thomas and Linus, the anxious thoughts arose again in her mind. She quelled them with her silent resolve. *You'll never find Isabelle and Charles! They're smarter than you, Abbot. They're smarter than me. God help me, I'm learning quickly.*

"Harry Winston's going to testify against you."

Barclay's words rang through Rogan's mind, spearlike, driving straight into the core of his emotions.

"He says he's been protecting you all along." Barclay's face, hard as flint, held a question.

"Liar! I'll kill him!"

"Keep it down, man! I know you're angry, but words like that will only hurt you worse."

"You believe me, Barclay, don't you?"

Barclay nodded slowly, his eyes assessing Rogan's every move.

Rogan cursed, turned, and raked his arm over the breakfast dishes still remaining. The glass exploded against the hard stone walls.

"Stop it! You can't react to them! Don't you see, you've got to rise above all this, have to be confident." Barclay grabbed him by the shoulders and shook him.

"I'm lynched before I ever get to trial, Barclay—which, by the way, is only two weeks from now! The decision's been made already. Dearborn's going to hang me and throw me to the dogs."

"Dearborn's not God! You've got to prepare to defend yourself. You've got to help me help you. Besides, I'm arranging a delay in the trial date."

"I don't want a delay!"

"I've requested that it be changed to April tenth. We need the extension. It offers us more time to investigate Winston. Dearborn had to comply or look suspicious. Now let's go over every detail."

"I've told you everything. If you haven't uncovered any evidence yet on Harry Winston, then you never will."

"I want you to think about everything, in minute detail. I'll return tomorrow and we'll talk then. You need some rest."

Barclay left and Rogan gripped his right hand. In his anger, he had gashed his small finger. He wiped the wound against his trousers. For over an hour he stood and paced, mulling over the events of the last few weeks. The Carraway sisters had not come to see him at all this week. Had it not been for his family, he would never have been given properly fitting clothes. He kicked at the bedding on the floor and realized that his death sentence had already been passed. He had wasted his grandmother's money on a lawyer for a hopeless cause. Frederick had to come for him; he had to help him break free. He lifted the newspaper clipping and read it again. Frederick had left it behind to tempt him. It worked. They would flee to California at once.

A sound outside the jail drew his attention. He stepped toward the locked door and listened.

"You're to remain on post until nightfall." A servant spoke in a hushed voice to the guard.

"Nightfall? Wot's that you're sayin'?" the guard asked.

"Judge Dearborn's ordered a permanent sentry for this prisoner until his trial."

"Why's that?"

"I don't know. But he'll be under armed guard until then."

Rogan barricaded the shock and fury that whipped his senses. He pounded against the door.

"What d'ya want?"

"I wish to send a message to my brother, Frederick. May I send for him?"

"No. No more visitors until your trial. Dearborn's orders."

Unable to quench his thirst for vengeance, Rogan drew back

his fist and rammed it against the door.

"I don't understand why you've chosen April." Visibly shaken, Annie stood before her aunt and uncle, still wearing the attire she had worn for her brothers' sendoff. Thomas and Linus had both been so strong when they waved good-bye, but Annie had wept.

Now the afternoon was upon her, and Harry Winston had dropped by unannounced. She stepped away from Harry, who had taken his place next to her. With all of them in the room staring at her, she felt confronted. He tried to take her hand, but she pulled away.

"Excuse her, she's been under great strain," Harry said.

"Don't speak for me, Harry!"

"I'm trying to help you, dearest."

"But how could we plan for a wedding in such a short amount of time?"

"I've arranged everything." Sybil held up her calendar.

"What would all of our friends say? That we rushed up our marriage, and for what reason?"

"They'll say that I was so in love with you that I couldn't wait another day," Harry answered without emotion.

"Shut up, Harry!" She turned to face him in a rage.

"Annie!" Sybil chided.

"Why are you forcing me to marry him, Uncle Abbot?"

"Force? I thought the two of you had made all the arrangements?"

"Why don't you both give me some time with her?" Harry again reached for her hand but only found air.

"No, Harry! You'll not manipulate me again. You've lied to me all along." She turned her wrath on Abbot. "And I've lied to myself."

"What's this?" Abbot yanked his cigar from his mouth.

"She's confused, sir," Harry said.

"I'm not confused. I'm more certain of my feelings than I've ever been."

"Abbot, Harry's right," Sybil said. "Let's give them both time to talk out the matter privately. It's only a nervous quarrel. All brides get a case of the nerves." Sybil straightened her skirts.

Posturing his shoulders, Abbot leaned toward them both. "I'll return shortly."

Annie looked away, sensing the heat of his anger. A silence settled on the room while they waited for Sybil and Abbot's swift retreat. She turned around and found that Harry stood over her.

"I'm about to be your husband and it's high time you stop embarrassing me!" Harry said. He took her wrist.

"Embarrassing you?" Annie tried to pull away, but he held firm.

"You don't know what's best for yourself. I'm going to start making the decisions for us and you're going to listen!"

"And I suppose you know what's best for me, Harry?"

"I do, and you don't!"

"This marriage is all arranged to shroud your past, Harry—"

"Annie, you're just confused. Your sister's death—"

"Don't bring Clarisse into this! Why did you come here?"

"Abbot summoned me, and my father demanded that I respond. He's right! You're headstrong and in need of guidance."

"What is it about you that these two can command your every move, Harry? What is it that you haven't told me?"

"I don't understand you."

"Don't you? Isn't there a certain trial in only two weeks that would decide a new fate for you if my uncle had not intervened?"

Harry shifted, hurling a wary gaze toward her.

"I know about the trial, Harry!"

"It doesn't concern you."

"This is all about you and Rogan Farrell, isn't it? This isn't about us at all."

"You're talking nonsense."

"You did it, didn't you? You took the money—"

"Shut up, woman! I've listened to you long enough!" Harry grabbed her by the shoulders, drew back his hand, and held it in midair, his eyes fiery with rage.

"Go ahead, hit me, Harry! Prove your love to me!"

He shoved her away and made fast for the drink cabinet.

"That's it, have a drink and see it all through clouded eyes!"

"You're ruining everything! You realize that Abbot will find your sister. He'll send her away for what she's done and you along with her," he said. "Then what of your little brothers?" He pulled out a flask and a glass.

"What interests me more is what will happen to you."

"I'll be a free man."

"Will you? Rogan Farrell's hired a lawyer, you know."

"I'm a witness to a crime, or haven't you heard?" Harry downed one glass of rum, then poured himself another. He laughed, low and full of himself.

"You're a known liar."

"Who doesn't lie, Annie? You're a liar, just like your deceitful sister who's run off to marry her cousin's fiancé. You're no different than any of us. You simply decorate your lies with pretense the same way you feather your worn-out hats."

"I'm no liar, but you're vicious!"

"I'm a desperate man, but no more desperate than you are. You'll storm about with your tantrums like a spoiled child. Then you'll do exactly what's expected of you. And we'll have a grand life, Mrs. Winston—"

"I don't want to hear any more!"

"Then you don't want to face reality. You're penniless without this marriage. That's why, in just a few weeks, you'll be walking the chapel aisle—"

"What are you talking about?"

"—all bound up with your proprieties and your lies under a white veil of resolve. You'll marry me, all right."

"I won't!"

He wiped the rum from his lips, pulled her against him, and pressed a hard, mean kiss against her mouth. She struggled to pull away, but his strength overwhelmed her. She felt the tears trickle down her face, felt him force himself on her, felt her will washed away with the reality of his words. She crumpled against him, sobbing, loathing him all the more.

Harry reached to stroke her hair and pressed his face gently against her own as Abbot and Sybil entered the parlor.

"Ah, look at them now." Sybil folded her arms at her bodice, smiling in a self-satisfied way.

"You were right all along, Sybil," Abbot said. "Looks as though things are all patched up."

"Just a misunderstanding. All better now." Harry held her on both sides of her face and kissed her once more.

Helplessness swarmed Annie's emotions. She had to find a place far away from them all to gather her thoughts, to think clearly again, and to pray.

24

THE RESCUE

"It fits so well. Don't you think so, Doris?" Sybil stood away from Annie, admiring the hat she had handed to her.

Doris said nothing.

"She'll make a beautiful bride," the shop clerk said.

"You'll be all the talk of England when you and Harry call on his family there," Sybil said.

"It's a visiting bonnet." The clerk beamed.

"I don't need any more hats, Aunt Sybil." Annie stood with arms folded as the shop owner's wife placed one hat after another upon her head.

"Why, you've scarcely any at all. I won't have the Winstons thinking you ill-bred, coming into their family without a proper trousseau."

Numb to the preparations of the past few weeks, Annie had begun to imagine herself as an object being fitted with things unnecessary, yet outwardly showy, for all of Sybil's friends to envy. Without comment, she handed the black velvet bonnet back to the woman and then turned to stare out the large glass window overlooking George Street. She ignored Sybil's impatient sigh and tucked the loose strands of her hair back into place, her face drawn and sullen.

"Annie, at least tell us which ones you prefer."

She offered no reply.

"Well, then, I'll pick them out for her. . . ."

More engaged in the talk on the street than her own wedding, she observed the group of merchants gathered outside the open shop door. A worse depression had settled on Sydney. The hotel business had completely collapsed. Trade had been hurt further by the separation of Melbourne from New South Wales. Many talked about the new colony, Victoria. She surmised from their talk that the citizenry there enjoyed their prospering new economy and cared nothing for the struggling Sydneyites. But most of all, her thoughts were drawn to Isabelle.

Annie stepped away from the doorway and called out for a newspaper. A tall smudge-faced lad accommodated her. The headlines heralded the mass exodus from Sydney to California for the gold rush. More than a thousand persons had left already. Annie felt as though everyone was leaving except her. The ships that did return to Sydney Harbor carried the newly prospering men, who only had returned to retrieve their families and leave again for California. Reading further only served to drive the dissatisfaction deeper into her emotions.

A buckboard rolled by loaded down with a family and all of their belongings. "Headed for Yorkie's Corner!" the husband shouted to his neighbors. "Not comin' back 'til I'm rich!"

Laughter ensued.

She rolled up the paper and stuffed it into a waste barrel. She hadn't slept, it seemed, in weeks, not since her fight with Harry. Her worried prayers hadn't ceased, but she had yet to hear any clear answer. Harry, cocksure of the verdict, had left no doubt in her mind about Rogan's fate.

His comely face would come to her in the night, and she would remember how he trusted her. Annie had gotten out of bed once to stare out her window at the jail. In her sleepy stupor, she had admitted to herself that thoughts of him had frequently occupied her mind. She wanted to run to him, unlock the jail, tell him to run away, to save himself. But then she would never see him again. Her selfishness would be the death of him.

She was so afraid Rogan would see the anxiety in her face that she had sent a servant with the bag of goods to the jail early this morning. She hoped her gift would speak to him, tell him he was in her thoughts. But she couldn't go and tell him herself. If he so much as asked her one question about the trial, she knew she would not be able to hold back. Implicating her own family now in a trial that was fast capturing the public eye would bring about more chaos than she could handle. But allowing an innocent man to be hanged was heinous. Either way she would hate herself.

Annie approached the husband on the buckboard. While he loaded supplies onto the back, she stood beside him, unsure of what to say.

"Hello, miss." He tipped his large hat and wiped his brow with his hand.

"I'm sorry to bother you, sir."

"No bother."

"Did you say you're going to Yorkie's Corner?"

"They's talk of a gold strike there, miss. Lots o' folks goin', not just me."

"Where exactly is Yorkie's Corner? Not in California?"

"No, miss! Gold's 'ere, right 'ere in New South Wales. Don't 'ave to go to no California to find it." He held out a map.

Annie studied his rudimentary scrawlings.

"Go past Parrametta, over the Blue Mountains—blimey, all you gotta do is follow the swarm o' wagons!"

"Is it near Victoria?"

"On the way."

"Thank you, sir."

Annie looked up to see Sybil staring at her through the store window. She swallowed hard, feeling nervous about what she had just done. Even more nervous about what she was thinking.

"Aunt Sybil?" She stepped back into the mercantile, gripped by her own boldness.

"Yes, dear, have you decided?"

"Yes, I have. I'll be needing some of these things." Her thoughts in disarray, she stopped at a table loaded down with kitchenware.

"But you can supply your kitchen when you return from England."

"I want to do it now. And I will have some bonnets, but not those." She marched to the aisle opposite where Sybil and the shopkeeper stood. Selecting some practical bonnets along with some cotton frocks, she bundled them up and handed them to the lady. "This is what I want."

"You can't be caught looking like that in England."

She ignored Sybil, continuing with her buying binge until she felt completely satisfied that she had all she truly needed.

"You surprise me," Sybil said.

"I've some money. I'll pay for it."

"No, I'll pay." Sybil blushed, smiling woodenly at the clerk. She drew out her purse.

"I believe we've only a half hour until we pick up my wedding dress."

"I believe you're right. We mustn't keep Mrs. Plenty waiting. Oh, and we should mail the wedding invitations. So much to do." She turned to acknowledge the shopkeeper.

"Mother, we didn't bring the wedding invitations," Doris said.

Annie saw the exasperation on Sybil's face.

"They have to go out at once!" Sybil said.

"I'll see they do. That should be my responsibility." Annie made a note and dropped it into her purse.

"Will this be all, Mrs. Dearborn?"

"I suppose we'll return later this week to properly select her trousseau items. My niece has always been the practical sort, but I'll help her out with these." She selected three hats along with enough laces to fill two trunks.

Annie protested, but it was now Sybil who ignored her.

"I only wish my young Dolly had some of her qualities," the clerk said. "She spends money as fast as my dear husband can make it." The clerk laughed.

"Aunt Sybil, would you mind? I've left my parasol in the carriage and the sun's come out."

"Not at all."

Annie couldn't determine if Sybil's gaze was suspicious. She waited for her aunt and Doris to step outside, then made her way at once to a different table, where she gathered up some more clothing items.

"Miss Carraway, did you know you've picked up a pair of men's trousers?" The lady's brow furrowed as she glanced over her spectacles at her.

"Yes, it's not a mistake. These are practical, aren't they?"

"Sturdy as they come." She shrugged and turned to tally up the total for Annie.

"I want to pay for part of this. Just don't tell her." Annie emptied her coin purse. She had her largest sum tucked away at home in a hatbox.

"If you insist, miss." The clerk gathered up the money.

Before Sybil could return, Annie tucked her selections under the cotton dresses.

"You are the practical one." The clerk began folding up the trousers first.

"You've heard all the talk about Victoria? I hear it's a lovely settlement."

A ring shone around the moon, electrifying the night sky before it became masked with fog. The Australian summer had begun to wane, turning the days cooler and ushering in the evening with skeins of gray fog. His face resting against the window bars, Rogan gazed up and listened hard to the silence. He wanted to hear Frederick's horse approach, wanted to tell him that he would go with him now without hesitation. But all he could hear was the restless shuffle of the guard's feet and a sour, breathy whistle the sentry made whenever the monotony had overtaken him. Barclay had come by again today. The April tenth trial date had only made him more restless during the last month. He backed away from the bars, and his movement set off a cicada, which in turn set off a chorus of them.

The bag of toiletries sent to him by Annie lay atop the table untouched. The fact that she didn't deliver them personally annoyed him. But everything she had said to him made him wonder if she could really go through with the wedding. Whether she did or didn't, he only knew that he had to see her again. If he could look into her eyes and know for certain that he had no chance with her—

"Farrell, you idiot!" He could kick himself for his wishful thinking.

Impatience got the best of him. He snatched up the bag and peered into it. Annie had sent him some more soap, a hair comb, even another shirt. He shook his head, then smiled. Whatever her reasons for sending him the items, he couldn't help but wonder if she ever thought about him.

After he had rolled up the bag and laid it aside, he stood at the window again to watch the moon. It had been huge and bright all week. He had found himself thanking God for little things like that.

Rogan picked up the news article from California, his eyes drawn again to the spot that Frederick had circled. The newspaper clipping had faded, along with the hope his brother had held for his escape to the gold fields. *I should have gone with you the first day you asked. You were right all along, Freddy.*

Rogan felt more helpless than he had ever felt in his life. His grandmother had dropped by that afternoon. Before she left, she prayed. Usually uncomfortable when she prayed aloud, he felt more at ease with it than in the past. This time he sincerely wanted her to pray, believing that God listened when she talked to Him.

He gripped the windowsill now and dropped his head.

"God, I know I haven't said much to you lately. But I sure could use some help—"

A hard, clattering noise shattered the silence. Rogan heard the guard shout and then watched as his shadowy frame rushed past the window. He ran, too, and stopped at the window to follow the man's trek into the dark woods just beyond the jail and stables. A howl arose. Rogan recognized the baying of the Dearborns' hunting dogs. He was so hardbent on watching the man that he didn't see the door handle twist.

"Rogan?"

He whipped around, startled by a woman's voice. "What in the w—"

"I've no time for details, but your life's in danger. Please come with me."

"Annie! Where are we going?"

"I'll explain along the way. I've a wagon made ready at the end of the Dearborn road."

"They'll hang me if I run off!"

"They'll hang you if you stay!"

Struck by the candor of her gaze, he studied her anxious stance, the way she stood poised and ready to bolt. Rogan snatched up his few belongings along with the bag she had sent him. He shot her a look of worry. She ran and snatched up his bedroll and draped it with a blanket to make it look as though he were sleeping. Baffled, he threw on his coat and hat and followed her through the doorway.

"I don't want to get you in trouble, Annie."

"I'm already in trouble. Let's go before I change my mind."

They traveled for hours, scarcely exchanging a word between themselves. Since they had left the jail locked up tight, their escape might go unnoticed until daybreak. Rogan watched her slumped on the carriage seat, her eyes struggling to stay open as she gripped the reins. He heaved a sigh, slid on his gloves, and took the reins from her. "My turn."

"All right, but keep heading down this road until we reach this fork in the road here." She lifted the hand-drawn map.

"Want to tell me where we're headed?"

"It's a new territory. They're calling it Victoria."

"It's a long way to Victoria."

"First we're stopping at Parrametta. Then on to Penrith, our stop just before we begin to cross the Blue Mountains."

"Mind telling me why?"

"To get to Bathurst. We have to cross the Blue Mountains to—"

"No. I mean, why are we headed to Victoria in the first place?"

"For one, I didn't want to see you hanged."

"Nice of you, Annie."

"Let's find a clearing and stop for a while," she said. "I want to rest."

"We should rest the horses too. Here's a clearing, but we'd do better to circle around it and hide our camp just behind that stand of trees."

"Let's not set up camp tonight, Rogan. We can make our beds in the carriage."

"Fancy bed."

"I was in a hurry."

Rogan turned the horses into the clearing but had to stop just short of a stream bed that he hadn't anticipated.

"What's wrong?"

"Not a good place. We're out in the open."

Annie alighted, then turned to make her way into the carriage.

"Where are you going?"

She hesitated, her voice wavering with a hint of worry. "I have to sleep for just a little while."

"Where am *I* going?"

"I urge you to keep to our course until you find a better stopping place."

"Thanks a heap."

Annie made haste to unfold the supply of blankets she had stashed inside the carriage along with her other personal supplies. Exasperated when the box of wedding invitations scattered out of the crate, she bent to gather them up. She had found them in Abbot's study. Sybil, in her absentminded frenzy, had left them there. To insure they weren't sent out, Annie had gathered them into her belongings.

As soon as they reached the first settlement, she would discard them. With all but one invitation stashed away, she snatched up the last one. It was smaller than the others and had a handwriting she didn't recognize. Annie turned it over and discovered it was not an invitation at all, but a letter to Abbot.

She started to put it away but feared it might be something legal, something important that he might miss right away. In her haste to gather up the invitations from atop his credenza, she had apparently scooped up this letter.

"Besides saving my neck, would there be any other reason you're doing this?" Rogan had stepped down and now stood behind, watching her.

"I also have reason to believe my sister may be in Victoria." She tucked the letter into her pocket.

"When did she leave?" Rogan asked.

"A few days ago."

"Left with that Lafferty chap, didn't she?"

"How did you know?"

"Lucky guess."

"At any rate, I don't know how long it takes to get there, so I brought along plenty of food as well as some pots and pans. We should be well supplied until we reach the settlement." Before closing the door, she heard him shout something she couldn't understand. She opened the door and peered out.

"Not to sound ungrateful, but have you any money?"

"A little. I've also a few things I can sell. Finery that the women in Victoria will pay a high price for."

"You hope. By the way, did you know people are saying that gold's been found in Melbourne?"

"I've heard about Yorkie's Corner. Do you believe it?"

"Sounds like something concocted to me. A half-witted shepherd can steal some jewelry, melt it down, hammer around on it for a bit. Looks just like ore."

"I've heard that."

"Nobody believes it, or else Victoria would be overrun with diggers."

"Rogan?"

"What?"

"They say Victoria *is* overrun with diggers."

"Let's get moving, then."

She popped a blanket in the air and pulled it over herself. "We will, after I sleep a bit."

"You're sure of that—about the diggers, I mean?" Rogan asked.

"Fairly certain."

"Does your family know you're headed that way?"

She snugged down onto the carriage seat, and her voice softened as sleep overtook her. "Well, they can't find Isabelle, which means they'll have trouble finding me."

Rogan kept driving while Annie slept. After a short while, the horses seemed to be having some difficulty, so he jumped down to check their hooves. He shook his head, turned, and glanced around, spying a side path. He would have to rest the team of horses or they would never make the next day's journey. Instead of rustling up a good sturdy buckboard, she had taken an expensive carriage. He hoped Annie realized that an elegant clarence would no more scale a mountain than would the queen herself. She at least had pilfered two good horses from Dearborn's best stable. *But we'll need tents and other supplies.* His speculative thoughts suddenly sounded ludicrous to his weary mind. He whipped the team into motion again.

Tonight's events had set off a war inside of him. Not several hours hence, he had daydreamed about being alone with Annie Carraway. Now that he had his wish, he didn't know how to act. Common sense told him that he couldn't up and run off with the niece of the man who planned to have him hanged. That gave Dearborn too many reasons to hunt him down. Besides, to hide from him, he needed more distance, the kind offered in California. He wished that Frederick hadn't been so long in coming back. By reading the newspaper, Rogan had studied gold digging with the same zeal he had studied architecture. He was ready for California, but if he couldn't make his way back to Frederick soon, he'd go without him.

Then he thought of Annie sleeping so peacefully in the carriage, trusting him to do the right thing. By including him in her plan of escape, she had endangered herself. Dearborn would send armed men out to bring him back, and Annie would be caught in the fray. He couldn't allow it. He would take her as far as the next settlement, help her find a trustworthy driver, and send her on ahead to join her sister. She wouldn't understand, he realized. But it would be better for them both if he didn't tell her everything.

A trickle of warm sunshine fell across Annie's hand. During the night, she had flung her arm half over the wagon's open window. She slept in a restful state, in spite of the anxiety that pursued her. She shivered and opened her eyes, half expecting Rogan would be gone. But the aroma of frying bacon startled her fully awake. She pulled the tangle of pins from her hair and spent a few moments refashioning her hair into a golden coif.

Noticing her rumpled dress, she decided to change. With Rogan busy preparing breakfast, it would offer her a few minutes to freshen up. She unfastened the cotton frock and dropped it to her feet. When she picked it up to fold it away, the letter fluttered from her pocket. Weary from their frenzied getaway, she had fallen asleep without looking at it again.

Annie picked it up and opened it. She could see right away that the letter was of a personal nature, the handwriting obviously female. The contents nearly took her breath away.

Dear Eugene,

I'm never certain if you receive my letters, since I've never gotten any from you. Our daughter, Abigail, has grown so much. She has your eyes and your temperament. I want you to know that this may be the last letter from me. Perhaps the news gladdens you, but as I've told you in the past, there's never been anyone in my life but you. You gave me the only family I've ever known, and she is precious to me. . . .

"You awake in there, Annie?"

"I'm not dressed! Just a minute!" She shoved the letter into the box of invitations.

"Might want to hurry. The morning could bring all kinds of problems down on us."

Annie pulled out another of the cotton frocks and threw it on. She grabbed her slippers and stepped out to find Rogan squatted next to an open campfire.

"Caught a few hours of sleep after all. I feel rested enough to get us going."

"You cook, I see."

"Not as well as you, I'm sure."

"I've had little opportunity, actually."

"You can do the honors this evening." Rogan stirred the meat around in circles in the sizzling fat.

"At the next settlement I'll seek out a Chinese cook." Annie slipped her feet into her satin shoes.

"If you've that kind of money, it would do you well to set it aside. You'll need it for your return home."

"I'm not going back home."

"Why? Has someone made you angry?"

"It's more complicated, actually. Isabelle's married now. My two brothers have been sent off to England to attend a boarding school. There's just nothing left for me at Dearborn Manor."

"What about a wedding?"

She hesitated long enough to make him stop and look up.

"There's not going to be a wedding," she said.

"Lovers' quarrel?"

"No. There's no love between us—and never has been."

"I'm glad to hear it." Rogan plopped the meat into the lid of the pan.

His words stirred a bit of contention inside of her, and she flashed him a questioning look.

"You never had the look of love in you; that's all I mean."

"Oh, that bacon smells good," Annie said, anxious to change the subject. "Let's eat, shall we?"

"We should eat on the run. If they haven't organized a search party for you, they'll for certain have a lynch mob out scouring the roads for me."

"But the sun's scarcely up. I say we give ourselves some time to eat first."

"Bottoms up!" Rogan handed her the lid brimming with bacon along with a billy of hot black tea.

She stared with distaste suddenly at the greasy meat and the scorched tin billy. It didn't look as good as it had smelled.

"You should keep up your strength. Just living on the trail's a hard day's work. Can't survive without sustenance."

"I'll have mine on a plate, thank you."

"You go and find the plate, then, there amidst your pile of boxes." He shoved the billy and the pot lid into her hands and turned to retrieve the horses.

She watched him march away with determination in his gait. His actions would have normally sparked a surly reply from her, but instead she felt surprised. She held the billy to her lips and sipped gingerly. She didn't mind strong tea, but this brew could sprout legs and walk. As she turned to sit down, a stone caught her slipper. Stumbling, she tipped the billy sideways, which sent the tea spilling to the ground. She looked around to see that Rogan had returned. His dark brows were pinched together and his mouth was tight. She saw she'd aroused his ire.

"You did that on purpose."

"I didn't. Really. Did you want that for yourself?"

"No, I've had mine already!"

"More of this, then?" She held out the greasy pot lid full of bacon. Not balancing the lid properly, it tipped too, although that hadn't been her intention either. Her fingers scrambled to catch it all, but the bacon found its grave next to the spilled tea.

"Are you going to tell me that was an accident as well?"

"I swear it was." She laughed.

"Then why are you laughing?"

"I don't know. You just—you're funny when you're angry."

"You're spoiled! You've had everything given to you."

Now his words did spark anger in her. She lowered her greasy hands and looked away. Exasperated, she climbed back into the carriage. Finding a cloth inside one of the boxes, she wiped her hands and began searching for her practical new bonnet. Occasionally she would glance up to find him watching her through the window, but then he would direct his gaze away. He gathered up the pots and kicked dirt onto the fire, his actions growing more and more intense. The longer the silence between them, the more furious he appeared to grow. She hadn't meant to anger him, but his mood suggested he wouldn't accept her apology. Silence, she determined, was her best weapon against his sharp tongue. She would make note to use it whenever possible.

"She's gone!" Ada stood in stunned silence in Annie's room. In a fit of hysteria, the maid had awakened Doris. The girl had muttered that Annie had retired early, but the bundle of blankets beneath Annie's sheets revealed an empty bed. Ada whirled around and shook Doris with vigor.

"Please let me sleep just a little longer, Ada."

"Did Annie go down to breakfast already? Have I just missed 'er?"

"I don't know, Ada." Doris tried to roll over, but the maid persisted.

She saw Annie's wardrobe door ajar and approached it with caution. She looked into it and found that it had been emptied of all of its contents. A panic swirled through her. Even the magnificent new bridal gown was gone.

Doris pulled the sheet over her head.

"Doris, run fetch your mum! Miss Annie's up and run off just like 'er sister!"

Doris merely sat on the side of the bed in a sleepy stupor. "Wonder whose husband *she* took."

25

THE MOUNTAIN'S SHADOW

Annie rode inside while Rogan drove the dusty toll road for forty miles. They reached Penrith after sundown. The mountain wall towered above them, rocky and tree shrouded, only a mile ahead. She tightened the ropes on her boxes as she felt the carriage heave twice before coming to a stop. Glad to leave behind the cramped confines of the carriage, she longed for the comfort of a soft bed. She had heard about an inn and a livery stable where travelers could rest their horses for the night. The money she had set aside in the past year, although meager, would provide for her journey until she arrived in Victoria. She had more than enough to get them to Bathurst. Once there, she would sell the wedding gown, as well as those pretentious bonnets that Aunt Sybil had insisted upon buying for her.

"Sun'll be down soon. We'll camp here for the night." Rogan opened the carriage door.

She couldn't help but notice how edgy he'd been all day, not at all like he'd been in the jail.

He began shoving her personals aside, broke open crates, and foraged for blankets.

"I'd be glad to show you where everything is."

Instead of answering, he heaved a sigh as though everything she said annoyed him.

"You realize we don't have to camp, Rogan. I have some money. We can stay in a roadside inn. I know of one—"

"Are you insane? I'm an escaped convict! They'll soon be circulating my picture around every borough, every postal stop, from here to California. The fewer people we come in contact with, the better."

A heaviness settled upon Annie. She had imagined that things would be so different between them. She hadn't bargained for his opinions being shoved in her face at every turn. "Rogan, I'm tired. You've driven all day and you're weary as well. I'll find us an inn, pay for it, and make the arrangements. No one will see your face."

"Too risky."

"You're so stubborn!"

"*I'm* stubborn?"

"You've little recourse. Everything belongs to me, you've no money, and—"

"I believe *you're* the one without options."

"Why do you say that?"

"A lady of your station wandering around the wilderness, a prime target for bushrangers. We'll do as I say." He pulled out two blankets and shoved aside the crates that she had placed on the opposite seat. Then he took one of the blankets and began making a bed of it.

"You needn't make a bed for me. I'm perfectly capable."

"This is my bed."

"You can't sleep in here with me!"

"Storm's coming. You neglected to bring tents in your haste to pack your—" he held up a red velvet bonnet, plumed in red and green feathers—"your *best* bonnets."

"I'm selling those!" She yanked the hat from him, ignoring his mocking stare.

"I would too."

"You needn't be so snappish!"

"No one leaves on a journey without tents is all I'm saying."

"I couldn't purchase tents in plain sight of everyone. We can make purchases in Penrith in the morning, if need be."

"We'll need to do more than that. This carriage will have to go. The road across to Bathurst is rocky. And after a downpour like the one headed our way, we'd do best with a couple of riding horses. Can you ride?"

"Of course I can ride. But we'll still need a wagon. I've got to have room for all of my . . . my things."

"I know, your bonnets. You can sell it all here in Penrith and be done with it."

"Penrith has few settlers, certainly no women of means. I've much finery to sell and I'll not give it away."

"Suit yourself. But the road through those mountains is treacherous."

"I believe you. We can trade this carriage for a wagon here if that suits you. We'll keep the team. Once we're in Bathurst, you'll see that a wagon's a practical means of transportation." Thunder rattled the windows. Annie placed the bonnets back into the straw and set about making her own bed.

"I'm going to unhitch the team and tie them up outside under that stand of trees. Not as good as that stable they're accustomed to every night."

"The horses will be fine." Exasperated and struggling to maintain a conciliatory tone, Annie watched him leave. Bristling, she yanked up one of the blankets that he had reserved for himself. By fastening the corners into the side windows she could create a privacy wall between the two seats. In spite of his wisdom in keeping their whereabouts hidden from any nosy locals, he understood little in the way of decorum. Their sleeping together in close quarters was not part of her plan. Once they reached Bathurst, she would pay for her own accommodations no matter what he said.

Lightning streaked overhead, followed by another chorus of thunder.

Rogan Farrell, you can sleep out in the rain for all it matters to me.

Rogan stroked the horses' necks to calm them. Between the wind and thunder, the oncoming storm had made the animals jittery. He also needed to calm himself. More than once, he should have bit his tongue, reined in his temper. But he had to prepare himself for their upcoming separation, had to keep his mind on placing Annie out of harm's way. But getting her there was half the battle. Having left with nothing but a knapsack of clothes, he had little platform to stand on when it came to asserting himself with Annie. But she knew nothing of traveling along wilderness trails. She wouldn't last an hour on the passes through the Blue Mountains. Hacked out by convict labor, the mountain trails had created the open door to the township of Bathurst and to further colonization. However, the road over the steep terrain and across swelling riverbeds offered little more than a footpath in some places. The fact that she had left with a costly carriage and a bagful of feathers and shiny buttons to ascend a mountainous terrain might have sent him into fits of laughter if the harsh reality of it all hadn't loomed so large. *I'll bet a bag of money she didn't bring any firearms.* He couldn't believe that he hadn't asked her sooner. He spotted her through the window bobbing back and forth like a peahen. In spite of her mulish ways, she cut a pretty picture. As much as she had layered yards and yards of fabric around her curvaceous frame, she couldn't hide her assets from the world or his discriminating eye. "Annie?" He used an authoritative tone, the one that always sent sparks flying from her glistening blue eyes.

"What do you want?"

He heard her cool reply, the tone that stood steadfast in the frozen etiquette of her correctness. She had used it on him when they'd first met. She never looked out at him but kept to her busy duties, however many she could find within the limited restraints of that infernal carriage.

"How many firearms did you bring along with you?"

"Firearms?"

He felt a swell of smug satisfaction. "Yes, firearms. You know, you put bullets in them, they go *bang-bang!*"

"But I was told that travelers don't carry firearms through the mountains. Bushrangers will kill you for them."

"Not if you kill them first."

"That's dreadful. I could never."

Rogan saw her raise her arms—graceful, slender arms that lifted the blanket up high and then allowed it to fall, so that she could bend and press its soft folds into the carriage seat with the gentle, feminine precision that few women he knew possessed. "More dreadful to be dead."

Instead of tossing back the caustic reply he expected, she turned her back to the window.

"It's going to be a long, cold night." He breathed out a sigh and pulled his coat around himself to block out the stormy wind.

The carriage rocked and swayed in the storm. It was a little unsettling to Annie, but she refused to let on. She waited for Rogan Farrell to disappear behind the blanket she had hung up. Then she pulled her feet beneath the quilted coverlet and slipped off her shoes. With her toes, she pressed her slippers into a corner. She wanted to be certain she could don them in a hurry if need be. She could hear him clearing his throat and breathing out a few exasperated sighs. She wondered if he felt as uncomfortable as she did, but she couldn't bring herself to ask him what he felt. That would be too intrusive, and exchanging pleasantries had proven impossible.

"Scared of storms?"

"No, I'm not afraid." His question surprised her.

"Good. Some women are afraid, you know."

"I'm not one of those women."

"Good."

She felt herself nod in affirmation, although he couldn't see her at all. She curled beneath the coverlet and pulled the quilt up close to her face, waiting for the chill to subside.

The wagon shifted in the wind. Something began to bang against the side.

She sat up.

"Just a loose rope."

"I know. Good night." She had spoken it every night to someone for as long as she could remember. Lonesome for Mussy, Annie felt a need to say it to someone, even if that person was not so desirous of hearing it.

"Good night, Annie."

"Rogan?"

"What is it?"

"Do you think they'll find us—my uncle and the Sydney authorities, I mean."

"I'm not an experienced outlaw, Annie. This is my first time."

"I know, but surely you've thought about it."

"Yes, I've thought about it. Did you mention to anyone that you were interested in Victoria? Did you ask many questions about it? You know, such as how to get there and the like?" Rogan asked.

"Not to anyone I know. I was careful in that regard, I believe."

"Any strangers?"

"I don't believe I mentioned it to a single soul. I read everything I know about it in the newspaper."

"That's good."

She snuggled her face against her pillow.

"So where did you get the map?"

"Oh no, I had forgotten . . ."

"I was afraid of that."

"But the man was a complete stranger on his way there, probably already on his way. Not to worry." She pulled up the covers around her face again.

"I trust you're right."

"So do you think they'll find us?"

"Maybe not. But if I know Abbot Dearborn, he'll search every inch of New South Wales and beyond. He's a calculating man. Hates to lose."

"That he does, but he hasn't found Isabelle and Charles." She closed her eyes and tried to see her sister's face again.

"You don't know that for certain."

"I just feel that he hasn't. Perhaps it's all just empty hope."

"That fiancé of yours and his family, they'll be looking for you too. Probably think I kidnapped you."

"Surely they won't think that, or would they? Harry won't. I think he'll know the truth."

"Harry?"

Self-annoyance shot through her emotions.

Rogan pulled back the curtain and cast a suspicious gaze her way.

"Didn't I tell you? I was engaged to Harry Winston." The fact that he didn't reply at once should have prepared her for his next reaction. Yet, when he yanked back the blanket curtain that separated them and yelled his response, she couldn't help but recoil.

"Harry Winston!"

"Calm yourself!" She sat upright, yet kept the blanket in front of her and up around her face.

"You've known all along then—you knew about Harry and me, knew about the trial, and didn't tell me!"

"I kept waiting for the right time."

"Yesterday would have been good!"

"Why yesterday? Why not now?"

"I wouldn't have come with you!"

"You didn't have a choice!"

"Didn't I? What's the difference between dying now or dying later?"

Annie didn't answer.

After several yanks on the curtain, Rogan had pulled it between them again.

Another lightning bolt made Annie cringe.

"How could I have been so thickheaded? *You're* the girl they picked to settle him down, aren't you?"

Again, she didn't know how to answer.

"You should have known better than to get tangled up with the likes of him."

"Abbot forced me—threatened to make Isabelle leave if I didn't."

"Why Isabelle?"

"Because Isabelle fell in love with Charles Lafferty. The Laffertys and the Dearborns had arranged the courtship and—Rogan, stop laughing."

"I can't help myself! It's all too unbelievable!"

"I'm going to sleep. You're incorrigible!" His cynicism aroused a spark of anger in her. Clutching the blanket curtain, she closed it the remainder of the way, then found her place on the seat in the pitch black darkness. She decided it best to ignore him and had all but settled back into her cocoon of angry piety when a jagged claw of lightning ripped through the sky. She bolted upright and shrieked, believing the carriage had been struck.

"It's all right!" he said. "Probably hit a tree, not us." He drew back the multipatterned throw.

She could see his face outlined in sporadic electric flickers. He had stopped laughing at her, and she could see a hint of concern.

"Why don't you let me keep the curtain open partway? That way you won't feel so alone."

"I . . . I don't feel alone." She cut her eyes to the floor.

"Well, I do. Let's just keep it open for my sake, why don't we?"

"If it makes you feel better."

She studied him for a while, nothing passing between them but a glimmer of mistrust.

"Time for sleep. Got some mountains to climb in the morning."

She watched him turn his back to her, then waited for the rhythmic breathing indicating he had fallen into a much-needed slumber. Anxiety pricked at her senses, teasing her with the fact that sleep had not embraced her so quickly. But the worries she had tossed aside in the daylight now came running back to whisper their dissonant song into her ears. Rogan had been more perceptive than she had been willing to admit. She did feel alone. She *was* alone. With Mussy gone and her brothers in England, God had answered her prayers—that they would all escape Abbot's control. But her answered prayers had left her feeling barren. God had made a way for everyone except herself. Isabelle had found love, the boys a future. But she had nothing except a stolen carriage, a broken promise, and an escaped outlaw at her side. *I thought my faith was strong, Lord, but it isn't. The more I try to find your will, the farther I run from it.* She drifted to sleep in spite of her worries, the thunder, and the rain, forgetful that she was tucked safe beneath the mountain's shadow.

26
A REASONABLE END

"Ada, come in here!" Dearborn sat at his desk.

"You be needin' me, sir?"

"I got a letter from England the other day. Have you seen it?"

"I haven't, Judge Dearborn. Would you like for me to ask about?"

"Don't do that. I'll keep looking. Did I just hear someone at the door?"

"I was just on my way to tell you, you've company, sir," Ada said.

"Who is it?"

"It's the Farrells' lawyer, that Barclay man. I told them it's Sunday an' all but—"

"What does he want?"

"He's brought Mr. Farrell's brother. They've requested an audience with you and—"

"Send them away."

"Abbot, I think you should see them. How would it look if you refused them?" Sybil stepped from behind the maid. She appeared nervous.

"Have they said anything, Ada, as to why they're here?" Annoyance shot from his face with a reserve of worry in his eyes.

"No, but I'm sure they'll be askin' the whereabouts o' Rogan Farrell. Most likely, sir."

"Have some tea made, Ada," Sybil said.

"They'll not be staying that long." Dearborn remembered that Frederick Farrell had visited Rogan on numerous occasions. The night they disappeared, the guard had reported a disturbance with the dogs. Someone had assisted Farrell. Wherever the convict had taken his niece, he had felt certain that the Farrell clan would know of it. So it surprised him to hear that the brother of the escapee had come to pay a visit. He reached for the newspaper clipping the guard had found atop the drafting table in the jail. He felt another surge of anger ripple through him.

"Judge Dearborn?"

"Mr. Barclay." Dearborn stood and extended his hand to the lawyer. Rogan's brother followed him into the room but didn't offer his hand.

"Thank you, sir, for meeting us on such short notice," Barclay said.

"What can I do for the two of you?"

"I want to know where my brother is!" Frederick said before Barclay could stop him.

"We all do, Mr. Farrell." Dearborn didn't like his tone.

"Please pardon us if we appear somewhat shaken," Barclay said. "But Rogan Farrell's disappearance has taken the Farrell family by surprise—has us all in a quandary."

"Is this true, Frederick? Have you absolutely no idea where your brother's run off to?" Dearborn held out the yellowed clipping.

"Rogan and I wanted to go to California, it's true." Frederick hesitated, then gingerly took the clipping about the gold rush.

"I suspected as much," Dearborn said.

"But he wouldn't speak of it until this trial was settled and behind him. He felt he could win in spite of the doubts I had about it."

"I believe that the judge has no more idea about your brother's whereabouts than you do, Frederick," Barclay said.

"It's all senseless. This isn't like my brother at all," Frederick said. "Dearborn, I'll be keeping an eye on you. If Rogan's harmed in any way, I'll be back here to ask you why."

"You think I killed your brother? Hid his body somewhere?"

"Frederick, I don't think—"

"Nothing would surprise me." Frederick ignored Barclay's warnings.

"Well, it seems we have a mutual mistrust. It does appear that we're both truly baffled. But you realize that with my dear niece missing, your brother Rogan is suspect to a kidnapping?"

"Rogan wouldn't kidnap your niece. She invited him here to dinner a few times in your absence. Perhaps you should ask her about her interest in him."

"If he told you that, he's a liar!"

"Ask your maid, then. She knows about it."

Dearborn studied Frederick's face and saw nothing but honesty staring back at him.

"Mrs. Dearborn asked us to bring this in, sir." A young maid entered with tea in spite of Dearborn's order.

"Mary, come here please," Dearborn said.

"Something wrong, sir?" She filled three cups for the men.

"No. I just want to know, during my occasional absence from the manor house, was the convict in the jail, Rogan Farrell, ever invited in for dinner?"

"Not to my knowledge, Mr. Dearborn. The missus would never allow it, I don't believe." She set the tea tray on a table in front of them and curtsied.

"Thank you, Mary. That will be all." Dearborn dismissed her.

"That doesn't prove anything to me," Frederick said. "If your niece had cautioned the maids about telling, well then, they'd fear they'd lose their position. Am I right?" Frederick looked to Barclay for his approval.

"It would all be hard to prove," Barclay said.

"It's meaningless!" Dearborn snapped. "What has it to do with finding my niece?"

"I believe Frederick's point may be that your niece went with Rogan Farrell of her own accord."

"It's a lie! She's engaged to be married—"

"Sir?" Mary stood in the doorway, her slender figure hidden partway behind the door.

"What is it?" Dearborn asked.

"There was that time that all of us were gone. Remember when the poor little girl fell ill, just before she died?" She genuflected out of reverence.

"Go on, Mary."

"But you'd have to ask Ada about it. She'd be the only one who would know. The rest of us, we up and left until we was told to return."

"Summon Ada, then." Aware of the anxious silence, Dearborn grasped the cup that the maid had filled for him.

"I was sorry to hear about your niece." Barclay bowed his head out of respect.

"It was quite sad, especially for her brothers and sisters. First their father and mother, now this." He looked up to find Ada staring at him from the entranceway. Her wan complexion foretold too much already.

"May I be o' service, sir?"

"Please, Ada, assure these gentlemen, if you will, that Mr. Rogan Farrell was never entertained in the manor house by my niece or anyone else." He hoped for her own sake that she could detect the veiled threat in his eyes.

Ada took a breath, pressed her lips together, and hesitated while they all awaited her reply.

"You traded the carriage—for this?"

"No one could buy it from me, didn't have the money. I had to take the trade or else we'd be traveling by fashionable carriage over yon divide."

Annie lifted her skirts from the washboard-stiff seat and picked splinters from the fabric. She gave the old farm wagon a look of disdain.

"We'd draw attention from the bushrangers for certain in the carriage. At least you had the sense to keep the horses."

"At least? You know, I'm surprised I can dress myself in the morning. It's a wonder I can remember my name." She knew her face must have drawn up into a frown, for he looked away awkwardly, a hint of regret in his dark blue eyes. At least, she thought it was regret.

"I didn't mean—"

"We should get going, eh?" She found her gloves and donned them.

"I'm sorry if I offended you."

Annie pretended to adjust her pale green bonnet, looking away from him. She wondered if he thought all women were stupid or just one in particular.

"What did you say, Ada?" Dearborn asked.

"I said that Miss Carraway did entertain Mr. Farrell during her sister's illness."

"Why didn't you tell me, or tell someone?"

"It seemed 'armless at the time. But please don't judge the girl. It was a 'ard time for 'er, tending to young Clarisse, what with 'er being all alone."

"She wasn't alone. She had you here."

"That's not the same. And what with the Farrell man bein' so polite an' all, seemed a pity for me to fix two meals and take them two different places," she said. "He was a perfect gentleman the entire week." She smiled at Frederick.

"Entire week!" Dearborn raged.

"I feel we should excuse ourselves." Barclay bowed, an uncharacteristic blush upon his cheeks.

"I think I've heard what I came to hear," Frederick said before offering a warm smile to Ada, an act that further ignited Dearborn's ire.

"Just tell me this, Frederick—do you believe your brother is headed for California?" Dearborn asked.

"I wouldn't tell you if I knew."

At the end of his patience now, Dearborn summoned the butler. "See these gentlemen to the door, please."

"Rest assured, Judge Dearborn, that we're doing everything in our power to see that my client is found. But I must agree with Frederick—I don't believe your niece was kidnapped."

"We'll see, won't we? Good day to you!" Dearborn bristled past, hurled Ada an angry glare, and headed for his daughter's room. Doris had slept in the same room with Annie and knew more about her than anyone. She would tell him what he wanted to hear, or she'd suffer the consequences. No more family secrets. He would be the first to find Rogan Farrell and end this embarrassment to both his family and the Winstons. He had waited too long already. Time raced against him. Rogan Farrell could be nearly to California by now. He would send some men to investigate around Sydney Harbor. If no one had recognized Rogan Farrell, they would surely remember if Annie had boarded in the last few days. He seethed at the thought. It would be the last time she embarrassed him. He should have sent her away long ago. But first he would use her to find the convict. He would only have need of a plain wooden box then to bring him back in, a reasonable end for an embezzler and a kidnapper.

Annie could find no comfortable place to sit. When she sat on one of the backseats, it jarred her body so hard she thought her head would come loose. Even more uncomfortable was how the front seat jostled her around. The leather dashboard behind the horses' hooves had become so worn, it scarcely kept the mud from splashing onto her clothes.

She settled into a blanket in the wagon's rear, then glanced up to be certain Rogan didn't see her pull out Abbot's letter. She continued reading:

> I've not had the means to send Abigail to a proper school, let alone provide her with everyday means. I'm very ill, Eugene, and am not expected to last much longer. Although you will have to explain matters to your family, I've decided to send her to you. I haven't the money right now, but once I sell the small cottage where we reside—you know the one—I'll have money for her passage with some to spare. I don't want her to see me this way, see me die, so I hope to send her to you soon. Please do not hate me for this, for I have no other resources. Trust me when I tell you that Abigail is your daughter, Eugene. Take care of her. See she is given every advantage.
>
> *Sabrina Madison*

Annie read the letter several times before she tucked it away. Her memory of the lovely, refined-looking young woman stuck in her mind along with her anger at Abbot. She wondered if he thought his secret would remain one. Now a little girl would appear on his doorstep, and Annie feared the consequences for the child. He would sweep her under the rug somehow, send her to the orphan's home, find a poor family in the borough he could pay to take her off his hands. Abigail couldn't be very old, not more than six or seven. Young enough to do as she was told.

"You're awfully quiet."

"Just tired."

Annie sighed at the long, winding road ahead that rose upward into the mountains in a snaky mire. Such a stormy deluge had been unleashed the evening before that the muddy stage road threatened to bog the wagon down to its rims.

"You look a little road weary."

"I'm all right."

"You want to stop?"

"No, we should keep moving. I can't have them arresting you before I get to Victoria."

Rogan turned around, one brow lifted. Annie smiled back.

"*Touché.*"

"I couldn't very well travel these mountains alone," she said.

"Of course not. You might scare the animals."

"Must you be so cynical?"

"Sorry, cynicism runs in my convict veins."

"If you're really a convict, then why don't you just run off? What's keeping you here?"

"I'm after your money."

"Can you be serious for one moment?"

"Money makes me very serious."

She couldn't tell if he meant what he said, or if he was making light of her again. Judging by the tilt of his head, the surety of his eyes, he had a way about him that could make him pass for an undertaker. But beyond his unbending and antagonistic ways, she wondered about the occasional moment when he looked straight into her, as though he wanted to read her soul. She always looked away, not willing to have her soul read.

"I notice you like to pretend that you don't like money. But let's see how well you fare without it."

"I can get along without my uncle's support. I know how to work, in spite of what you think."

He scanned her critically.

"Those lovely hands don't know work."

"I haven't always lived with the Dearborns, you know. My father farmed."

"Now, there's something I didn't know about you."

"Not everyone wants to spill their life out all at once."

"Tell me more."

"Not now."

He heaved a sigh and tipped his hat forward to block the sun.

Or perhaps he just didn't want to look at her anymore. She didn't know for certain because he had taken to becoming as silent with her as she had been with him. He had seemed so docile in the jail. Perhaps she had made a grave error in rescuing him. Annie made her way to the front, balancing herself as she went. She climbed up the back of the seat and planted herself next to him.

"Maybe you are a farm girl." He looked away while she straightened her skirt.

Annie took a breath and prepared to comment in as reasonable a voice as she could manage. She hoped to clear the air between them. But he stiffened his back and brought his arm across her lap.

"Don't speak."

She would have protested, but the way he whispered it sent a warning through her. The horses slowed somewhat, and she saw that he tightened his grip on the reins. She heard him mutter to himself.

Both horses nickered, and their heads bobbed out of their usual rhythm.

"Is something wrong with the horses?" A voice in her head told her the answer was no.

Uneasy, she shifted and felt her slipper bump her purse. She lifted it with the toe of her shoe, then scooped it into her lap, where she hid it under her shawl.

"Look out!" Rogan ducked when two men jumped in front of the rig waving pistols in the air. He drew back his hand to smack the whip against the horses' flanks, but the youngest highwayman yelled, "Stop or I'll put a bullet in 'er 'ead!"

"Stop the horses!" Annie saw that he leveled his weapon straight at her. Rogan had already pulled back on the reins. She grabbed the seat to steady herself while the wagon jolted to an abrupt stop. With her eyes fastened on the highwaymen, she saw that one man was older and walked with a pronounced limp. Once he had laid eyes on her, he never took his gaze from her.

"We don't have any weapons. Don't either of you get nervous with those pistols." Rogan held up his hands.

"What do you want?" Annie asked.

"Let me do the talking." Rogan gripped her wrist.

"Search the wagon!" The younger man ran fast to Rogan's side of the rig as he barked out orders to his anxious companion. He had a hard frown and a merciless expression that challenged

Rogan to react. "Give me one reason to pull this trigger and I will."

His dark hair was pulled back in an oily queue, and Annie noticed his habit of raking his fingers through the crown of his head in a nervous manner. She pulled her shawl closer, keeping her bag hidden beneath it.

"Look what we got 'ere! We got us a bride!" The oldest bandit rifled through her boxes of finery. He held up the spotless white train of her wedding gown.

"Put it back; you've no need for it!" she said.

Rogan turned his face toward her so only she could hear. "I said, don't talk."

"You been needin' yourself a bride," the youngest one said to the other.

Her body tensed when she saw the icy stare of the youngest man.

"You can't mean her," Rogan said. "She's as mean as Lucifer. That's why I'm taking her off to Bathurst. Our father's arranged a marriage for her." Rogan offered the man an incredulous look.

"Rogan, don't!" She couldn't believe his words.

"I like the mean ones," the older man chuckled.

"She's your sister?" said the other one.

"Then you wouldn't mind me borrowin' 'er for a bit?" His eyes widened and the old man began making his way around the wagon.

"Rogan!" Annie wanted to hit him.

"Afraid I can't let you do that, mister." Rogan stood up in the wagon.

"Don't you move!" the other bushranger threatened.

"She's unblemished, if you know what I mean. I swore I'd get her to Bathurst unharmed. It's not for me, you understand. But I've made a vow to my father." Rogan held up his hands as proof that he meant no harm.

"He'd never know if you didn't tell 'im."

"Are you out of your mind?" Annie asked.

"Go ahead, take 'er down for me," the old man said.

"Now, why don't you show me where you've 'idden your money?" The youngest one offered his first smile of the day but kept his pistol trained on Rogan.

"All right, just don't shoot." Rogan made a great show of removing his coat.

"Don't leave me!" Annie exclaimed.

"Now, you just go with this man and we won't be harmed."

"I hate you!"

"That's right, come with me. Nice and easy-like come down off that wagon, pretty girl," the old man leered.

"Here, don't muss your shawl, dear sister."

Betrayal swam through Annie, but then she felt Rogan's hand slip under the shawl. Even more surprised, she felt his fingers curl around the small pistol she had hidden in her grasp. She released the weapon into his steady hand. On impulse, she fell to the wagon floor.

27

A WILDERNESS GENTLEMAN

"Looks like your partner's abandoned you." Rogan held the older gunman at bay.

"Don't shoot me, mate. This gun ain't packin' no bullets!" he said. "Herschel an' me, we didn't mean no 'arm. We just needed some way to get to Bathurst ahead of them other blokes." The gunman's pistol dangled from two quivering fingers. He held it out for Rogan to confiscate.

"What others?" Rogan showed only mild interest, keeping his suspicions high that the other highwayman, who had run off at the sight of Rogan's pistol, might reappear with ammo.

"Why, the ones wot's goin' to the diggins' at Victoria."

Rogan shot a glance at Annie.

"They say there's gold in Victoria." The gunman tried to make small talk.

"I'm going to count from one to three. If you're still here when I finish, I'm shooting the buttons right off your blooming shirt. One . . ."

Still visibly shaken, Annie covered her face with her hands. "The lady thinks I should do it anyway. What do you think, mate,

306

think she's right?" Before he could finish his statement, the robber had disappeared into the eucalyptus woods.

Annie picked up her purse and began stuffing the contents back into it. Then she recounted her money.

"What do you make of that? They were bluffing all along. Not a bullet between the two of them."

"You're a beast!"

"What's this? Gratitude?"

Suddenly and sharply, Annie slapped him.

His face stung and he had a good mind to retaliate—teach her some things, things she should know about a man. She had a fierce temper, one he suspected had rested dormant for a while, stifled within the confines of Dearborn Manor.

"I'm sorry, Rogan, I—"

"You just keep surprising me and you'll find yourself wandering the Blue Mountains all alone!"

"You've no right to threaten me! You were going to hand me over to that filthy monster!"

"If that's true, then why did I bother saving your ungrateful *reputation*?"

"*I* saved *you*!"

"You? You couldn't save a drowning fish." He saw she battled to hold back the tears but couldn't restrain his tongue to save his own floundering soul.

Annie clambered over the seat, wiping her tears with her sleeve and putting distance between them as fast as she could move.

"Those blokes are just like all the men bumbling around in the wilderness. They're starved for the sight of a woman, any woman. One as pretty as you comes along and they'd kill their own brother to get at you," he said.

"Would you be so kind as to shut your mouth?"

"I've a good mind to leave you along the road! It would teach you to appreciate someone like me." He heard his own mind shouting, pleading with him to stop.

"Why don't you, then?"

"Because I'm decent, that's why!"

"Decent?"

He saw she laughed at him with her eyes, and it ignited his anger all the more.

She shook out her bridal gown, then lifted the veil to inspect it, but she would no longer look at him.

"Yes, decent! Not arrogant, or . . ." The words spewed from his mouth, spearing her with intense indictments as he felt his emotions sinking into a mire of regret.

"You're implying that I'm arrogant?"

"As though you—" He stopped, seeing one tear slip down her cheek, leaving a white-hot scar across his heart as it went.

"You can stop now, Mr. Farrell. I feel we should be on our way. We've wasted enough time as it is."

Rogan hadn't heard her call him Mr. Farrell in months.

She dismounted the wagon. She never did fully cry as he thought she might do. The one tear had escaped, he imagined, without consent. He watched her go but wanted to stop her, to make her listen to how he really felt about her. Instead, he sat muddled up in his own mute stupidity. After Annie had folded up the pure white gown, she pressed it back into the clean paper she had wrapped it in and returned it to the crate. With strength and precision, she grabbed a tool from the rear of the wagon and began to hammer nails into the crate's lid, sealing the box as though it would never be opened again. Not once did she ask for his help. He wondered if she had done the same thing to her heart, nailed it up tight to keep out the violators. He suddenly realized that he had mishandled her feelings the way that creep had manhandled her wedding gown.

"You need some help with that box?" he asked.

He heard the hammer fall into the back of the wagon with a loud thud. "I suppose we'll be on our way, then." He took the reins.

After she found her place in the farthest reaches of the wagon, he kept his eyes straight ahead, brought out the whip, and used it on the horses, in spite of the urge to lay it to his own hide.

For miles Rogan felt as though he traveled alone. Annie had fallen even more silent, but he didn't want her to know how much it frustrated him, so he remained quiet too. He pushed the team farther up the tree-tangled summit. All the while he noticed more and more travelers along the way. One man walked with what looked to be his family, all their possessions piled into a wheelbarrow. His wife had a child that straddled her back, and they had harnessed their young son to the wheelbarrow to help pull it along. Ahead he spied a group of well-to-do men dressed in spurs and opera ties. In the event that they might later be asked if they had seen a man of his description along the road to Bathurst, he allowed his team to slow so that the horsemen ahead would soon leave them far behind.

By the time the sun began to slip behind the highest peak, he had counted throngs of travelers. Sound reasoning told him to hide himself among a company of seventy men, half of whom were drunk and skirling bagpipes. He pulled alongside their six wagons.

Annie pretended not to notice.

"Evening, sir!" he called out to a Scotsman.

"Evening to you!" the man answered, his body stretched out in the rear of the dray.

"Just wanted to enjoy your fine playing." Rogan referred to the bagpipes that wheezed out a cacophony of high ancestral strains.

"Enjoy it, then, and have a drink!" The man held out his jug.

"Thank you, good neighbor!" Rogan reached over the side of the moving wagon. He could feel the bore of eyes upon the back of his head. He knew Annie Carraway hated the sight of strong drink. After taking a swig, he took another for good measure, just to show her she had no say over his life. The home-distilled liquor shot through him, inflaming his insides.

"You like it, lad?" the Scotsman asked.

"Prime vintage!" Rogan coughed into his hand.

"Thought you'd like it, laddie." Outwardly pleased with Rogan's good nature, the man leaned back over to retrieve his jug.

"Where you headed?" Rogan finally asked what he had wanted to know all along.

"Ophir. We're headed for the new diggin's. Aren't you?"

His interest whetted, Rogan prodded him. "Certainly. Isn't everyone?"

"Everyone with two legs and a back for carrying a cradle and a pick," said the Scot.

"But I'm a little confused—don't know up from down. Where exactly is this Ophir?"

"You know of Yorkie's Corner?" the Scotsman asked.

"I've heard of it."

"Well, a couple of prospectors went and found so much gold dust in that place, they renamed it Ophir."

"Ophir?"

"Ophir, as in the Bible. First Kings, Hiram brought gold from

Ophir." Annie spoke from the rear of the wagon, but she never looked up.

"Oh yes, I remember," Rogan said. His comment caused her to look up.

"Well, thank ye for jonnin' me in a drink, laddie. May you find the treasure you're lookin' for." The Scotsman waved farewell, laughing at the bumps in the road, his companions, and anything else that offered an excuse for levity.

"I'm famished," Rogan said. "Let's stop and eat. No need to set up camp just yet unless we decide we like this place. But I could do with a walk, stretch out my legs. They're paining me." With a side road spotted ahead, Rogan steered the team into it. He knew she wouldn't answer, but he kept talking anyway as though he fully expected a reply. The team rounded the bend. He could see that other travelers had gotten the same idea to stop and eat. A dozen or more drays hitched to great lumbering bullocks speckled a green field, which was turning gold in the bath of yellow that preceded dusk. Yesterday's rain still dripped from the foam green vista. A watering hole overflowed its banks with water the color of cocoa that smelled of overripe earth. But all of it had been touched with ribbons of sunset. Rogan knew it wasn't the prettiest sight in the world, but it felt wide and open to him, and he would never take a spectacle like that for granted again.

Sometimes the night had brought a slight chill to the air. So he stopped the team out in the open to soak in what little warmth he could. He tipped his hat to a passing gold seeker. He could tell by the camp outfit he hauled and the "California hat" cocked back on his head that the man was headed for the diggings. Rogan lifted his feet in the air and spun around to face the wagon's interior. He started to call out, but would have spoken to nothing but an empty wagon. Annie Carraway had already disappeared out the back. He sighed and resolved that he should accustom himself to eating alone.

Annie's arms cradled a loaded crate of food. She looked around for a flat grassy place to spread a blanket. The wagon canvas had shielded her from the heat, however, and she had wrapped her shoulders with a shawl. Her skin sweated from the heat. She would have returned the shawl but didn't want to return to the wagon until absolutely necessary. She passed several large-eyed women with wild urchins in tow. Rogan had chosen a noisy place to stop, but she understood why he would do such a thing. Traveling alone in the Blue Mountains had indisputable hazards. By following a group headed for Ophir, they might possibly be better hidden than if they went alone.

"Some bread for the child, mum?"

A woman had stepped in front of her. She looked to be not much older than herself. On her hip she carried a toddler who had angelic eyes and a smudged face. She set down the box so she could dig through it, handed the woman some dried beef, and tore off some bread for her child. But before she could close up the box, she found that a few more women lugging children had gathered. They surrounded her, and some of the older children pressed against her and begged for food.

"I'm sorry. I can't feed you all—" Annie tripped backward. The wooden box fell open and the women and children all scrambled in a greedy frenzy. She tried to sit up and snatch away the crate, but too many of them already had their hands in the food.

"Here! Away with you all!" A tall comely man, dressed in a dark suit, pressed through the shrieking, fighting mob. He tossed a couple of older boys aside and snatched up two others by the shirt.

Annie stood, brushing the grass from her clothes.

"Leave this lady alone! Out of here, all of you!"

The greedy throng scattered, but not before stuffing their tattered pockets and clothing with their pilfered spoils.

"Thank you, sir." Annie, grateful for his help, took his outstretched hand. She dusted off her frock, then scooped up the crate.

"Too late, I'm afraid, miss. It's empty."

"That was foolish of me, I suppose," Annie said, embarrassed by her naïveté.

"Sorry, miss. I saw you offering food to the beggar woman. I suspected this would happen, but I was too far away to stop you."

"Try to be Christian in these parts . . ."

"We do best to extend Christian charity to our own kind. Beggars will take what you offer and rob you of the rest."

"I hope that's not always true."

"Perhaps not in civilized society, but even then, it can happen."

"Well, I thank you." She didn't entirely agree with him. But he had a refinement about him, and a warm smile and soft brown eyes that welcomed her.

"Let me carry that for you. Name's Jacob Fitzroy. As a matter of fact, I've more bread in my wagon. Why don't I replenish what was stolen from you?"

"That isn't necessary."

"Not to worry. You'll need every crumb to make it to Bathurst."

"How far until we reach Bathurst?" she asked.

"In that wagon? Looks as though you've got a good team. If you leave at sunrise, you'll make it by midafternoon tomorrow."

"I'm glad to hear it."

"So you're traveling to Bathurst with your husband?" he assumed.

"No."

"Not to Bathurst?"

"Not my husband. He's my—he just works for me. I'm a settler."

"Not a gold digger?" he asked.

"Gold digging's not for me. I'm perfectly satisfied with a roof over my head and a comfortable bed."

He led her straight to his team and outfit. "Here's my wagon. I'll only be a minute."

Annie watched him disappear into the enormous covered wagon. It was a large affair, expertly finished, with room for many more supplies than he appeared to carry. He reappeared bearing an armload of food.

"So you travel alone?" she asked.

"I know what you're thinking. Why the large wagon? Well, I'm meeting my brother and his family in Bathurst. I'm going to help them build a homestead. They've few resources and I've done well for myself. So I've agreed to help them out. I can't wait to see their faces when they see this beauty."

"How kind of you."

"And in the process, I hope to find a wife as good as he's found. I'd like nothing better than to settle down and have a family, and build a fine house for a deserving woman."

She couldn't help but notice the glint of interest in his handsome face.

"For you." He handed her the bread.

"So you don't plan to prospect for gold?" she asked. His philosophical ways piqued her curiosity.

"Not me. I've made my own way through hard work. Let the fools have it, I say."

"I agree completely. I plan to set up a business as a laundress until I join my sister."

"With those lovely hands?" He cupped his palm under her hand.

"No, not do the work myself, of course. I want to hire women to work for me," she said. Actually, she hadn't thought of it until just now. "Then once I've established a steady supply of work, I want to open a mercantile. Victoria's going to need a good one." She felt the gentle way he cupped her fingers in his own. His amused expression caused her to laugh, and she savored his compliments.

"Victoria, eh?"

"Or Bathurst. I haven't decided. Not yet, anyway." She blushed and didn't know how much personal information she should divulge. But Rogan was nowhere in sight. If this man were as trustworthy as she thought, then what was the harm in telling one person? Rogan would never know, and she would be more careful in the future.

"Here's your food. Careful with it, now. Keep the lid on good and tight until you make it back to your wagon. Should I walk you back, Miss . . ."

"Carraway. Not necessary. But thank you so much for your kindness."

"Pleasure's all mine, lovely lady."

She basked in his approving smile. Perhaps traveling with this group would have more advantages than she realized. Contrary to what some believed, the wilderness did attract a gentleman or two. She believed she had met one.

The wagon just ahead, she felt a tinge of dismay to see Rogan standing out in front, his arms folded and his face twisted in sour disapproval. She tried to rush past him but felt him grip her arm. "Let me go!"

"I saw what happened just now. You can't just walk away without an escort. This isn't Sydney."

"I don't remember asking you your opinion."

"I know you're stubborn, but you could've gotten hurt."

"That would be the day, now wouldn't it? Two filthy armed men threaten me, and you see no harm in that. But let some hungry children accost me and let's call out the Royal Brigade!"

"You're twisting the details."

"Am I? Or are you just looking for ways to try to dominate me?"

"Dominate you?"

"May I remind you that I'm the one person keeping you safe from the law? I would think that you would appreciate my offering you such ready employment."

"Now, you wait, I didn't agree to any employment."

"You've no choice, Mr. Farrell."

"Stop calling me that! And I've every choice!"

"Do you, now? Knowing my uncle, it's only a matter of time until your face is circulated to every postal stop, every borough, every township, from here to England. You take me to Victoria, though, and you'll be free to go anywhere you please."

"Awfully nice of you."

"I'm offering you freedom!"

"It's not yours to give. I can find employment with any of these men. They'd all hire me."

"Then go! I don't need you!"

"I will!"

A swell of despair rose up in her as she watched him storm back inside the wagon. He made a great show of gathering up his belongings and stuffing them into a box. "Those are my things," she said when he lifted a box of hers. He slammed it down and she flinched.

"Miss Carraway?"

"Oh, Mr. Fitzroy." She knew her face reddened this time, but she sighed with resolve.

"Is there a problem?" Fitzroy asked.

"I seem to have lost my driver." She said it loud enough for Rogan to hear.

"Not to worry. I'll find you one before sunup tomorrow," he said. "Join me for a stroll?" He offered his arm.

"I'd be delighted."

Rogan's head bobbed out of the canvas. She saw the way he glared at her.

"Lovely sunset, Mr. Fitzroy. What would I have done if you hadn't chanced by?"

28
THE BEST-DRESSED LAUNDRESS

Rogan hitched up the team bright and early. He had found work with a well-to-do farmer, Hank Jamison, who, like all the rest, had fixed his sights on the goldfields. Jamison had considered his offer of work a stroke of luck; it was not easy to find a good driver and someone willing to help haul around a camp outfit and digging equipment. The various companies of gold seekers had been a motley lot, most heading toward Ophir without any forethought for sufficient supplies. But the already wealthy Jamison had it all—panning cradles, gold-washing pans, one crate brimming with nothing but picks and other sharp tools fit for pounding the gold out of the tightfisted Australian rock. Jamison had wandered off early in hopes of convincing a desperate indigent of parting with his whiskey.

Temptation lured Rogan to gaze toward the group of wagons where he had left behind the most stubborn woman alive. But suspecting she might catch him gawking in her direction, he kept his head down and his hands to task. Not since the war last night between himself and Annie had he spoken to her. She had sashayed off with that dandy of an Englishman, flinging Rogan a haughty gaze. Her equivalent, he decided, of a good kick in the teeth. *She can pair up with every dandy in the camp,* he decided. No amount of begging or persuasion would send him crawling back to her. He had gotten her this far. A rare feat, he decided, for any self-respecting man. But she wouldn't hold him by the collar again. Not ever. Nor would he stay with this company of travelers if she decided to do the same. He would bide his time with Jamison until this group crossed paths with another company. Then he would disappear and keep moving, the best strategy for keeping Dearborn's hounds at bay. Ophir would be his destination too, he decided.

Gold fever had been in his blood since the day Frederick had waved that newspaper article under his nose. Once he had struck gold, he would send for Barclay. Together, they would do to Harry Winston what the Winston family had done to him. If the truth wouldn't work, money would buy him his freedom and then Rose Hill would be his next priority. With a little luck, he might entangle Dearborn in a public scandal he wouldn't be quick to forget. He couldn't think beyond that point. But he wanted his life back, might even kill to regain the autonomy Abbot Dearborn had stolen from him. Freedom to return home to Rose Hill, set up a practice, maybe give old Mason Hale a run for his money. Under no circumstances would he allow the likes of Dearborn or Winston to run him off his family's land. He'd die first, he resolved. But he wouldn't be hanged for something he didn't do.

The bright yellow fabric of a woman's billowy skirt caught his eye. He turned his head and saw Annie weaving in and around the wagons, her eyes wide and the soft tendrils of her golden hair fluttering around her cheeks and forehead. She dashed around like a scalded feline. The troubled look she bore caused him to stiffen his back. In no mood for another brawl with an overwrought kitten, he narrowed his eyes and decided that he wouldn't give her the privilege of a fight. Not before his ritual cup of black coffee, anyway. She laid eyes on him, then bolted straight for him. When she opened her mouth to speak, he looked away.

"Mr. Farrell!"

He had never heard her so breathless before. She sounded like a frightened little girl, and it stirred something in him that he felt he had best keep hidden. He blew out an exasperated breath, then looked at her.

"It's terrible! You won't believe!"

"I might."

"It's that Englishman, Mr. Fitzroy. He's run off with my horses!"

"Sorry to hear that." The news stirred his ire, but he held his opinions about the Englishman, although he felt it worthy ammunition. But that kind of artillery was better saved for later. It took every ounce of intestinal fortitude he could muster to not bolt for the road and hunt down Fitzroy. But he continued strapping up Jamison's team, scrutinizing the harnesses, surveying the horses' legs with great interest.

"Mr. Farrell, did you hear me?"

"Yes, Miss Carraway. I'm sorry to hear of your misfortune." He said it evenly for effect. The effect satisfied him to his core.

"But you've got to do something, go after him! Call the law!"

"Think of what you're asking. You want me, a runaway convict, to approach a lawman? Why don't you tell me how I would go about it? 'Now, listen here, Mr. Lawman. I'm an honest criminal and I want to report a theft. Some crook stole our stolen horses—' "

"Stop it, I say!"

"Annie, I don't work for you anymore. Now, I suggest that you find yourself another whipping boy to order around. I've found a new situation."

"You can't leave me stranded like this!"

"Buy yourself a new team. You're rich."

"I'm not. I've only enough for food until I reach Victoria. All I have is—"

"Bonnets? Feathered bonnets?" He felt the light of humor spill out inside him.

"You're a cruel man. I hate you!"

"I knew that."

Humiliated, Annie traced her steps back to the horseless wagon. All the while she relived the events of the prior evening. She had realized too late that Jacob Fitzroy had charmed the common sense right out of her. "For safety's sake let me hitch your horses up to mine for the night. I'll keep watch over them for you." Fitzroy had said all that to her and she believed him. He had arranged a driver for her, or so he had said. Like a fool, she hadn't insisted upon meeting the driver. Obviously, the man had never existed. When she awoke, she had found the empty spot once occupied by Fitzroy's wagon. Her team of matching Cleveland bays had vanished along with Fitzroy. She seethed at the thought. To make matters worse, and against her better judgment, she had gone running back to Rogan Farrell for help. She regretted her latter actions almost as badly as she lamented trusting the conniving Fitzroy.

Her approach to the wagon revealed a sight that unnerved her even more. A gang of young hoodlums had invaded her unmanned wagon. She could hear their glee as they rifled through her personals and ravaged her food supply. No longer wary of anyone or anything, she slid her hand into her handbag and pulled out the pistol. "Put it all back or I'll blow off your heads!"

"Don't shoot, lady! Hey, mates, bloomin' woman's got a gun, she 'as!"

"Drop the booty!" another boy shrieked. "Run or she'll kill us!"

Annie waited for them to scatter. She climbed back into the wagon to survey the damage. Plumes had been yanked from the bonnets. The laces strewn around looked soiled, and if she hadn't been too weary to count, she felt certain that many were missing. But worse than that, all of her food supply had been pilfered. She stared out at the wagons that had begun to pass her by, none of the riders offering her so much as a glance. "I need my food! Who took my food?" she shouted into every wagon that rattled past her. But her pleas were ignored.

"I don't think they're listening."

She jerked around to see a wagon stopped in front of her. Rogan stared at her.

"What do you want?" she glared at him.

"Nothing." He tipped his hat at her and whipped the team he drove.

"Don't mind me. I'll just walk to Victoria!"

"Beautiful day for a walk."

The sight of him smirking at her sickened her, and she turned away.

"Oh, by the way, like you to meet my employer, Mr. Hank Jamison."

An older gentleman peered from inside the wagon, sipping from a silver flask. She nodded at him but cut her eyes askance.

"Mr. Jamison is in need of a laundress. Don't suppose you know of a good one?"

More than any other time she could remember, she wanted to cry. Maybe even scream. But she found herself offering the man a weak smile. It took her a moment before she could speak.

"I suppose not, Mr. Jamison," Rogan said.

"I do know of a laundress, Mr. Jamison." Annie's words sounded wooden, and she couldn't look at Rogan.

"Do you, now?" Jamison asked.

"Yes. I'm a good laundress." Her teeth on edge, she nodded.

"What a relief! And Farrell here says you're the best cook he's ever seen."

"Oh, he did?"

Rogan winked at her. She remembered she had one last bullet, then asked God to forgive her for such thoughts.

Rogan folded his arms across his chest and avoided her eyes.

"I can cook, if you need a cook."

"We both need a good cook," Rogan said.

The silence that passed between them said more than words. Disdain seeped into her mind as she surveyed her belongings.

Rogan accepted Jamison's offer of a drink, taking a sip from his flask.

"What about my wagon?"

"Good-bye, old wagon," Rogan shrugged.

By the time she had gathered all of her belongings into Jamison's wagon, she could see the last rig ahead of them pulling onto the sticky mud-caked road.

"We need to pull out unless we want to travel alone," Rogan prompted Jamison.

"I've no intention of traveling alone, lad. Miss Carraway, I've never seen a laundress hauling so many frilly belongings. Are you quite ready?"

Annie shoved the crate containing her wedding dress against the other crates. She smoldered. Rogan had not stirred from his seat or offered her so much as a thimbleful of help. Sweat trickled down her brow, making gritty rivulets. For the first time since she had departed Sydney, she saw the folly of her plan. The chances of finding buyers for such overpriced finery in a wilderness colony would be close to impossible. Yet, with so many miles behind her now, she had no choice but to forge ahead and pray she'd find some women of means in Victoria, or somehow locate Isabelle. If not, she would be the best-dressed laundress in all of Victoria.

"Miss Carraway, are you ready?"

Jamison's tinny voice annoyed her, but she knew better than to express her disapproval.

"Time's a-wasting."

"I'm ready, sir."

The next sundown brought the company of wagons into Bathurst. Annie peered from the back of the wagon and surveyed the townspeople. She saw a mix of men and women, but few ladies would have matched up with some of the finer Englishwomen of Sydney. However the town had been characterized in the past, the influx of gold seekers had given it a whole new face. Hordes milled about the town square wearing red-and-blue "California hats" and "California shirts," and showing off their firearms to one another.

Jamison had Rogan drive the wagon up to a small mercantile. Glad of it, Annie would organize her laces and bonnets out of Rogan's sight while they gathered supplies. She might even find luck in selling her things from the back of the wagon. Although bound by her obligation to cook a few meals for Jamison, Annie decided to part company with him once they made it as far as Ophir. As they traveled, she would keep watch for the Cleveland bays. If Fitzroy had his sights set on the goldfields, the likelihood of catching up with him would be good. Once she spied Fitzroy again, she would take her chances with the law and have him arrested on sight, in spite of what Rogan had to say about the matter. Rogan Farrell had proven that his loyalties were only to himself. She'd not be fooled twice.

Jamison staggered from the wagon.

"Mr. Jamison, I can't be washing your things in a bucket, not if you want me to get them clean."

"What is it you be needing, then?"

"A large washtub and a bar of lye soap."

"I'll take it out of your wages."

"Not to worry. I can find work elsewhere. Lots of people in Bathurst will be needing a laundress." She saw the exchange of glances between Fitzroy and Rogan.

"I'll get you your washtub, but don't be asking me for anything else. I won't make any money in Ophir if it's all spent before I begin."

"Thank you, Mr. Jamison."

The men disappeared into the mercantile. Annie could see why the man had so much wealth already, but she couldn't finance his foolhardy excursion. Once she had sold enough finery, she would offer to buy back the tub at a reduced price. After a moment's hesitation, she tore open the crates packed with the trousseau laces. One by one she laid them across the back of the wagon. She smiled at a group of women who passed.

"What you be sellin'?" one of the women asked.

"I'm selling my trousseau laces if you're interested."

The three of them, dressed in tatters and patched attire, stopped, looked up at her, surprised that someone of her station would address them. One of the women stepped forward, a glint of interest in her eyes. "Your trousseau laces, miss? Why?" the lady asked.

"I was wise enough to call off a wedding." She waited for their reaction, then saw the look of approval she expected.

"We ain't got no plans for a 'usband."

"Surely these items will bring you better luck than they did for me." She smiled when she had evoked some laughter from them.

"Let me 'ave a look." The lady who spoke wore a frayed pale blue bonnet. She had a worn face and wore soiled gloves that may once have been white.

"I've some bonnets as well." Annie held out the petticoats to each woman and saw the approval in their faces.

"Might as well 'ave a look-see at all of it."

"I'll get them for you." After fetching two of the new feathered bonnets, she offered to place one on the head of one woman. The woman removed her dowdy-looking brown bonnet and allowed Annie to adjust it and tie it for her.

Her friends voiced their approval, flattering her. Annie could sense it was all too much temptation to deny herself.

"How much for the bonnet and this lace petticoat?"

"I feel you should know that they're of the best quality—"

"How much?" the woman persisted.

"Half a crown each."

"Wot's that? Half a crown? Why I never paid so much for a bonnet! That's nigh two days wages."

"But look at you, Molly. You be lookin' so fine." The other two handed the laces back to Annie.

"Do I, now?"

"You do!"

"How about two shillings each, then?" Annie put the other bonnet back in the box along with the other laces. She felt sorry for the woman, knowing she had probably never had anything nice to wear her entire life.

"I'll do it! Let me fetch the money. I don't carry it around, but me room's just down the street 'ere."

"We'll wait 'ere with the lady," one of the woman's friends said.

While time passed, a few more women gathered, but none could afford the imported finery. Then Annie looked up to find the other two women had slipped away. She stood in the back of the wagon to get a better view around the square, in hopes of spotting the culprits before they got away. When she had first watched the ragged customer walk off, her goods in tow, a small voice had warned her to stop the woman. But watching the lady's glee over her newly found treasures had stirred something in her, causing her to trust the woman.

"Looking for something?"

Rogan's voice startled her. She stammered, not wanting him to know of her misfortune. She turned to replace the lids on her crates. Then she shook her head.

"I got to thinking—I probably shouldn't have left you alone in the wagon. Too many unscrupulous folks around in Bathurst."

"I . . . I don't need your escort every minute of the day."

"Would you like to try to sell some of your bonnets here? Might be a few ladies who could afford them, although not many."

"As a matter of fact, I've tried to sell them and—"

"What's the matter?"

He must have read her face, but she could already imagine his reaction. She hated to tell him.

"Someone stole your frillies."

"How did you guess?" She looked at the ground.

"Annie, you can't let someone walk away with your goods like that."

His voice had taken on a softer, gentler quality. She gazed down into his eyes, a blue so deep it pricked her heart.

"You're too trusting."

"I—you would have done no differently if you'd been here. The poor woman was in tatters and she—" Her voice broke.

"Tatters or no, you can't let someone steal from you. You needed that money for your business." Rogan stepped up into the wagon.

"I'm well aware and angered, but what can I do about it now? Once again, we can't call the law."

"Don't be so hard on yourself. You just have to remember, you can't trust anyone."

"What's happened?"

Annie saw the red-eyed Jamison standing on the street cradling the new washtub.

"Miss Carraway's been robbed of her finery."

"I'll call the law, that's wot!"

"No need. It was just one bonnet and a lace garment. I'll just have to be more careful in the future."

"You're certain, Miss Carraway?"

"Thank you anyway, Mr. Jamison."

"Well, Rogan, here's some money. You'll go down and buy that ammunition for me?" Jamison shook some coins around in his hand.

"I'll do it now. You lock up those bonnets of yours, Annie. The next time you get it in your head to try to sell them, you let me know first. I don't want you doing it alone."

She felt his hand cup her arm. The tenderness of his touch startled her. She backed away.

"You've some ammunition to buy, Mr. Farrell. I suppose we should be fast on our way," she said.

Rogan turned away but kept his eyes on her. She felt a strange tingling around her heart, and she couldn't take her eyes from his. All she could do was breathe out a whispered, "Hurry now, Mr. Farrell." She watched him go and hated herself for wanting to run after an outlaw.

29
NIGHT OF A THOUSAND STARS

Rogan had to maneuver fast to talk Jamison into camping outside of Bathurst. Skittish about the wilderness, Jamison had planned to lodge in town. But Rogan knew full well that the longer they remained in Bathurst, the more time they gave the local folks to memorize their faces.

"Drive a little farther. Get us a bit ahead of the others." Jamison, now fully convinced that they should lead the way to the gold diggings, urged Rogan to stay on the road.

"Mr. Jamison, your horses need the rest and so do you. Why don't we camp along the roadside tonight? We'll still be ahead of most of the wagon companies in Bathurst."

"I suppose you're right, Rogan. I am feeling a bit woozy. I should lay myself down." Jamison finished off the remains in his flask and nodded his agreement. He turned to crawl into the rear of the wagon.

"What about Miss Carraway?" Rogan asked.

"You won't be asking me to give up my own bed for the likes of a laundress, now will you?"

Rogan could kick himself. He hadn't thought of the sleeping

arrangements until now. He unhooked the lantern, saw her tiny frame curled up motionless inside the wagon, the faint touch of light kissing her cheeks and her full rosy lips. In spite of her quick temper, she had an innocence about her. To look at her like that stirred him. He felt protective of her as he had that night in the jail. Jamison had proven himself a likable sort, but any man in his cups couldn't be trusted sleeping next to a woman as pretty as Annie.

"Wake her for me, will you, Farrell?"

"I could set up tents for us."

"You can set up a tent for the wench. I'm sleeping in the wagon."

"Mr. Jamison, I'll do that, but don't call Annie a wench."

"It's all right." Annie's drowsy voice arose from the back.

"You're awake." Rogan looked surprised.

"I'll set up my own tent." Her assertions always had a way of seeping into his emotions, fanning his ire. She wouldn't let him do anything for her unless desperation forced her.

"How difficult can it be?"

"All right, Mr. Jamison. You go on back and make up your bed. I'll wake you at dawn for breakfast."

"Don't want no breakfast, Rogan. Just allow me rest. You go about your business and get us on the road to Ophir."

Rogan stood to stretch. Even a bed on the hard, unforgiving ground wouldn't keep him from slumber tonight. Still gripping one of the wagon's lamps, he stepped gingerly through the well-loaded vehicle. He tipped back a crate that was stamped with the word "tents."

"All the stakes are packed with it," Jamison said. "Just take the lanterns with you. I can sleep in the dark."

"Thank you, I will." Annie had finally stood, arms folded like a prim matron, her soft blue eyes still heavy with sleep.

"Annie, I'll tote the tent wherever you want it. But I think you should allow me to set it up for you."

"I assure you, Mr. Farrell, that I can set up my own tent."

"Go ahead, then!" He hefted the cumbersome tarp and tossed it out onto the ground. Annie clambered out of the wagon in a way that let him know he had angered her again. He could see her slender silhouette in the early twilight. She first yanked up a corner of the tarp and draped it over her frail shoulder. He saw her take a step forward, heard her emit a faint groan. It pained him so to watch her struggling, but not enough to keep the mirth from his lips.

"You'll be needing this lantern, won't you?" Rogan asked.

Annie wrestled with the tarp, then marched back to where he stood. She glared up at him until he handed the lamp down to her. Her manner of getting what she wanted never ceased to amaze him. Purposeful, she staggered across the clearing, flitting about, her arms encumbered with the tent and the lantern. The tarp jerked and twitched as it dragged behind her. With some distance between them, she still yanked and fought, looking like a wounded firefly.

Rogan busied himself with hunting for the other tent but took time occasionally to peer out at her. After a tremendous struggle, she finally managed to find a place to land about a hundred yards out from them. "Don't go too far," he said.

"That isn't possible, Mr. Farrell."

He decided to stop handing her so much ammunition.

Carrying the tent such a distance had winded Annie. She felt dizzy in spite of the meal she had prepared for them earlier in the wagon. Certain that she could lie down on the ground and sleep under the stars, she yet persisted in showing Rogan Farrell that she could set up camp. She waited, hoping to catch her breath, then emptied the sack of stakes onto the ground. Her brothers had set up tents before, out on Uncle Abbot's land. She stretched out the tent just as she had seen them do. But she needed a hammer. By lantern light, she picked through the stakes and came across a small hammer, one just right for her grip. Grateful that she didn't have to return and ask Rogan for a hammer, she selected a long iron stake. The weight of the stake surprised her, but she aimed it at the tent corner just the same. It wavered in her grasp. Every swing she took at the stake top had little effect. The stake teetered back and forth. With each wobble, she grew more frustrated. She finally drew back and pounded it with all the force she could muster. It sank into the ground, but only by an inch.

"I'm sorry to tell you this, but I can't find another tent."

She whipped around to find Rogan standing over her.

"Did you hear me? Jamison must be mistaken. I couldn't find a second tent."

"Sleep in the wagon with Jamison."

"He's passed out drunk, sprawled all over. I'd have to unload half the wagon to make room for myself."

"What are you saying?"

"Nothing. I'm not saying anything at all." Rogan turned away.

"You can have the tent, if that's what worries you." She felt relieved to tell him that, but would never admit it.

"No, I couldn't do that to you."

"Go ahead. It's a clear night. I'll make my bed between you and the wagon."

"I can't let you do that."

"You can't stop me."

"I'll vow, you've got some pluck about you, but you're fragile, just like all the rest."

"I can't imagine what you mean by 'all the rest,' but I'm weary and too tired to argue. Good night, Mr. Farrell." Annie dropped the hammer into the pile of stakes and ambled toward the wagon.

"Be sure you fetch that other lantern from the wagon."

"I'll do just that." The remaining blankets bundled into her arms, Annie first decided to make a campfire. A chilly night breeze whistled around and under her skirts. One by one, she gathered some large rocks and made a circle atop a patch of dry, barren soil. Then she collected kindling, followed by some logs that she heaped atop the brush pile. She had kept a matchbox in her bag for just such occasions.

"Want me to start that fire for you? I can do it with stones."

Self-satisfied, she never acknowledged his lame offer. Rogan Farrell, no different than any other man, had it in his mind to thunder through life the hard way. She struck a match against the box and tossed it into the kindling, not offering him so much as a glance. Her mouth poised at the base of the woodpile, she blew out a few strong puffs of air. Persistence soon offered the desired results. A satisfying crackling sound preceded some rolling curls of gray smoke. After she had stoked the woodpile, she watched the new flames lick up and around the logs.

The slow clapping sound of Rogan's hollow applause made her stiffen. She could see him standing out in front of the tent, offering a cynical ovation. She ignored it.

Jamison's bedding supply coupled with her own quilts made a good bed, softer than she had imagined. She slid between the downy folds and turned her face toward the fire. The starry sky drew her gaze. The sun long extinguished, a dark blanket of blue rolled out the night, a velvet carpet that cradled diamonds of every size. A bright streak, distant and traveling faster than lightning, caused her to look eastward. But by the time she looked east, it had vanished. Her lids grew heavy, and she felt a sleepy inward sigh lull her toward the slumber she so coveted. But another trail of fire crossed the sky, and she bolted upright to see the shooting-star display. With the quilt bundled around her shoulders and body, she watched the spectacle, a fire-dance amid the celestials. The sight of it dazzled her as more of them zigged across the diamond blanket.

"Everything all right?"

She could see Rogan's face, yellowed by the lantern light, as he peered out of his tent. "Nothing wrong. Just, well, see for yourself," she said.

"See what?"

"Look up." She said it through clenched teeth.

She watched him twist sideways and crane his neck. He had loosened his hair from the queue. It tumbled about his rugged face, making him look like one of the apostles pictured in her Bible.

"Sometimes at night in the jail, I would see one. But not often. I've never seen so many at once."

"Nor have I. I'll bet there's a thousand of them."

They both watched for a while, never a word passing between them. Annie had never really studied his face before. He had a classic countenance, she decided. Seldom had she met a man with a face as comely as his, or one who possessed half his wit. Nor had she ever met a man who would take to stargazing—not even her own father. Isabelle had pegged Rogan Farrell as an egotistic heathen, a man deluded by his own fleshly desires. Isabelle was right, of course, but Annie wondered if he were really any worse a sinner than herself.

Jacob Fitzroy lifted the old mattress and stashed his money under it. Self-satisfied with his plunder this week, he felt secure in sleeping on top of it. The fact he had crossed paths with the young woman from Sydney had been a stroke of luck. She had played into his scheme quicker than a green poker novice. She'd been easy to pick out of the crowd. It was those golden locks that caught his eye, and the gullible glint in her trusting blue eyes. Annie Carraway stood out from the others as a lovely poised flower, if not the most beautiful victim he had ever met. If she hadn't been such an innocent, he might have tried to keep her around. But a girl like her would hand him over to the law in a blink. Even prettier than the girl was her team of Cleveland bays. He wondered how she had managed to acquire such a fine breed. He couldn't get her to say much about herself, only that she would need to find work when she arrived in Victoria. He was baffled at how a woman of her obvious breeding would be out traveling in such a way. He had sold his older team at once and hitched up the gleaming carriage horses to his wagon. Once he felt he had allowed sufficient time and distance between himself and that last wagon company, he would head for Bathurst and buy a fitting carriage for the team. No need to ruin the bays in their prime. Just one more job, he kept telling himself, and he'd turn honest.

The secluded inn behind the mail-stage station had offered him the fastest place to lie low once the familiar wagon company had passed. The innkeeper had complained of the low cost of wool keeping the pastoralists away from his hostelry. But upon close inspection, Fitzroy could see the ill-kept accommodations might be the greater deterrent.

With the lantern extinguished, he undressed himself and climbed onto the sagging mattress. A kookaburra's screech unnerved him, so he sat up for a while, lit a cigarette, and waited for the wilderness sounds to quieten. The air grew still, and he tried to recall if ever the night had been so silent. He sucked on the moist quid for the last time and then settled into the bedding, the white cloud of floating smoke a comfort to him.

He had so drifted into a deep slumber, it took him a few horrifying moments to realize that the sudden explosion of splintering wood and gunfire was not a nightmare. He threw himself to the floor and tried to crawl beneath the bed, but something big grabbed him by his thick graying hair. "Don't kill me!" he shrieked just before feeling his head slam against the floor.

"I think it would be best if I set up my sleeping quarters in the tent." Annie told herself that it wasn't the night sounds that caused her discomfort; she just hadn't realized the evening would be so cool.

"Gets rather noisy out here, doesn't it?"

"I'm not afraid. But it's chilly out here and—"

"Come in."

"I've brought the other lantern. I'll hang this blanket from the top of the ceiling like I did that night in the carriage."

"Suit yourself."

"Any other arrangement would be unseemly."

"No one is watching."

"God is watching, Mr. Farrell." She opened her bag and pulled out some large pins. In a straight line, she fastened the edges of the blanket along the tent ceiling. While she moved across the tent attaching the blanket, she could feel his eyes on her.

Annie would have jumped between the quilt folds and fallen straight to sleep, but she sat down on something that lay hidden underneath the covering. She groaned.

"Is something wrong?"

"Feels like I've sat down against a stone."

"Odd. I thought I had cleared the area well beneath the tent."

"Why, it's Isabelle's Bible." Annie lifted the quilt and held the lantern over the spot.

"Oh, that, I—"

"Don't tell me you've been reading it?"

"I haven't."

"Are you telling the truth?"

Rogan shrugged.

"Mr. Farrell, you needn't feel ashamed for reading the Holy Scriptures."

"Who said I feel ashamed?"

"Do you?"

"I didn't know what else to do with it. I should have given it back to you, but it slipped my mind."

"But you've read it?"

"Just thumbed through it. Not a crime. You keep it, though."

"I think Isabelle would rather you keep it."

Annie heard Rogan breathe out a sigh and roll away from her.

"Good for her. Maybe it'll earn her points with God," he muttered.

"Have you always been so cynical, Mr. Farrell?"

"I don't remember."

"I'm sorry if I'm being intrusive. I'm not as adept as my sister in sharing my faith."

"Give yourself some credit. If I wanted to be religious, I'd choose to be like you."

"Why is that?"

"You're not self-righteous. Jesus wasn't self-righteous. Ate with the sinners and the publicans just like you."

"You *have* been reading. But I'm no comparison to Jesus."

"What about the way you cared for your sister? Everyone ran from the house like a bunch of spooked rabbits when that child fell ill. But you stayed."

Annie remembered the morning she had taken him into the room. In reflections later, she felt it was Clarisse's way of saying she would be leaving them soon.

"Clarisse would have done the same for me."

"Perhaps. What about the way you tolerated Abbot's control over your life?"

"Tolerance is not the best word for my relationship with Abbot Dearborn."

"Whatever you choose to call it, you did it out of pure love for your family."

"You're quite observant. We should sleep now."

"Sorry, didn't mean to get so close to the real Annie Carraway."

Annie shook her head and closed her eyes. She pressed her face into the pillow, settling herself. Rogan stirred restlessly for a while, then fell silent.

Her mind drifted, and she felt peaceful and headed for a sound slumber.

"Annie?"

Her eyes flew open.

"You asleep?"

"Almost, why?"

"Do you ever wake up feeling like a fraud?"

"What do you mean by that?"

"Don't get all flustered. I don't mean that as a personal indictment against you. I mean, do all people wake up sometimes feeling like a fraud, or is it just me?"

She weighed his words but didn't answer right away. He didn't notice.

"For example, does your uncle Abbot ever feel like he isn't really what everyone thinks he is? Does Isabelle really think she's as good as you see her? What about the vicar?" he asked. "You see, we allow others to see us as we want to be seen. But inside, we know who we really are, if that makes any sense at all."

"It does." Annie didn't know why Rogan had turned into a philosopher at so late an hour, but she understood him.

"So answer me. Do you, Annie Carraway, ever feel like a fraud?"

No one had ever asked her such a thing. She drew the quilt next to her face, contemplating his question.

"You always get so quiet on me."

"Rogan, I don't just spit out my words like you. I think matters through. Is that a crime?"

"You called me Rogan."

"All right, yes, sometimes I feel like a fraud. So who are you, really?"

"I'm a wanted outlaw, a kidnapper, an embezzler—"

"You're none of those things, are you?"

Rogan drew back the curtain.

Annie felt surprised to see him staring at her.

"Must we talk like this? I feel like a Catholic at confession."

Voluntarily, Annie pushed back the curtain, then seated herself cross-legged in front of him.

"My family all hails from an emancipist line. I've told you that, though."

She nodded, eager to hear him speak. He hadn't been this civil since their last breakfast together at the manor house.

"Rose Hill made my grandfather a rich man. My father took it over for the family. He had a brother, but he didn't want anything to do with sheep ranching. Father managed well, until the fire. Then came the depression."

"It has affected many."

"Not you."

"That's where you're wrong. My mother tried to farm here. Her failures took what little life remained in her."

"That's when you had to come live with Abbot. You're fortunate, really, if you consider what might have happened."

"Clarisse might be alive."

"You can't blame yourself for that, Annie. I watched you that morning pouring yourself into that little girl. Sometimes children get sick and don't recover."

"I know," Annie said. "Is it getting cooler?" She pulled the blanket around herself.

"Let me give you one of my blankets."

"I have enough—"

"I said, 'let me.' " Rogan took a blanket, stood on his knees, and wrapped it around her.

"Thank you," she said. When he took charge in this way, it comforted her. No man had ever had such an effect on her. Especially Harry. She glanced down and saw Isabelle's Bible between them. "Rogan, would you mind . . ."

"Mind what?"

"What did you read?"

"In here?" He pointed to Isabelle's Bible.

"As I said, if you don't mind." She saw the hesitation of his gaze, then he reached for the Bible and opened to a dog-eared page.

"I can read, you know."

"I believe you." She waited while he cleared his throat.

" 'Again, the kingdom of heaven is like unto treasure hid in a field; the which when a man hath found, he hideth, and for joy thereof goeth and selleth all that he hath, and buyeth that field.' "

Annie lay on her stomach, resting her chin on her fingers.

" 'Again, the kingdom of heaven is like unto a merchantman, seeking goodly pearls: Who, when he had found one pearl of great price, went and sold all that he had, and bought it. Again, the kingdom of heaven is like unto a net, that was cast into the sea, and gathered of every kind: Which, when it was full, they drew to shore, and sat down, and gathered the good into vessels, but cast the bad away.' "

"The words of Christ."

Rogan nodded.

She studied him, remembering that he came from Katy Gabriel's lineage.

"I'm not a complete heathen, Annie."

"I'm sorry if I've—"

"Don't apologize."

"Why did you choose that passage, Rogan?"

"It's made me think about some things, is all. I grew up with religious training, just as you did. But poverty changed me. After seeing how my father struggled—sensed his humiliation when he failed—I decided it wouldn't happen to me."

"Riches change some. Poverty changed you."

"You want to be poor?"

"Not really." Annie laughed at her own confession.

"In some ways, you're richer than the Dearborns," Rogan said.

"You're right."

Rogan yawned and stretched out his brawny arms.

Annie smiled, then bid him a good night. Before she could react, he closed the curtain for her. Instead of falling to sleep at once, she knelt and prayed for her sister and brothers. Then she whispered a prayer for Rogan—that he would find the treasure he so earnestly sought.

Above her prayers, Annie wasn't sure, but it seemed as if she heard him whisper on the other side, "God, take care of sweet Annie. My dear, sweet Annie."

30
SAINT ROGAN

"That's not Rogan Farrell's body!" Abbot tossed the cheesecloth over the dead man's body.

Next to him stood Harry Winston, his eyes red from drink and his face etched with weariness.

"But he had your team, your horses! The innkeeper showed me his room." The man a common laborer, he kept lifting and dropping the grave cloth.

"Did the innkeeper give you a name?"

"He didn't offer a name, but he fit Farrell's description exactly."

"Don't you know what Rogan Farrell looks like?"

"It was dark. The room was black as pitch, it was! I shouted at 'im something like, 'Where is Miss Annie Carraway?' and he answered, as if he knew 'er 'isself. Didn't he, Ralph?" He turned to his partner, pleading for him to concur.

"Who else would know Annie Carraway but Rogan Farrell?" the partner asked.

"The man must have come upon them in the mountains. Maybe Farrell sold the man my team. All I know is that Rogan Farrell could be anywhere by now," Dearborn said.

"You didn't see Annie anywhere?" Harry asked.

Both men shook their heads.

"Find out what those posters say. I want a manhunt from here to California. Rogan Farrell is to be shot on sight!" Dearborn said.

"We don't know where else to look, Judge!"

"An innocent man's been murdered here. You find Farrell and bring him back dead, or I'll have you both arrested for murder."

"Listen to me—you said the man told you where Annie had gone to? What did he say?" Harry Winston loaded his pistol.

"He said the girl was headed for Victoria," the laborer said.

"I'm going after her." Harry inspected his weapon.

"I think you should, and take two of my men with you." Dearborn dismissed all but Harry from the parlor. "You realize, don't you, that if that witness testifies about hearing you slip at that card game, it could draw attention away from Rogan Farrell's prosecution? He needs to be brought to justice at once."

"I'm not worried about a drunken witness. I just want to bring Annie home. She has no business running off with the likes of him."

"Don't ever let anyone hear you say that! She's been kidnapped, and everyone must know why you had to shoot Rogan Farrell."

"I can't shoot him! I've never killed anyone."

"It's your own neck if you don't."

"I trust the judicial system will lean my way in the matter."

"I can't control the courts, Harry, not to that extent. Remember, Farrell's found a slick English lawyer. These men I'm sending with you—they're dead aims. With a reward out on Farrell's head, and the threat of losing their own, they'd kill each other to be the first to pick him off."

"I'd rather go alone."

"It's not safe to cross the divide unaccompanied. I'll have your horse and a pack made ready. Bring me back Farrell's body along with that surly niece of mine. If she wants those young brothers of hers well provided for, she'll cooperate."

Dearborn's butler entered and cleared his throat.

"What is it? I'm busy!"

"Judge Dearborn, you've another letter from England, sir."

"Burn it! I want no mail from England!"

The butler bowed, red-faced, and turned away.

Harry watched Dearborn storm from the parlor. His fingers curled around the loaded pistol. His arm dropped limply at his side as he slumped into a chair and buried his face into his other hand.

"Yes sir, this 'ere's Yorkie's Corner."

Rogan thanked the local pastoralist.

"We should ask him about a mercantile." Annie counted the money that Jamison had paid her so far.

"Jamison! Wake up, old man. We've made it clear to Ophir!" Rogan said.

"Ophir? Is it Tuesday already?"

"It's Wednesday. You slept through Tuesday."

"Did I miss anything?"

"Three of the best meals I've ever had."

"Thank you, Rogan," Annie said.

When she said his name, it caused a smile to peek out from his sun-blistered face.

"Wake me when we get to Lewis Pond's Creek, Farrell." Jamison slumped back into the wagon.

"Let's find an inn for you, Annie. I don't want you sleeping on the ground again tonight. Jamison and I can set up camp near Lewis Pond's Creek."

"I'd rather keep moving, Rogan. I think I should go on to Victoria. I'll find another wagon going that way."

"Annie, your sister may not be in Victoria. If she is, you'd be better off showing up with a little gold in your purse." It made him feel anxious every time she mentioned going off on her own. If three common street women could take advantage of her, worse things could happen to Annie. He wanted her safe.

"I don't care about the gold."

"Why are you so afraid of being rich?"

"I'm not afraid. But I'm not like Abbot either."

"You think all wealthy men are greedy."

"Aren't they?"

"Maybe they're just smart. Smart enough to hang on to what they have."

"They could spread it around, share it with those less fortunate."

"They should do that, I agree."

"You agree?"

"Surprised?"

"I'm not certain. When did you start caring for unfortunates?"

"You've taught me some things." He spoke to her in a more gentle tone now. He could see a glint of suspicion in her face.

"Such as?"

"I'm not too old to learn, Annie Carraway. You think you're the only one who prays?"

She snapped closed her purse and cut him a dubious gaze.

"I've been talking to Him some lately."

"Him. God?"

"God. You think I'm too bad to pray, don't you?"

"No one is too bad to pray, Rogan."

"So I've heard."

"I've been given a lot of second chances."

"Not you, Annie."

"Especially me. I fail quite often. But Isabelle assures me that something good will come of it."

"Bah! If I could be as good as you, they'd make me a saint. How's that for a name, Saint Rogan?"

He loved it when she laughed.

Yorkie's Corner afforded a choice of one inn. Annie spent most of the afternoon curled up on the smallest bed she had ever seen, although she didn't sleep a wink. Rogan had insisted that he pay for the room, a small indemnity, he had said, for all she had done for him. He had taken on different ways of late, she had to admit. A loud pounding knock brought her to her feet. She stood at the door but didn't open it. The pounding continued, so she finally opened the door slightly.

"Afternoon, ma'am."

She offered a nod to the man who stood hammering a rusted nail into the building wall.

"Sorry if I disturbed you. The mail office asks us to put up these 'ere posters. I'll be finished in a bit."

Annie closed the door before he could get a glimpse of her, latched it, and returned to the bed. After sitting up for a few minutes, she wished she had gone with Rogan and Mr. Jamison. The hammering had stopped for several minutes before she ventured out again. She saw no sign of the man, so she crept over to where he had nailed three posters. It didn't surprise her that they all had drawings of wanted men, but the sight of Rogan Farrell's face unnerved her to the core. *Wanted for kidnapping?*

Rogan had predicted Abbot's next move with frightening accuracy. The sign claimed Rogan was dangerous and armed. It said he was "wanted dead." Abbot always took measures to extremes, but killing an innocent man sent him over the threshold of decency into darker paths. She ran back into the room and stuffed her small bag with her overnight personals. Anxiety made her peer through the scanty curtains more than once. But she saw no wagon, which sent a wave of anxiety through her. Rogan had to know right away. In a few minutes, their stomachs would haul them back, wanting her to fix another camp meal, she hoped. Rattling wheels made her flinch, but it proved only to be another load of gold diggers headed for Lewis Pond's Creek. The posts would be seen at every mail stop, she realized, and every inn from Sydney to Ophir. Soon Lewis Pond's Creek would be swarming with men whose money-hungry eyes would size up the features and build of a stranger in their midst, a man whose face matched one they'd seen at the mail stop. One of them might want to pull out a gun and cash in on Judge Abbot Dearborn's handsome bounty. *Wanted dead.*

No sign of Jamison's wagon.

"Rogan!"

"Find any color, Jamison?" Rogan asked. It hadn't taken him long to master the panning cradle once Jamison had demonstrated its use a time or two. "Rock it like a baby," Jamison had said. His eyes felt the strain of trying to spy the "color," a speck of gold that indicated there might be more where that speck came from. So far, the specks had been few and far between.

"One or two. Not enough to buy a beer," Jamison said.

"Some gold rush, eh?"

"Patience, Farrell. We're finding signs of it. We've just got to find Mother."

"Mother? I'd settle for little sister." Jamison's gold-digging jargon made Rogan laugh. Rogan panned for another hour until his eyes hurt. He had followed Jamison down a bluff. He hoped that when they returned, the horse and wagon would still be safe at their secluded camp. They had stopped where the stream grew sluggish. Alone except for the occasional duckbill platypus that paddled around the reeds and rushes, the two of them had pulled the cradles from their packs and begun scooping the sand, swirling it, emptying out the gravel, and counting the occasional color. Rogan had counted only five specks so far. He saw Jamison empty another flask—couldn't help noticing he'd been looking a little pale of late. "You should take it easy on that stuff."

"This stuff? It's medicine."

"You drink that much and it's poison."

"I drink. I'm honest about it. More than I can say for you."

"You saying I'm dishonest?"

"I am."

"I thought you were my friend, Jamison."

"That's why I'm telling you, mate. You're lying to yourself."

"Well then, tell me, Reverend Jamison. How have I transgressed?" Rogan knew Jamison had tippled all afternoon and was well in his cups by now, so he humored him.

"I see the way you look at the lass. See the way she looks back at you. You're falling in love with her, aren't you?"

"In love with her? You're drunk."

"Any drunk could spot love in your eyes. Why don't you just up and tell her?"

"Because it isn't true." Jamison annoyed him now. Not for any other reason than the fact that he didn't like men meddling in his private affairs.

"I heard her say she might go on to Victoria. How do you feel about that?"

"It's not safe, that's all."

Jamison laughed.

"What's funny?"

"I'll wager you a bag of gold, if that lass up and runs off, you'll be fast on her heels, faithful as a hound pup. Old Jamison'll be left to fend for himself, that's wot!"

"You don't have a bag of gold to wager." Rogan stood, arms folded at his chest, waiting for his booming laugh to subside.

"I will. I smell gold. It's here somewhere. You see all that quartz? It's waving its fists and shouting, 'Look here, look here!' Quartz and gold. John the Baptist and Jesus. Where there's one—"

"You keep panning then, bloke. I'll run back and see how fares our laundress—bring us back some tucker and nibbles." He wearied of Jamison's rambling.

"I could go with that and some tay. Someone should keep an eye on her. She's apt to run off, and then where would you be but crying in your beer with me."

He ignored the cynical smirk and the mischievous glint in Jamison's eyes.

John the Baptist and Jesus. Jamison's comment had stuck in his brain, rolled around, back and forth. Finally he got the meaning of it. He chuckled to think of Jamison offering a biblical parallel. Annie would call it sacrilegious, he decided. *No you wouldn't, would you, Annie? You're too busy judging yourself to judge others.*

He neared the main road that would take him to the inn. Soon he would see her again, see her smiling eyes. But he wouldn't ask her to cook. Jamison could eat beans, just this once. She'd worked harder in the last few days than most men he knew. He would buy them dinner from the innkeeper's wife. That was that! They could dine together, and in a proper way, he decided. He felt a deep satisfaction. The thought of sitting across the dinner table from Annie Carraway sent his emotions stampeding through his head without a rein.

He leaned back, and there on the splintered floor, tucked beneath his boot, was a single lace glove. It seemed a sacrilege to him to be resting his foot on it in this way—like a stack of old magazines piled on top of a Bible. It reminded him of the night she had left her gloves in the jail. That blasted maid had burned them along with everything else. He scooped it up and dusted it off. Since no one was around to see, he held it to his nose. A faint aroma, something akin to spring and baby's breath, tickled his senses. No doubt about it. She smelled good.

An explosion of pure white disturbed his quiet reverie. A flock of cockatoos, startled by his sudden approach, took flight, sweeping upward, their loosened white feathers scattering behind them like wedding petals. Rogan watched them for a while until they disappeared.

Finally, he spotted the ragged little inn. He pulled right up to Annie's door. The curtain on her window flashed, swung around, then just hung there.

"Rogan! Hurry inside! Hurry!"

Annie had never looked so pale and shaken. Rogan leaped from the wagon. Something told him he shouldn't speak until he got inside. He closed the door behind him.

"Look. They're posting these notices all around."

He took the poster from her, saw his face, big and undeniably his.

"They nailed it right outside my door. I tore it down, but I'm sure it's not the only one."

"Did anyone see you, ask you any questions?"

"No. I stayed hidden. But we've got to get you out of here."

Rogan nodded, then jerked back to face her.

"We could go to Victoria. Find my sister and her husband. They would help us."

"Us?"

"Stop it, Rogan! We've no time to waste!"

He took a moment, then sighed inwardly.

"What's wrong now?"

"I can't risk it. I won't risk your getting hurt, or worse."

"They won't hurt me, Rogan. It's you they're after."

"It's too risky. I'll find you a good family, one who wouldn't mind offering you a ride to Victoria."

"You're so stubborn!"

"And you aren't? Annie, I couldn't bear the thought of your getting—" He stopped, noticing a curious gleam in her eyes. Perhaps he'd said too much already, but he couldn't deny what he was feeling right now. He stepped toward her.

"Why couldn't you bear it?" she whispered.

He remembered Jamison's accusation. All at once, he realized the man was right. He would follow her anywhere, like a hound pup. His hands reached out, touched her arms, then gripped her small hands in his.

She looked at him without a word.

"I couldn't bear it because I care about you, Annie. I don't want to let you go."

She swallowed hard, as though she had trouble believing him.

He wouldn't let her turn away. The longing in her sapphire eyes told him to trust his instinct, even if it made him look like an idiot.

"Rogan, I don't know what to say."

By now he could feel her soft breath like a caress against his face. It felt sweet against his sun-toughened skin. She didn't pull away this time. He smoothed the hair from her face, allowed the gold tendrils to caress his ink-stained fingertips.

"You're pretty, Annie. You ever get tired of hearing that?"

"No one's told me that since my father died."

The way her voice trembled put him at ease with her.

"Harry Winston's a fool, but I'm not." His hands now slid around her shoulders, explored the soft hollows of her neck, then pulled her close to him.

"Rogan, we—"

"I'm going to kiss you, Annie Carraway." He saw her lashes flutter and her eyes close; then she lifted her face to meet his. Heaven and earth could have rattled to the foundations in that moment and he wouldn't have noticed. All he knew, all he felt, all he wanted to be, was tied up in that first kiss. Annie's soft lips met Rogan's with delicate surrender. They kissed again, and it reached into his soul. He desired more of her but knew he had too many things that needed to be made right. "I've been praying, Annie. I never told you that I know your ways, your ideas about faith. My kinsmen, they've taught me right from wrong. But more than that, they taught me about a personal faith. I turned away from it—went my own way. I was a fool."

"We've all made mistakes."

"It's not the same, Annie. You make mistakes, but then you make it right with your Lord. I turned my back on the very One I needed all along. But He's been talking to me about my stubborn ways. I can't get away from Him. I can't pretend He's not there. God came after me and, you know what? I surrender. He wins!"

Tears brimmed in her eyes and ran down her cheeks in joyful streams.

"You believe me, don't you, Annie?"

She nodded.

"It's hard for me to say this, but—"

"Rogan, I love you."

"Oh, Annie. . . ."

He burned to have her lift her face to him as she had just done. She must have sensed it, or felt it too, for their lips found each other again. He allowed a few moments to pass, not wanting to ruin it all with too much talk. "I'm taking you to Victoria. I want you to find your sister so you can stop worrying about her." He rubbed his bristly jaw against her tender porcelain skin until he felt her lips slip once more over his. Annie raised her mouth from his; she smiled and it was brilliant to him. A satisfied sigh welled up from inside her, and he felt her tiny frame respond to it.

"Rogan? What about the gold?"

"What gold?"

"The gold."

"I don't care about the gold."

"You mean that?"

"I swear it. I just want you, Annie."

"I'm so happy, Rogan. I want right now to last forever."

He watched as the contentment faded from her eyes, replaced with anxiety.

"But it won't. They're coming to get you. You can't go to Victoria. You'll have to hide someplace safe. Someplace where only I can find you."

"I can't ask you to live in hiding, Annie."

"Just for a time, until we can get things straight."

"I want to tell Jamison. He might even help us."

"Rogan, hold me once more; then we'll go. I promise."

"I've been meaning to talk to you about your bossy ways."

"Hold me now, Rogan. Hold me for a long time."

Rogan gathered Annie into his arms, cradling her next to him. Then he rested his chin against the crown of her head, closed his eyes, and prayed.

31
WANTED DEAD

"Say, Orvil! Where in blazes did you put that Wanted poster?"

It was the last thing Annie heard the innkeeper shout, right as they pulled away. She never looked back and kept a tight grip on Rogan's forearm after he had whipped the team forward. Rogan's picture would be replaced within moments, she felt certain. The innkeeper had never laid eyes on Rogan. She had seen to that. His wife had prepared a meal for her, but Annie had taken it to her room and split it with Rogan, just to quell suspicion. Soon the creek banks would spill over with the gold seekers. Rogan had to flee all the curious eyes.

Glad that she had rested somewhat, she had slipped all of her belongings from the room. No one would suspect that she hadn't slept in the room overnight.

"Are you scared, Annie?"

"Yes, I'm scared. But only scared I'll lose you." She pressed her face into his shoulder. Rogan's musky scent drifted through her nostrils, and it comforted her somehow. But she couldn't quash the worry altogether. The sooner they left behind the inn and the main road, the faster she might relax. Her head nodded on his shoulder, and she felt herself counting his breaths. She couldn't sit close enough to him.

"If I die today, I'll die the happiest architect on earth."

"You are an architect, aren't you?"

"Yes, but just until the embezzlement business takes off."

Annie laughed and heard his deep resonant laughter join hers. She had never allowed herself to laugh at him, and she suddenly realized it was because of her pride. "Did I ever tell you, Rogan, you're a funny man?"

"What else am I?"

"Fairly handsome."

"Only fairly?"

"All right, exceedingly handsome."

He kissed her forehead.

"I love your wit. You've intelligent eyes—"

"We're going to get along quite well, it seems."

She felt as though she had spilled a long-harbored confession. A bit more time passed and she kept speaking softly to him, affirming out loud what she had denied herself in private.

"You know what you are, Annie?"

"Tell me."

"Irresistible."

Finally, he steered the horses into a thicket and stopped them just beyond the edge of a bluff.

"Annie, we have to stop here. Unless you want to climb down a bluff, you'll need to wait here in the wagon while I go for Jamison."

"I can climb. Don't leave me here alone."

He lifted her from the wagon, but instead of putting her on the ground, he held her close and rocked her.

"I'll carry you down."

"You don't have to do that."

"Let me decide."

She relaxed against him, glad she could finally trust again. He had carried her halfway down the gradual decline when he stiffened.

"What's wrong?" she asked.

"Jamison's on the ground!"

"Go to him, Rogan! Put me down!" She could see Jamison herself. He was sprawled facedown on the sandy shore. No sooner had her feet touched the ground than Rogan had bolted for the foot of the bluffs where his comrade lay motionless.

Rogan searched for signs of life, then turned Jamison onto his back.

"Is he all right?"

"I think he's alive, but come look at him!"

Annie lifted her skirts and raced toward him.

"It's that blasted liquor and the way he lives. I told him he'd poison himself." Rogan felt his pulse.

"Where can we find a doctor?" She knelt next to Jamison and gripped his wrist. His skin was cold, his face ashen, and he had a weak pulse. Panic rioted through her.

"Back at the last mail stop. They'll know."

"But you can't go!"

"I have to, Annie! I can't leave him here. Not like this."

"I'll take him myself! You load him into the wagon. I can drive a wagon the same as you." She saw the way he shook his head at her.

"Hang on, old man. Run ahead, will you, Annie? Some of our gear's still lying about our camp. We should leave behind as few traces of our presence here as possible." Rogan hefted Jamison into his arms.

"I will!" Annie meandered up to the camp, tripping on her petticoats, skinning her wrist against an imbedded boulder. Just as she had stumbled forward again, a sound, unclear to her, ricocheted down into the stream bed, ringing off the rock-encrusted vales.

Rogan cried out.

"Rogan, what was that?" Breathless, she pulled herself up by the next stone. She stopped to take a breath, then realized that Rogan hadn't answered her. "Rogan?"

The bullet shot through Rogan, searing, numbing, as it tore through his shoulder. Caught by surprise, he felt his arms go limp. The last clouded glimpse of Jamison reeling from his grasp pierced his mind with despair. He couldn't speak, and for a moment felt himself drifting away from all he loved. He thought of his grandmother, how she had prayed for her heathen grandson. His mother's face, his father, both came to mind. Then he thought of Annie. If she would draw near, he would tell her to kiss him just once more, and that would be his last taste of heaven on this earth. He figured that if He saw the face of Christ Jesus, his time was finished. But He wanted to ask Him, plead with Him to give him more time with Annie. A few hours of bliss was time too short. Surely God could find one reason to leave him here for just a little while longer. *Don't take me yet, Savior. Mercy . . . mercy . . .*

"You alive, Farrell?"

He felt his body nudged by the toe of a boot. His mind raced to recognize the voice.

"Rogan! Rogan!" Annie said.

Her voice sounded like a nightingale's to him. He felt her throw herself on him. The weight of her body sent a ripple of pain through his chest and across his shoulder. He groaned inwardly.

"So is this the way it is, Annie?" The man's voice queried her in a way too familiar. That ignited Rogan's ire, but he still felt paralyzed.

"You killed him, Harry!" Annie accused.

"Not I, but your uncle's manservant."

Finally, the name Harry Winston swirled around Rogan's semiconscious state. But Harry's voice surprised him. He sounded shaken, when he should have been victorious at having bagged his fiancée's captor.

"Why, Harry?" Annie wept while she wiped Rogan's brow with her skirt.

"You can't blame me for this, Annie! I wanted to come alone. But Abbot blackmailed the manservant."

"In what way?"

"He mistakenly killed another man thinking it was Rogan Farrell. The man had Abbot's Cleveland bays, the ones you took from the stables."

"Jacob Fitzroy?"

"You are the one who took them, aren't you? Not Rogan?"

"Yes, I took the bays! I ran off like a coward. I should have stood up to you."

"Did you love Rogan Farrell?"

"What if I did?"

"I didn't come to kill him, Annie. This incident . . . well, it went too far, got out of control. I couldn't see Farrell die for it."

"Then why come at all?"

"I . . . to save him from Dearborn's men. That's why I climbed down here. But one of them got trigger happy and—"

"You're such a liar!"

"I'm not, for once. And if I aim my pistol up there . . . well, the gentleman's kinsman is with him, and he wouldn't take too kindly to my having shot him. We're in a bit of a dilemma."

Rogan stirred.

"Don't move, Rogan," Harry whispered to Rogan.

Rigid, Rogan began to wiggle the fingers on his left hand, which was hidden beneath his crumpled body. He wanted to know just how much of himself was alive. It appeared not much.

"I want those men to think you're dead. They'll head down here upon my signal. When they do, I know for certain that they can't see you when they round that gully. We've got to get you to your horses," Harry said.

"Harry," Rogan said through clenched teeth.

"Yes, Rogan?" Harry stooped slightly.

"I stole your girl."

"Yes, I know. You always win, don't you?"

"They'll never stop looking for us, Harry." Annie sounded worried.

"They will when I confess."

Rogan opened his eyes and gazed up at Harry Winston through his cloud of pain.

"Rogan, old man, you're alive."

"If I live, Harry, remind me that I owe you a punch in the jaw."

Annie paced outside the room where Rogan lay in the physician's home. It had been a three-day vigil of pacing, eating very little, and sleeping in the physician's parlor on a small sofa, where his wife had made Annie a bed.

Before the men had lifted Rogan from the back of the wagon, he had passed out from the pain. Jamison had awakened on the way and kept muttering things to Annie that she couldn't understand. Rogan hadn't spoken since. Harry tended to the horses, having sent Dearborn's men back to Sydney. He had assured the hired gunman that he wouldn't be hanged for shooting a horse thief, then had relieved him of his obligation by paying him off.

While Annie waited, she separated Rogan's personal belongings from Jamison's into two crates. A leather bag with a rawhide strap caught her eye. Since it had been wrapped up in Jamison's coat, she assumed it was his. She lifted it to place it into Jamison's crate, but the weight of it drew her suspicions.

"What's in here, rocks?" Annie lifted the flap on the bag and looked inside. The three rocks nestled in the folds of leather proved her notion right. She turned the bag upside down, dumping the rocks onto a rickety three-legged table. At first sight, she thought they were quartz. But the dust that crumbled onto the tabletop had a distinct color, one she had heard Jamison describe often during his sporadic moments of sobriety.

"Jamison, you did it!" She recalled his ramblings in the wagon. He had been trying to tell her the whole way back.

Annie hastily raked the gold nuggets back into the bag, paying careful heed she didn't leave behind traces of the sparkling grains.

The door opened and the physician stepped out.

"Any change, doctor?" she asked.

"Not yet. You'd best go and get some rest."

Annie trudged from the room again. It seemed her lot in life to be forever waiting at a bedside.

She prayed God would grant her one request—that she wouldn't be left alone again.

"Miss Carraway, someone would like to see you."

Annie looked up from her bed on the sofa. The physician's wife stood over her, unsmiling, which was always her way.

She was halfway out of her bedding when she heard the doctor's voice. He had stuck his head into the room.

"He's awake," the doctor said.

"Rogan, he's—"

"He took a pretty mean bullet, but the wound's healing well and he should recover soon."

Elation swept through Annie. After the doctor and his wife had left the room, she pulled on a linen frock and combed back her hair. Then she darted into the bedroom where Rogan had been sleeping for three days.

Wrapped in a white sheet, Rogan's head was being lifted by the physician's wife as she held a glass of water to his lips.

Across the room in another bed, Jamison offered Annie a weak smile.

"Rogan, you're alive!" Annie ran to the bedside.

"You're certain?" Rogan asked.

Annie kissed his face.

"I think I just might be dead—because you look like an angel to me."

"Doctor says you'll be fine, up and about soon."

"How long have I been here?" Rogan asked.

"Four days, and you've had me worried."

"I opened my eyes once and could have sworn old Jamison was standing over my bed looking at me—thought we'd both passed over."

"I *was* looking at you, fool—seeing what I could steal off the body."

"Glad you're feeling better too, Mr. Jamison." Surprised that Jamison had so much pluck, Annie gazed over at him and offered an encouraging smile.

"She's been hovering over you, waiting for you to come back from the dead, Farrell. You're one lucky bloke. I don't have no pretty young thing hanging over me."

"Thank you for pointing that out, Jamison," Rogan said.

"Just want you to know you're lucky, is all."

For three more days, Annie kept bathing Rogan's face with cold cloths. He didn't care much for the chilly baths, but he loved her nearness, the way she hovered over him as though she could breathe the life right back into him. From time to time, she would kiss him. When she did that, he knew beyond any doubt that he would live.

Jamison sat up, drank his soup, and complained he couldn't find his flask. When the physician's wife walked from the room, he gestured to Annie with his arm.

"You need something, Mr. Jamison?" she asked.

"Keep your voice down."

"He's up to something," Rogan said. "Watch yourself, now."

"Bring me my leather bag," Jamison said.

"All right." Annie left the room, then returned at once with his satchel.

Jamison took it from her and rifled through it. His eyes large, he took on a look of panic.

"What's wrong with you?" Rogan sat up, adjusting his pillow.

"I had something in here, something important!"

"You mean those rocks?" Annie asked.

"Yes, dear, where are they?" He looked relieved.

"I cleaned up all your things and threw out the bad. I saw the rocks and threw them out—"

Jamison's head fell against his pillow. He closed his eyes, emitting a pitiable moan.

"You didn't want those rocks, did you?" Annie took the bag and shook it for him once more. Then she turned her back on him and winked at Rogan.

"Those weren't ordinary rocks—they was gold, woman!"

"You can't be serious!"

"Jamison, are you telling us you up and struck gold?" Rogan sat up.

"Three big rocks, and there's more. But we have to get back to our claim before someone finds it."

Annie stooped beside his bed and reached underneath it. She pulled out a small trunk with a lock on it.

"What's that you got?" Jamison peered at her, suspicious.

From a key she had in her pocket, Annie opened the lock. She popped open the lid and showed Jamison the contents.

"Oh, girl, you almost stilled my heart!" Jamison lifted the gold chunks out of the small trunk.

"Sorry if I scared you. They weren't safe in that bag. I locked them up and put them under your bed for safekeeping."

"You're a gem, that's wot!"

"We struck gold? You saying we struck gold, Jamison?" Rogan stood and staggered to Jamison's bedside. He took one of the nuggets, turned it over, and held it up to the light.

"Rogan, you can't get up yet," Annie said. "Lie down!"

"We're rich," he said. He examined each rock, and each time the realization seemed less like reality and more like a dream. He raked it across his palm . . . saw the glistening "color" Jamison had told him about.

"We *were* rich anyway, Rogan. Remember?" Annie's eyes glinted with an uncertain worry.

He knew Annie's thoughts, seeing distress all over her face. She had a fear of money; she could remember a happy time in her life when she did well without it. But he couldn't allow Dearborn or anyone else to take his family's land.

"Jamison, grab your trousers. We've got to get back down there!"

"Why do you have to go, Rogan?" Annie asked.

"Not for the money, Annie. You know why, don't you?"

Annie's eyes locked with his, and he felt their souls commune. He wanted to promise her that he wouldn't become like Dearborn. In the past, he could never have sworn such a vow. But he had found something much bigger than Abbot Dearborn, and he would never let ambition conquer him again. Neither would he fall prey to circumstance like Annie's family. Not if he could help it.

"I understand," Annie said.

Rogan had his encouragement now. He gathered up his clothes and his courage and aimed his bruised body toward Lewis Pond's Creek.

32
LEWIS POND'S CREEK

Annie didn't go with Rogan. He and Jamison cashed in a part of their gold and found two good mounts for the trip. Annie took the team and wagon into the small borough nearby. Her desire to find Isabelle outweighed any gold rush. She spent the morning at the mercantile, asking the various settlers and gold seekers if they'd seen a young bride with violet eyes and auburn locks.

"Who you be lookin' for, lass?" An older gentleman stood examining a farm tool.

"My sister, Isabelle Carraway. What I mean is, she's married now to a man named Charles Lafferty. So I'm looking for a couple by the name of Lafferty." Annie described Isabelle and Charles.

"What did she do, run off?"

Annie hated to answer.

"Lots o' young folk doin' that nowadays. Does she know you're lookin' for 'er?"

"No, but if she did, she'd want to see me."

"Anyone else lookin' for 'er?"

"Yes, my uncle, Abbot Dearborn."

"He's with you?"

Annie shook her head.

"So it's just you, no one else?"

"Just me, sir." His questions, the way he pressed her for details, piqued her interest.

"I might know where she is, or I might not."

Annie felt exasperated. Then she remembered something personal that might bring meaning to the conversation. She excused herself and returned to the wagon. As she went, she breathed a prayer that God would help her find favor with the man. Then she said a prayer for Rogan and ran back into the mercantile. She saw the farmer, who stood over a bag of grain haggling with the merchant.

"Excuse me, sir. I hope this helps," she said. Then she held out Isabelle's Bible.

"What you got there, miss?" The farmer took it, opened it, and read the inscription.

"It belonged to my father, Ralph Carraway. His father gave it to him. Now it belongs to Isabelle. I want to take it to her," Annie said. "And I want to see her again. Desperately."

The way the farmer brought his hand to his chin and scratched his head let Annie know that he weighed her request, took it to heart, but struggled to divulge what he knew.

"Sir, are you going to help me?" she asked.

Rogan sat on the creek bank with his head in his hands. Lewis Pond's Creek swarmed with diggers, some ill-equipped, others loaded down with picks and pans.

Four men stood over the place where Jamison had found his gold. Each had a cradle, swirling it, rocking it with as much care as they would a newborn infant.

"They found our gold," Jamison said. He stood with a cane in one hand, his new silver flask in the other.

"I'm sorry, Jamison. Hard to understand the circumstances, I know."

"I understand fully."

Curious, Rogan turned his face to look up at him.

"It's my luck. I always fall just short of the prize."

"What's that supposed to mean?"

"Did I ever tell you I was once a man of the cloth?"

"You, Jamison? You a preacher?"

"Had a wife, two sons."

"No wonder you're always quoting from the Bible." Rogan recalled the way he'd referred to John the Baptist and Jesus.

"We started us a church, pretty little chapel, about a mile or so between Bathurst and the Blue Mountains. People really came to hear me preach."

"Where's your wife?"

"Name's Hedda. She lives with her family in Bathurst. They've got a nice spread. The boys love ranching."

Rogan shook his head, confused.

"Don't look at me like that, Rogan. Hedda used to look at me the same way. Rips my heart out, it does."

"You don't have to say any more if you don't want to, Jamison."

"Confession's good for the soul, all that. I worked long hours, would spend days at a time visiting all the members and then some. Bought us a fine farm. Still live there myself. But along the way, I lost myself."

"Lost yourself—how?"

"Having all those people looking up to you makes you feel like you're more than you are. I started believing that I was their answer to prayer. Even began to think I deserved something better than Hedda."

Rogan realized what he was implying. His brow lifted, but he felt sad for Jamison. Too sad to judge him.

"Just paint 'fool' across my forehead."

Rogan felt a prick at his heart. He'd never discussed such matters with Jamison, had never asked him about himself.

"You start trying to take the place in people's lives that belongs to God and you place yourself on a pedestal that's too high. Well, all's I can say is that it's a long drop down when you fall." Jamison pressed the flask to his lips.

"Your wife left you?"

"She had no choice. Never saw me. Must have been like being married to a ghost. That's when I found another new lover." He held up the flask and winked at it.

"I'm sorry."

"Don't be. Just learn from the mistakes of an old fool. Try to take the place of God and you'll be booted out the door faster than Lucifer himself."

"You sound like a wiser man now in some ways."

"Some ways?"

"You still got the flask."

"Keeps me warm at night."

"Lay it down, Jamison. Start again."

"Gettin' too old."

Rogan stood and gathered up his belongings.

"Where you going, Farrell?"

"I'm going to find Annie. When I do, I think I'll hold on to her really tight and never let her go."

"Look out, all! I see wedding bells for Farrell."

"Is that so bad?"

"Downright intelligent of you. About time."

"Annie's taught me a lot about life, about what's important. I love her so much, it hurts."

"You'll give her a kiss, then, from an old fool?"

Rogan nodded and shook Jamison's hand.

"Take this too," Jamison said. He handed Rogan the leather knapsack with the gold inside.

"I can't take your gold, Jamison. That one piece is as big as my fist."

"It's a wedding present. For Annie. I'll find more."

"Thank you."

"You keep the wagon too, Farrell. I'm going to stay down here awhile . . . keep panning. Maybe I'll make myself worthy of a good woman—one like you found."

Rogan walked away feeling pity for Jamison. The man had been so close to the truth once but had gotten sidetracked by his own ambition. All at once, he saw himself in Jamison.

He saddled his horse, secured the gold in the satchel, and headed off to find Annie, with the greatest treasure of all hidden inside his heart.

"You suppose I've found them, Rogan?" The map in Annie's hand trembled. She studied the poorly scrawled ink marks drawn for her by the pastoralist in the mercantile.

"Only the Lord knows, Annie."

Once she had shown the Bible to the man, it sparked something in him. He indicated that he had met the newlywed couple calling themselves the Laffertys. But the young woman said her family would be looking for them. Didn't want her uncle to find them. According to the man, they had quite a large spread of land, though. That fact surprised her.

She fussed with Rogan's bandage until he snapped at her. "I'm sorry. You've grown so testy of late."

"It hurts!"

"I just wanted to have a look. Needn't be such a child about it. Doctor says we have to change it once a day, or more if it needs it."

"Please leave it alone, Annie."

"All right. Look, there ahead. I see the twin groves of trees that man described to us." She straightened the bodice on her new lace gown.

"Let's have a look."

She could scarcely sit still as Rogan wheeled the carriage onto the land. A curl of smoke signaled the chimney top ahead. Out front, she could see a man and woman cultivating a small garden plot. "Is it them?" She almost leaped from the wagon.

"Good morning!" Rogan called out cheerily to them.

But as the wagon drew near, Annie could see their blank stares. "It isn't them, Rogan."

"Well, let's ask them if they know the Laffertys."

Disappointed, Annie slumped against the back of the carriage seat. Rogan stepped from the carriage to extend his greeting. He queried them carefully, she could tell, but she couldn't hear their bashful replies.

"Annie?" Rogan called up to her.

"Yes, dear."

"These folks say their name is Lafferty."

She tried to offer a smile, but the discouragement was too great. "We've come all this way for nought, I'm afraid."

"Sorry to have troubled you," Rogan said to them.

Annie felt the seat shimmy as he climbed up next to her. "I give up. I'll never find my sister."

Rogan cracked the whip.

"Ma'am?"

The woman's voice surprised her. She turned her head to acknowledge her.

"Did you say you're looking for your sister?" the woman asked.

The way the woman's husband glared at her concerned Annie.

"It's all right, sir. Please allow your good wife to speak," Rogan said.

"What is your sister's name?" the woman asked.

"I call her Mussy, but her name is Isabelle Carra—that is, her name's Isabelle Lafferty."

"What's your name, ma'am?"

"I'm her older sister, Annie."

"Then you've come to the right place. Your sister's been worried sick about you, ma'am."

"I don't understand." Rogan shot the man a skeptical glance.

"My wife and I are employed by the Laffertys. We use their names only when strangers are afoot."

"Mrs. Lafferty has got some monster of an uncle she's watchin' out for." The woman nodded.

"Don't I know it!" Annie said. "Can you take us to them?"

The evening's fare in the Lafferty home was a bounty greater than Annie could have imagined. She and Isabelle finally found a moment to themselves.

"You look well, Annie. Such a beautiful bride."

"What about you, Mussy. You're being kept as well as Queen Victoria herself."

"Charles' family found it in their hearts to forgive."

"I didn't know."

"Once Mrs. Lafferty heard a wee one was on the way, well—"

"Mussy! You don't mean, you're expecting a child?"

"I know I don't look it in this dress. But come Christmas the Charles Laffertys will have their first addition to the family."

The sisters hugged from the settee on the front porch.

"But you've shown up with your own surprise, Annie. I never imagined you and Mr. Farrell, well—"

"Would marry?" Annie held up the finger graced by the new shining gold band. "Yesterday's ceremony was no more secretive a ceremony than Charles' and your little fiasco."

"We Carraway women do manage to get our way."

"Not our way, Mussy. God's way." Annie loved hearing her sister laugh again. She felt Rogan's fingers grip her shoulders. She lifted her face, meeting his eyes with her own.

"Annie, Charles and I are talking of expanding their spread, making a joint venture, raising sheep. After we return to pay off Rose Hill's debt, Charles has invited us to come back."

"I can't believe it!" Isabelle took Annie's hand.

"But is the settlement large enough to support an architect?" Annie asked.

"Victoria is begging for an architect," Charles said.

"Annie, it's true," Isabelle said. "Rogan's skills as an architect will be desperately needed here in Victoria. The hills are teeming with new families in need of houses, barns, businesses."

"But first we've that other business to settle." Annie gave Rogan a knowing glance.

"It will be settled. I promise you, Annie."

Isabelle looked at them both, too curious for words.

Charles gestured toward the stablehands who approached with their mounts.

"If you ladies will excuse us, we're going out to inspect some of the land now." Rogan donned his hat.

"Yes, Rogan here has an interest in a quartz outcrop on our property."

"Quartz?" Annie couldn't decipher the curious glint in her husband's face.

"Quartz and gold, John the Baptist and Jesus." Rogan grinned.

She stared after him.

"I'll explain later, Annie." Before he reached the horse, he turned on his heels. "I almost forgot."

"Forgot what?" Annie asked.

"My treasure." Rogan bent and kissed her gently.

Still baffled by his anxious behavior, she returned his kiss and watched him ride away with Charles Lafferty, the two of them chuckling like giddy schoolboys.

"Annie, you're not going to leave me like this, are you? What business have you to settle?"

Annie pulled out a letter and handed it to her sister.

"What's this?"

"A very long story."

33

A SEASON FOR LOVE

"Rogan, you're back!" Katy Gabriel ran from the front porch toward Rogan and Annie's wagon.

"Grandmother, you're a sight to behold!" Rogan clambered from the wagon to greet her.

Annie laughed to see the excitement. The Farrell family poured from the house, all shouting that the eldest prodigal had returned to them.

"I want everyone to listen and listen good!" Rogan said.

His mother, Meredith, embraced him while Donovan soaked up the presence of his son.

"Frederick, come here!" Rogan ran to him and gathered the family around.

"He's something to say; now let him say it!" Katy winked at Annie.

"Please meet the new Mrs. Farrell, my wife, Annie!"

Annie blushed, fully expectant of their surprise. She stood, smoothed her traveling dress, and waited while Rogan ran to assist her down from the wagon. Her thoughts reeled with so many emotions. They had just come from her uncle's home, having shared the news with him of their marriage. All the embarrassing charges had been dropped, and Rogan was free to leave with his new bride. Harry had settled his debt with Mason Hale in private. When Abbot had heard all that Annie had to say to him regarding Sabrina Madison, his whole bearing had changed toward them both. Abbot's sudden spirit of cooperation had surprised Rogan. But not Annie.

The Farrell women grew giddy with excitement, all of them wanting to meet Annie.

"Did you hear? Rogan's married!" Frederick exclaimed to all of them.

Annie felt herself jostled and squeezed as the Farrell women surrounded her with their glad approval.

"I knew it!" Katy said.

"How did you know?" Annie looked at her, baffled.

"God tells me everything." Katy looped her arm in Annie's.

"I feel so fortunate to be part of this family," Annie said.

"Will you build a home right here at Rose Hill?" Katy asked.

"I'll let Rogan tell you." Annie saw the anticipation in her face but didn't want to spoil Rogan's reunion with his family.

The afternoon buzzed with the sudden activity of the women's cooking and the men catching up on Rogan's adventures in the gold diggings.

Annie listened as he shared of their good fortune, how he and Charles Lafferty had made the biggest gold strike in all of Australia. Their plans for a joint sheep operation would be realized. But the resignation on Katy's face saddened Annie.

"I'm sorry to be the one to take away your grandson, Katy."

"Annie, I want Rogan to be happy. I've never seen him like this," Katy said.

"You must attribute it in part to your prayers."

"I know. I give thanks to God for all of it. For you too. You'll come to see us, though? Bring me back some great-grandbabies to spoil?" Katy dabbed her eyes.

"I promise." Annie hesitated again, not sure if she should divulge their next bit of news. She decided to wait. The next few days would offer them opportunity to share everything with Rogan's family. Time had now become their friend.

The summer harbor air refreshed Annie. She held to Rogan's arm, anxiety rippling through her. Morning had sent them away from Rose Hill to finalize the matter that had nagged at Annie for so long she could scarcely sleep. But last night she had slept more soundly than any night she could remember.

Rogan and Annie watched as the boarding plank from the large ship was fastened into place. Soon they would meet the child whose dilemma had filled their thoughts so much of late and brought compassion and resolve to their hearts.

"You know what she looks like?" Rogan asked.

"I believe I do. She has her father's eyes, poor child."

Twenty or more passengers scurried down from the ship, some embracing waiting family members, others stepping foot onto a shore they'd never seen before.

Annie watched as a severe-looking woman approached, holding fast to a little girl's hand. She appeared to be searching for someone.

Seeing a note fastened to the child's summer dress, Annie stepped forward and leaned down to read it. *Dearborn.*

"Look, Rogan. It says 'Dearborn'."

"You're right, Annie," he said. Then addressing the woman, Rogan asked, "Ma'am, are you looking for Abbot Dearborn?"

"I am. Are you Abbot Dearborn?"

The woman had a coarseness about her, but Annie saw the wisdom of offering her respect. "I'm Abbot's niece. We've come for the child."

The little girl, large brown eyes wide with fear, tried to pull away from her guardian.

"Behave yourself, girl, or I'll have to clout you!" Accompanying the harsh words were a scowl and a yank of the arm, causing the child to cringe with downcast eyes.

"That won't be necessary!" Rogan pulled some coins from his pocket and handed them to the woman. Annie could see that the child's guardian had rankled Rogan's ire, and she moved forward to meet the little girl, bending to look into her face.

"Abigail, I met your mother once. You are just as lovely as she."

"Mama died," Abigail said, her chin quivering. "She's with the angels." Tears rimmed her eyes and threatened to spill.

"My mother died too. But I have a family now, and Rogan and I would like you to come be a part of it. Will you come be our family?" Attempting to control her own trembling emotions, Annie held out her hand in invitation.

Rogan turned to Abigail's guardian. "Thank you for bringing her to us. You'll be on your way now?" he said, dismissing her.

Frowning, she replied, "Yes. But see that you take proper care of the child, now."

Watching the woman walk away, Annie held Abigail close and said, "You won't have to see her ever again."

Abigail buried her face against Annie. Then taking the girl's hand, Annie put her arm through Rogan's and said, "Let's go home."

As they headed out, Rogan said, "Your uncle seemed pleased at your proposition, Annie."

"He had no other choice. And neither did I. Abigail won't have to grow up as I did."

"No, she won't. She's beautiful," he said.

"She's ours, Rogan. Our little treasure to have and to hold."

Rogan cradled them both in his arms and held them as though he would never let go.